Bridge of Dreams

Bridge
of
Dreams

Book One: Selling Water by the River

Chaz Brenchley

ACE BOOKS, NEW YORK

THE BERKLEY PUBLISHING GROUP
Published by the Penguin Group
Penguin Group (USA) Inc.
375 Hudson Street, New York, New York 10014, USA
Penguin Group (Canada), 90 Eglinton Avenue East, Suite 700, Toronto, Ontario M4P 2Y3, Canada
(a division of Pearson Penguin Canada Inc.)
Penguin Books Ltd., 80 Strand, London WC2R 0RL, England
Penguin Group Ireland, 25 St. Stephen's Green, Dublin 2, Ireland (a division of Penguin Books Ltd.)
Penguin Group (Australia), 250 Camberwell Road, Camberwell, Victoria 3124, Australia
(a division of Pearson Australia Group Pty. Ltd.)
Penguin Books India Pvt. Ltd., 11 Community Centre, Panchsheel Park, New Delhi—110 017, India
Penguin Group (NZ), Cnr. Airborne and Rosedale Roads, Albany, Auckland 1310, New Zealand
(a division of Pearson New Zealand Ltd.)
Penguin Books (South Africa) (Pty.) Ltd., 24 Sturdee Avenue, Rosebank, Johannesburg 2196, South Africa

Penguin Books Ltd., Registered Offices: 80 Strand, London WC2R 0RL, England

This book is an original publication of The Berkley Publishing Group.

This is a work of fiction. Names, characters, places, and incidents either are the product of the author's imagination or are used fictitiously, and any resemblance to actual persons, living or dead, business establishments, events, or locales is entirely coincidental. The publisher does not have any control over and does not assume any responsibility for author or third-party websites or their content.

First edition: May 2006

Library of Congress Cataloging-in-Publication Data

Brenchley, Chaz.
  Bridge of dreams / Chaz Brenchley.— 1st ed.
    p. cm.
  ISBN 0-441-01324-4
  I. Title.

  PR6052.R38B75 2006
  823'.914—dc22   2005036261

PRINTED IN THE UNITED STATES OF AMERICA

10 9 8 7 6 5 4 3 2

Part 1

Chapter One

**D**OWN in the Shine was Issel, dreaming.

It was a very real dream, because he lay curled cold between the ribs of the boat, nested in the old wet smells of fish and weed and netting, and the air was sick aglow.

His eyes were open because he was afraid, because he was listening, because he was dreaming; no one has their eyes closed in their dreams. At first he thought he'd woken up, because he was listening, because he was afraid. That was all part of the dream.

He'd heard footsteps in the shale, which had woken him, or so he'd dreamed. He'd been afraid because no one who meant any good walked on the strand in the Shine. That's why he was here, why he was let sleep in the boat. He had a knife, and he was fierce when he was afraid.

He lay curled cold in the boat, and if any thief came to steal it or the nets or himself, then the haft of the knife was in his hand, and the blade would be in their belly if he could get it there.

He lay and listened to the footsteps, and then the stillness after; and so he heard the long soft cry of the waterseller, "Suu-uu!" with the bubbling shrill at the end like some marshbound bird, and so he knew he was dreaming.

He lay in the boat where it was drawn up on the strand, a few short paces from the lapping lip of the great river of the world, and here stood a man selling water. In the night, in the Shine.

And here came people to buy, footsteps in the shale. Issel was still afraid, but he was dreaming; he lifted his head a cautious span above the planking. A boy should see what he dreamed about. How to understand it, else?

There were the people come to buy, a handful of them: slave and merchant, mercenary, lady, lad. Only a dream could bring such a foolish, unlikely group together. There could be no meaning in this, unless there was a great deal of meaning, too much to fumble for.

There was the waterseller: not tall, not potent, strong and squat, with no significance to him. He wore the proper dress, though it had no colour in the pallid shimmer of the air. He had the proper stoop beneath the weight of what he carried, the battered urn of beaten tin; he had the cup on a long chain, and the proper turn of his wrist, twist of the spigot to fill it. Issel knew.

No one drank his water. They paid him, and at first Issel thought he poured it into their cupped hands, but they each of them held a little bottle or a flask. They bought the water and hid it away as though it was precious and pricy, as though a massive river were not running just beyond their feet. And then they went quickly, each in a different direction, no words to say between them.

And then the waterseller turned his head to look directly at Issel, where he was spying from the boat. No words, only a smile; but the smile had enough to say. The man had the teeth of a dog.

Issel screamed, because that's when he knew he wasn't dreaming.

Chapter Two

I T was Jendre's privilege, one of Jendre's few privileges, to live and sleep not among the children, because she was not a child, and not among her father's women, because she was neither wife nor concubine nor slave. She was his daughter and a woman grown, or nearly so. There was no precedent. She had asked for, begged a chamber of her own, just the short time she would have in this house. Her father was a kindly man, or could be so, and perhaps a little touched with guilt; he had given her key and command of a tower room, the first and last that she would ever call her own. A casement window overlooked the city, her own private view of the world; a second door opened onto a small roof-terrace, her own private garden in the sun.

It was Sidië's privilege, one of Sidië's many privileges, to sleep with her sister Jendre, simply because she was Sidië and other people's privacies meant nothing to her.

Jendre was sixteen, and ought to have been married by now. Her father's overleaping ambition, coupled with his native caution, not to spend his wealth unwisely: those were all that had kept her free, or kept her caged. All the girls of her generation were wives long since, most of them mothers. She was castaway, adrift, out of time with her proper music, doomed; she was owed, she felt, a little consideration.

Sidië was eight years old, and was owed nothing. She did not barter, and she would not sacrifice; what she wanted, she took.

Often and often, what Sidië wanted was Jendre. Big sister, little sister: they were twin souls, Sidië said it frequently, because she'd heard it in a story once and liked it, and so taken it to herself. To Jendre they seemed more like slave and mistress. Small and brutal mistress, who rode imperiously over any will but her own.

So, night after night, Jendre slept this badly for this reason, that there was a hot body in the bed beside her. When she was awake Sidië demanded amusement or information, sherbet or water, Jendre's attention entirely; when she was asleep she claimed as much attention and space besides, squirming around like a starfish and tangling the covers, snoring or muttering in her dreams.

Tonight her dreams had woken her, in a gasping sweat. Jendre had woken too, necessarily. She had given the little girl a drink, bathed her sticky skin with cool rosewater, soothed her with soft words, soft hands until she slept again.

Jendre could not sleep so easily. She lay quiet for a while, in a futile pretence that she could. Then she abandoned pretence and sister and bed all three, slipping carefully out between the curtains and padding barefoot over rugs towards the window.

Opening the shutters was a risk, the grate of the fastening and the squeak of the hinges. Jendre held her breath as though that could help at all, caught herself doing it and almost broke down in giggles, almost gave herself away altogether. There was no break in her sister's breathing; reprieved, relieved, she opened the window also and leaned out to catch the vagrant breeze that came off the Insea, always before dawn.

Not so long before dawn now. There was a far hint of indigo around the eastern stars and first touch of a horizon below, a line drawn between sea and sky. She might kneel here in the window seat and watch for an hour, two hours, while the colours rose and ran around the great fierce glare of the sun; she had done that before, and never mind the great fierce glare of her sister when Sidië woke to find herself alone.

First, though—always, though—Jendre's eyes were drawn closer, lower, looking more down than out.

They hadn't lived long so high on the hill. This great house was still new to her, its broad gardens were still a revelation; so was the view, so was the idea of having all the city fall like a skirt below her. Looking out in daylight, she could see their previous home with ease. She could see figures if they moved in the garden, children with their nurses running about. She knew those trees, those paths, those little lawns and ponds; she remembered how fine it felt to have such space to play, so many rooms within. Once she saw a man down there, who must have been the officer promoted to her father's place and power. She envied him and his family, and hoped he would not prove to be too good a soldier, or too ambitious a man. Not like her father, who was both.

If she stared and squinted, she thought sometimes that she could see the house that had come before that, its roof at least, squeezed in among so many others, down towards the docks. She was born in that house, and so were all her father's dreams.

Now those dreams were realised; they lived in the Sultan's shadow, and could rise no higher up the hill. Now they had to pay the price, or she did. She could see no houses in the darkness, only points of light that faded as they fell away towards the river, towards the bridge, where it cast its glow over the lower town and the dark shimmering waters, over the sister-city Sund on the southern shore.

Points of light came closer, grew brighter, were lamps and torches carried by a squad of men. They came up the street, and the gates opened; they were expected, the house was waiting for them.

Jendre had been waiting for them weeks now. They always came in the earliest morning, that was common knowledge. It was the other reason, the real reason why she slept so badly. Not the unfamiliar bed, nor familiar Sidië within it; not the heat nor the rain, not the shine of the bridge breaking in unwelcome through the shutters. She blamed them all, but in truth she was wakeful because she was waiting. Now at last they had come, and she was terrified, not ready, not at all relieved.

She listened, and heard the slow rhythm of her father's voice at the foot of the stairs. Dismissing the guard, no doubt. This tower was outside the women's quarters, and her father was no fool; she and her sister were rarely unwatched, never unprotected. Except now, when they most needed protection.

She heard footsteps rising, and not her father's. Unfamiliar men: they would have to explain themselves, or let their uniforms explain them. Her father would stay below, to witness as they left.

They were at the door. She ought at least to pull a robe on over her sleeping silks; she did not, could not move.

They came inside, heavy-footed, heavy-breathed. The lamplight would wake Sidië; she should have thought of that, and gone out to meet them on the landing.

Too late now. She heard her sister stir, sit up, cry out in grizzling wonder to find the bedroom filled with men, grim-faced and silent.

Jendre tried to go to her, but she was not allowed even so much time or kindness.

They were the High Guard, the Sultan's own janizars, and they would give their lives for any lord of Maras or any man of rank. Or for his family, for his children, for Sidië, for Jendre. Except that they had this duty too, that they must take one child from every man of rank and give that child over to the bridge.

Jendre knew that she was destined for this. Why else had her father never married her away, in all these years? He was keeping her dispensible, to be invested later. In their previous house, in his previous rank, he had been a man of fame but little influence: too junior, too poor. Now he was a general, and he must give his hostage to the Sultan. She wished that she thought he would be sorry.

They came in the earliest morning to catch the child sleepy, ill prepared. Jendre had been preparing for months, for years; she was not ready, but at least she was not surprised. She wondered if that was an advantage.

I wish you had come sooner. She wanted to say that, but her lips were dry and her throat was choked; she could not frame the words. She could barely stand, though she did that much at least, she came to her feet and stood there, even nodded faintly in response to the young officer's silent salute, a finger touched to his brow.

She was awake, she was the sacrifice, she understood; she had always understood. She had forgiven her father long since for all his ambition, all his inexorable rise. Of course he must be more than a simple soldier, of course he must be a great man at the court; of course there was a price that must be paid, and she must pay it. That was the way of their world. If a man had daughters, he must use them as he could, to buy wealth or alliance or prestige. If the cost of a place at the Sultan's side was a child, boy or girl, who must be lost to dreaming, then of course let it be a girl; in this family, now, let it be her.

Which was why it was so wrong, so cruelly wrong when the men of the High Guard left her standing in all her unready courage and took her sister Sidië instead.

Chapter Three

ISSEL was still huddled in the belly of the boat as the Shine faded, as the sun came up.

He didn't know, he wasn't looking. Enough of courage, too much already. He was all the way down in the slime and the stink, where there was always a finger's depth of foul water; he had squirmed beneath the folded nets, for what poor added shelter they could give. He lay with one side soaking heedlessly in the bilge, prickling all over. His head was wrapped in his arms, and his shapeless greasecloth gaberdine was pulled over to make it oh so abundantly clear that he could see nothing, the demons of the Shine could parade themselves and all their congregation and it wouldn't matter, he still wasn't looking.

He didn't see the dawn. He didn't watch how the fireworm glow of the Shine was beaten back by sunlight, like salt water yielding to fresh where the river ran into the Insea. If he heard voices, footsteps crunching along the strand, all the sounds of men coming to their boats, he didn't stir in response.

It was a kick that shifted him at last. He'd felt the boat shift under a man's weight, and still he hadn't moved. He'd known the kick must come, and still he hadn't moved; and he was usually so quick to see a bruise on its way, so swift to dodge . . .

When it did come, it came with a curse. Then he had to scramble, not to find himself more cursed than he was already.

"Up, hound! What manner of dog are you, to lie sleeping in the sun while honest men are at their work? Is my boat your kennel, pup . . . ?"

And so on, and on; and Issel was tangling the nets in his struggles to avoid, to avert, to deny the names he was given, and that made the boat's master angrier still. Hard boots and harder words: it was pure relief to tumble over the side onto dew-damp shingle, and see his urn and his little things thrown after. For a moment it was just relief, nothing but that.

Then it was something more, relief and worry mixed. He'd lost his sleeping place, his shelter. The man would find another boy to guard his boat, he made that clear: a boy of his own blood, not a beggar's brat, a dogtooth scavenger too fine to fish . . .

That was unfair, untrue. Issel would have been a fisher's boy and glad of it. He had tried. He'd spent one full day in the boat, working the oar and hauling the nets and gutting the little fish there in the bilge before the sun could turn them. All the day, he had thought that he would die. By the day's end, he was almost wishing to.

It wasn't the work, the sweat and the ache and the weary weight of the day; work was survival, work defined his life. It wasn't the man, with his casually brutal hands; Issel was more than used to blows and bruises, they had seasoned every day's work he'd ever done, which meant every day he could remember. It wasn't even the mingled smells of slimy net and riverweed and fish guts allied to the strange uprooted rocking of the boat, bringing him a sickness. He did feel sick all day, but it wasn't that.

It was simply the water, so much water and himself so small, so precariously poised above it. He had always stood in awe of the river, never felt comfortable coming close although he could never keep away. To crouch in a frailty of wood and pegs and rope, to feel the surge and suck of tide and current, to wonder how far the river reached below his feet, how dark and strange the waters ran—it was a day of constant terror that the work, the beatings, even the smells and sickness could not disperse. He had begged his nights in the boat regardless—"I cannot fish for you, but let me be your eyes at night, your guard"—and every night he felt the river's rush disturb his dreams.

And now he was a waterseller and even that, even the urn's weight on his back could drag at his mind, like a constant hissing in the shadows.

Even the quick spurt of water from the spigot was like a blade in his belly, a sudden whipping chill across his mind.

———————

THE river seethed and bubbled on the pebbles of the strand. He couldn't fill his urn, though, not from this. Those who bought water would never buy what rose in the Shine or ran under the long arch of the bridge. He tried not to drink it himself.

His eyes lifted to the bridge, where it lay like a bar across the white of the sky, dark and perilous. His tongue ran across his teeth, to find how sharp and strong they were. Sharper than yesterday, stronger than last month, last year . . . ? He couldn't tell. He knew someone who might tell him, but he didn't trust her word.

He gathered up his little things, wrapped them all in his gaberdine and tied it with a length of rope. With that awkward packet tucked inside his shirt, he slipped his arms through the straps of the urn and hoisted it empty to his shoulders, turned his back on the river and set out to walk thirsty to the public fountains, the broken heart of Sund.

Hungry he was used to; thirsty was always hard, especially where he must walk away from water. That was a wrench that he felt in his bones, as if they were poured full of lodestone and had to be hauled against the pull of north. He had never told this to anyone. He knew someone who would understand it, but he thought she surely shouldn't know, unless she knew already.

———————

ON the bank above the strand, the upturned hulls of bigger boats made huts for fisherfolk. Those boats had been the pride of Sund, in days before the bridge. Marasi governance forbade them now. Those not swiftly gutted and cut apart for housing had been burned; some few of their great spines still lay black and half-buried in the shingle.

Issel picked his way between the hulls, conscious this morning of how twenty years out of water had barely touched them. No sign of rot, no worm: old blessings still held good, it seemed, even in wind and sunshine, even without the rip of current and the bite of salt.

He was watched every step, every morning, to be sure he stole nothing that could be eaten or sold. Time was, when he would have done. Never in the Shine, but mornings when the mist was thick he used to sneak among the patchy gardens, taking what nimble fingers found, a little here and a little there. Of course he did; what else should a hungry boy do?

They knew. He'd been seen and chased, caught and beaten, seen and chased again. What they didn't know, these silent and suspicious folk, he'd sooner go hungry than eat their produce now. He couldn't sell it anywhere in Sund, he wouldn't feed it to the rats. Rooted in the shadow of the bridge, grown in the Shine—no. He wouldn't. He'd rather starve and die. His tongue touched his teeth again, and he hurried barefoot over paths of mud and stone. Somewhere in the huts, a dog was barking. Didn't these people *know*? He wanted to burn their crops, stone their dogs and drown the puppies, drive them from the river's edge entirely.

But of course they knew. Many of them knew nothing else; even the oldest had lived half their lives beneath the bridge. The worse half, to be sure, but what could they do? There was nowhere safe their little boats could take them. They fished in poisoned waters and grew crops in poisoned soil, sold what they could where they could and ate the rest regardless.

BEYOND the fishermen's huts, a road was all the city had for border. Once there had been a wall, high and strong, not strong enough. After the bridge came, after the Marasi had marched across the river, they had obliged their new subjects to demolish it. Soldiers and citizens, councillors and elders wielding bars and hammers while the tavern bands played in the streets. It was unification, the governor said, not conquest; what did Sund need of walls, against its brother Maras? If Maras kept its own walls, that was only sense, for the better safety of all; but there should be no more quarrels in the family. They were one people now, one city, Maras-Sund.

In Issel's childhood there had been mounds of rubble where the old wall had fallen. Other children had played on them, while he broke his nails digging out insects from the cracks. Highborn young ladies paid money for those in the markets, live food for their singing birds; stallholders would give him broken copper coin for a bottleful.

These days even his slender fingers would have been too broad for the work, but the mounds were long gone anyway, robbed out for building stone. There was only the road to show where the wall had run. Issel crossed the road and walked into shadow, into the lanes and alleys of the poorest quarter of the city.

NO dogs here, in the dubious margins of the Shine. Here the people were more equivocal, or simply more afraid. Kittens played in an open doorway, hissing and pouncing and darting back; one great scarred tom crossed his path, luck to the lucky, not to him.

Other eyes were less neutral than the cats'. He was Issel, he was known, not everywhere for selling water. Never here in the river quarter, Daries; here women walked to the public fountains to fetch their own. They knew him, though. A few looked on him with favour, more not, but they all looked.

Some unseen girl chirruped at him from a half-shuttered window. He flashed a dishonest smile into the shadows of the room and sent a scathing insult rolling after. That was all habit, heedless; it still drew a burst of giggles in response, like a cloud of butterflies rising from a bush that's shaken by a stone that's thrown.

A voice came at him from across the alley, low but carrying: "Hold that tongue, little *saka,* little waterseller, if you want to keep it. Let the young ones be, they're not fit for you to play with."

"And who is fit, then, is it you? Old mother?"

She was, perhaps, old enough to be his mother. She sat crouched by the doorway of her house, her hard, gnarled hands dipping into a mortar of pounded chickpeas to make balls of the paste, which she rolled in a spiced flour after.

She clucked a time or two and showed her bad teeth in a mock politeness. Issel kept his mouth closed, for fear of what she might see.

"Well. Better me than those simpering virgins. Why pick corn in the green, where there are golden kernels to be gleaning?"

"Why do either, when you can beg your breakfast of a woman as gentle in her heart as she is ripe in her body? Just a handful of your tamasseh, there, for a man with a hard day's work before him . . ."

"A boy with a day of idleness and thieving," she snorted. "But aye, start now, why not? You'll not steal my heart, so you may as well steal my food instead."

"Beg your food, with your blessing, mother."

"And offer blessings back, and lie and flatter and lie again; it is thievery, with you it always has been. I know you, Issel. I always have known you." It was true, she always had; he knew how hard those hands were. But she was using them now to pat half a dozen of her small cakes flat for easy carrying, spreading a fingerful of fiery harissa on each one as she went.

This was all instinct, it was almost the theft she called it; he took her cakes and left her nothing but words as heart-hollow as they sounded. He was heart-hollow himself, and good rich warm tamasseh could do nothing to fill that void. He munched as he walked, and eating seemed as meaningless as the banter of his begging. He had lingered too long in the Shine. Corruption was in his blood, and the dogs were hunting.

One dogtooth had been not hunting but selling water. In the Shine, and by the water's edge . . .

AND he was a waterseller himself, and he needed to remember that. He needed money. He might have begged a breakfast, old habit with an oily tongue; it would be harder to beg a bed. Beneath a roof, out of the Shine— that kind of generosity came at a price. Pickings were good here in Daries, where the people were as poor as himself, but Daries lay dangerously close to the bridge. Further into the city, where the merchants and the craftsmen congregated, they knotted their purse strings tighter.

A stable would do, a hayloft would be grand, but horse boys were notoriously jealous of their privacy. There were few horses left, in any case, and still small chance of finding a stable empty. Nothing was wasted, nothing went unused in Sund.

Nothing was wasted, not even time, but he was wasting that. Already he could hear distant cries in the still air, "Suuu-uu!" as if birds called to each other across the city. Others in Issel's trade were so far ahead of him this morning, they had been to the fountains and filled their urns and carried their water far enough to be selling it already.

He scowled, and hurried forward. Swift feet on a hard road, shrill whistles and soft calls that made him dawdle not at all, bullock carts and peddlers to be dodged around as the ways grew wider until at last he came to the constant babble and press around the public fountains.

ONCE it had been the fountains themselves that had babbled in their gardens. So he'd been told, at least, by men who had been old in his trade before ever the bridge had come and the Marasi over it. Old themselves now, bent and toothless, strong; they held their place with sticks and curses and with guile. And talked, of course, as old men will, of how things were before: how green the gardens and how sweet the water, how it leaped in jets as high as the city wall, no, higher, and fell again to flow like living crystal in streams and rills from the central basin to every corner of this broad parade. Paths and lawns surrounded it, trees overhung it; bridges spanned it, cut from the same veined marble as the channels where the water ran, but it was always the water that held eye and heart. It seemed to be veined itself, shot through with gold and silver. It gleamed even after it was drawn into urn or jug or bucket, it shimmered even in the tin cups of the *sakalar*. So they said, at least, the old men who had drawn it, borne it, sold it then.

No longer. There was no power now, to make water leap and sing. The Marasi had forbidden it. The jets were stopped with leaden plugs, the bridges broken, the channels blocked by rubble, clogged with the slime of years. The trees had been felled, and the lawns ran reckless with weeds and wild grasses. This was a place of fear, a display of raw power, Marasi might triumphant over defiant, defeated Sund.

The public gardens where the fountains played, here had been the living heart of the city; here had been the gleam, gold in the water, the affirmation of Sundain strength and soul; here was—of course!—where the Marasi had brought their bridge to ground.

It looked like a bridge in mist, in the soft monochrome shadows of first dawn, when there would be light but no sun yet. It steamed, or smoked perhaps, lending an acrid tang to the air. It seemed to be no work of man, no honest build. It lacked a parapet; it had no piers, no trusses to support it. It might have been poured of molten stone, if stone could melt like glass and be cooled like glass and look so insubstantial. It defeated the mind and the imagination; it defeated the eye altogether, rising through its own fog to overleap where the walls had stood, rising higher and stretching further, overleaping all the width of the river beyond, the great and unbridgeable river of the world.

It looked like a legend, a picture from some ancient tale; it should have been a legend and nothing more, a thing impossible. The wrath of Maras had fallen upon Sund in a single night, half the population of the city swore it, all those who had lived through and survived that night and the morning, the many mornings, the days and months and years that followed. They had gone to bed secure, because Sund ruled the river and so the Sultan could never come at them; they had woken to find the river bridged and the armies of Maras already within their walls.

The armies of Maras were with them still. There was always a squad on guard at the foot of the bridge; there were always troops coming and going across it, during the hours of daylight. Never at night. Even the Marasi would not treat their own men that unkindly. At night it gleamed like a rainbow sickly twisted out of true. Its light fell through the mists of its own making, brighter than moonlight beneath its arch, seeming to make the air itself glow. That was the Shine, which cut a swathe of terror nightly from the dead gardens here to the strand below. After twenty years, the Sundain were still learning how slow its poison was, how deep it ran. Only fools disregarded the dangers of the Shine. Fools and boys, and Issel was both; fools and boys and watersellers, seemingly, after last night, and Issel was all three. Small wonder that he worried about his teeth.

———————

ISSEL had heard how strange it was to cross the bridge, that strangest of bridges, even in daylight; but he'd heard it from people who couldn't possibly know. What he'd seen for himself was Marasi troops fresh off the bridge and staggering, sweating, dizzy, confused. Some sank to the ground despite their sergeants' screaming, others pushed straight through to the fountains and drank, or dipped their heads in the water and came up gasping. Some vomited, before or after; some were crude enough, debased enough to vomit into the water. Deliberately, sometimes. There were Marasi who could never taint enough of Sundain water; they must piss or spit into every pool, every basin, every wellhead.

The great central basin was all that was left whole among the fountains. Hot lead had destroyed the jets, but not choked off the water; it came bubbling up still, clean and pure. Half the city fetched its water from here, now that every source below the bridge was tainted.

Once, long ago, the watersellers had filled their urns at spouts, a line of gushing lion-masks set in a wall of marble at the gardens' eastern gate. Now that wall was gone, and the gate too. The pipes that took the water there were shattered and dry; watersellers must jostle with the women and slaves at the basin's rim, and give swift way to any Marasi trooper.

Elbows and knees and a sharp chin, a hard head for butting: Issel used them all this morning, squeezing through a pack of bodies, blessing those men who would let themselves be bullied out of their places and cursing those who would not. The women were easier to offend, swifter to retaliate; he offered them honeyed words in whispers, eyes and smiles, and still yelped at their pinching fingers as he slithered past.

He carried the bulky, awkward urn like a child in his arms, the stopper already between his teeth, so that when he reached the basin's rim he could thrust it immediately hard under the water's surface. Best not to linger, not to anticipate . . .

A slow tingle in his fingers, in his arms, starting where they were under the water but rising higher, running all through his body, fizzing in his spine. It was always like this, building to a cold clean ache like a blade in his bones, in every one of his bones. He'd been a dirty child, because washing frightened him; he'd never learned to swim.

Bubbles rose as the urn filled. As they burst, he felt the same thing happening inside, all his fear and confusion squeezed out of him by the rising touch of water, the deep possessive feel of it that was so nearly pain, so nearly pleasure and yet neither one of those. This was why he sold water, why he lingered near water, why he had slept on the strand. Even the slimy rankness of the boat's bilge had offered him this, last night in his terror.

This morning as every morning he was overcome, stilled and chilled by the wonder and insignificance of himself against this simple potency. He stood and felt nothing of the world around him, felt everything inside his skin, the pulse and flow of everything that was wet and living and bound by his own name.

The urn was full, he was full and overflowing, shivering, fit to scream. He didn't scream. He hoisted the urn out of the basin, knocked in the stopper, thrust his arms through the straps, let the weight of it swing him around—

———

—AND found himself alone, all that press of people gone from behind him, from beside him. They might have touched him as they went, tugged at him, whispered or shouted or shrieked; he had not noticed.

So they had left him, and here came a booted Marasi sergeant with a swaying, muttering troop of men behind, fresh off the bridge and craving water, and he was standing in their way.

Men had died for less. Too late to dive aside; the sergeant's hand was on his sword hilt, and Issel couldn't move fast with all this water on his back.

All he could do was stumble forward, towards the soldiers, already reaching to his hip for cup and spigot: "Sir, sir, I have drawn you water, sir, to save you having to stoop and drink like animals, like we do from our hands, sir, you can drink from my cup; save you getting mud on your boots, sir, and your men slipping in the wet of it . . ."

The sword hand lifted and the sword with it, a hand's span from the sheath; then it slammed back and the man grunted, scowling beneath his tarboush. His moustache seemed to purse as his mouth pursed, and he said, "Well, boy. Are you so keen? Serve me water, then, serve the men and be quick about it . . ."

Dry-lipped, sweating but still sharp, still scintillant, Issel served water to the Marasi as though he poured it from his bones. Leathery veteran though he was, the sergeant drank three cups without drawing breath between; then he glanced at his men, grunted and thrust the cup back for another refill. This one he sipped, watching his troop over the rim. It was discipline, nothing more. He drank what he did not need, while they were desperate and must wait. It had never been a surprise that these soldiers were brutal in their turn, when they had the chance to be.

At length, the sergeant let the cup fall on its chain. To Issel's eye he looked invigorated, brightened, like a snake in its new skin. Issel had seen this often and often, where a simple cup of water bought from him could slough off all the drag of a weary day. A bucket of well water would not do as much, his clients said that again and again. They thought there was some virtue remaining in the fountains, a residue of what had sparkled once. He never claimed that, he made no claims at all.

Something else that he had seen often and often, right here in the gardens, at the bridgehead: Marasi soldiers in trouble, sick and unsteady. That was one reason why there were always guards, why a battalion was garrisoned around the square, why so often a riot would flare just here. Hotheads saw men weak and vulnerable, the chance to strike a blow for Sund; they never saw the consequences, the counterstrike. Mostly they did not live to see it.

Day after day Issel had seen these men or their brother soldiers swaying, kneeling, puking. He'd never seen them close at hand, like this: never smelled the acid in their sweat and in their vomit, never felt the tremble in their fingers or the fever on their skin. They snatched at his cup, struggled for it until the chain snapped; then they crouched below the open spigot, gulping like frogs, thrusting their faces into the thin stream of water and gasping for more. So much for the sergeant's discipline; so much for not having to drink like animals, they made animals of themselves. Issel could have walked away and they'd have followed him on hands and knees, anywhere he led, so long as he would give them water.

Anywhere but back across the bridge. These were raw boys, recruits, bought in fresh; they were bruised all over, but their eyes were darker with the terror of what they'd done in this last march, or what had been done to them.

He could almost feel sorry for them. They were still Marasi soldiers, though, and he was Sundain. As the flow from the spigot faltered, one of them reached out to snare his ankle. A swift, sharp tug, and he was falling. The weight of the urn pulled him backwards; he heard it crack as he hit, and even through the arching pain of that he felt the touch of chilly fizzing wetness.

Then, for the second time in an hour, he was being kicked. Hard to curl, with the rigid urn still strapped to his back; impossible to roll away and stupid to retaliate. He managed not to be stupid, despite the pins and needles in his skin. He only lay passive under the boy-soldier's boot and waited for whatever would come next.

"Filth, were you smirking at us? Dog? Teach you to stand above your betters, show you where your place is, gutter boy . . ."

A fisherman's boots were harder and his legs were stronger, but these soft toes sought softer targets. Issel was past sobbing for the pain of it, sobbing only for breath before he heard anything above the boy's monotonous cursing. At last it came, the hiss and crack of the sergeant's whip, the yelp in response and then the snapped commands, "Stand up, what are you, soldiers of the Sultan or a mewling pack of puppies? On your feet and follow . . ."

One final kick to the gut, and Issel was left alone. Altogether alone, there in the sticky trampled mud around the basin, and better so. It meant he could pick himself up slowly, which he did; straighten himself with caution, to find where hurt the most, what damage he was carrying; bend over to retrieve his cup and then unsling the urn while his feet took him unsteadily to the water.

Cupped hands made a bowl, a little gathered pool between his fingers made a mirror. Scrapes and scratches, nothing worse, no great run of blood from nose or scalp. He ducked his face into his hands and felt the tingling shock of water, more than cold and wet together. A quick rub to shift the worst of the dirt, not to foul the fountain, and then he leaned over the rim and plunged his whole head beneath the ever-stirring surface.

And came up swiftly, shivering, gasping, shaken. After a long moment, he ran his hands over chest and belly: muck and aching soreness everywhere, bruises to come but no deeper hurt. He thought this was his life, to be brutally unlucky and to come out better than he might. Like his city, he thought, clinging to the edge of disaster but never quite slipping over, always surprising, always surviving somehow.

The urn was in worse shape than himself. It was no great work of craft, sheets of hammered tin shaped into a rude cylinder. One of the long, soldered seams had split; he slid wet hands down wet metal, pressing the open edges together and working the lead seal with his thumbs until it was warm and pliable, willing to grip again.

That was easily done, but the least of the damage. The spigot had been crushed out of all shape by the stamp of a soldier's boot; he couldn't fix that with wet fingers. And the cup was buckled also, and the chain broken. He needed a tinsmith, a man with an anvil, tools and skill.

And had no money to pay one, no way to earn money without the urn, a reputation across the city as a thief and trickster. It was well deserved, but it could trip him up today. Women he could charm, sometimes, some of them; men were harder.

Well, if they couldn't be paid and wouldn't be charmed, they would only have to be cozened. That was another use for wet fingers and a wetter tongue; and this was Sund, where nothing useful ever went to waste.

Chapter Four

ENDRE hadn't faced down her father for a long time, not like this, with a fury running far, far out of all control.

Not since she was Sidië's age, she thought, small and vulnerable and given to reckless rages. The thought was like oil, poured recklessly onto her flames.

"She's a little girl, a baby, and you gave her, you just gave her to them. You stood there and watched while they took her, and she was so scared . . ."

"It is the law, Jendre. You know this. You always have known it."

"The law of ambition, the law of greed. I have always known that you wanted this, yes, of course—that you ached to see your daughter taken away in the mists of the morning, that you thought it was nothing, a common market price, no cost that mattered. But it was to be me, not Sidië! That was, I thought that was understood between us . . ."

"Jendre, they would not have taken you. You have grown too old to be a dreamer."

"Too big, you mean." Actually she thought it had worked the other way, that he had grown smaller since the last time she had shouted at him, shorter, so that she could see now how his hair was growing thin. He seemed broader in recompense, pressed down, spread out; and heavier for sure, every word and thought more weighty. "What, would they be afraid of me, those brave soldiers, would they think I might have fought them down the stairs, so that they had to take a little child instead?"

In fact she had chased them down the stairs while Sidië fought and screamed, and the men had taken her regardless. Jendre had been stupid with shock; by the time she understood, it had been too late to fetch a knife, knives to defend her sister with. By then the men had been almost to the foot of the tower stair with the little girl kicking in their arms, and her father waiting by the open door. Even then, stupid still, she'd thought he might do something to stop this cruelty. All he had done was let the men through and then close the door, close it in Jendre's face and bolt it too.

———————

THAT had been early in the morning. Now the sun stood high enough to sneer at her folly: how her hands were sore from pounding and her throat from screaming, how her belly roiled with hunger because he had let no one come to her until she was calm.

She had calmed at last, and he came himself with a tray of food, but she could not eat it. Not while he watched, at least. Now he was here, she was angry again and more than angry, a very long way from being calm.

"You should have sent one of the women with this," a flailing hand above the dishes, not quite stupid enough to catch hold of them and hurl them, hurl all the tray at him. "Buy peace at a distance, with weaker bodies than your own, why not? If that's how you buy your influence at court, why not your domestic quiet?"

"Sidië buys me nothing, Jendre. You know this. She is a hostage, not a gift. Yes, they will use her while they can, and no, we will not see her back again, or never as she was; but that is to ensure my loyalty, not to win me advantage. The court commands, it does not sell its favours."

She snorted. "It commands those who beg to be commanded. You have begged and bribed and killed when you had to, to be allowed to stand where you are. You chose this day to come."

"I have done what I had to, yes, to rise in the city. With no great family at my back, it was not easy; it has taken longer than it might, and it has cost me more. Sidië was a part of that price, but no more than any man in my position is required to pay."

"You could have been less greedy for position. You could have stayed where we were happy," down there, in the lower levels of the city, in the houses she could see out of her window. Her little sister was too high a price, for a high place and a far view.

"Children want to do that, always. Adults know better. You cannot keep contentment in a cage."

"For a while, you can. You can try. You could have waited till she too was too old to be a dreamer . . ."

"She must still have been a hostage. One of you must, and I have other plans for you. Jendre, she is gone; accept it. Try to be grateful."

"Grateful!"

"Yes. I would not have chosen this for either of you, but as it cannot be avoided—well, better her than you. As I advance, so too do you. You can have a life now, and a good one. Be glad of that and thank me for it later."

She would not do that, she would never do that. It was his gift, to rise on others' backs and see only the step ahead, never to look down and see the broken bodies, broken lives of those he left behind. She refused to inherit what she despised. Be grateful, for Sidië's terror now and her years of imprisonment to come? Imprisonment and worse: only rumour spoke of how the dreamers lived, and she thought the blackest rumour not black enough. She would sooner die than be grateful. Right now she would sooner kill her father. Wise to herself, though, she had locked her knives away. Nor had he come close, or relaxed his watchfulness. Even among his own, he was a cautious man. All she could do was throw food at him, and that would win her nothing better than a beating and the loss of this precious little privacy, her room in his house.

He was leaving her now, giving back that privacy, closing the door behind him. She heard his footsteps on the stairs; she heard the lower door opened and then closed; she listened for the sound of the bolt, and wasn't sure. And was too proud, far too proud to go down herself to check. She would assume that she was locked in, by her own hand: that she had bolted the door herself, against any return of her father. She wasn't sure that there was a bolt on the inside, but she would assume that too.

At least for a while, she would. For as long as it took to eat and eat, to gorge herself on soft bread and olives, on chicken cold in a sauce of pounded walnuts, on dates and pomegranates and figs. Sidië would scream herself sick in a rage and turn away from any food; half the women of the house would cry themselves out of all appetite for any reason or for none at all. Not so Jendre. Food was fuel, and she burned it like wood in a furnace. To be angry was to be hungry, passionate meant starving.

There was nothing nice, nothing delicate about her when she ate. Not much at any time. Sidië's mother was a fine-boned and fragile creature, her father's pet for a season, not so now; Sidië had been shaped in that same mould, light of touch and light of temper, capricious and quicksilver. Jendre had something of her own mother in her, and she had her father's strength of will, everyone said so, and a fair share of his body's strength as well. Which must needs be fed, and so she had his appetite also, unless that was her mother's.

When she was done with eating—when the dishes were empty, by and large—she took the last handful of dates out onto her little terrace and spat the stones out over the balustrade, trying to send them all the way to the street and watching them fall short one by one to lose themselves in the plumed grasses on this side of the wall.

She used not to be so feeble. Time was, when she would have been out of her casement and over the roof and away, to find her least reputable playmates and run wild half the day till someone found her and brought her home for a whipping.

But they'd lived down in the city then, in the city's heart, where one house butted against its neighbours on either side and the roofs made a playground and a highway, half a home. Here she was isolated, penned beyond hope of any freedom. Their great house stood in its own wide gardens, where men watched every pathway; around the gardens was a wall, and that was guarded too. The guards weren't family men, too new. They came with her father's position, from his army friends; they were loyal to him alone, or else to him at best.

She pined for her old and easy life, going when and where she chose, coming back when and how she must. She had always liked her home, she had always loved her father; she never ran for long, and never far. He used to call her pigeon, because she liked to flock and she had to fly. He could have caged her then, bars on her windows and a watch on the roof; he never did.

She'd meant to have some birds here on the terrace, birds in cages, so that when the High Guard came to fetch her she could open the doors and let the creatures fly, her last bright wishes sent abroad. But she couldn't ever bring herself to make a pretty thought real, if it meant caging beauty even for that little time; and now they had taken Sidië instead, untutored and untamed.

Jendre couldn't see the old palace from this side of the house. She could send thoughts like birds winging towards her sister, but only blindly. Nor could she say what they should seek. Not the peremptory, demanding little sister who teased and tormented her and all the other women of the house unheedingly, unhindered; not the soft, sweet-smelling, cuddlesome little girl who shared her bed, all whispered secrets in the darkness and elbows in the morning. Nothing that she would recognise, Jendre thought. Not even the familiar sight of Sidië frustrated, Sidië in distress: her face bruised with fury, her eyes swollen and her yellow hair matted to her head, fists and teeth and screaming. Not that.

Little was known about the old men who kept the children who dreamed the bridge. Much was murmured, little known. Where they were exactly, which pavilion—well, perhaps. Jendre had been shown it, at least, more than once: looking down into the palace gardens from the crag that overhung the wall, her companions—younger, wilder, wiser—had pointed and said *there, there they all are, in there* . . . Several times, different companions, always the same pavilion.

Little was known, but this was certain, that what went on in there could not be learned from those few who came out. Sometimes—when it didn't matter, when the family had lost its property, its influence, its men—a child might be returned. When it was no longer useful, either as dreamer or hostage. Never the same child, though, never the proud boy or the pious girl who had been taken. They disappeared into their father's harem or away to some far family farm, and nothing was said aloud, but of course there were whispers: *fat and feeble, feeble of brain and body, barely aware* . . .

She didn't want to think of Sidië like that, not yet; but why would they wait, those old men with their smoky skills? A screaming, sickening, starveling child would be no use to them. Her sharp little sister dulled and stupefied, lulled into somnolence, a waking sleep—it was a dreadful thought, Jendre couldn't bear it. But was it better to hope that rumour lied, that Sidië was still screaming, sobbing herself into a fever, refusing all food and comfort?

She didn't know, she couldn't choose. She wished for her father's mind, all steel, traps and cages. He could close off that place where he kept Sidië: all his memories, all his affections locked away, not to be a trouble to him. That was how she thought of him, his mind like his house, divided.

Jendre thought her own mind was more like a tree and tender yet, slender yet. She could be afraid for herself, in those little breaths of time where she could stop being afraid for Sidië. *I have other plans for you,* he had said. If she was not to be a dreamer, she must necessarily be a wife. That burden she'd always thought was Sidië's to carry. *You have your daughters all the wrong way round, father . . .*

But no: if Jendre was too old for dreaming, then Sidië was too young for marrying, right now when he needed both a hostage for the Sultan and an alliance for himself. It was ill timing, nothing more; he should have been swifter to rise at court, or else more slow. As he was not, no doubt she should go through to the women's quarters, to learn what man she must be married to. Someone there must know.

As soon as she could face it, she would do that. There would be tears and lamentation, though, more tears than she could bear just now. There might be accusations, too: *why her, why our little pet instead of you? It should have been you. Did you plead, did you beg, did you give her over with your own betraying hand?*

There would be some at least who thought that way. Well, she had scowled down half the harem half her life; she wouldn't be intimidated now.

One last look across the tumbling roofs of the city to the far wide water and the bridge that arced above it like a strung bow, a rainbow with an oily sheen, slippery with shadows and sickly even in sunlight. She could not see it now, she could surely never see it again without thinking of Sidië. Sidië and others, all those taken away to dream.

She shuddered and turned away, stepped back into her chamber. There were footsteps coming up the stairs, and she wouldn't be intimidated by those either, although she knew the slow shuffle of them as well as she knew the pace and beat of blood in her own body. If her father had locked her in again, she'd never know it now. It would have made no difference, anyway; Clerys could walk through any door, locked or bolted, barred or sealed. And would do it, of course, a day like this. She should have come sooner. No doubt she'd been busy with Jendre's father, but even so, she should have come sooner . . .

She came now, with her arms full of colours and no easy comfort on her tongue, no idle words to dull the edges of the day. It was Jendre who spoke first: who looked at what Clerys carried, silks and satins, and said,

"What, does he seek to distract me with pretty gifts, does he rate my anger—or my sister—so cheaply?"

"Why would he rate your anger at all, then, what is that to him? This day would come; if you had listened to the world and not clouded yourself in trouble and foreboding, you would have known that it would come like this. It is always little children who are taken."

"It's always the firstborn," she said sullenly, still trying to cling to what was already lost.

"Not so. With the great families, of course, that is known from the day of the child's birth, if it survives; but for men such as your father, who need time to climb so high? Always a small child, it must be. If there is none, such men do not climb. You should have known."

"Oh, and you? You are slave here, it was your duty; what did you say, who know so much?"

"Slave, am I? Well then, let me be a slave. No part of my work, to warn my mistress that she blinds herself to what is true and clear."

In truth, Jendre wasn't sure what Clerys was. Only that she stood at the heart of the family, more so than Jendre's own mother or Sidië's, far more than her father's current favourite. Clerys' life was told in whispers, in rumour and exaggeration; she would say nothing herself, just that she was here now and meaning to stay, so how could it matter where she had been before? Jendre's grandfather had brought her to Maras and to his house, or so Jendre had heard: a captive in war, a young concubine to please him in his age. She had also heard that it was Clerys who first introduced her father to the pleasures of the body, either before or after the old man's death. Either way it was a scandal, that a son should enjoy his father's woman: harem gossip, never to be flung about beyond the wall. Even now, there could be harm to come of that. Especially now, when he had his place at court.

And had given his daughter to secure it, and the wrong one, all unready. Jendre glowered at Clerys. Whatever the woman had been in the past, whatever she might be now, she lived the life of a slave: she wore the dress, did the work, played at obedience while her tongue ran free. Throughout Jendre's life she had nursed and tended all the children of the house; the girls especially had always looked to her for comfort, for discipline, for security.

So now, "Truly, Clerys—if you knew it would be her they took, why didn't you say something? To me, at least, if not to Sidië?"

"What would you have done?"

"I don't know. Something. I could have prepared her a little, it needn't have been such a cruelty . . ."

"Jendre, for Sidië that was the kindest way, not to give her time to think at all. For you it's different, you need to plan, to see your road ahead and understand it. Then you will accept, and that is good. For her, not so. If she saw what waited, she would have been very afraid."

"She would have grown accustomed, in time . . ." But Jendre's voice faded, under the weight of the lie. Not Sidië, no. It wasn't in her to be quiet, to accept. She would have screamed and wept, and gone on screaming.

"When would you have had us tell her," Clerys went on unremittingly, "a week before they came, a month, a year? How much terror would you put your sister through? Better this way, let her have just the one morning and farewell. By now she will be easy."

"You can't know that." It was rumour, all rumour, what the old men did with their smokes and spells. Slaves and daughters, what could they know for true?

"Your father can. Or do you imagine him to be as ignorant as we are? Do you think that he would send his child into the dark, where he has not been with a lamp already to see what waits her there?"

That was right, of course; he would have learned long ago what really happened to the children of the bridge. It would be important to understand it, if he was to rise. Likely he would have been to the old palace to see for himself.

"Well, but you could have told me, at least. You said yourself, I need time to prepare . . ." And perhaps that was the true cause of her rage now, her own shock and hurt, and not her sister's suffering at all. She didn't want to think so, but perhaps.

"And how long could you have held the knowledge secret, you? You never could keep anything from her, that she wanted."

Here, in this room that was meant to have been hers and hers alone, that Sidië had appropriated simply by the force of being Sidië, Jendre had no arguments left. She slumped onto the bed, onto the dresses that Clerys had spread there, and said, "Well, what's to do, then? Why all the pretty things if he doesn't think to buy my temper back, if he can send you here to do that so much more cheaply?"

"There are important guests in the house tonight," Clerys said calmly, chivvying her aside with little gestures of her fingers, picking up one of the dresses and giving it a shake, "and they will expect to see you."

"To see me? Whatever for?"

"Jendre. Even Sidië would have understood this."

"Oh. Yes, of course." Sidië especially would have understood this. Jendre's mind still hadn't caught up with her change of status, from sacrifice to marriageable daughter, valuable stock-in-hand. "Prompt, isn't he?" There was a bitterness on her tongue and in her voice that surprised her with the sharpness of it, she who had always been so acquiescent.

"It's for your good as much as his," Clerys said, all unmoved, unstung. "He is of the court now; if he lingers, you and he may find the choice made for him. We are all at the Sultan's disposal."

They always had been, but now they were in the Sultan's eye. The woman's arguments went on making sense.

"Well. So who comes tonight? And which of these shall I wear?"

"The green will look best, I think, by the time I have painted the day's tempers from your face. The dresses are a gift from your mother and her women; they have been at these for months, knowing that this day must come."

And had said not a word to Jendre—but that was ploughed ground now, let it lie. "You have not said who it is."

"What, should I know which lords wait on your father tonight?"

"Yes. Of course you know. Don't play with me." Jendre was learning distrust, learning quickly and from the woman who had taught her most and best; by the glint in her eye, Clerys was watching the lesson sink home.

"Well, perhaps. The pasha Obros is expected, his son Salem, their retinues. The pasha is—"

"The Sultan's old good friend, I know."

"I would have said married, Jendre, married several times to several wives and declares that he is tired of women; but that other is true too." She pursed her lips then, and would clearly say no more without prompting.

Impatiently, all unlike herself, Jendre prompted.

"And the son, then? Salem?"

"Is known also to the Sultan, I believe, and likely favoured by him."

"Not that," though that would not have escaped her father. "I mean, is he married?"

"Salem? Not that I know. He's a young man yet, though no doubt he has slave-girls and concubines."

"No doubt," but it was deeply indelicate of Clerys to mention them. Shocking to do so, to one who might be his bride. There was no point in a rebuke, but Jendre could and should be cool, chilly even, crushing in her silence.

"You may not be offered to either one, of course," Clerys went on, seeming quite uncrushed. "There will be others with them, who stand less high in the Sultan's favour; perhaps your father is seeking an understanding there, not overreaching so soon."

"Perhaps so," though it was no description of her father that she could recognise. That man had never fallen short of overreaching. She had half a wish to say so, she liked the sound of it in her head, but she was still in an icy mood and would not play.

"Or, of course," Clerys went on blithely, still unheeding, "it may be none of these. I said you were to be seen, no more than that. Perhaps he only seeks to remind the court that he has a marriageable daughter; it may be that he looks elsewhere to marry her."

That seemed less likely; she favoured the suggestion with no more than a grunt. Which won her no more favour in return than a wry look, and, "Come, you'd best spend what's left of the day in the bathhouse. A cold plunge will freshen you, and stop your head from aching; and then you can trouble your mother with questions and spare me to my work."

Which was entirely the worst suggestion that she could have made, and Clerys knew it.

Jendre stood patiently and allowed Clerys to undress her, to pose her in the new green silk, to fidget with the sleeves and folds and hems of it; she even gazed at her image in the glass and agreed that it was a lovely dress, and that she would look well in it when she didn't look so pale and puffy around the eyes, so like a child after a tantrum. In her utter determination not to be seen that way, she was perfectly quiet and perfectly behaved. And if that period of calm gave her time to dread the evening to come—and perhaps it would be the pasha after all, and not his son: men did grumble about the weary weight of their women, and yet did buy or marry more— then at least that dread could be eclipsed for a time by the nearer and so greater dread of spending hours in the harem, in her mother's company.

Chapter Five

HE Street of Smiths must have been vivid once, bright and busy, and not so long ago. Sund had been famous for its metalwork; all the world's traders came in pursuit of it, *caravans and caravels* as the saying was.

All the signs of that lost trade were here still. The street was gapped like a mouth of bared bad teeth, half the workshops standing open and empty, stripped to the shell. Even their doors and shutters had been taken. Some had a name still, fading letters on the brickwork, but Issel had never learned to read.

The goldsmiths and the silversmiths were gone, along with all the armourers who survived the bridge and its invasion. There was money in Maras and none here, and only a toll to pay, some extra taxes, perhaps a little pride or however you reckoned the costs of betrayal. In Maras, good work could bring high prices from the same men who would take it in Sund at a sword's point.

This was a long street, and seemed longer because it ran so straight and empty. The tinsmiths congregated at the further end; none had thought to move into the abandoned shops closer to the centre, to the fountains, to Issel in his need. Still, the trudge of it gave him time enough to break off a piece of lead solder, time enough to spit on it and work it wetly between finger and thumb until it was soft and warm and willing to take a shape, time enough to shape it into a rough round like an ill-struck coin.

Ironsmiths to left and right, then the workers in brass and bronze and copper, those who had stayed and could find work. At last the tinsmiths, and even here the finer craftsmen were gone, lured or fled away. No matter. Issel needed no delicacy, even if he could pretend to afford it. He bypassed a couple of workshops on general principles, to seem to be seeking the best. Then he spat again on his little lead roundel and smoothed it gently as he ducked under the awning of another. "Ohé, man, mastersmith, here's work for you . . ."

In fact, he'd chosen this shop because there was no sound of hammer on tin, only voices, which ought to mean that his urn could be mended quickly. It might also mean that the man was known to be a shoddy worker, but never mind that.

If he'd listened to the voices before he stepped inside, he'd have chosen another tinsmith, busy or not. Too late now. He was still blinking at the bright glare of the furnace, could still barely distinguish one figure from the other when they both spoke.

One said, "Work from you, is it, water-boy? I'll see your money first, before I lift a hand to it."

And the other laughed shortly and said, "Most men would lift their hand to him first. Any man who knew him. But you take his money, do his work. Swiftly, now. He should not be here."

That was true, of course it was true; he should be far up into the city by now, hawking his water. People would be looking for him. Others of the *sakalar* would be invading his beat already, stealing his customers. But Issel thought the opposite was also true, that she should emphatically not be here. He didn't want to talk to anyone today, beyond *take my money, do my work, suuu-uu, buy my water,* but most especially he did not want to talk to her.

And was not in the least surprised therefore to find her waiting for him, where he had not expected to find himself. The more unpredictable his day, the more likely she was to inhabit it.

It had always been this way. First and last, she was the only constant in his life; hers the first voice that he remembered, the only face to last from then to this. And from then to this, he had heard that voice from unexpected corners and seen her face where he would never think to look for it.

If she was a familiar sight in Sund, it was an exotic familiarity. Wherever she stood she seemed unlikely, a fat woman among a lean and hungry people, a poppy among grasses. She wore colours of flame in this drab and desperate city, as if to declare how little she belonged here; she turned her eyes on the future, as if to avoid looking about to see where she was now.

It was her master's food that kept her fat, of course, and her master's silks that dressed her. Presumably he didn't mind, though he was seldom in Sund to say so. One of those wealthy merchant-lords who had always traded with Maras, since the invasion he spent most of his time across the river; his property here was left in care of a steward and a small household. Which Armina his slave-woman ruled, by sheer weight of will. Issel had been in and out of that house all his life.

And had always only gone there when he must, had always left as soon as he was able. Reluctant to enter, and as glad to get away as she was to see him gone. Hers was no open-handed, open-hearted charity. She would feed him, clothe him, even shelter him at need, but the need had to be absolute. Better he sleep in a doorway tonight than beg a bed from her; she would agree. She watched over him more like a hawk, he thought, than a hen.

Which meant trouble coming, more trouble, if she had troubled to seek him out.

He didn't bother to ask what trouble. He barely bothered to look, let alone to look guileless, as the tinsmith took the cozening disk of lead from his fingers, frowned at its shimmer and tested it with his teeth. Satisfied, he grunted and tucked it into his belt pouch; Issel had been sure that he would. It was soft like silver, heavy like silver, now it had a shine like silver. It would keep that glamour only until it was dry, but long enough. It might be days before the smith found it again, dull and worthless, and he might never connect the slug with the boy. Issel had always been lucky in the small things, he would never have survived his life else; and he might need a tinsmith again.

He might not. He might never sell water again, he might not dare to. Last night might have been his own vision of his own future: poisoned and perverted, his body slumped into a new shape as his bones changed, his jaw stretched into nothing human. Issel had rarely glimpsed a dogtooth, under a hood or behind a slamming shutter. Mostly that kind hid until they could run, ran before they were found and driven out. Where they ran to, Issel didn't know. He'd always been afraid he might find out, learn by doing. There was no telling how long a boy need linger in the Shine before the poison seeped into his system, before his spine would bend and his legs bow, his face twist and stretch, his teeth grow long and sharp. Nothing showed to his own eyes yet, and he saw himself daily reflected in water. He checked his teeth more often, many times a day, and couldn't tell.

Maybe last night was just a warning, to drive him from the strand. He might keep from the dogs if he never went back to the Shine. His bones could be wholesome yet, young and strong and resisting; perhaps he could go on selling water. He wasn't sure that he could give it up, anyway. He was branded, soul-sealed, possessed; how could he walk away?

He didn't know. No one knew, unless it was Armina, and she wasn't telling.

The smith took the urn, hissing under his breath. Issel heard a shake of bells, all the little silver bells she wore knotted into her hair among the beads and the rags of colour and the leather strings and the shells; she said, "Learn from this, Issel. You should have learned already, not to stand between a thief and his silver."

He opened his mouth to say that he hadn't, and then thought that perhaps he had. Sundain water in a Sundain fountain, and the Marasi coming for it . . . Never mind how she knew what had happened or where he would go to mend it. That was Armina; and meanwhile the smith had lifted his head rather than his hammer, and was scowling.

"Issel, is it? That's a Marasi name."

Issel forced himself to relax, to let her answer for him.

She was vast and sweating in the furnace heat. She said, "It is; and what of that?"

"I won't serve a Marasi."

"Does he look like a Marasi?"

"He looks like a starveling beggar brat."

"That he does," she said, "and that he is. Do the Marasi beg? In Sund? If he looked like a Marasi, you'd serve him fast enough, for fear of his sword's edge against your throat. But he looks like a Sundain water-boy, which is what he is; and he has paid you for the work."

"What's he doing with a Marasi name?" the smith grumbled, laying the urn on his workbench and taking a chisel to it, peeling back the last of the lead that held the spigot.

"Trying to wear it out, if he can't outrun it. Perhaps his father was

Marasi; perhaps his mother was. He doesn't know, so how should I? I know there's no sense blaming a boy for the name he carries. Blame him rather for what he does with it—or with what else he carries, that he hasn't the sense to take care of."

"Not my fault," Issel muttered. "The soldiers came while I was at the water, what could I do but serve them?"

"You could have stayed alert and run, not been idling when they came."

"I wasn't idling, I—" He'd had his arms in the water, which was a very different thing from being idle; but he couldn't explain that, he didn't have the words, even if he'd wanted her to know. Anything she didn't know already, he wanted to hug closely to himself.

"You were late in any case, you've been kicked more than once today. If you'd been early to the fountains, you wouldn't have been caught at all."

He thought that was obvious. It wouldn't do to say so. He said nothing. Into that little silence, the sound of the tinsmith's hammer fell like a hard rain: sharp and perfunctory, invasive, meaningless.

"Well," she went on, "at least you're swift to duck when you have your eyes about you. And quiet under a kicking, you'll need that more. What's coming to you can't be ducked. And you know where to look for help, that's good too, and how to pay for it." Her eyes were dark and strange, and never flickered. She was telling truth, not teasing. This was why he feared her: because of what she saw. "But you'll need to be swift-heeled away from here. You should have been up early, boy. You must run now to catch the tail of the day, or else it leaves you lying in the dust."

When he'd been small, when he'd been hungry he'd chased rats and caught them by the tail. And been bitten for it, fair payment for his supper. Sometimes, often he'd been a moment late in his leaping, and his fingers had barely closed around the stiff twisting thing as it slipped away. He'd lain there and sobbed at failure, at disappointment, at another night with a gnawing belly. She knew, she'd seen.

Again, he said nothing. She said, "I'm fat and slow, I'm leaving now. He won't listen," with a jerk of her head back towards the smith, meaning *I won't try to tell him,* meaning *he is doomed already,* "but you do. You do that, you listen to me. Don't be slow away, Issel, or this day leaves you in the dry."

The poor of Sund—which meant almost everyone in Sund these days, himself and everyone he'd ever known—laid their dead in caves and holes in the hills behind the city, a far cry from any source of water. She was saying *listen or die, get away from here swiftly,* but she wasn't saying *come with me, come now.* He glanced to where the smith was working, and said, "It's only an urn, Armina. Why should I wait?"

"You need it."

He had thought so too, until this minute. But, "I can live without it." He could beg and steal and run errands, as he had before. The urn was always heavy, a weight on his back and a weight on his mind also, what he had done to get it.

"No. You must not. It is needful, Issel. Save the urn, save yourself; there is no more you can do today."

"I could take it now, come with you, have it mended tomorrow . . ." She was urgent for herself and urgent for him, but separately; it was starting to prey on his courage.

"*No!* You must wait, you must see it mended, you must take it with you when you go. But you must go swiftly and carefully, as soon as may be. I must go now . . ."

She gathered her pots up into a sack and then she did go, but not out into the street. Deeper into the shadows of the workshop, rather. It was curiosity as much as frustration that drew him after.

The tinsmith lived behind his shop, a single life in a single squalid room. Issel looked, Armina sniffed, they both moved on. An open door led out into a yard heaped with broken things: kettles and castings and the stuff of his trade but not that alone. There was ironwork and woodwork and more besides, bricks and stones from fallen buildings. The smith was a gleaner, and a hoarder too. Many in the city earned coppers from what they could scavenge or steal; much of what he saw here, Issel could sell tonight if it were his. To have gathered so much and not sold it suggested a man not as hungry as he was greedy, wanting to keep what he possessed.

Issel didn't see the point. He owned the clothes he wore, the things he carried and the urn on the tinsmith's bench; all else came and went again, for money or food or favours.

A gateway in the yard led out to a narrow alley, gutters and shadows and dank stone. Armina plucked up her skirts and picked her way between the puddles. He stood and listened to the bells in her hair, random music like slow rain on water; he watched her in her rolling rush, like an overladen ship beating against wind and current, much effort for little gain; and he thought how much effort she put into his life, and how little he gave her in return.

Slave herself, she had fought to keep him free: free to hunger, free to crawl from one filthy mudhole to another, free to be a thief and a beggar and whatever else he could achieve. When he saw her in the streets, it was always a portent. She had come to find him, to fetch or send him somewhere, not always to his comfort. Whenever he went to her master's house in search of her, she would make play with her bells and cards to mark out his future path. Sometimes it was hard to be sure which he dreaded most, her hand directing his life or her eyes foretelling it.

Sometimes, though, he could be grateful. Today, this morning, now. She was never clear in her warnings, but when she said *don't be here* he took her seriously. He had good reason to.

Back into the workshop, then, and glower at the smith, *hurry, hurry . . .* Out into the street, a glance up at the sun in case the smith was watching, *see how the morning rises, feel the heat, there are thirsty men abroad and me not selling water, hurry, hurry . . .* And then a look left, a look right, try to see the real trouble coming.

Nothing in sight, nothing yet. All he could see was a street not full of people, craftsmen not overbusy, bringing their work out into the sunlight. No one seemed alarmed; the only urgency was his, and that was truly Armina's. She had seen, and not said, what was coming; it might be anything, sickness or accident or sorcery. It might be nothing that he could see at all. Better not to tease himself with looking; better just to tease the smith, *hurry, hurry . . .*

But the man in the workshop over the way was pouring molten tin into moulds of sand, and it jagged at Issel's eye like liquid fire as it flowed, like a distillation of water, essence of spirit. He saw the weight of the earthen crucible, he saw the shimmering heat in the tongs, he saw the smith's caution in pouring and his boy's in tapping each mould for air. Above all he saw the metal's fierce gleam, the heavy milky run of it and the radiant stillness after where it peeped through sand and steam together.

He didn't see the Marasi before he heard them, the tramp of booted feet and voices muttering. Too late, he jerked alert: a sergeant and half a squad, young and dirty-pale in the sun. Another fresh draft, newly brought across the bridge. Still shaken, still uncomfortable inside their skins and untrust-ing in the earth beneath.

Their dress was casual, their boots dragged in the dust, they talked in soft voices and stared about them as they went. It looked to Issel as though they were simply being shown the city, the major streets, the districts they would need to know, the markets and the foodstalls and where to find a whore.

He stood still against the pressure of Armina's voice in his head, the al-most physical pressure of her hands invisibly, insistently against his body. The smith had hoisted a new crucible, a fat and clumsy pot without a han-dle, glowing coals and cinders still clinging to its base. Too dull to glow it-self, too dry to hiss or steam, it made the air ripple with its heat. The smith gripped it with long tongs; his bare torso steamed and ran with sweat, while his muscles flexed and stretched like living things beneath his skin as he managed the arm's-length weight and the danger of it. Puckered scars were scattered over his skin and his boy's too, arms and ribs and faces, where all their wary care had not been enough.

The soldiers had reached that workshop, and were passing by. The smith's boy spared them a quick, nervy glance, his master none at all. It didn't seem to matter; the sergeant was paying them no more attention than they were him. Maybe Issel was wrong to look there for trouble. Maybe Armina was wrong altogether, though that would be a first . . .

Except that one of the soldiers, one of those blond lads who looked barely older than Issel himself, one of them was losing his grip on what was solid and true. Issel could see it happen: like seeing a man drunk on alcohol or smoke, just in that moment when he feels his body or his tongue slide away from him. The lad shivered suddenly, and his skin glistened; his feet stumbled and his eyes lost their direction. He shook his head to a com-rade's question, and blundered out of reach of a steadying hand. His own hands tried to snatch at a balance that wasn't there; he seemed sure to fall, but doubled over instead to spatter a thin bitter vomit before his feet.

And was still moving, still trying not to fall and not to tread in his own spew, and so he strayed blindly into the smith's back, just as that man tipped his brimming crucible above another mould.

The smith kept his feet, kept his grip on the tongs, even kept their grip on the crucible. Better if he'd let all fall. Instead he jerked forward, one short and deadly pace. The crucible swung in a slow arc; tin spilt in a silver rain. The smith's boy had just time to start a scream as the thin stream of it ran up his leg where he was kneeling beside the mould. He never finished his screaming, because the body of the crucible struck his head and the weight of it might not have been a killing blow but the heat of it surely was.

The boy dropped down across the filled moulds, spilling several. He lay there while the still-molten metal poured and pooled around him; there was a hiss and stink of burning, cloth and flesh, but nothing in him moved. The side of his head looked bald and boiled, where the crucible had struck.

The smith stared down at him, and then began a keening of his own. *Not just his boy,* Issel thought, *his son, surely . . .*

He had time to see what happened, and to see quite clearly what would happen next. He had time to wonder, *is this how it is for Armina, all the time, seeing time so clear, like a road laid out ahead and our feet set to march along it?* He had time even to be surprised how much time he had to think these things, how slow time seemed to run.

The smith had still not loosed his grip on the tongs, nor theirs on the crucible. Now he turned, and the muscles in his shoulders strained to whip his arms around with that fierce weight dragging at them.

The soldier had staggered on, just a pace or two, not far. He was dragging his hand across his face, blinking about him, trying to understand. And then the crucible found him and crowned him, uptipped, disgorging; for one terrible moment Issel could see the flow of shining tin running into his eyes and burning deep while his mouth gaped wide below, screaming in silence, bereft of any sound at all.

His was another death and worse, more stupid, lethal.

WARNED and ready for it, Issel at least could move against the shock that stilled the street. His feet were already carrying him back into the workshop while sergeant and squad, smiths and customers and passersby were all still staring, rapt, appalled.

Out of sight was good but not enough, not by a distance. As much distance as possible. He gestured at the smith for silence, for speed. The man just gawped at him, hammer in hand, his head turning foolishly one way and the other. He must have heard the screaming; now there were other noises, steel and shouting, running feet . . .

He was too slow, this smith. Quick with his hands, the cup reshaped and back on its chain, the spigot in place and looking practical; slow in his head, though, where speed mattered more. He was a burden that Issel couldn't afford.

Just the urn, then, take the urn and go. The smith hissed at him, stood in the way, shook his head. He was going to speak, he was going to say *not yet, I haven't finished,* and *what's your sudden hurry, what's happening out there?* Issel could see his own death spelled out in the words, in the delay.

He ducked under the smith's raised arm and snatched the urn off the workbench, and was too late already. There was a shadow coming in from the street, a soldier, sunlight catching the blade in his hand.

"You, boy, put that down. Both of you, into the street. Now."

He was barely more than a boy himself, his voice tight and strained. He had seen two swift and cruel deaths, and there were more to come, some at his own sword's edge. A Marasi death would be paid for in numbers; as many as the sergeant's men could round up, they would kill.

Issel set the urn down again, and let one hand drop into a small quenching-trough where it stood on the workbench there. He did not, he did *not* want to do this, but his life was a thread held at the flame's edge.

He felt dizzy, he felt a searing rush down his arm to his hand as though all the blood of his body were being drawn there. He must have looked pale, scared, sweating, as any boy might when he saw the steel that would slit his throat.

"Out," the soldier said. The smith made a gesture of bewildered helplessness and started forward, doomed already, dead already. Issel waited until the soldier turned back to him, impatience rising, ready now to kill him here in the shadows; and he waited a moment longer, until he felt the water seethe and surge like a live thing against his open palm, until he felt the heat of it and the steam of it all up around his shoulder and he saw the soldier's eyes widen with a sudden fearful shock.

He thought *forgive me* to the soldier, to the smith, to all the others who must die today; and then he picked up that iron quenching-trough one-handed, water-handed, and he threw it with a strength he didn't own, which also belonged to the water.

He saw the square black tank turn in the air so that the water boiling inside it fell like a weight of flame onto the soldier before ever the iron's weight thudded against his skull.

Issel was moving already, urn on his back and run: through the workshop and the room behind, and so out into the yard. Armina had left the gate wide open. He ignored it, turning instead to where the smith's hoard was heaped and piled up. A foot here on a broken stone quoin; grip a bed frame and stretch a foot there to a slant of planks and keep moving, light and fast and nothing will fall. Maybe, nothing will fall . . .

Nothing did fall, Issel included. He went up that accumulated junk like a rat in lamplight, and so over the wall and onto the flat roof of the workshop.

———————

HE might just lie flat behind the parapet and hope not to be found. More soldiers must come, but they should see the open gate and chase out into the alley. They were fresh from Maras, they wouldn't know about the roofs here, boys on the roofs. They might not think to look.

But Issel was of Sund, he was a boy, he was on the roofs and he was in terror for his life; none of that preached stillness. The roofs ran like roads to a boy like Issel, clear and unguarded. The water might have drained him, but he could still run.

Indeed, he was running already. His feet had chosen for him, even before his mind could decide that running would be best.

Any boy growing up like Issel knew the roofs of Sund as well as he knew the alleys, the back rooms and the brothels. They made another plan of the city, a web of highways and secret access, swift escape.

Here in the Street of Smiths, every workshop crowded close, wall to wall. An easy leap took him from one to the next, all along the street; and each had its forge and so its chimney, height to dodge behind and shadows for shelter . . .

Issel ran and jumped, ran on and heard no sound of chase behind him. He didn't pause to look. He ran to the tanners' yards, where he could drop down from roof to wall and hope to lose himself in the swirling steam that rose from the pits below.

Lost or not, safe or not, he kept running. The Marasi might bring dogs; they might have magic means to hunt a quarry down, swifter and more lethal than a dog. Any dog would lose a scent in this; he choked on a sudden foetid rush of air and almost lost his footing on the uneven coping of the wall. Fall, and at best he'd come out black-and-blue after a beating from the vatmaster. He might come out green or purple; he might not come out at all. The liquor in some of those dyeing pits was poison, he could smell it like a slick of rancid oil over what was foul and stinking already. Pity the men and boys who had to work down there, but pity them from a distance, further than this . . .

Had his nose always been so sensitive, to separate poison from decay? Maybe that came as a gift from the Shine, to a dogtooth in the making. It was something new to fear as he kept on running, this time a fear that he could not outrun because he took it with him.

WALLS and roofs, higher roofs broken up with walls, more climbing than running now; he stopped, because he had to. What made him strong drained him also, it ran out of him like water. Terror could only drive him so far beyond his strength. He subsided, breathless and shuddering, just barely wise enough to slip the urn off his shoulders before he toppled back.

He lay sprawled in sunlight on a roof of tiles and gasped for air, for security, for comfort. Air was all he could find, but that at least came free, there was only the pain to pay for. When at last he could crawl a short way, he had a chimney of baked bricks to lean against and all his own wide world to watch.

From up here he could see every quarter of Sund the slave city, from the desolate fountain gardens to the richly green estates of the governor and his friends. He could see the markets and the traders' streets, and more smoke than there should be in the Street of Smiths. Fire was a stupid punishment for the dead, but the soldiers wouldn't care if they burned all of Sund, though their masters would. He could see no sign of pursuit.

He could see the crowded tenements of Daries, the river quarter; the beached and upturned boat hulls beyond, the long white finger of the strand; and then the world's river itself, broken with rocks and islets but as broad as a plain, as deep as a mountain valley, a wall too strong for Maras to breach, unbridgeable until they made a bridge.

He could see the bridge too, but he didn't like to look at that. There was no Shine to see in daylight, but it was still an evil thing, a wrong thing, owning no place in the world. Sometimes he wondered if the sun only hid its poison, not burned it off as they believed in the city, as they needed perhaps to believe.

Maras was too much to see, too potent, a stain against the sky. The Insea was too much water. After a little while, so was the river. Over his shoulder he could look south all the way to the enclosing hills, a defensive wall where they had no need to build one, no use for it at all except to hold their dead at their backs, like history.

Closer than that he could see the merchants' quarter, vast houses in their own gardens and no roof-run between them, only the streets where he should be selling water. Where other men would be stretching their own beats now, not hearing his defiant voice, "Suu-uuuu" to warn them off . . .

And so he was up on his feet too soon and slinging his empty urn, no speed left in him but a sullen determination not to lose this last thing that was his. It was hard to be a thief or a beggar where he was too well-known as both; if he couldn't be a waterseller, he might as well walk all the way to the burial caves and lay himself out in the dust.

He came down from the roofs and walked the alleys like an innocent, towards the shaded avenues of his beat. There was no water in his urn, he had nothing to sell, but he knew how to remedy that.

Most of the greater houses sheltered Marasi officers and their personal troops of guard, the original owners dead or dispossessed. Some few still held Sundain families, those prepared to buy influence or betray their friends. Issel despised both, and had sold to both. To some he sold more than water on the street.

Indeed, they were poor customers for water. All those houses had cisterns for the rain; many had their own wells. Which were watched over, jealously guarded, a sign of high status in Sund and not, emphatically not accessible to a young waterseller whose urn was dry, who must walk a mile otherwise to fill it.

Except that one of those houses lacked the busy household that would have time to watch its well. One impoverished aristocrat from an old Sundain line still clung tenaciously to his house, although he had no money to staff it or maintain it; he found his servants among the city's beggar children, it was said, food and a roof in exchange for rudimentary duties. Issel had seen them sometimes, boys and girls worse dressed than himself, out of place in these broad avenues and seeming to know it, slipping nervously off on errands or fetching foodstuffs home.

They'd avoided him, and he them. Ordinarily he'd have done the other thing, tried to befriend them, to trade, to win their trust; instead he kept his distance, for his own particular reasons. The house had a well, and they weren't likely to keep any careful guard on it, and none the less he had promised himself time and again that he would never use it: that he would haul his weight of water from the public fountain, go back and come again. Today he could not, dared not. If one of the soldiers had seen him with his urn, if the smith had said a word before he died, if anyone had spoken of a waterselling boy, he could be watched for. Despite Armina, despite his own hopelessness, he thought he ought to lose the urn, lose himself in the crowded city. Better that than lose his life in some Marasi darkness, slowly.

He thought he should—but not today. Not now. One more day to cry water in the sunlight, sell restitution to the thirsty, feel the spark and flow about his body . . .

THE gardens of the house were walled and he wouldn't go near the great iron gates, but there was a small wooden door in the sidewall. The lock of that was broken. He knew. Paint had peeled from the sun-faded wood, but a great dark stain remained, low down. He knew about that, too.

He forced the stiff hinge open with his shoulder and slithered through.

All the garden was overgrown, uncared for. There was a clear path, though, leading him between shrubs and under hanging branches. He'd expected to search for the well, like a man who seeks a wonder in a tale and must suffer first before he finds it; in fact he was brought straight to it. In a clearing in the shadow of the house was a low stone wall, set square to the four points of the compass and holding a long fall into darkness. Beside it was a bucket on a rope.

The windows of the house were shuttered, blind, as though it stood quite empty. It must be a strange poor service that the children gave, or their master demanded; Issel listened, and heard nothing from either house or garden. Quickly, then, he dropped the bucket down, and heard its splash. It was only as he began to haul it up that he realised that his hands were fizzing, as they did when they were wet.

His hands were wet. Because the bucket had been wet, and the lower stretch of rope. And it was a hot day, and the sun fell clear onto the wellhead. Issel might have seen no one, heard no one, but someone had been here on this same errand too recently for comfort.

Someone was standing directly behind him; he could hear breathing now, too late. Heavy, hungry breathing. He could feel a hand on his arm, sharp nails digging in.

He could hear a voice, oddly thick and slurred; it said, "You should not be here," which was almost what Armina had said before. She had been waiting for him, and so had this one too, perhaps.

He turned because he could, because he had to; and looked up into the face of his dream, dog teeth and smudged eyes a long, long way from the Shine.

Chapter Six

SHE plunged like a fine needle into a bolt of silk, piercing deep and leaving no mark behind. Like her life, the way she'd thought her life would be: all swallowed up, nothing to show but memories. She'd hoped to be remembered, sighed for, sheltered in the hearts of those who loved her. Those few who truly loved her.

Feet like a needle's point, toes pointed, striking down; and the sudden jarring contact too soon, like needle's point stabbing into thimble, unyielding. And now, now she felt the bitter chill of it, no more warm thoughts of silk, of love, of dying. She felt her lungs squeezed and her heart stilled, as if a brutal fist had closed around her chest. Her legs cramped, and she thought she groaned beneath the pain of it, the weight of it, the sheer crush of water.

She pushed against the bottom with a tremendous effort, driving herself upward, it might have been against all the waters of all the oceans of the world. And came slowly, unbearably slowly to the surface, and broke through, and opened her mouth in a desperate gasp, a breathless clamour, a thin weakly wheeze that no one close could hear. For that at least she could be grateful, as she paddled feebly to the plunge pool's side.

Dragging herself up the steps and into the welcome steam, she found warm towels awaiting her, more welcome yet. Welcome most of all were the hands that held the towels. Mirjana: one of the slaves here and a friend for years, a girl in their last house when Jendre too had been leaving her childhood behind her.

"Oh! *Oh!*" Briefly, all she could do was moan and shudder. Control of her jaw came back to her—*typically*, her father might have said—before the rest of her body, allowing her to clench it against the relentless chattering of her teeth, and then to grunt, "Rub, rub harder, idleness, don't pat at me! What do we keep you for . . . ?"

"Do you want me to begin to answer that question?"

"No . . . No," leaning back into the strong hands, beginning to sigh instead of shiver as the room's heat and the rough handling worked some warmth into her body. "You'd take forever, and never give me space enough to say *I know*, or *thank you*." Her bones still ached with cold, but there was some perverse pleasure to be found in that. Like creeping into bed when she was utterly weary, tearful with simple tiredness: to lie still and warm and comfortable gave a welcome even to the biting edge of exhaustion. Even so, she said, "Tell me instead, why do we do this? Why freeze ourselves, when we can wash warm and still be just as clean?"

"Why do you ask the same questions day after day?" Mirjana countered, wrapping a towel around Jendre's long hair and twisting, squeezing out a spatter of chill water. "Most of these don't do it, your father's precious flowers," with a wonderful acid sear in her voice, "they're far too tender for such treatment. You do it because Clerys tells you that it's good for your skin, because I tell you that it's good for your soul, because you have such an easy life you have to be reminded that other people suffer."

"Do I, really? Is my life so easy?" All the burdens of her day were in her voice, welling out all unexpectedly. Mirjana heard, she could not help but hear; and in a moment the towel was gone, forgotten, and her long arms wrapped around Jendre in nothing more than a hug.

"Most days it is, my love. And it will be again. Today is hard, I know. We will help, all of us who can. Even your mother, if you will let her. Come now, be good, go to her . . ."

Mirjana pulled her up onto her feet and held her steady while she stepped from thick straw matting into her rosewood pattens. Pretty with scarlet straps and silver nails, they lifted her a wide hand's span, a crucial span above the floor, above the scorching heat and the constant swirl of water. She did Mirjana the same service in return—simpler pattens for a slave, a plainer wood and linen straps fixed on with studs of bronze—and then they walked hand in hand through steam and shrill to where Jendre's mother held court.

––––––––––

THERE was a small squeeze of bodies in that corner, but they made room for Jendre on the dais. Mirjana knelt behind her as she nested into the cushions at her mother's feet, murmuring, "Sit up straight now, and let me oil you."

Jendre felt the slow, steady strokes of slippery thumbs rising up her spine, and was grateful: grateful to all those who loved her and would make this as easy as they could. Sometimes she wondered what there was in her that deserved such love, from those who should resent her. Today, now, she could only wonder why she was so needy, faced with this woman who ought to love her most and best.

"Jendre, daughter, what have you been about, fighting with your father and weeping at nothing, spoiling your beauty on this day of all the days there are? You, girl, put her back in the cold water, it will draw up those hanging bags beneath her eyes . . ."

Mirjana paid no attention. Jendre had known her mother longer, long enough surely to know better by now, but still she said, "What, is it nothing, that Sidië is taken from us and given to those who keep the bridge?"

"Nothing to me, nor to you either, unless you say that she was taken in your place, and try to be grateful at it. Girls go where they are sent; your sister is ahead of you, but only by a breath, if you can be wise tonight."

There it was again, that call to be thankful. Somehow it was easier to hear it in here, and from her. In this place conspiracy was as natural as breathing, the air was thick with it, the marble slick with it; someone else's suffering was always to be welcomed, as a sacrifice to forestall one's own. And if Jendre's mother cared little enough for her own child—women loved sons, perhaps, if you had to make a rule for it, and bartered daughters— then why should she care more for the pampered daughter of a rival?

Jendre looked about her, already sure not to see who she was looking for. "Where is Sidië's mother?"

Teres: a concubine, blonde and slender, frail, never thriving in this world, clinging to her one child as her only security. Even Jendre rarely used her name, she was identified so widely by her daughter's; but then, the same was true of Jendre's own mother. Women without sons trod uncertainty for their daily penance. And when their daughters were gone or given away, what then, what could they rely on?

"Oh, her? She will be in her quarters. Howling. No cause for you to do the same."

"No? And when I am gone in my turn, mother, will it be your turn to weep alone?"

"Why would I weep, with my child married so high above us, and I, Ezerria, known to be her mother?"

For a moment, a dreadful possibility thrust itself into Jendre's heart. When she left to join her husband's household, did her mother mean to come with her? Like Teres, she was concubine, not wife; she had no rights, no property, no family to watch her honour. She had never seemed to cling to Jendre, but she could change at need . . .

Jendre gazed at the square face and heavy hair, the determined bulk of her, and might have laughed at the thought of so solid a figure clinging to the slender reed that was herself. What need had Ezerria of her, of anyone? That woman would survive a cataclysm, by her own strength; she would survive any upheaval in the harem. New wives, new women, they never had shifted her and never would; nor would she be lessened by the loss of a daughter.

She would make it magnify her, rather. Her daughter—her husband's only surviving daughter, in any way that mattered—married into one of the great families, high in the court and in the Sultan's eye; oh yes, she could invest herself with a great authority on the back of that. There was one thing at least that she shared with Jendre's father, and that was ambition. In different ways and to different ends: he looked outward and she inward, he was restless where she was settled, he wanted power and she prestige. But they would both wait and wait until it came, and they would both spend ruthlessly of what they had, to reach it. Little Sidië had gone, in pursuit of it; now, swiftly, Jendre was to follow.

And she was surprised, if only a little surprised to find an equal stubborn patience rising in herself. Not the ambition, no, or not yet; she didn't know what she wanted to achieve. But she would wait until it was clear, until she had an aim. And then she would wait, and work, and spend as ruthlessly as she must until she had it in her possession.

She thought perhaps that people would be sorry then, although she wasn't certain who, and couldn't yet say why.

HER mother talked and for a while, for a wonder Jendre did listen. Perhaps she even learned.

Then Mirjana nudged her to her feet, and they left Ezerria still talking, still building futures in the steam. In the disrobing room Jendre was rubbed down with rough towels and oiled again, oiled all over, while she lay on a soft-cushioned couch drinking small cups of coffee for her dizzy head and great draughts of water for all the sweat she'd lost. Mirjana sprinkled perfume in her hair and left her in the firelight, warm and drained and dozy.

Now was the time when Teo should come to her, with all the gossip of the harem in his soft voice and sharp blue eyes. She'd gentled his accent and his thin temper; he'd brought new horizons to her imagination with the games and songs of his people, stories of seas and hills and cities far away. For a while, they'd been inseparable. Sidië had been jealous of their play, trying often to squeeze between them. It was the move to this house, though, that had forced them apart. The harem door lay between them, that she could pass through and he not.

Even so, he should come to her now. This was his time with her, always. No one was better than Teo, after she'd spent time with her mother. Clerys took her apart, to show her the core of what she was; Mirjana drew her close, to show her the deep reach of what she knew; Teo built her up, to show her the strength of what she had. Her mother simply ground her into incoherence, like meat in a mortar.

She waited, waited, closed her eyes and waited longer. Still the next voice she heard was not Teo's, nor Mirjana's, and not her mother's either.

"Well, are you sleeping, then, and the sun so low, so much to be done before we lose the light?"

"Clerys."

"Indeed. Up, up; clean is clean, but only half the need."

Jendre rose slowly, feeling towels slip from her body and hearing herself groan at the simple heaviness of it, astonished that so little meat and bone could weigh so much where it had seemed so light before. Stupid with sleep and scents and soaking, she stood and let Clerys wrap her robe around her, even guide her feet into her slippers.

"Where, where's Mirjana?" Clerys had long outgrown these fussy little services; it was always the younger woman who tended to her, in the baths and after.

"Mirjana is busy. So am I, but I am busy with you. Come."

A strong arm around her back, and she stumbled forward at the urge of it: out of the bathhouse and through one court, through another. She blinked against the glare of the sinking sun, and said, "Where's Teo?"

"What, will you ask after every slave in the harem? Teo is at his work, I expect. I would not know. I have trouble enough watching the women under my care," with a squeeze of her waist to say *you are one of those, the chief of them, the most trouble by far.* "The chief eunuch keeps his boys at a run."

The chief eunuch here was as new as the house, a gift from the Sultan. Jendre wouldn't think to challenge him so soon, to overrule his orders on a whim. *Later, later . . .* It was a promise to Teo or to herself, and made in silence: the kind of promise that could be withdrawn without harm, if it had to be.

But she was waking up in this fresher air and frowning, saying, "Clerys, where are you taking me?"

"To your mother's quarters, of course. You do not leave these walls tonight, girl. Did you think you'd be let wander, with the house arush with visitors and you the prime reason for their coming?"

Not wander, no; she wasn't a giddy girl anymore, she was growing up fast today, and any highborn man looking for a bride would be scandalised to find her casually footloose, even in her father's house. But, "I could wait in my own quarters. With you, or with Mirjana . . ."

Clerys snorted. "You will wait where you are told to wait, where you should have been kept in the first place, and saved my weary feet that endless climbing. Get used to it, Jendre: you are your father's daughter, and you will be a great man's wife, and it's time to stop these tricks and tempers. The life your father has made for you, your place is behind the wall, here or elsewhere."

And if she did not choose to accept that place . . . ? But no, that was a nonsense, no thought at all. The choice did not lie with her. There were always stories alive in the city, daughters strangled for that kind of disobedience, refusing to marry where their fathers chose. She had thought she would have less than this, a slow dead time in the old palace with the old men; even that had seemed better, anything had to be better than a eunuch with a bowstring and a swift, choking, shameful end.

"Must I go to my mother's rooms? Could I not come to yours . . . ?"

She liked the slaves' quarters, their closeness and comfort and the easy, endless chatter.

"Now you're being foolish. Your gown is waiting for you where I left it, where my workbox is, where your mother will expect to find you, in her robing room. She will expect to find you ready to help her, so come on, girl, hurry . . ."

———————

JENDRE was not ready by the time her mother joined them, she was a long way from being ready; but in truth neither she nor Clerys had ever expected anything else. Ezerria's expectations were another world, which they did not inhabit. And it took time, it took an age to prepare a girl for a night like this. She must try on the dress again, to allow Clerys to adjust all the little adjustments made before. Then she must slip it off again, and sit still to have her body powdered and her hair brushed out; and then on with the dress again and a great napkin tucked around her neck to protect it, the hair tied and wrapped and rolled up out of the way so that Clerys could begin to paint her face from her box of coloured pastes and powders.

Sidië had loved to play this game. When Clerys was indulgent, half the slave-girls in the harem might be going about with gaudy cheeks, giggling or scowling according to their mood, flaunting their colours or else scurrying to the baths to oil and scour clean. To Jendre, it had never been a game. She had seen those same colours used to hide pocks and blemishes on sickly sisters who had died, and brothers too. She had seen her mother use them daily, to bring life to flabby skin. When she was little she thought that was a simple truth, that paint could make a dead thing live; she thought that was why her siblings had to be painted with white, staring faces and bright red cheeks, to keep them from the long parade towards the family tomb. It never worked, and so she watched her mother carefully and all the women else, to see if they would fail also and so die. And she watched her painted toys, her dolls and animals with equal care, to see if they would stir and shift in their boxes, toss and moan and disturb her nights.

By the time she was old enough to understand the art, she was too late to love it. Only rarely would she endure it, even. Tonight, there could be no argument; she sat rigid and resentful beneath Clerys' soft brushes and hard fingertips.

Another woman, almost any other woman would have crooned and fussed, and driven her perhaps to screaming. Clerys worked in silence, something to be thankful for. And something else, she worked with skill and subtlety, nothing like the vivid crudities Jendre had seen on some women's faces. Jendre wouldn't look in a glass, but at least she could trust Clerys to paint her with a living beauty, not a mask. There was some comfort in that.

Small comfort in her mother when she came rolling in, slow and heavy from her long day in the bathhouse but still not done with talking. No more than Clerys would she croon or fuss; Jendre would have liked to scream regardless, except that she had learned years earlier never to do that, never to waste her furies against her mother's flab.

". . . Loyalty can be bought and sold, remember that. It's something you trade for, not something you trade with. It isn't coin, it's not dependable. Like love, it can be bought away from you, or stolen. Use it where you can, but never trust it . . ."

This was her mother's world, and a lesson on how to work within it. Jendre listened and learned and still wished her mother to hell and all her wisdom with her. She wanted none of it: none of the secret skills, the seductions and manipulations, the hidden hatreds and the whispered wars. Denied the bridge, she must be spent where she could be most quickly useful. Well, so be it: lacking any choice else, she would endure it. For her own protection, she would win whatever love she could achieve and buy whatever loyalty she could afford. But she would never follow her mother, to relish the struggle and find pleasure in each little gain, despair at every loss. She would never be a player.

———

BY the time Clerys was satisfied and her mother also, the sky outside the window held all the colours of an old bruise, yellow and purple and black. Jendre had already lit lamps within the room, setting them in mirrored alcoves to harvest all the light that they could shed. Now a boy went by the doorway with a rushlight, leaving more lamps burning in his wake; it was Teo, but she saw him too late to call. Or recognised him too late, rather: at a glance the boys were all alike, all dressed in skullcaps, tunics, trousers, with their heads shaved and their feet bare. Seeing him move in the corner of her eye, briefly she had not known him; he had not moved like little brisk Teo. His walk was slow and cautious, as though he carried a beating on his back. Perhaps he did.

She'd have gone after him to ask, but she wasn't allowed the time. They were suddenly in a tearing hurry. It was always so, in the harem: long languorous hours lost in a desperate rush, when nothing could be right or ready. Jendre was swept out of her mother's chambers as though these two strong and determined women wanted to race the sun to its bed, after lingering all afternoon to let it run. With one before to lead her and the other at her heels, with her long, rustling skirts gathered up to let her scurry ahead of a whipping tongue, she was bustled and chased through corridor and court to the dining room.

Silk hangings on the walls, low tables on the tiled floor, many cushions and carpets spread about, but no food yet and no attendance. The hurry to be here had nothing to do with appetite.

All the end wall of this chamber was an intricate grille, painted and gilded, curtained on the further side. Beyond that curtain was her father's dining hall. On either side of the grille, stairs led up to a gallery; that was where the interest lay, where half the women of the harem were clustered, whispering.

Her mother would be taking note, who was here and who was not. It was nothing to Jendre, not now. She climbed the steps, hanging back at the top to let her mother's bulk and authority squeeze a way through the crush, where she could follow in her shadow.

As below, so above: here was another grille, but here the curtain hung on the women's side, and had already been drawn back. There were soft carpets underfoot, and a splendid view beyond the curls and twists of the ornate grillwork. Jendre's fingers locked around cool gilt iron and she peered through the petals of a delicately worked flower, ignoring the elbows jabbing at her as others fought for space and sight of what lay spread below.

This was the women's privilege, their sometimes-privilege, to look down on their master and his guests at their feasting. Sometimes it was the opposite of privilege, forbidden. Some nights the curtains were drawn, with the new eunuchs standing mute guard at the head of each stair. Those nights there was music and laughter beyond the grilles, lasting late and late; the whisper said that Jendre's father would hire in a troupe of dancing girls for the entertainment of his army cronies, and serve wine behind the locked discretion of his doors. Dancing girls were not famously discreet, but no one cared what tales they might tell. Besides, it was said—by dancing girls, and others—that the Sultan himself had a great cellar full of wine, and served it to the Hierarch after weekly prayers.

There were many things said about the Sultan, and not all could possibly be true, but Jendre had always privately liked that one. It suggested that the old man might be at least in some part honest, if it was only an honest hypocrisy he had.

IN the men's dining hall the dishes, the decorations, the walls themselves glittered under a thousand lights. Tables and couches stood on a raised dais at the further end—to leave space at this end for those dancing girls, Jendre thought with an indulgent smile, not yet out of the habit of indulging her father—and half a dozen men sat among the cushions there, eating idly while they talked, while guards stood watchfully against the walls, while slaves and pages passed plates from hand to hand to save their masters' stretching. There were goblets of gold to drink from, and certainly no wine in them tonight; her father was no fool, to risk all his rising on a bold or premature gesture. For this meeting everything would be formal, proper, as perfect as he could contrive.

Herself included, he had contrived that too. She still nursed her fury, and forgiveness lay a long, dry road ahead, but she was too much her parents' daughter not to see the advantage of a good match now. For her, too, there could be advantage. She would do nothing to harm her own future, or her father's. She would be the ideal virgin bride when the men came to look on her; for now she could look on them, and see where her father's choice had fallen.

Six men, and one her father; another an army friend of his, old friend of hers, Tukus, who used to play with her when she was small. The two men had risen together, but her father always a little further, a little faster. Not Tukus, then. He was here by her father's courtesy, a gesture, a favour, to draw him to the attention of great men.

One great man, at least. Great men were easy to identify, even at a little distance. Sitting at her father's right hand, served by his host, grizzled in his beard and scarred in his face—that must be the pasha Obros, shield-friend to the Sultan.

Young men too were easy to identify, or one young man at least. At her father's other hand, with a slim moustache and no beard, no scars, no harm from the world at all, that must be Salem, with the quiet demeanour and the slender hands, drawing no attention to himself, speaking to Tukus when he spoke at all. And smiling his thanks to the pages and the slaves as they served him, and listening gravely to the older men: all breeding and no pride, and if she had to marry one of those men, she felt a surge of hope that it might be him. And told herself that was only wisdom, a lesson well learned from her mother; better to be first wife to a young man than junior in a long-established harem, trying to make a place for herself among too many, trying to please an old man with jaded or sophisticated tastes. Better to help a boy make his own place in the world, with a corner just for her . . .

She said nothing, and didn't know if her thoughts were written brutally clear on her face, or subtly so, or not at all. It didn't matter. She only watched, and only cared to watch; she feasted with the men, every mouthful, every unheard word and every gesture.

She had to be nudged and then shaken, when at last the men had finished eating: when they were having perfumed water poured over their fingers, when they were picking a last rose-scented sweet from the sugar dust in the bowl, when they were beckoning a boy to bring more coffee. When it was the women's turn to eat, and to be watched.

They must move down from the gallery to the floor below, where more boys were fetching in more food. They must gather around the tables there, and Jendre must be pulled and pushed discreetly close to the grille wall, to sit with her face in the light. She must not stare at the grille, she must seem oblivious to the men on the other side of it. She must eat little, talk little, smile not too much; and yet she must be animated, interesting, attractive. She must shimmer like an opal and shine like the moon, quietly compelling, fit to catch a young man's eye or an old man's fancy, both.

Half the ordeal was not to let it show, how much of an ordeal this was. Clerys helped, fetching her little dishes and sweet drinks, distractions for fingers, eyes and mouth; Mirjana was there too, helping too, cross-legged in the corner with her cither in her lap and playing soft melodies from her own far country, occasionally singing low and sad, the songs of exile and loss; remarkably, astonishingly, Jendre's best help came from her mother. Sat heavily beside her and free to talk where Jendre was not, where modesty demanded attentive obedience, bright eyes and a quiet tongue, the older woman was loud, garrulous, playing shamelessly to their unseen audience—and yet, as ever, she was subtle where she seemed to be most coarse. Like the worst kind of harem mother, trying to rise on her daughter's luck, she alternately praised and scolded Jendre; but somehow her praise seemed to bite more truly than she meant it, and all her scolding only served to throw more light on her daughter's better qualities.

". . . You should smile more, your smile's good and you waste it, showing it so seldom; and that slave should have painted you more striking, demure colour is no use on a demure girl, I can barely tell the paint is there at all . . . Talk to me, I swear my caged birds talk more than you do. Not when you've something to say, of course, oh no, I've heard you when you're passionate, when you're pleading, and your tongue is swift enough then, so why let it dangle now? How can you charm a man, if you cannot flatter him? Your voice is not unpleasant, all softness and low notes, like that girl singing, I've heard you two sing together when you thought no one was listening, and it's just as pleasing when you speak. *When* you speak. What, is there something holy in that mouth, that you will not sully it with talking? Nor eating neither, I suppose. It's a wonder you've lived long enough to marry, picking at your food the way you do. You need to put some flesh on, no husband is happy long with a scrawny girl. Happy enough to start with, I grant you, with his slender new beauty—but that won't last, neither the beauty nor the happiness, if you don't get some meat on those bones—"

And so on, and on: lifting the weight from Jendre's shoulders, freeing her to nibble on what Clerys brought, to listen to Mirjana, to nod and murmur and do little more while she was exhibited, described, lauded, all in the guise of exhortation. She had seen slaves sold at market with less clamour; she supposed it must feel quite a lot like this. Except that she had almost stopped feeling at all, she was exhausted of emotion. Perhaps being a slave at market felt almost exactly like this, like not feeling at all, only living through other people's choices, enduring it all because in the end endurance was easier than its opposite.

Smoke and spices, she would long remember those: the tingle of pepper on her tongue, the tickle of sweet smoke in her nose where it came wafting through the grille, to tell her what the men were at. Drawn close to the grille now and sharing a pipe of *khola,* they would be talking, no doubt, discussing her: her features, her accomplishments, her character. Would she make a suitable, no, an acceptable wife for the pasha, or else for his son? If they hadn't thought her suitable, they would not have come. Perhaps her father's status counted for more in the pasha's eyes because he had achieved it in the wars; the pasha was a soldier too, and famous for it.

Oh, let it be the son . . . She had lived all her life as a soldier's daughter; if she must be a soldier's wife as well, at least let him not be her father's senior. Let him be a young man with a beauty fit to spoil, not scarred and damaged yet, not wearing the story of his life written on his skin. Let her have a fresh skin to work upon, a boy where she could write herself a story, part of his, as he no doubt would write himself on her.

On her and in her, inside her, his seed to grow and shape her as her mother had been shaped, into someone new and strange, strange to her, Jendre-mother to his heirs—and oh, let it be the boy, unmarried and no father yet, let her children be his first, his preferred, his chosen loves . . .

Smoke and spices and those dreaming wishes, those she would remember. Of the rest, not much. It seemed to last for hours, till she was disgusted by food, by drinking, by talk and smoke and music too. She thought it was all betrayal. Conspiracy had swallowed her, and would spit her out; at whose feet, she had still not been told.

She endured, she let it all wash over and around her, and eventually even her mother began to lag in words, to show her weariness. Clerys came to sit with them and ate from Jendre's plate, "a shame to waste such food, why let boys and dogs fight over such a treat, if you won't eat it?" Mirjana stilled her cither and slipped away. Jendre saw Teo among the boys as they cleared dishes to the kitchen; there was no smile in him and no sneaking titbits like the other lads, he seemed to have lost his appetite with his voice. He used to look for her, and now she couldn't catch his eye. *Later* became *tomorrow,* and would do.

Tonight she would have been glad of her bed anytime now, her bed or anyone's, she would share gladly with her mother or with Clerys. There was no talk of sleeping, though, no small talk at all; they were waiting, and they none of them felt any need to say so.

They waited, with glasses of tea that no one drank; and at last, at long last her father came.

He came in smiling, clapping his hands, delighted; there was only one question to ask, and she was too tired to be delicate, to wait even a little longer while he spread compliments and thanks among his women.

"Father, which one must I marry? The pasha, or his son?"

Her father laughed shortly, a little cough of surprise. "Which . . . ? What, little bird, do you not understand yet, not even yet? The pasha was not choosing for himself—no, nor for his son neither. The boy came in his father's retinue, no more; the pasha came on his master's behalf.

"I mean you for the Sultan, girl. And so now does the pasha. That will be enough."

Part 2

Chapter One

ISSEL woke dry-mouthed in a dry place, dry and dark, and didn't understand it.

He knew where he had been before this, what he had been doing. He had been in the garden, by the well; he had been screaming, because the dogtooth had him. Had he fainted from sheer terror at the teeth, the clawed hands, the eyes, all so close, his private nightmare made flesh? He had fainted before from a dizzy hunger, or once in a sudden rainstorm, the exalted rush of it, black thunder and a river's weight of water falling. But to faint and then to lie unconscious while he was carried into the dusty dark—that was something else, and he didn't believe it.

Perhaps the dogtooth had a magic, to make him sleep. He'd never heard that there was any power in their blood, though, only corruption. The Shine brought no blessings. He himself was proof of that. He did have power, and the Shine's taint coursed all through it.

Besides, his head hurt. He pushed his fingers through his hair, and flinched when they found the sore spot behind his ear. No stickiness, no blood, but a definite lump. Perhaps he'd fought the dogtooth, fought and lost. Surely he would have fought . . . ?

He'd fought before, when he was in terror. He had the scars to show it, and the knife— No. He used to have the knife. A quick rummage through his clothing proved that other hands had rummaged first. The knife was gone, and his other things. He guessed that he could crawl all through this darkness and not find them. Nor his urn.

Which Armina had made him wait for, when she knew that there was trouble coming. And so he had run from that trouble into this, when he could have left the urn and left with her and so avoided either. Which she must have known, she who felt the breath of the future like a wind in her face. He could feel the weight of her hand on his neck, pressing and pressing.

He got to his feet carefully. Only his head hurt, and that only when he touched it or moved it sharply. Good enough. In the dead dark, he reached out his hands like a blind man to feel for walls and door, what kind of room this was. No hope of a window: there was no light in here, nothing from the world outside. All his life he'd lived with the smell of water, *in the river's breath* they said in Sund; here he breathed sour dust and stillness.

Cracked stone flags beneath his feet; walls of brick, with mortar crumbling at his touch. A small room, a storeroom empty but for him, its low door fixed fast and no keyhole, no hinges that he could find, only the bare planking with not a stud or a nail, not an iron fitment anywhere. It might have been made to hold him. His mouth was too dry to spit, and still wetter than anything else in here. He could make water, but nothing pure, nothing potent; it might have worked on metal, but there was none. Wood and water had little to say to each other at any time. Old wood like this, iron-hard and bone-dry, it might as well be stone; he might be better trying to soften stone.

Still, he pissed into a corner and let his fingers dabble in the spurting stream of it, feeling the warmth, feeling the tingle. Light ran from his wet hand and down the damp wall into the puddle of his piss, like fire running down a spill of oil. It was a thin light, a sour light, as his piss was thin and sour, no true water; but it was light enough for comfort.

Light enough to creep through the darkness of his cell, if not to beat it back. He saw what he had found with his fingers, and little more. The floor was grimy with long neglect, dustballs gathered in the corners; the walls were hung with cobwebs and curved inward above his reach. Small room, no window, vaulted ceiling: a cellar, surely. All that Issel knew about cellars had to do with dampness, with earth floors and earthen walls, but all his knowledge came from houses far less grand than this. Brick and stone were a revelation, an astonishment.

And something more, he thought, a statement: *I know what you can do, boy.* This place might not have been made for him, but it had certainly been chosen.

He sat and gazed at the barren cell while his piss-water dribbled away into cracks between the flags, leaving a damp dust that flickered faintly with a ghost light as it dried. Let it go; there was nothing here that needed watching. He waited, and the light died altogether, and he sat in the dark until at last he heard shambling footsteps outside, grunts, a wheezing breath, a soft cry of "Suu-uuu!" to tell him who it was that came. Not a kindness, that, and not a warning: just a taunt.

A scraping sound, metal on metal, the key in the lock; a slow, stiff grating. The door swung outward and the dogtooth was there, a silhouette in lamplight, the lamp held by a boy at his back.

Issel came slowly to his feet. He had been afraid of this before, he would doubtless be afraid again; right now, not. Not even as a shadow, a harbinger of his own future, *you too will come to be scuff-footed and heavy-jawed, slump-shouldered, strong and stupid, strong and sick for sleeping in the Shine . . .*

"You will come with me. Boy."

"Who says so?"

"He does. Your master now," which was all the confirmation Issel wanted. This creature wasn't worth his terror; he had a better reason to dread a better man.

It was an effort to say, "Take me to him," and a greater effort to leave the hollow safety of that cell for the lamplight and uncertainty of the house.

———

IT was the same house, he was sure. They had caught him by the well and carried him indoors, no more than that. Even the cellars boasted wealth and position, like having a well in the garden, here in Sund where water was not rare but more than precious. How many such houses could there be, where such a creature could hide?

He was afraid of more than the dogtooth now, but the boy with the lamp was not. Just a boy, with a shy half-smile; and he wasn't cowed and he didn't seem hungry or beaten or accursed. Issel might have looked for hope in that if he had dared. And Armina must have seen him here, sent him here, meant him to come here somehow. There could be hope and comfort in that too, but hope had always been a dream, and comfort was futile. He turned away from the thought as he did from the boy, gazing at the dogtooth's broad bent back and what he could see beyond, his first shadowed glimpses of the house.

HIS cell was one of half a dozen opening onto this passageway. Out here again the walls curved inward above his head to make a vault of the ceiling, to arch like a cat's back against the press of the house above. Out here, though, the walls had been washed white; the floor had been swept and scrubbed till its flags too were bone-white; other storerooms stood open, and they too had been scoured. A couple held sacks and boxes, jars on shelves, but the rest were simply clean for its own sake. Issel thought that his cell had been left deliberately in the grime of its disuse, deliberately for him, not to bring any water anywhere near it.

He thought that wasn't a precaution, so much as a message: *I know you for what you are, boy, as well as what you will do, where you will be, where we can find and fetch you . . . .*

It was Armina's skill to see his future course and try to shape it. If his captor had that too, then Issel had more cause to be afraid. Except that he had no fear to spare, he had used it all already. A boy could be no wetter than a fish, no hotter than a flame, no more afraid than Issel. He was used to fear, as a fish is used to water, as a flame is used to being hot; this was only more intense. Fear was like pain, he thought, you could learn to breathe through it, to walk against it, to master it moment by moment and never to let it master you.

He'd had a lifetime's learning, and he was using it all today.

The passage opened into a wider chamber. There were tables here and troughs of stone, great hooks in beams that spanned the ceiling. It might have been meant for meat, for butchery, but there was no sign of use, only that pervading cleanliness. From one corner, a staircase rose up into dim shadows, a suggestion of daylight. The dogtooth led the way; Issel heard the boy blow out his lamp and saw the shadow vanish from his feet, felt the darkness close in at their backs.

The stairs brought them into a scullery, sinks and cisterns and a long, scrubbed table, showing in what light sneaked in through an open doorway and a single high, small, shuttered window. That was light enough, to a boy who had spent too long without. He didn't need so much, he didn't need any light at all to know that there was water here. He could smell it, he could taste it in the air, feel the damp on his lips like the breath of another.

His feet tingled where he trod, where a trace of wet lay streaked across the flags, but that was nothing. A stray beam of sunlight through a crack in the shutters raised a gleam from a puddle in the bottom of a basin, and that was still nothing next to the dark weight of water in the vast stone cistern below the window. A wooden lid covered it, but it was there; he knew it, he could sense it.

He took a step, two steps: not meaning anything, perhaps, as mindless as a plant that turns towards the sun. A sudden cruel grip arrested him. The dogtooth had Issel by the arm, sharp nails digging deep.

"Not there, that is not for you."

"You could let him wash, Baris," and that was the boy with the lamp, his voice sharp and clear against the dogtooth's slur. "He is wonderfully dirty."

"No. He comes as he is, the master has said so."

"Later, then," the boy murmured, this time to Issel. "Patience, be good and you'll be given water enough, all the water that you need."

All the water in the river of the world wouldn't be enough, Issel thought, to quench his fear. Did this boy also know about him, did all the house know? And what then of the world beyond? He had always tried to be careful. Armina must know, but she ought to be the only one. Indeed, he spent time hoping—or dreaming, or pretending, perhaps—that even she knew less than she thought. He'd never confessed, tried never to let her see; but he didn't know how to cloud the eyes of someone who could watch his steps before he took them. Most likely she knew it all and was just too wise to say so.

Unless she had said it here, to these. That made better sense, worse sense, another kind of sense: that this was betrayal, that she had sold him at last, after so many years of paying to keep him free.

———

FROM the scullery to the kitchen, vast to Issel's eyes and almost empty, the great fire pits long cold. He saw bread and vegetables, a cooked chicken on a marble counter, and his dry mouth tried to water. His belly stirred and groaned aloud. The dogtooth only grunted and tugged him on faster; he heard the boy chuckle at his back, and thought the laugh was kindly.

He could use some kindness here, if Armina had abandoned him. If he had time to benefit from kindness. It might be death that waited for him in this house; it might be worse than death.

Except that the boy seemed neither cruel nor afraid. Issel didn't want to look for comfort, but this boy thrust it at him. He seemed to be playing servant here, as the rumour was; well, Issel could do that too, and perhaps that was all that was wanted, a boy off the streets to fetch and carry and wait attendance on the master of the house.

The master whose other servants included a dogtooth who sold water in the night, in the Shine. There was truly not so much comfort there.

———

FROM the kitchen to the hall, broad and open with a high door bolted shut, tiles underfoot and a staircase rising. Across the hall and through a wide, arched doorway, moving from the servants' quarters into the master's now. Here too the windows were shuttered, so that they walked through a foreboding gloom.

One room led into another, and he didn't understand what all these rooms could possibly be for. Even if they'd been filled with furniture and carpets, with light and wealth and people: how would they be used, what could happen in this room but not in that? They seemed not to be for eating in; he was sure they were not meant for sleeping nor for bathing, and after that his imagination failed him.

His courage had failed him long since, but his pride would not. He could be humble, he could grovel where it might help, but not here. He walked tall, when he walked through the last of those confusing rooms and into the gaze of a dozen, a couple of dozen people.

Here they were at last, the people this house needed, though nowhere near enough. This was an audience chamber, meant to intimidate: long and shadowed, dark around the door. All the light was at the far end, where the sun struck down through tall, unshuttered windows onto a dais, where a man sat on a high chair while the others—his entourage, his servants?—stood or lounged against the walls or squatted at his feet.

Issel tried to shrug off the dogtooth's grip, not to seem hustled or dragged before this court, not to seem scared or reluctant. He couldn't shift those nails, so he walked forward like a prisoner, like the prisoner he was: proud and scared and doomed, he thought, with his captor at his side and only a boy behind him.

The silence seemed to meet and marry with the shadows, handfast and untouchable. This end of the hall wouldn't seem so dark, if it weren't so bright at the other; the silence wouldn't seem so loud, so pointed, if he couldn't hear the footsteps walking into it. The boy's soft and easy at his back, the dog-tooth's shambling at his side, his own nervous and trying to hide it.

Bravado was pointless, but he had nothing else. He always spent what last little coin he had, even if it was only a slug of lead made to shine with spit and glamour. He squinted into the dusty light to see who these people were, and found that he could still be surprised. Except for the man on the high chair, they were all young: boys not past their first soft beard, some not yet approached it. And girls too, and all of them dressed patchily, as though their clothes had first clothed someone else. They looked like himself, Issel thought, as though they snatched a living from the blade's edge. A school for thieves, perhaps, a beggars' court?

But no, surely, he would know of that. No one lived closer to the secrets of Sund. Or so he'd thought, till now. These children were a mystery beyond his understanding, and they seemed to be making mock of his own most hidden secrets. The youngest of them—no more than eight or nine, a bone-thin boy as worn and dirty as his dress—was blowing spit bubbles into a heavy beam of sun, just to watch how they sparked and fizzed in the light. Another, a dark girl, was on her feet with a little cup of water in her hand, stirring it with one finger, and he thought the sparks and fizz were in her eyes. Something twisted deep in the pit of him, down in the dark there, which he had long thought hollow and dead and empty.

Servants or acolytes, slaves or worshippers or free, young and younger, they might be watching him, but they all looked to the man in the chair. Their silence waited on his word. There was a stillness too that wasn't touched by all their little movements, nor by Issel's walking into it with his ill-matched guard. The man held the stillness as he held the silence, quietly to himself.

He was in his middle age, grizzle in his long hair and his short neat beard. His face was lined and marked by years of hardship. His dress was little better than the urchins' at his feet, a robe of drab grey with darns around the hem, but there was still a highborn air to him, the arrogance of lifelong authority.

"Baris, thank you. I think you can leave him now." The voice was light and casual; the gesture was absolute, a minimal movement in a single finger. The dogtooth snuffled and stepped aside.

The man had a goblet in his hand, filled near to the brim with clean water, well water, Issel could smell it.

"Did no one offer you a wash, lad? Well, too much water can be as bad as too little, when you're not ready. You must be dry, though. I've a drink here, if you'll take it."

Oh, he was dry, yes; and he would take nothing from this man yet. He thought there might be more danger in this quiet room than he had faced before. He might be standing closer to his own death than he had to the Marasi soldier in the tinsmith's shop. All the strength in this room knew where it belonged.

"No? No matter. Even a dog takes time to trust. And every dog can be taught in the end, though it costs a bite or two."

Was that an insult, or a prophecy? Or neither? The man was highborn, no doubt he had trained dogs and servants and thought them much the same. No doubt he had never walked in the Shine. But he kept a dogtooth servant and sent him to do exactly that; he couldn't pretend to be ignorant. No one in Sund could pretend with any credibility. All through Issel's childhood the city had watched its poor, its displaced, its river-folk and rebels changed by the poison-light leaking from the bridge.

It was an insult, then, or else it was a prophecy. Issel reacted to neither. This house should be safe—but Issel might have the taint deep in his bones already. He was sure he had it in his blood.

"My name is Tel Ferin, and I am master here. You have nothing to fear, from me or any of mine."

"I am called Issel," and he didn't believe Tel Ferin for a moment, there was much to fear here; but his voice croaked only because his throat was dry, no other reason in the world.

"I know that. Now. As does all the city, I think." There was a shade of humour in the voice, but it was turned inward, not inviting anyone to laugh. "We've been looking for you a long time, Issel. For someone whose name is widely known, you are particularly hard to find."

"You have me now. What will you do with me?"

"No more than you would like us to," though that plural was surely aristocratic manners and nothing more. Tel Ferin would do what he wanted, with Issel or with any of them. "We fetched you here to offer you a new life."

"With you?"

"Of course."

"Here?"

"For now, you would live here."

The man was offering a change, but not a choice. Issel wondered what would happen if he refused; he thought the answer lay in the silence.

Pride still asked for a show. He said, "Why?"

Tel Ferin smiled thinly. "Because you would be welcome; because you have been sought; because you are one of us. People in this city talk of Issel the waterseller, who has been Issel the thief, who is also Issel the thief of hearts, the silver-tongued, the slippery. All of that. But there is another boy who can do tricks with water, whose blood carries the memory of Sundain honour, from the days when we were strong. That boy people do not speak about at all. It took us too long to learn that his name was Issel."

"I don't do tricks," sullenly.

"Only when you have to." His voice suggested that he knew all about the Street of Smiths. "You have the skill. Every time you dabble your fingers in Sund-water, the city speaks of you. And we listen to the city. Did you think that you could hide from us?"

"I don't know who you are."

"Yes, you do—only that you have not stopped to think. Many people learned the water-magic, Issel, in the days when we were free; they learned from us, those of us in whom it was inborn. They did do tricks, and little more. It was we who purified the water for them, we who watched the river, we who raised up storms against Marasi fleets and kept our city safe. I was still apprenticed, not yet adept when they made that dreadful bridge overnight and marched across in the morning. We could do nothing; it does not touch the river, and our water could not find it because it lives in dreams, not in the world. They killed my master, they killed all the adepts they could find. A few of us escaped, mostly the young. The schools were burned, the fountains broken, but even the Marasi cannot kill the spirit. For twenty years, my friends and I have sought out children who show a native talent. We offer shelter here, and training. We have not found many—well, as you see. These are all our recent harvest. But now we have you also, if you will."

And if I will not . . . ? That was still the question he would not, need not ask. There might be chances later to ask it of himself. If he could find yet another way to live. For now he shrugged, and wondered how much of this Armina had known or seen or plotted. "I will stay," he said, as though it were a great condescension. "Where are my things?"

"Ah yes, the parcel. We took it from you." Tel Ferin was not apologising for that. His gesture produced the bundle of little things, but it was Tel Ferin and not Issel who received it from the dark-haired girl.

He laid it in his lap, and reached two fingers into his goblet. Those fingers drew out a scoop, a ball of water that held itself together, shimmering, until his hands reshaped it into a blade, a water-knife whose edge gleamed sharper than Issel could ever grind his own.

Tel Ferin held the knife for a moment, smilingly; and then he cut the rope and unfolded the gaberdine, brought all Issel's little things out into the light.

Chapter Two

THE Sultan was no longer young, but he was still swift in his decisions. Swift and ruthless in politics and war, that was his reputation; now they could say that he was swift and ruthless in matters of love also, if they chose to pretend that love had anything to do with marriage.

Jendre was too honest. It was politics, no more than that; unless it was a little about war too, the readiness for war, keeping the generals loyal. For sure it was not about her. These were her wedding days, and she had not yet met her husband. At least she had seen him, in street processions and at court a time or two; so far as she was aware, he had seen neither her nor her likeness. She had sat for no portraits. Perhaps he trusted the pasha's eye for beauty; perhaps he did not care. She was uncertain which to hope for.

If this was politics, though, it was politics dressed in silks and rubbed with scented oils, like herself. Also, and more unusually, it was politics conducted in the open, under the city's gaze. Like herself.

Maras would be four days *en fête*, to celebrate the Sultan's latest marriage. This was the second day; he might not have seen his wife-to-be, but half the city had. To Jendre it had always seemed one of their stranger customs, to parade the new bride before the people. The custom was said to have its origins in war, when conquering sultans would lead captive women in triumph through the streets. That might be true, but Jendre thought that this was politics again. Let the people see the Sultan's wife, and welcome her; let everyone pretend the city had a voice its lord would listen to. He governed by custom and decree, he could afford to marry by acclamation.

Yesterday she had been carried through the city on an open litter. Gilt wood and soft cushions offered small comfort against the stares of thousands; all her guards and attendants had been a frail palisade. Fine robes, a sheer veil, those meant nothing. She'd felt as naked as a slave at market and almost yearned for the gates and high walls of a harem.

That was yesterday and worst, being shown to the people. Today she was to take ship at the royal dock and sail downriver to one of the great waterside estates, to be shown to the lords of the empire.

The pasha's pavilion was their ultimate destination; the pasha's son was her honour guard, he and two dozen of his chosen men. Again she must go in the litter, but he rode close on her right-hand side, and his sworn-brother on her left. Between them they offered a welcome protection and the opportunity to look about. Yesterday she had sat rigid and stared ahead, seeing nothing, only desperate for the ordeal to be over. Today she might still feel like an exhibited prize, but she could at least try to enjoy the exhibition.

It was years since she'd been out so far in the city: not since she was a child, running with unsuitable friends in pursuit of childish and unsuitable delights. Older now, she gazed around her with new eyes that had no expectation of delight, but could at least appreciate beauty.

There was Salem on her right and Mussun on her left, young men dressed in their finest, crimson and blue with gold and bright stones to catch the sun, to catch her eye. There was beauty of a kind, two kinds, the works of man and God together; she could lie on her cushions and turn a languid head from one to the other, appreciating both.

But there were beautiful young men in every harem, if all you wanted was to look. Whatever thin pleasure there was to be found in it, she could save for later, for the rest of her life. Today she'd rather look at the city; a last chance was not for wasting. She sat tall and straight and looked out over the heads of the people, over the heads of her guards, even over the bobbing feathered headdresses of the handsome friends who rode beside her.

Maras held beauty in its bones, in brick and masonry and marble. Broad avenues and ancient narrow alleys, domes and towers, long walls and open markets, high arches and monumental tombs: skinned with gold and white and jewelled colour, plaster and marble and a thousand glazes, the city dressed itself in light as water does, shimmer over shadow.

Downslope and out of sight were the strange and misty colours of the bridge. They must go that way, she and her party, but not directly. The city's major streets ran parallel to the river, one above another like the strata of society that her father had always been so eager to climb. There were twisting stairs and plunging lanes to link them for folk in a hurry, folk on foot; those on horseback or in litters must take a slower way, winding back and forth between the houses. This high in the city, those houses and their garden walls were tall enough to hide Jendre from any sight of the bridge.

Besides, she was looking up. All her life she had looked out onto a horizon of hills beyond the river, beyond Sund; she knew its rounds and rises, its sudden crags, like clouds seized in a storm's moment. There was nothing here like that. The hills of Maras were contained within itself, annexed to the Sultan's needs or his people's whims. Even in the parks and gardens, little had been left untouched. The city's silhouette was all straight lines and measured curves: spires and cupolas, temples and great houses. Beauty was built, never found. Even a jewel had to be cut, a pearl set or threaded into its right place in the pattern. God had made the world, but it wanted the Sultanate to render it immaculate.

Up at the height, there was the Sultan's own estate, the New Palace they called it still, though it had been built by his grandfather's grandfather. In two days she would climb that height and not come down again. The next rising hill had its palace too, nestled into the crown. All around and trying to engulf it was a park, a long-dead Sultan's desperate gift to the city that none since had dared reclaim. She knew that park, she had spent stolen hours there with her stolen friends; they had climbed trees and walls and sudden rocky outcrops, seeking vantage points to peer down into the palace grounds. That was the old palace, the Sultans' former residence. The Palace of Tears had been its unofficial name for generations. Whenever a Sultan died or was deposed, all his wives and women had to leave the imperial harem; that was where they were sent now, to live out their lives in perpetual mourning for their lost lord. Or so the story was told. Jendre thought it more likely that they would mourn their lost wealth and influence, those who would mourn at all.

The old palace was also where the children went, who were taken to dream the bridge. There was Sidië, somewhere there; she would be like a reflection of Jendre, the two sisters each of them locked away on a hilltop, except that Sidië's cage would be not at all like Jendre's. Caged in her dreams, caged into dreaming: rumour was a nightmare in itself, leading imagination in a frenzied dance. Jendre was old enough to distrust rumour, but not to disbelieve it. Rumour could be moderate, where the truth was dreadful. Harem life was a scented, suffocating tedium, but nothing so bad as what little Sidië might face in the shadows of the old palace.

Jendre's head turned sharply away from low roofs and hidden cruelties; and so she found herself unexpectedly face-to-face, eye to eye with Salem, just where she had sworn she would not be.

Her abrupt movement must have caught his attention. She should be glad, she supposed, to be so carefully watched. She might smile, bright enough for him to see it through the transparencies of her veil; she might make a dismissive, self-mocking gesture, pitch a murmur for his ears only, *Nothing, it's nothing, I was startled by a bird, a thought, no more . . .*

She might have done; she did not. She looked, and felt herself snared by looking, and saw him caught by the same sharp snare. His gaze rooted itself in her, as hers in him. And she'd been so determined not to do this, she had to think *not my fault, no. Him,* she thought, *blame him.* He blushed and then paled, and she thought that he blamed himself mightily, and still he didn't wrench his eyes away. Which was his to do, he was the man and should be stronger.

Which meant that it would be insulting in her to look away, unforgiveable. Her solemn duty not to offend her host, her guard, she hoped her friend; she went on looking.

The eyes were dark and wide and anxious, but they would be dark in any mood. They had a sheen like moonlight on water, the same shadowed beauty that his city owned. The brows above were fine and black and made her think again of Maras, of the city's arches and domes and the hills it stood on, that defining rise and fall. His nose was straight and not too sudden, not thrusting itself ahead of him. His jaw was strong but not stubborn, his skin was smooth and olive, his moustache was a boy's effort, sparse and foolish; that must embarrass him among his men, but she found it endearing.

So long as she was demure and not blatant, she might be allowed a brief endearment. But this was not demure, this slow staring, this long draught of boy in sunlight. She thought that she had drunk so deeply, she could close her eyes now and see him still in every living detail, she might never need to look at him again.

Which would be just as well. She was going into a strange house, to live among strangers; she couldn't afford to arrive with gossip or suspicion dragging in her train. Worse, she was going to marry the Sultan, master of the city, master of them all. His eunuchs were said to have waxed their bowstrings for more than one of his women. Survival demanded care; this was foolish, careless, worse. She should pray for his horse to peck on the cobbles or for her own bearers to stumble, anything to pull their eyes apart. Someone to speak, Mussun, that should be enough; or a voice from the crowd, a shout, people had shouted before . . .

There was shouting, she thought, but that was too far ahead to save her. She'd have to save herself, then. Save them both. In the bodice of her gown, thrust into the beauty of the embroidered silk was something more beautiful yet, a jewel, a gift from the Sultan: a circle of emeralds enclosed by a circle of sapphires, the green of her abundant youth engulfed by his overmastering blue, eternal possession. The thought of it might have been enough, and was not; a glance at it should have been enough, but she couldn't move her eyes to look.

The stones were set in gold, in a brooch, a pin. A long and savage pin, that Mirjana had been wary with as she forced it securely through the worked silk, in and out. It should have had a sheath, she'd said, to save scratching herself or her mistress. Jendre had said that the Sultan never did sheathe his blade, except in another's body. And then she had blushed, while Mirjana snorted. But she was glad of it now, lifting her fingers to find where that point jutted from the silk and slamming the heel of her hand into it. The sheer brute pain of the moment dragged a gasp from her and jerked her head, her eyes away from his, shattered that web of spun glass—so fine, so strong, so transparent—that had held them gaze to gaze.

And now there was indeed shouting ahead, and it was growing louder.

Her escort was concerned; both young men were moving forward, one of them glad of the excuse, perhaps. She thought that perhaps she glimpsed armour under their bright finery, a glint of something more steel than jewel. Their horses were the same, wearing good strong leather and chain beneath all the pretty harness and the bells.

They were fit horses for the city, too, small and wiry, hardly more than ponies: light on their feet and swift to turn, none of the grand showy warhorses she'd seen so often in parades and exhibitions, bred for weight and power, wonderful in the charge and all but useless in the steep and narrow byways of Maras. Two cocky, showy young men riding in the people's eye, she'd have expected finery and nothing more, their gaudiest cockerel colours in oiled silk over oiled skin and the proudest beasts in their stables, blades in their belts only because the hilts were jewelled.

———————

IT was as well that she'd been wrong. The road took another of its sharp turns down and around, and here was the source of all that shouting. Here was a place of trees and shade beside the road, a place for rest and contemplation, with far views down over the tumbled roofs of the lower city and out across the river, to Sund and beyond.

It might have been those views that inspired some captain to set a military post here; it might have been the shade of the trees that inspired a contingent to settle here with or without orders. There were soldiers everywhere in Maras, the slave-soldiers called janizars. Taken as prisoners or hostages or tribute from the far fringes of the empire, the best of them were trained from children to be the swift instrument of the Sultan's will, the High Guard, vicious and cruel and loyal beyond life.

Those were the elite. By her father's report, more made sullen and reluctant recruits, hardened under their sergeants' whips into a mindless soldiery, fit to guard the borders and keep the Sultan's peace, fit to fight the Sultan's wars when needed. Here in the city, they were as liable to fight each other for the easier duties and the more comfortable billets. Sent out from barracks to watch the traffic on the road, bored and hungry, what more natural than to claim possession of this little park? They could argue, gamble, set up their kettles over cooking fires, doze in the shade, kill time as soldiers always had.

Janizars were trouble, that was understood: restive at the best of times, liable to mutiny if they were ill fed or ill-used, or if their officers were weak. This troop was in full riot, and her escort had been slow to understand. Noise on the street, in their own city, on a feast day? No doubt they'd thought of nothing worse than drunken men dancing in the road.

These soldiers might be drunk, but they were not dancing. Their encampment was a wreck of steam and sludge, where the kettles of meat and grains had been tipped over onto the fires beneath; that in itself would have been warning enough, if someone had only seen it. Always it was the first sign of a revolt, when the janizars overturned their kettles. She'd heard her father tell of a dull booming thunder rising from the camp, where the inverted vessels were being beaten like great iron drums. Not here, no need: this was one small contingent with a grievance, and they weren't trying to rouse the city.

Perhaps they only wanted to rouse themselves. That much they had achieved, with drink and shouting and throwing things about; now they were in the road and not inclined to let anyone past, merchant or servant, cleric or girl.

Especially not girl, where that girl came with an escort of guards and nobles. They might not recognise her, but they understood court dress when they saw it. Here were men with access to their masters the generals . . .

That might have been all they wanted: a message carried, their protest heard. But they were armed and raging drunk, and Jendre's guards were determined to see their ward safe through to the river. And their lord's son too, whom they had loved and guarded all his life, and his sworn-brother, who was no less a part of the family, no less urgent to protect.

When they saw a band of men in the road with weapons raised, swords and halberds, arrows nocked to bowstrings, of course they drew their own swords in response. And when Mussun pressed his horse forward between them to speak to the rioters, when one of those soldiers snatched free-handed at his bridle and snarled up at the young lord with his sword lifting in the other hand, the nearest of the pasha's men swung his long scimitar with concentrated purpose.

Jendre thought the janizar was only gesturing, no intent to harm. Too late to say so, to cry out *no, stupid, don't!* Too late for him, perhaps too late for all. Nothing would stop that sword, nor what must follow. She could see it all, in the snare of the moment. Not the detail, not who must die and how—but death certainly, folly and death.

That soldier, clinging on to Mussun's harness: his death should have been the first, and might have satisfied. Swift punishment for a swift offence, the janizars might have accepted that. Half their life was ruthless discipline, where the other half was slack indulgence. But doubly stupid, he didn't die, that scimitar wasn't striking at his neck; and stupid again, trebly stupid, it took his wrong hand, his bridle-gripping hand.

She watched it happen and knew that it was wrong, so many kinds of stupid. She saw the blade like an arc of light where it swung and bit and cleaved clean through. She saw the first flick of blood that followed, and then the sudden spurt as the hand fell away, still obscenely clinging to the bridle of the tugging, turning horse. Her eyes wanted to follow the horse, and could not. They were rooted to the man, the soldier, the running stump of his wrist. She'd seen one-handed men before, though never newly made; it was horrific, but it wasn't that which held her in a cold grip.

It was his other hand, the hand he had, the one that held a sword. It had been moving already, in reaction perhaps to the scimitar's glitter in the corner of his eye. Now—too late again, like everything today—it drove that long straight soldier's sword hard and clean into the throat of the guard who had maimed him.

Blood gushed bubbling down the blade, and that was the first death, come too late; too late to save anyone, she thought. Mussun had his horse in hand, too late; he had his own scimitar also in hand, and brought that slashing down to take the soldier in the neck, almost to take his head off, and too late. Too late the soldier died, and too late Mussun saw his own peril through his anger.

———

NOW everything was too quick, too soon. All those archers with their arrows nocked, they all let fly at once. Jendre saw Mussun jerk and jump in his saddle. She saw how his fine clothes sprouted suddenly with bare black shafts, like a pollarded willow in a bleak spring. She saw him sway, she saw his fine hands lose their strength so that the reins of his horse slid free and his sword fell, to swing loose and useless from a halyard. She had time to think how unfair that was when he'd been so careful, he'd worn armour beneath his silks and never thought to meet a dozen arrows at point-blank, from recurve bows that could drive a shaft through steel.

Then his horse was wheeling and he was toppling sideways, someone was screaming—not her! which was a relief somehow, to find herself at least quiet in her fear—and her bearers were struggling to turn the long litter in the narrow road. Each man might simply have turned where he stood and carried her backwards, and part of her stupidly wanted to explain that to them even while the litter was swaying and tipping wildly and she was clinging on, stupid again, far wiser to abandon it and run.

But they were in a mêlée now, caught, surrounded. Her guards, the pasha's men, they might have run from janizars; surely, with their lords and her to protect, they would have retreated. Now not, they could not; they pressed forward, blind to any other duty than revenge. And Salem was among them, above them, ahead of them, charging the rioters with a cold, killing fury.

The janizars' fury was the hotter, and they were made for this heat; they were nothing if they were not fighting. The battle might be a mindless idiocy, but they would kill regardless. Bodies barged back and forth, men yelled above the clash of steel, men died below the stumbling feet of their brothers or their enemies or the hooves of Salem's horse.

Despite that horse's work, despite its rider's, it was the pasha's men who mostly did the dying. They were too few and not ready for this, their dress half-ceremonial, their minds on the river trip as much as the dangers of the street. They would have been watchful for assassins and armed against disorder, but never fit to meet a troop of janizars.

That much Jendre could see and understand. She saw hacking, darkened blades close and ever closer, and here came something else that she could understand, another folly of her city's long history to be written in blood. How the Sultan's young wife was slaughtered almost by accident, for no reason that anyone was ever able to draw out . . .

The janizars were close enough for her to see what men they were, sweating and frenzied. They terrified her, but terror brought clarity, detail, a dozen separate voices in the brawl, the rising stink of these men who meant to kill her. She had never thought that a battle would be so slow, so messy or so loud. All that grunting and shoving: half the time they seemed to wrestle more than fence, too many bodies pressed too close to use their weapons easily or well.

Still, they used them well enough. The litter lurched and tipped like a ship in storm; one of the bearers was down, killed as casually as a sheep for meat. Caught in the press of men, his brothers had no space to ground the litter; they had no weapons and no skill to fight, and no one now to guard them. They could die, but they could do little else.

Another man did that, dying beneath his pole, and the litter did find room enough to fall then, twisting as it went so that she fell first onto the stones of the road and the litter came down on top of her.

That was good, perhaps, after the bruising shock of the fall. It was a slender and delicate device, a frame of sapwood and leather straps beneath a gilt-and-velvet cope, so that it lay lightly enough across her back. It concealed her, and it looked more robust than it was; fighting men would eye it askance and do their best to step around it.

Even so, this was only an illusion of shelter. The janizars had seen her. When they had pulled Salem down and overrun the last of the guards, as they surely would, they'd look for her. And find her, cowering here like a mouse in a live trap for their pleasure, the perfect hostage against their safety . . .

When she was younger, when she was free, she never went out into the city unarmed. Now she was a woman, she wouldn't have been let near the Sultan with knives in her bodice and needles in her hair. The best she had was the jewelled pin, to scratch at any hand that reached for her. It wasn't much.

She crouched and waited within her darkness, her tent of soft cloth and skimpy wood. She heard all the sounds of battle louder, harsher, closer now that she could see nothing: the smithy sounds of metal against metal, the butcher sounds of metal hacked through bone, the gasps and heaves and screams of men.

Then it was the sudden stamp of horse that she was hearing, right by her refuge, and a voice that called her name.

"Jendre! In God's name, Jendre, are you there?"

The voice was hoarse, frightened almost, charged with passion. She hurled herself to her feet, throwing the litter back and looking nowhere but up, looking for nothing but what she saw, Salem still miraculously mounted. There was blood on his face but not his own, a mask too thin to hide his feelings. He held out his left hand while his right drove his sword at the nearest janizar, while his horse stood magnificently still. It was wild-eyed and trembling, awash with blood and much of that its own, she could see cuts that bled freshly as she scrambled all ungainly up Salem's arm.

Sprawled across its hindquarters, she cried, "Now, go now!" as she clutched the leather crupper, desperately insecure with her silks sliding at every movement of a rump slicked with sweat and blood, but determined not to fall. Not unless he did, and his horse also.

Instead she hauled herself upright, to sit sidewise across that narrow rump and cling to the cantle of his saddle. Being high again, she could see again, and what she saw was mayhem. There was no order to it; if these men had been trained for war, they must have forgotten whatever they once knew. Men died for lack of discipline, as much as lack of skill or lack of friends; on both sides they died, and perhaps even man for man, but it meant nothing. There could be only one outcome. The janizars outnumbered the pasha's men, and always had. Now they were half a dozen to one, half a hundred to a handful . . .

A handful and Salem, who had seen his sworn-brother cut down and had led his men into this fight, who should have stayed to lead them also to their furious death. He had another duty, though, to his father and his Sultan if not to her. She thought she could feel the reluctance in him as he kicked and spurred his horse away, up the road towards a near safety.

SO near, just the turn in the road and they were clear of danger, only the sounds of battle following. Salem brought the horse to a slow walk and now she could shudder, now she could feel dizzy and sick; she could shift her grip from the cantle to the man, hug herself close enough to smell the oiled steel hot beneath his silks, the sweat in the perfume in his hair, all the smells of man and horse and battle . . .

And then abruptly he stiffened within the circle of her arms, and the horse came to a dead halt in the middle of the abandoned street. Startled, she peered past his shoulder to see another troop of janizars running down the hill towards them.

"Oh," she murmured, desperate again, "what shall we do? You can't fight these too, you on your own. Set me down, at least, you can't fight at all with me to cumber you; and see, they have riders with them, they would catch us double-mounted. Set me down and flee; I can, I can hide in the buildings here . . ."

"Lady," he said, and bizarrely he seemed almost to be laughing, "your courage is as bold as your eyes, but my horse is so hurt, they would catch me anyway. And there is no need to flee. This is help. Look closer."

She used her veil to wipe her eyes of sweat or blood or tears. Indeed, these janizars did wear another uniform, the green and gold of the Sultan's own, the High Guard; and they followed the riders as loyal men follow their officers.

Salem flung up an arm as they drew close. A voice called an order; all the troop came to a swift and ready stillness, through which she heard a voice with an easy weariness to it. "Oh, what, Salem, is it you and yours making merry in the streets, then? And have you all found a girl to jaunt about at your saddle's back, or is this the young lord's privilege?"

His levity won him short answer. "This lady is the Sultan's bride and your general's daughter, Hedin, and we were escorting her to my father's barge for a day on the river. My men are dead by now, and so is Mussun, whom you knew and I loved."

"I heard there was trouble. Rumour runs fast, up the hill." That was a saying, all through the city; and this must be Hedin the wazir's son, from that family that was not noble nor rich and yet somehow still the spindle that all the city turned around. All his steely, mocking lightness was gone in a sentence, forgotten in two.

"Janizars," Salem said, "from the town guard. One troop, not so many as you are. Not now," and he cast about for a rag to wipe his sword blade and could find none, and so went on holding it a little out from his body and his mount, a fastidious gesture that she loved in him when they were all three of them so gouted in blood that it could make no difference what he wiped it on or where he held it.

"Very well." A confident young man, this Hedin. "You stay here with the lady, Salem. We will see to this."

"No, it is for me—I told you, they killed Mussun."

"Indeed; but your horse is too hurt to fight, if you are not. Set the lady down, and dismount before he dies of it. There's no shame in letting others pursue your vengeance."

He said it as though there were, great shame. Jendre thought he meant it as an insult; so too did Salem. She could feel that, even through his mail.

The man was right, though. She had passed through her own shivering fit, she realised, or else it had been shaken out of her. It was the horse that shuddered now, deeply, violently. She realised too how troublesome she must be to Salem, under these courtly but scornful eyes, that courtly but scornful voice: he had left his men to die, he had abandoned his friend's body for her sake, and she clutched at him like a street harlot . . .

She unwound her arms from Salem's chest and sat straight. Immediately he was swinging his leg forward and over the horse's neck in an awkward dismount, her fault again but there was no blame in his manner as he reached to help her down.

She felt anything but steady on her feet, but the horse would fall before she did, she was determined on that; and she thought the horse would not fall, not now. Strong like its master and trained to war, tough as the hill ponies it sprang from, it sweated and stank but stood firm, as she did. Salem stood rock-still at her side and said, "Go, then. And send a message to the harbour, to my father's barge; say that we will see the lady home . . ."

"No," she said, the word in her mouth before the thought was framed in her head, but she knew it was right. "We will wait till the streets are clear, Salem, and then we will go down as we intended. Let the people," and the janizars, all the discontents and rebels in the empire, the world, "let them see that I am not frightened," though she was, "and that their Sultan rules his city as he always has."

Impossible to creep home, to shame her husband before she had even married him. To their credit, the young men understood and nodded. Then Hedin wheeled his horse away, crying orders to his men.

A dozen of them stepped aside, to stay with Jendre and Salem. A confident young man indeed, this Hedin, unless he was only the perfect soldier-citizen, more careful of his Sultan's possessions than he was of his own life. Some in his family had had that reputation; their long record of service was illuminated by tales of sacrifice, as it was also blotted by betrayal.

He rode around the corner and out of her sight, with what remained of his troop trotting readily behind him. Salem had already turned to the bleeding, trembling horse and was stroking it, talking to it, working what healing there might be in voice and hands. Sympathetic magic, perhaps. Jendre felt herself shiver again as those low tones penetrated. Guilt, sorrow, comfort, distress: aimed at another, they still reached deep into her.

One of the men came forward to take the horse from Salem. Perhaps he was the troop's horse doctor; perhaps he was only a groom, or had been before he was made a soldier. He led the animal away to the shelter of a wall, stripped off its heavy saddle and ripped the caparison into rags and padding.

Jendre would have been glad enough to stand quiet and watch him work, as Salem clearly wanted to. But Salem was a boy, he couldn't keep from blundering in to where pain waited. Or else his manners were too nice, he couldn't stay silent in her company; or else he wanted to distract her from what they could both hear, war and death on the road below.

He turned his head and said, "Lady . . ."

"Jendre," she insisted, this little at least, "you must call me Jendre now. I think we are blood-kin," with a tight little laugh.

"You are not hurt?"

"No," only scraped and bruised and burned with fear, scalded all through. "But the same blood has soaked your dress and mine, that must mean something. We have been in battle together, my lord."

"And fought side by side," he said, lying magnificently, "and so you shall call me Salem as my brothers do."

She saw the shadow touch his face, and knew that he was thinking of his sworn-brother Mussun, who was dead, whose revenge had been taken from him. It wasn't the horse that had kept him back, he'd have gone afoot but for her; she knew that, if he did not.

"Salem," she said, and dwelt on it just for a moment before she went on, where she had to go. "You left your men to save me. I can't thank you for it, it's beyond thanks, but . . ."

Boylike, he turned his head away. "You were my charge, my duty, the Sultan's bride; every man there would have died for you, every man would have saved you if he could."

Every man did die, all but you, and you it was who saved me . . . "Your friend died, Mussun. I wish I'd known him better. I do know him to have been a brave man and a handsome man, but little more. Can you tell me . . . ?"

"Ah, Mussun." This would be hard for him, but it might be easier than the silence, the sheer weight of things that must remain unsaid. Easier than either, a man came with a pail of water, fetched from a courtyard nearby; she sacrificed her veil to make a cloth and washed face and arms with cool well water. Salem waited until she was done, then plunged his whole head into the pail.

He rose dripping, and shook his hair like a dog; and then he said, "You will never have been over the bridge to Sund, Jendre, you can have no idea of how our people live, south of the river."

No, of course not, the bridge was a nightmare—Sidië's nightmare now, but let that pass—and Sund was a myth, built of a thousand myths. But, "Mussun was from Sund?"

"Oh, yes—or perhaps no, not truly so. Had you asked if he was Sundain, I would have said that the other way around. But I did find him there." For a moment, he seemed to feel that he had said enough. Then he grimaced, and went on, "Not everyone in Sund feels it necessary to hate us. Some thrive under our protection. Some have married into Marasi families, but yet stayed on in Sund."

Indeed, some Marasi families had moved their entire households south of the river. Old families, mostly, with long lineage and high position and no money to support it. In Sund they could live as their rank or their pride demanded. "And Mussun, then—he was the child of such a marriage?"

"Alas, no," but Salem was smiling as he said it. "Mussun's mother was Sundain, daughter of one of their merchant families. Well, they are all merchants in that wretched town, but she came from a wealthy house. She was unmarried, and she bore her son; they are careless of their women there. But she claimed that she was seduced—raped, she said—by a Marasi officer. She named her child in the Marasi style, and raised him to believe that he was one with us. When I found him he was fourteen, and angry, and brawling in the street with friends of mine.

"My father had taken a party of us across the river, to teach us how it was for the men who must serve there. I had wandered apart from my friends, up a promising alley"—*after a promising girl,* Jendre heard, and gave no sign that she had heard it—"but it was a dead end," *she wouldn't play,* and he was too kind to force her. "I went back to find my friends at dagger point, this one lean boy trying to hold all six of them, spitting defiance in their faces. They had swords drawn, and he would have been dead in a moment; but I spoke for my father, and they waited for my word.

"He was Sundain, they said, and had not given way as he ought to, not shown them proper respect; and he was armed, two long daggers he had, and the Sundain are forbidden to carry arms in the streets. So they had challenged him, and he had scorned them, and so this.

"I calmed them, I had them put their weapons up; and then this boy, this merchant's son claimed to be Marasi, one of us, and Joquil laughed at him.

"So there was a fight after all, only they used fists and not blades, because I forced them to it. Nor would I let the others help Joquil. He was older, bigger, stronger, better trained; but that half-breed boy was savage, brutal, ruthless. Joquil was on his back in the filth of the street, winded, stupefied, beaten—and the boy's heel came stamping down to crush his nose.

"And that was Mussun, our first meeting; and I suppose I saved his life twice that day, because Joquil's friends would have killed him then despite me, except that I stood between them with my sword drawn while I swore Mussun to my side and I to his. So then he was Marasi in truth, and of the best family, sworn-brother to the pasha's son, and none of them could touch him. And he laughed at them as they helped Joquil away, and then he pulled a handful of dates from his pocket and shared them with me, and that was Mussun too."

"Quarrelsome, impetuous, vicious in victory, the bastard child of our city's longest enemy?"

"Yes, all of that."

"You don't paint an attractive picture."

"Do I not? He was an attractive man, I thought. And my sworn-brother, and my friend. Will you take him away from me?"

"Not for the world, my lord. Keep your friend, you earned him; and you saw him clearly, which is unusual." *Unusual in a man* she would have liked to say, and did not quite dare. Talking to Salem in this mood, with his friend freshly dead and all his men besides, she felt as though she walked on paper, laid over something dark and viscous and terrible. One missed or heedless step could rip through and submerge her, overwhelm them both.

He was holding on to that mood, soft-spoken and easy, with a bitter grief beneath; he said, "I thought you were to call me Salem?"

"So did I, and so I shall, when it's appropriate. Sometimes you must be content to be my lord," and not because these men of Hedin's were listening.

"Well. Only if you will consent to be my lady. Sometimes."

The skin around his eyes was pale, his lips were tight and strained beneath that boy's folly of a moustache, his hair was dripping water down his neck. "It would be an honour," she said, "so long as you remember also that my name is Jendre, and yours to use."

He gave her just a little nod, with a wealth of significance at its back; and then there was a clatter of hooves on cobbles and that was Hedin, riding back himself to tell them that the road was safe and they could make their way on down to the harbour, "with my escort," he said, as though to underline the disaster that had been Salem's escort before him.

Salem ignored that. To Jendre he said, "We could no more ask your bearers to take you further than we could my horse, even if your litter has survived. Will you be content to walk, my lady? I can perhaps show you views of the city that you have not seen before . . ."

She laughed, and was delighted with how natural it sounded. "I doubt that, Salem. I think I have explored every lane and rat-run in this city, barefoot and more bedraggled than my company."

He raised an eyebrow with the air of a man expressing an extreme of surprise, and murmured, "I believe it is your turn to tell a story . . ."

———

SO they walked all that slow and winding way down through the city to the river's side, and as they went she told him of her reckless childhood. At first her telling was determined, as they walked round the corner and past the place where they had been waylaid. Mussun's body was there still, laid out with men at head and feet; Salem stiffened, but walked on without a pause. Tonight he might go sleepless, Jendre thought, watching and praying over his friend, but for now he still had another duty.

The bodies of the other fallen were there too, all mixed in a heap, bearers and guards and janizars, as though it did not matter which was which. And—what was worse, she thought, what gave her voice its steel as she drove her story forward, as she drove her feet—there were prisoners also there, no more than a dozen of the rioters. No more than a dozen now, and fewer with every minute. As they passed, as she stared she saw one stripped quickly of harness and armour and valuables, pushed to his knees with his hands bound; she saw how young he was, how drunk and how afraid, how he was sobbing almost with the fear; she saw the knife drawn swift across his throat, and the gush of blood that followed.

She had seen men die before at the hands of authority, stranglings and beheadings in the public square, and had watched with a child's detached fascination. This was different: less sophisticated, more brutal, closer and more immediate, far more personal to her. These men had attacked her, killed her escort, would have killed her and Salem too; and yet . . .

She turned her head aside and somehow kept on talking, but even gazing into Salem's face was no remedy. She thought she could see it reflected in his eyes, that line of men, stunned and silent, slumped and drained and only waiting for this most casual of roadside executions.

Chapter Three

O many rooms: and there were so few people, of course they couldn't use them all, and why would they want to?

Even so it was strange to Issel, how close-packed they chose to be, like dried fish in a box. Not Tel Ferin, the master had rooms of his own; but all the young people cooked together and ate together, washed together and worked together and come the night they slept all together in the one big room, and Issel didn't understand it.

More, he couldn't do it. Alone all his life, he could not sleep in a crowd. He lay in the dark and listened to their breathing, hours of breathing and snoring and occasional soft voices; at last he stood up with his blanket and his bundle, he picked his way across the unfamiliar softness of cushions and pallets and rugs, between sprawled bodies and out into the stillness of the house. The first night he wandered a little from room to room, finding his way by little glimmering spitballs, fainter than fireflies, until he settled in the first hidden corner that he came to. The second night he was bolder, he ventured a little further. By the week's end he had explored every corridor, opened every unlocked door and found a place to claim his own, a wide window ledge with a padded seat of fraying silk.

He didn't announce it, he didn't say, "This is where I sleep now." He still settled down with the others at night, but always close to the doorway.

There was no door. He lay quiet until they were asleep, most of them, enough; then the quiet rise, the blanket and the bundle, the slipping away. Unnoticed, he hoped. He did try very hard not to be noticed.

———

IT was the middle of the night, and Issel was not sleeping. Worrying, rather, in the solitary comfort of his window bed; and here came something else to worry about, someone else, footsteps in the passage. *Tulk*, he thought. That quiet, unworried boy who had carried a light for Issel, who had shown him that it was possible not to be afraid. There had been other lessons since, and time spent together that was nothing to do with learning. Issel had never had a friend; he wasn't sure what the signs were. Perhaps it was enough to sit and share food and talk. That first, and now this: Tulk woken to find him missing, come in search. Tulk could find his way in the dark, slow but unhesitating, listening at every doorway. He was the best listener in the house, except perhaps for Tel Ferin, who reckoned to hear everything in the city. Before it happened, sometimes, news flown ahead of its event.

Issel sat up and threw his blanket back, turned to welcome his friend, surely they must be friends to seek each other out in the dark; and the first thing he saw was a subdued glimmer advancing down the passage. Not Tulk, then. A tall, slender figure carrying something cupped between the fingers, that cast more shadows than light. Briefly, he thought it would be Tel Ferin. The master, picking out a gifted pupil for special, private teaching . . .

But this was not Tel Ferin, for all the height and the long loose hair. Too young, too slim and the body speaking differently, more curious than commanding . . .

"Rhoan." The name was a sigh; it might have been relief or disappointment, but was neither. She was here, and that was enough. She filled all the space there was.

"Indeed." She came close and set down the light she carried, a softly shimmering bowl of water. She obviously meant to stay a while. He scrambled hastily into his shirt, not looking at her, not needing to look. He could feel the smile on her face, light and mocking as the flick of a whip, there and gone and only its sting surviving. Was she decently dressed, or wrapped in a blanket, or naked entirely? He hadn't noticed, and still wasn't going to look. "So this is where you slope off to every night."

"Yes."

"It's unfriendly."

"I thought you were asleep."

"Did you really? All of us, every night?"

Well, no. Not really. He shrugged, gazed down at his bare feet, his thin bare legs rising to the tattered hem of his grubby shirt.

"It would still be unfriendly, even if none of us knew. You'd still be doing it." She sat down beside him, so that now he was looking at her feet next to his. Equally bare, slender but somehow not bony, tough but not ugly; and there were her ankles and then thankfully the hem of her own shirt, as old as his but fresh, laundered, neatly darned.

"I can't sleep," he said. "Not with other people." Nor wash himself or his clothes with others watching, all that water and him trying to be so uninteresting. No street boy could be body-shy, he'd begged naked when he needed to, but these people might see what they shouldn't. Faced with the rush and plunge of so much water, he might do what he shouldn't, and then he thought half Sund might see the consequences.

"What are you afraid of?"

"Nothing!" Indignantly, untruthfully, transparently.

He went on staring at his feet, and hers; and so saw her intent, saw it coming and could do nothing to forestall it. He watched her foot walk teasingly on its toes, across the flagstone floor till it found his. A nudge from her, from him a jerk away.

She chuckled, and said again, "So what are you afraid of?"

He could say *you*, and that would be true but not true enough, although she might accept it. He could say *everything* and that would be true too, but she'd never let him get away with it. He didn't say anything, and the silence hung between them like a lie, another lie.

At length, when it was obvious to them both that he had no answer, she said, "Never mind, then. Will you show me those things of yours, that you brought with you?"

At least that made him lift his head, to stare at her. "You've seen them already." Everybody had.

"I've seen Tel Ferin laugh at them. I don't know why he did that."

Neither did Issel. Of course the great man wanted to see what was being brought into his house, but once he'd seen, why he'd choose to make a public mock of such poor treasures, that was a mystery.

"Everyone else laughed too."

"Not everyone."

That was true. There'd been no sound of laughter at his back, where Tulk stood. The rest he couldn't judge, he hadn't been looking. Squirming in humiliation, rather. The wound was still raw. And his little things were hidden now, and he meant to leave them so.

"They're nothing," he said. "Why do you want to see them?"

"Because I want you to show them to me. They're not nothing to you, and I'd like to understand that."

That was all. She didn't bully, she didn't press. She only waited, while he fumbled through all his reasons for refusing and found that none of them would do.

Reluctantly, then, he reached under the window seat's padded cushion, where the upholstery was torn. His fingers found the coarse, slick fabric of his gaberdine and drew it out. Her eyes rolled a little, and he thought he'd need to find a better hiding place.

No matter. He started to unfold the gaberdine—and then stiffened, gestured Rhoan to keep quiet and flung a corner of the greasecloth over her little bowl of water. The light died; she sat quite still beside him in the darkness, while he listened.

His ears had always been sharp; he could hear it clearly, even over the pounding of his heart. There was a heavy snuffling just behind him, just the other side of the thin shutters where they opened onto the garden. Footsteps too, the weight of a body forcing through tangled undergrowth.

Rhoan's hand on his shoulder seemed to be saying *don't worry, that's nothing to be alarmed about*—but he waited until the snuffling had faded, until the footsteps had followed it out of hearing before he dared begin to breathe again.

She was laughing at him. "Issel, it was only Baris. He keeps watch in the garden at night."

"I know what it was."

"You shouldn't be afraid of him. He's a servant here."

She'd never had to sleep out in the Shine; she didn't know any of the many reasons Issel had to be afraid of Baris. There was a world of stories, how this dogtooth and that had run mad or turned cruel as their bodies changed, how their minds were tainted too. None was an old story; the people who told them were the people who knew, who had seen their own friends or family deformed, debased, corrupted beyond measure. It was only sense, to fear what was fearful.

For Issel, it was only sense to be afraid of his own future. Baris was a shadow, an omen of what could come to him. A shadow made flesh, an omen that didn't only haunt his dreams: that was with him day and night, hot-breathed and heavy-footed, malignant and knowing. Better than anyone, better than Tel Ferin or Armina, Baris knew what Issel was afraid of.

To stop Rhoan finding out, Issel deliberately took the other path she'd offered. "Aren't we servants too? The master treats us that way." And had them call him "master," as though to make the point.

"Pupils," Rhoan said determinedly. "In a strict school, sometimes. And of course we have to do some of the work around the house, there isn't anyone else, but we're still pupils. Here to learn, not to serve. And we are allowed to talk in the early morning, whether Baris is listening outside or not; and we're allowed to make a light to talk by." She nudged him in the darkness, a not-so-gentle hint.

"You do it," he said, uncovering the bowl again.

"No, you. You put it out. And it's your turn, anyway. I'm tired."

Then why aren't you sleeping, why are you troubling me? He knew better than to ask aloud. And he'd run out of excuses, of arguments, of anything. He reached a finger down to touch the water, just the lightest skimming contact; his mind reached at the same time, just a flicker of a thought, the barest spark leaping from flint to tinder.

The water flared into stark actinic light, brighter than the sun in summer and far more fierce. Black shadows leaped and danced. His own yelp as pain lanced through his finger and ran up all the bones of his arm was echoed by her astonished gasp.

"How did you ever . . . ? Quick, cool that down or never mind Baris, you'll have the whole house come to stare."

This was why, one reason why he was trying to be so quiet, so unobtrusive; it was one reason why he found that so hard. He flung his gaberdine across the bowl again, but the light still flared through the fabric.

"I'm sorry, I don't know how to make it gentle. Tel Ferin says I need to learn subtlety, but . . ." But he'd never had the chance, in a lifetime of trying not to use his gift at all except when he needed it urgently, and then being reckless in emergency, lashing out with everything he had.

"Well, let it go, then. I'll do it."

He nodded and felt for that little thread of connection in his mind, where the memory of his touch still stirred the memory of water. And snapped it, and the glare died. He was blinking at the after-image when he felt Rhoan's fingers move his gaberdine; a moment later, a soft glow lit the window seat again.

"How did you ever manage to hide for so long?" she asked. "From us or from the Marasi, from anyone? If that's what happens every time you get your fingers wet . . ."

"I didn't do it much," he muttered. "Tried not to. But it's not that fierce, anyway, out in the world. Tel Ferin's water is different." Sund-water was supposed to be different, special anyway. Issel could work with anything, rainwater or river water or whatever came to hand, but the water in this house was as different as oil is from coal. He hadn't been thinking, or he wouldn't have reached to touch this; he could sense it now, fiery in its bowl.

"Even so. You're different too. It doesn't feel the same to me, even, since you touched it. Sort of greasy, somehow? I wouldn't want to drink it now. And it hurt you, too. Didn't it?"

"Doesn't it you?"

"Just a tingle. Pins and needles, nothing more. Not enough to make me yell."

"Well, I said, it's different here. Not like in the world. I thought you wanted to look at my things?"

And he opened up his gaberdine to make a display of his oldest, closest secrets, just to stop her prying further.

HIS little things, his privacy, all that he knew or trusted about himself: they were five small pieces, and they were worth nothing to anyone but Issel.

A stone, river-washed and rounded, greenish-grey and flecked with cream, veined with a darker purple; pretty enough, but not enough to pick it out from a million other pebbles on the strand, if anyone were fool enough to go picking pebbles on the strand. "I had that from my mother," he said. "It's all I have," and even that might be a lie. He couldn't know; he had no memory of his mother. It was Armina who gave him the stone, and the story with it.

"Who was she, Issel?"

"No one knows. She was dead when they found her." Actually it was

Armina who found her, but no one used names if they could help it, telling stories in Sund. "I was with her, holding on to her skirts, half-wild and half-starved. I don't remember. I was very young. I knew my name," or so Armina had told him, "but not hers."

"Oh, that's sad . . ."

Issel shrugged. He had learned to do that. The city made its victims, as the river did. Time and history and water, it was all implacable, everything that flowed.

A string of tiny shells, threaded onto silk: pretty for their own sake, iridescent like mother-of-pearl, like raindrops slicked with oil as they fell. If he'd lived another life, where pretty things were common, they'd need no legend to explain them. As it was: "I used to gather those," he said. "There's a place I know, at the elbow of the strand, where it turns into the current. You can find them if you look, among the pebbles. And there was a girl," half his life ago, when he was still a child, "who sold pretties in the market. Cheap things, shells and feathers. Not for the rich, just for people who had a little more than she did. And she had a little more than I did, so I found them for her and she fed me or patched me a shirt or told me where to find a woman with an errand or a house with an unlatched door."

"What happened to her?"

"I don't know. One week she wasn't there. I asked, but no one knew, or else they wouldn't say. She never came again." People came unknown from nowhere, as he had himself; they vanished too, and there might never be a body, an empty room, anything to show where they had been. "I had a pocketful of shells for her. I should have tried to sell them, maybe I could have taken her place," her blanket, spread on the ground in the little space she fought for, "but I was upset. So I made a heap of them for anyone to take who wanted; and I just kept these, and threaded them for her."

"Issel, that's sweet."

He shrugged again. It was Sund, that was all: his Sund, the city that he was beginning to realise that she had never lived in, for all that she was born and spent her life here. Perhaps no one inhabited his city, except himself. When people came and went, perhaps they only moved between his Sund and someone else's.

A brass buckle, from a page boy's shoulder-strap: "I had this from the man who might have been my master," who might have changed his life.

"I was in his laundry, stealing what I could snatch, some shirts and a box of this brasswork; but they caught me, his servants did, and took me in to face him. If he'd been Marasi, he might have had my hands off, there and then. But he was Sundain, he knew how the city was, though he lived in a house like this. And he was young, and romantic; he said he would spare me even a beating, if I ran a message for him and fetched him an answer back. I did that," across the roofs to a family that had lost its wealth but not its pride, that huddled bewildered in a tenement in Daries but still kept guard on its doors and windows, on its daughters. Once he was free of his captors he might just have shrugged and forgotten it, but he had his own unexpected pride; he carried the message and the answer too, perilous both ways. "I don't know what he would have done if he hadn't liked the answer. But he did, he smiled. And then he gave me this," just a buckle, worth nothing on its own, "and said there would be other errands, and other brasses from the box. When the box was empty, he said, when I had them all, then he would give me the uniform to fit them, and I could be one of his pages proper."

"So what happened?" Rhoan prompted, as he fell quiet under the weight of a life unlived, undiscovered.

"I went back next day, but one of his other pages stopped me in the kitchen. And took me out into the garden, and beat me," and the dew had been wet on the grass and Issel could have used that but he hadn't, he'd been trying so hard not to be noticed, not to be different from any other thieving beggar boy, "and said that if I went again he would break my elbows. He was a big man, he could have done that," or Issel could have stopped him, but only brutally, with water; and then he couldn't have gone back anyway, so what was the point? "So I stayed away."

"Never mind. You wouldn't have liked it anyway, being another man's servant. I don't think you'd do that well."

He thought she was wrong, maybe; or maybe he only wanted to think it, in this new world. She might say that they were pupils here, but it didn't feel so to Issel. He wanted nothing more than to serve Tel Ferin, to please him, to satisfy him. And however hard he tried, he seemed to come up short; and so he tried harder the next time, and he thought the most demanding master should find that satisfactory.

A token, a talisman, a little wooden figure, crudely carved: a crouching frog, whittled from some tarry scrap of timber. "Someone I used to spend time with," Issel said, "he made that for me."

"Why a frog?"

"He said because I was green and wet," when Issel first went to live up on the roofs. Later it was *because you sit there so still and quiet and I never know which way you're going to jump, and you always surprise me, little frog.*

"This loop your friend's cut into the back, that's quite clever, it means you could wear it on a string . . ."

"Yes," though he wasn't a friend even when he made it.

"You don't, though."

"No."

"Did you ever?"

"Yes." All the time, around his neck; they all called him *little frog* then, it came to be his name among them and he thought they were his people. For a while.

"I think you should again. I've got a leather thong I'll let you have . . ."

"No."

"No. I thought you'd say that. Why not? Why do you keep it, if you don't want to wear it? You don't keep much."

He didn't keep anything, except these little things and what he needed for today, perhaps for tomorrow too. He supposed he needed these for yesterday. That must be why he couldn't throw them out.

The last of his little things was a knife, or it had been once. Bone-handled and bound around with cord, not so much for added grip as to hold the bone together, where it had split and split again; even that cord was rotting now. And the blade so worn, so hollowed out with grinding against any stone that would give an edge, it was more a needle than a knife blade. Four fingers'-length of stained, exhausted steel, no match for the other knife he wore.

"Well," she said, "I can see why you don't use that anymore."

No, she couldn't. It was still strong, still sharp, still trustworthy. Something more than overuse had stained that blade, in ways she couldn't see.

"Again, though, why carry it?"

"In case I lose the other."

"Issel, the day you lose your knife will be the same day I forget my name, my city and everything that makes me who I am." She hadn't known him a week, but she'd seen that much, the street boy's determined grip on what was crucial. "Oh," she went on, "keep your secrets, your little treasures close. I won't pry," as though she hadn't been doing that already. "But find a better place to keep them, because there are others here who will pry and spy and bully if they can. And don't let anyone see you work with water, until Tel Ferin's taught you to be gentle."

That much he didn't need telling. He wouldn't have let her see, if he'd been thinking. She made it hard for him to think, sitting close beside him in this private light. She had a sleepy smell to her, and a warmth that he could feel through her shirt and his own. And she was leaving him now, standing up and walking off, taking her little bowl of light with her. Leaving him in the dark, where there was nothing to do but think, all the hours till the morning came.

BEING alone at night was something he had to take steps to achieve. Being alone in the morning came as easily as breathing. All his life he'd been used to early rising, up with the sun, as soon as the Shine had faded. Here was no different, whether he had slept well or not. Everyone else—his schoolmates, he supposed he ought to call them—slept late or very late, as late as they could, clinging to their blankets and their dreams.

Come first light, then, he would be up and doing. A bucket of water from the well, for a quick and private wash—and never mind that the others taunted him with being dirty, he didn't dare join them in the bathhouse—and then he busied himself in the kitchen, lighting a fire under a small cauldron of a kettle that would take an hour to boil. A little pan sat directly in the coals, and was seething in five minutes. He took pinches of dried leaf from a white porcelain jar decorated with images in blue glaze, scenes from an unimaginable life, he supposed it was Marasi. The leaf went into a matching pot, which he filled with the simmering water.

He set the pot and some biscuits from yesterday's baking on a tray, and carried it to Tel Ferin's private door. He'd not been let beyond there; so far as he knew, no one was. When not teaching or supervising his ragged school, the master kept himself strictly apart. One thing was certain, though, that he would be awake and about. He, his servant Baris and his newest pupil, all three of them alert to the day. Issel could see all manner of significance in that.

A scratch on the door, on a panel where the varnish was quite worn away, where generations of servants must have done just this before him; footsteps from the other side and the door swinging open, the master there, Tel Ferin in his old fraying robe which must have been gorgeous once, so many colours of silk embroidered so densely. Now it was hard to see what those embroideries depicted, what animals, what flowers had been made to live before age and dirt and usage conspired to break the threads and dull the vibrant colours. These days Tel Ferin belted it with a mismatched leather cord, and only ever wore it in his apartments and in these early mornings. Issel suspected that no one saw it now, except himself. That was something to hold on to, another little thing that no one in the school could mock at if he never said.

At first Tel Ferin had nodded and taken the tray and said not a word. Yesterday, he had bid Issel good morning, that at least. Today he stood thoughtful for a moment, before he took the tray; and then he said, "Self-appointed duties will win you no friends among your peers."

"No, master."

"You don't mind that?"

"I don't need friends." He had come this far without. What he needed in this house was one man's approval, nothing more.

"That may have been true before; you seem to have had a special providence watching over you. You will likely find it different here. Fetching my tea in the mornings won't fetch you any special favours from me either, Issel, but the others may well suspect that it does. They will pick up reasons enough to dislike you, without that."

"I don't care what they think."

"Even so. You may learn to care; they may teach you to. Most of them were much younger when they came, and they fitted in comfortably," little kids to be teased and bullied and protected, all three at once. Issel had seen that already, understood it, decided not to play. "You don't. You stand out already; I'm afraid you may suffer for it. It is a great pity that we were so late in finding you."

"You found me when it mattered," when he needed finding.

"Perhaps. Providence again, perhaps." Tel Ferin said that with an air of resentment. "Well, let be. You are here, finally, and matters will fall out as they will. I will do what I can."

A nod, and he turned and was gone, and the door was closed behind him. Issel wondered if Tel Ferin had been doing what he could from the first, from Issel's arrival here: if that public mockery of his little things had been a deliberate attempt to make him seem ordinary, smaller than his legend, nothing worth the fuss they'd had to find him.

He could perhaps be grateful, if he could believe it. He spent his own days trying to achieve the same effect, at least among his schoolmates. He could learn to believe it, perhaps. He wanted to.

It was hard to credit how far his wants had shifted, in these few days. He didn't want for shelter now, for food or dress or comfort. He had more company than he could ever want. He wanted Tel Ferin to be satisfied with him, to give him praise and favour, to train him in person, in secret, behind that private door. He wanted the others to leave him alone, and Baris the dogtooth to vanish altogether. Disgraced or dead or run away, Issel didn't care, if he was only gone.

In all his life, whatever Issel had wanted, it had always ended up out of reach. He thought that was the definition of want. As here, now: Baris wasn't about to disappear, any more than Tel Ferin was going to adopt a preferred apprentice. Any more than his new companions were going to let him be solitary, it seemed. There was Rhoan, who tempted and tormented him in equal measure, who sought him out in the darkness, and he wasn't sure why; and then there was Tulk.

Now, there was Tulk. Here indeed was Tulk, shambling in from the dormitory with his hair awry, scratching and yawning and arching his back in a desperate stretch, his every move saying that it was too early to be out of bed. His body needed to say it for him, Issel knew; it was far too early for Tulk to be talking.

So far from the neat, quiet, self-possessed boy who had carried a light for Issel on his first walk through the house, this incarnation of Tulk peered hopelessly into the great kettle and grunted, seeing how the water barely steamed yet. Issel knew what came next, and might have forestalled it; might have gone himself to fetch a goblet of goats' milk from the jug where it sat cool in a ewer of water, to tear a double handful from yesterday's greasy flatbread and give them both to the other boy. It would have been kinder, quicker, easier far than watching Tulk's awkward progress: how many empty goblets he knocked off the shelf, how nearly he spilled the milk, how the bread almost defeated him altogether.

But it would have been a statement too, an assertion, *we are friends, we look after each other.* Issel was still shy of making any such declaration, even here, privately between the two of them. Friends shared their secrets, that was inherent. Now that Rhoan knew so much about him, he'd have to tell Tulk also, maybe tell him more; and Issel had secrets that he never told, even to himself. The less guarded he became, the closer he let people come to the heart of him, the more danger they brought with them.

So he let Tulk fetch his own breakfast, and let him slump on a bench alone to chew his slow way through it. There could have been a happy joke between them, how hard Tulk found these mornings; but he still dragged himself out of bed long before he needed to, long before the others roused to join them. Issel saw no joke in that, and couldn't laugh about it.

———

FIRST duty of the day—once Tel Ferin had his tea—was always to fetch in water. The cistern in the scullery would be in high demand; if it started full and was kept topped up, then come nightfall no one would be shouting at the younger kids to go out and haul buckets from the well. Even at this distance, where the bridge was only a shimmer low in the sky, Issel thought they should not be carrying water in the Shine.

It was too late for him, he carried poison in his blood already, even if his bones showed no signs yet. It showed in his work, and in the water after he had worked it. It was one reason why he liked to act the servant, the water-boy, the disappointment. The more people saw him fetch and carry, the less they would remember the reputation that had preceded him, the reason Tel Ferin had hunted him in off the streets. If they thought he was ordinary, dull, untalented, they'd have no reason to watch him; perhaps then they might never see the reality of him, the twist that made him a creature of the Shine.

Besides, he still craved that simple closeness. It was better to carry a bucket from the well than to play with a palmful of Tel Ferin's fierce product. The master called that purified, but Issel preferred what came pure from the earth, Sund's proper water.

———

BY the time Tulk was fit for talking, they were usually no longer alone. It might be Rhoan who came through next, or a couple of the younger girls. They tended to get up before the boys, one or two of whom would cling to their beds past reason, past noon if they were allowed to.

Girl or boy, their routine was more or less the same. They would dip a pan into the steaming kettle, and carry it through to the scullery to wash. Damply back with fresh water, cold from the cistern, to top the kettle up; and then a beaker of milk and a bowl of millet porridge, and the start of the long day's talking.

It was easy to be quiet, Issel had found, among so many. They would talk and talk, in twos and threes and all together; most would never notice that he didn't.

Tulk talked to Issel all the time, and never really needed answering. He could be quiet when he was told to be, as he must have been on that first day, walking Issel through the house; he could be quiet when he had to be, the first hour of every day, when his mind and his mouth were both still clay, thick and sticky. Otherwise he talked, his voice ran on and on.

Like water round a rock, Issel thought; and like a rock in water he felt no tingle from it. A stream could roll a rock along its bed, and sometimes Tulk said something to move him, to make him change his mind or his intentions. A stream could dry up and leave a rock exposed, and sometimes that happened too, the flow of Tulk's monologue was cut off and Issel felt himself suddenly naked in the silence. Most of the time, though, he bathed in that wash of words and never heeded it except as disguise, *see me, I'm busy here, all this talking . . .*

It didn't fool Rhoan, he was sure, but she would leave him alone when he was with Tulk. That was good enough. Issel might not want Tulk's friendship but he was happy to use it, if only to ward off someone else's.

The boys' early work didn't excuse them from further chores. Rhoan could insist all she liked that they were pupils and not servants; Issel wasn't the only one who found it hard to distinguish, when they spent their mornings running errands and scrubbing floors.

For him, it was generally scrubbing. Tel Ferin was reluctant to let him out beyond the garden wall. Other boys, younger boys, would be sent to run a message across the city or else to take small coins to the marketplace, to come back with flour and a sheep's neck and a weight of lentils and onions. Issel was kept withindoors, with a bucket and a brush.

If he minded, he didn't mind enough to make a fuss about it. He was restless in confinement, but he was fed and sheltered here, which was worth a lot. Besides, when he scrubbed, he was still intimate with water. If he was watched, he took it steaming from the kettle in the kitchen; if not, he drew a bucket cold from the cistern and heated it with a touch. Because he could, perhaps, or just because they couldn't.

Tulk objected to being penned up, far more than Issel did. "I'm your friend, so they think I have to do what you do; and they won't send you out because they're not sure you'd come back, or because someone out there is looking for you, or whatever reason it is, and so they keep me in too. I've had enough, I'll tell you . . ."

He had told him, over and over, these last days. Issel had told him the obvious solution, but only once—"Tell them you're not my friend; or better, show them, stop spending all your time with me"—but Tulk had heard it as a joke and laughed, and shaken his head with a sigh at the terrible unfairness of it all, and shown no signs of abandoning Issel's side.

———

EARLY to rise, Tel Ferin was late to start the day's teaching, those days when he taught at all. Sometimes, often, it was the older students who passed their skills and knowledge down to the younger or the less experienced; often and often, those skills were more about survival than the proper use of water.

There, at least, Issel could allow himself to shine. These people might dress like street children, but they were only playing at it, games of disguise; they pretended to themselves as much as to the city. He had lived that life for real, year after year, and he could show them all the scars of hunger and misadventure, all the damage they'd avoided. Their skills were common citywide, how to live under occupation, how to be Sundain: hard lessons, necessary lessons, but not exceptional. His were in a different class. He might have paraded them to win respect, to earn himself a place; in fact he tried to use them otherwise, to disparage his own legend, to help the others think that he had survived by meanness and beggary more than magical talent. It was true, but it was also another game of disguise.

When he did study magic, he mostly sat with the younger children to learn what was most basic here. That helped, as so much of his own water-working had been desperate, violent, extreme. He had never thought to weave a rope of water, or to make a mirror, or to fold water like glass around a candle's flame and make a lamp of it; he had little idea how to use his talents peacefully or quietly. And then there was Tel Ferin's purified water, exaggerating his lightest touch until he was scared to touch it at all. All of that was good, he thought; he looked clumsy and ignorant and slow, nervous and unskilled, even compared to little Ion, whose talent was only starting to come through.

Tulk sat with Issel here too. He had an awkward gift, just enough to mark him out. It was for his protection that Tel Ferin gave him shelter, as much as his ability; Tulk admitted that himself. "If I stay ten years, I'll still be struggling to keep up with the bright new kids. I'm just a glimmer-worm. It doesn't matter, though. It's only the tricks I'm not handy with. I'm as smart as anyone, I can learn how things are done, even if I don't have the strength to do them well myself. There'll always be a place and a need for knowledge, Tel Ferin says . . ."

TODAY, the master came striding into the kitchen, where they all seemed naturally to gather once the chores were done. He sent the seniors away on several errands, except for Rhoan; to her he gave a small flask and asked her to fill it from the scullery cistern. "With a ladle, please, and carefully—don't just dunk it under the surface. I want it dry to the touch."

"I know what you want, master."

Tel Ferin nodded, waited, tested the flask with his fingertips when she brought it back. Then, as Issel, Tulk and the younger children all sat facing him across the width of the table, he took another identical flask from his pocket and set the two down side by side.

"One of these holds our own common water, well water," he said, "ours by right of birth, but special only because it is Sundain. In the other is our own particular water, purified by me, ours by right of birth and blood and usage.

"The one is good to drink, good to cook with, good to bathe in, Issel." A nudge and a snort from Tulk, outright giggles from the others at the table, even little Ion. Issel knew that he was acquiring a dirty reputation in the school; he hadn't realised that it had reached Tel Ferin. He felt himself flush, and didn't look up to see if Rhoan was smiling.

Tel Ferin went on, "The other is good, of course, for much more than that. You all have the ability to use it, in differing degrees; that's why you're here. But you're still clumsy, greedy with it, snatching like children for pretties and sweets."

"Well, but they are children, master." That was Rhoan, from where she leaned in the scullery doorway, and Issel still didn't look up; this time he was entirely sure that she was smiling, and directly at him.

"Not all. And young or not, they need to learn control, restraint, delicacy of touch. Even those who strain to touch the power at all, mmm, Tulk? Even they can understand the difference between a blade and a bludgeon."

That might have been Issel's cue to nudge back, to snigger in his turn. Perhaps he should have done it, just to nudge Tulk away from the friendship that he himself so surely did not want. Instead he sat quite still, and let Tulk interpret that as he chose.

"I will teach you to work with a feather's touch, like the kiss of silk on the skin," and likely no one at that table had ever worn silk, but this was what Tel Ferin offered: glimpses of another kind of life. It was more than hope, better than hope. Any beggar, any thief can hope for change, but Tel Ferin had it in his gift. Issel had turned his back on hope, and even he was a believer here.

"Tell them why, master. They won't ask, but there's one at least who won't understand the lesson unless you explain it first, and again afterwards," and she did absolutely mean Issel now, she might as well have named him. He clenched his fists beneath the table and struggled to show nothing on his face; if there had been any water spilled on the planking, it would have been seething by now from the simple intensity of his glare.

"Only the one, Rhoan? This must be a better table than I've had before. I remember one girl, dullest of a dull year, who had to have this particular lesson cuffed home separately into each ear. I'm still not sure that she hears me when I tell her to tread more lightly."

"That's because you left her halfway deaf, master."

"The more reason she should cling to the half she has, in hopes of learning something even yet. But there is more art in a fingertip's touch than there is in a fist; and if art alone is not enough, there is quiet too, and secrecy, the chance to do your work and slip away in safety. Why break a bottle to get at what it holds, when you can melt the seal and take what you want and seal it up again and be gone before the loss is noticed? Our city having been stolen from us, we must needs steal it back; and every good thief works unseen, unheard and undisturbed. Issel could tell you that."

He could indeed, although he didn't want to. He might have told them more. More than once, Issel had set a wet palm to a pane of glass in a casement window, in a house like this. Feel the glass soften and melt against his skin—like butter, like lead, like iron, like anything that had a liquid form, like water—and so reach through to the catch and pull the window open. Climb in and look for what treasure might be there, what to take or who to give a message to. Or both. Oh, Issel knew all about treading softly.

He was a little surprised that so did Tel Ferin—but then, the whole school was here, and Issel hadn't known about it. That bespoke a softer tread than he could imagine, softer almost than he could understand. Of course it must be hidden from the Marasi, who had spies and informants throughout the city; but if no whisper of its existence was let leak out, then there must be those like Issel whom it would never find.

If Issel had known, if he'd heard a rumour, he'd have made it his business to find this place years ago. More than that, he'd have seen hope for his city. The Sundain wore their defeat like a brand, immutable, because they had no hope. The water-magic had been their beating heart, their strength, their authority, and they believed it dead. Let just a murmur run through the streets and markets, down to the strand and out to the fields and farms, let one person say to one other that there was an adept still in Sund, teaching the young; hope was a river—of course! what else, here, in this city of all cities of the world?—that would start as a trickle and end as a torrent, to sweep away the Marasi and their cursed bridge with them.

"Two flasks," Tel Ferin said, setting them down in front of Tulk. He'd been holding them while he spoke, turning them between his hands; latterly the long loose sleeves of his robe had fallen down to conceal them altogether.

"Yes, master."

"One of them holds purified water, the other simple well water. Can you tell me which is which? Without opening one to touch the water?"

"Not me, master," positively, as though he couldn't imagine such a skill, as though it was quite unfair to ask him. "You know I don't have that much talent."

"I know no such thing. It's only you that's certain." Tel Ferin was never the most encouraging of teachers; his voice snapped like a lash to drive his pupils to greater effort. "I know that you have not tried. An adept can sense the potential within the water, before ever his fingertip is wet. All of you here at this table have that ability, latent; yes, Tulk, even you. It only needs belief and practice to bring it out. Touch the flasks if you want to, feel where one is singing with the water in its darkness, where the other is quiet yet . . ."

Issel could feel it from where he sat. He could feel both, the blessed and the unblessed, the candle's flicker against the furnace heat; he couldn't understand Tulk's hesitation, how the other boy scowled and handled one flask and then the other and then the first again, while Tel Ferin murmured, "Lightly, lightly! You won't learn more by squeezing. Try with your mind first, before your fingers—reach through the leather there, feel how potent the water is, how it feels for you, how it wants your strength to touch it . . ." And then, at last, when Tulk seemed utterly disinclined to say anything at all, "Well, this one or that? You have to make a choice."

"Do I, master? This one, then, I think. I think my fingers tingle, when I touch it. But . . ." But he clearly wasn't certain, even of that little; he doubted himself extremely, although the one he nudged back towards Tel Ferin blazed in Issel's senses.

"That one, is it? And so unsure a judgement . . . I'll test you again, Tulk. Daily, until you learn to trust yourself. Issel, is he right?"

Yes, of course he was right. Issel could have faced the test blindfolded, in the dark; with his hands bound and muffled, insensible, he would still have known exactly where that flask was, and where the other. Alone with Tel Ferin, he might have said so. He wanted never to lie to that man. But here, with the others watching, when he was trying so hard to be small, unregarded, nothing special—

"You know better than I do, master."

"Of course," though Rhoan for one didn't believe it; he saw her stiffen in the corner of his eye, he almost saw how her thoughts ran back to last night, to the brutal flare of water in her bowl. "However—"

Tel Ferin picked up one flask and tossed it without warning. Straight towards Issel: and that was not so far at all, and he didn't have time to think before his hands were reacting, reaching to catch.

And it was dropping into the cup of his palms before his mind caught up with his body, before he understood. This was the purified flask, and it was going to hurt if he caught it; he was so attuned by now that even without touching, it was going to burn like molten iron on his skin. And if he pulled his hands back, if he let it drop, everyone else would laugh at him but Tel Ferin at least would know it was deliberate, and so would Rhoan . . .

And he had no time to think of any other choice, so he did catch it; but he caught it stiff and scared, with all his mind turned against it, trying to repel it even as his fingers closed around the leather that contained it.

Stupid, *stupid* . . . !

Even without touching it, surely without meaning to, he was tapping into that water's power. Trying to turn it against itself, to squeeze it from all directions at once . . .

The rigid hide shattered in his hands. Issel had seen a pot explode once in the fire, in an eruption of steam; this was like that, and he yelled once from the ripping shock of it, and again as all that twice-potent water seethed against his skin.

Others were yelling too, and not only from the shock. A hail of leather shards had stung several of them, in more tender places than Issel's street-hard hands. Faces, mostly, and forearms flung up to cover eyes.

And here he was trying to be quiet, to seem weak, to hide what he was and what he could do . . .

Chapter Four

ENDRE was in a litter again, and passing through the streets of the city again; but this time was nothing like the time before, and nothing would ever be like this again.

This was no pleasure trip for the Sultan's young betrothed; she had no lighthearted lords for company, though Salem must be somewhere in the parade. She hadn't seen him since the day of their adventure. Today she had struggled to keep her hopes downcast like a modest girl, her fancies crushed to ashes like a wise one.

It was the last of her wedding days, the day of the wedding itself, when celebration went over to solemnity. She had spent all morning in the temple, being washed and oiled, censed and scented, perfumed in the gaze of heaven to make her fit for marriage here on earth. There had been prayers, hours of praying, herself on her knees before the altar and prayed over by a rota of indistinguishable priests while her eyes drifted where they could, her mind further.

The temple had been built for a different faith entirely, long ages back, before the first Sultan besieged and took the city. He drove out the native priests and their gods with them, even stripping the roof off to let the last echoes of an alien rite fly free before he had his builders replace it with the widest, the highest, the finest dome in the world. Three architects had died amid the rubble of their failure, before the fourth had triumphed.

All around the rim of the dome were set the words of God, as was proper. Those aside, the dome itself was all the beauty and all the decoration that it needed, blue marble vaulting almost out of eye's reach, out of light's reach into shadow. The walls still bore the murals and mosaics of the old religion. Sultan Abeyet had fought his own priests over that, not to let them tear down or cover up what had come before; rather let it stand, he had said, to show how God's truth had overtopped it . . .

That was long ago. There had been lesser sultans since, and stronger priests. Hangings had appeared one by one to cloak the walls: silks and velvets embroidered with the name of God, the banners of the faithful, a hundred bright designs that were yet holy.

A hundred hundred banners might not have been enough. But all the warlike sultans brought back trophies from their wars and left them here. The banners of defeated armies, hung low beneath their vanquishers' arms; and armaments, and mighty drums and trumpets from the battlefield, robes and royal vestments, great candlesticks of gold from plundered chapels, silver plates and suits of foreign armour.

There was so much, Jendre could have lost herself in all those boasts and tokens, the story of this dynasty she was marrying, the Abeyids in their pomp. But among the massed swords and spears behind the altar, there was a massive shield with a bronze boss. The way the shield was hung, the polished boss acted as a mirror to show an image of the whole wide temple floor. A priest standing before the altar could keep a view of all his congregation.

So too could any supplicant—any bride, say, on her knees. Jendre was grateful. It meant that she could hold still and seem to be obedient while in fact she watched all the ranks of empire coming in to see her wed.

Always, always the Sultan must be seen by his people. In everything he did, he must be seen. How could the city trust what it did not witness? Sons of the royal house were carried through the streets at birth and circumcision; so were wives before they wed; at his elevation, the heir must take the crown from the dead Sultan's hands, and the common people must be there to witness. Every week he must ride the streets in procession, to show the people that he was not dead himself. Sultans had died, and their bodies been kept in pickle till one claimant or another could be fetched from the far border of the empire. There were kingmakers in every generation and more in the palace harem, scheming mothers and ambitious girls; the people had no faith in rumours, reports, anything that they had not seen.

Whenever the Sultan married, the people must be there. Not all, of course, and she didn't know how the lucky few were selected: by lot or by repute, by their masters' choice or their own election? One way or another, some few hundreds of the city's poor-but-worthy had won their day among the great. They came in early, herded by soldiers. Not all the Sultan's enemies lay outside his borders, nor inside his court. More than one of his ancestors had fallen to a citizen with a grievance or just a madman with a knife.

After the common folk came the merchants, all in a pack together: neither one thing nor another, neither poor nor noble, freemen who knew their own worth but were not sure that others did.

And then the army, squads of janizars to line the walls while their captains and captains-general strode among the pillars.

And after them the nobility, the men of true rank, the source of all her father's aspiration. The young men preening in their finery, their elders more dour, more soberly dressed, the habit of old men everywhere. It dawned on her about then that she was and would be the only girl to enter the temple today, the only woman to leave. To see the Sultan married was an affair for the whole city, by which it meant its men.

Thinking of old men, young men, of course she thought of Salem. There was no point looking for him in this bright distorting mirror—and so she did, but only because she knew she would see nothing but swathes of colour in the bronze, no man's face.

The mingled colours parted like meat before a blade, and here he was at last, a gleam that was the Sultan in his robes of gold, come to claim his bride. She couldn't move her eyes from him, that little speck that grew till it took over all the mirror, more, till it became a man and was beside her, a great bull bear of a man, the Man of Men.

The Sultan knelt to no man. To God, perhaps, in private, but not before the priests. He stood, and the marriage service seemed to defer to him more than to religion; he would not be patient, standing all day in a temple to be prayed upon.

———

SHE was swiftly married then, before he lifted her to her feet and set her veils back and kissed her on the brow in token of possession. She kissed his hand. And then he turned and left with that same old soldier's stride, to take his place at the head of the wedding procession. There would be chaos now, she knew, as the stewards tried to order who came after: nobles and merchants all fighting over precedence, forgetting or ignoring what they were told. He would sit his horse and turn in circles for a little while, and then ride out regardless and there would be a mad scramble at his back and it would never quite sort itself out however long the route or slow the ride.

For herself, she was glad for once to be led about, to have someone to follow. Stewards from her husband's household bowed to her and called her by gracious titles: courtly men, political men, their faces as neutral as their voices. Were they satisfied with her? She could not tell. They handed her over to palace eunuchs, who kissed her feet and ushered her outside.

The eunuchs were older. She couldn't tell their ranks, but for sure these were not body servants, nor guards from the harem. She thought there must be power vested in their soft hands and fluting voices, in their bland bald heads and unrevealing eyes: perhaps the only power to which she might have access now. She would need to learn, and quickly.

At least she had no need of body servants. She had been told she had no need of anything; that was just as well, as she owned little, but she was taking less. One trunk of favourite clothes and shoes, one jewel box, the simple precious gifts hoarded through her girlhood; she thought they would be too plain for the Sultan's wife to wear, but she would not willingly part with them. One other box, all her life's saving of things not precious at all: toys and trinkets, mostly. At the last minute, she had added an old dress of Sidië's, a beloved fierce blue that had been worn almost to rags before the little girl could outgrow it. Sidië had had no chance to take her treasures with her; Jendre would keep this one at least, on her behalf.

If it wasn't mislaid or diverted or simply forgotten, as she feared being forgotten herself behind the high wall of the Sultan's harem. She had seen the cart leave her father's house this morning with all that was now hers, all that she was allowed to keep and take; she only hoped that she would find all safely waiting.

SHE was making her own journey in a closed palanquin, fit transport for a married woman. It was hot and almost airless inside the heavy curtains; she kept her face as close as possible to the panels of white gauze that let in a little light, what little breeze there was. Even so, she could see nothing of this great procession, though the histories would describe it all as hers. Just the bobbing heads of eunuchs all around her and the guards outside them, some on horseback and more on foot, holding back the crowds.

There were crowds, but they were quieter today, subdued by days and nights of revel, or frightened in the presence of the soldiers. She was still subdued herself, and more than a little frightened; glad of the curtains to hide behind, glad not to have to walk this final stretch between her old life and her new.

She might never walk anywhere again, except in a garden. She thought she might grow fat; she wondered if the Sultan would like it if she did. Fat women were more beautiful, they said, to older eyes. *A girl should be slender, like a sapling; a woman should have girth, like a tree full-grown.*

By that rule, Salem still had a boy's tastes, he still liked girls. But she was a wedded wife now, and it was her duty to grow plump and lovely. Plump with children too, no doubt, to give her husband sons. Men liked that, and so did courts, and so did harem servants. Never mind the Sultan, it was the eunuchs she must please from day to day. No simpler way to do that, than to breed boy-children for their master.

THE slow sway of the litter, the tramp of the bearers' feet, the softer rustle of the eunuchs in their robes and slippers, the occasional snort of a horse or the jingle of its harness, the molten murmur of the crowd and the air like molten glass, hot and thick and heavy—she startled herself by dozing and rousing, one time and again and then again; and then she dozed and didn't rouse, didn't wake at all until someone called her name.

The world had changed, beyond the curtains. The palanquin was steady now, set solidly to ground, but it wasn't that. All the sounds were gone, that had lulled her into sleeping. There were other, fresher sounds out there, voices and birds and water; the air was still close within her curtains, but she felt cooler already; the light beyond the gauze was shadowy and muted, as though the hard sun had no welcome here. A new world indeed, and she must rise to meet it like a new wife, like one whose place was here. She must not be proud, youngest come of least significance; but yet she must not be craven nor sullen nor weepy.

As soon as she reached to draw the curtains back, other hands were there to do it for her: beringed and manicured fingers, peeping through the long sleeves of a eunuch's robe. No, more than one. A flurry of eunuchs beckoned her out. Their faces glistened, their robes were sticky with dust and sweat from their jogging shuffle all that way through the city and up, always up towards the palace while she dozed. They were not young; nor were they men to inspire sympathy. She had been given over into their care, and they would be careful of her. They would watch her and guard her, guide her, spy on her and report on her; as much as the walls of the harem, they would be her cage and her protection.

And infinitely useful, cruel, fickle, true. She must learn their names and win their favours, she must make them love her if she could. It wouldn't stop their spying or their cruelty, but better far to have them do it with a tender heart. She reached out, took the first two hands that offered, and stepped as lightly as she could from the palanquin and into—

INTO what? She couldn't say. Was it a court, or a garden? A terrace, perhaps, high on the hill here, level ground falling away beyond a palisade; but that fall was a dozen paces, no more, and there was the wall, behind and above the trees that could not mask it. A terrace should have a view. And there were buildings on all other sides, which should make it a court; except that the open space was wide and the buildings low, and there were paths between them all, and flower beds and shrubs, trees in pots and fountains in a pool and surely it was altogether a garden . . .

"Lady Jendre, welcome to the Palace of the Shadow of God." However the eunuchs might reckon seniority between them, there was no doubt in her mind nor in his, that the one who spoke was senior. "We thought you would like to rest after the excitements of the day, so we have brought you directly to your house."

"My . . . my house?" She blinked about her. Pavilions on every side, and any one of them large enough to house all her father's harem, and with room to spare . . .

"Indeed, lady." He gestured, they all did, making a path between them to usher her easterly. She saw that the building ahead seemed low only because it was so long; there were high windows on two storeys, and more in the roof above. A shaded gallery ran all its length, making a balcony also for the upper floor. Doors and shutters stood wide, allowing glimpses of rich colour within, tiles and fabrics and furnishings.

"*My* house?" she said again, whispering, bewildered.

"For the present, lady. His Magnificence commands it. All his wives come first to these apartments," and *apart* was the word, she realised, "to ease their welcome. Later, some other accommodation will be found for you, closer to the heart of life."

She was beginning to understand. She was in the harem, but not yet of the harem. She must be tested yet. The Sultan was not at all an old man, but he had been long on the throne. He had wives and wives. Some must have been desired, passion snared and trained to pleasure; some certainly were political, some almost historical. There would be a hierarchy, ranks and rights, a constant wrestling for power and influence and place. Every new marriage must threaten that tense and careful structure. It might be that she faced more than one trial, and more than one judge.

This attentive eunuch who walked beside her, he might have his own voice in those judgements.

"What is your name, sir, please?"

"You should call me Ferres," he said, as though others might call him by other names or titles. Now was the time to ask questions, to show how willing she was to learn; she drew breath, and then didn't know what to ask. She knew her father's harem to its bone, which was Clerys; to its soul, which was her mother. This next to that was a city by a hut. She thought it was a city indeed, and wished she were a traveller, curious and uncommitted, passing through.

She must ask something; she stammered the first question she could think of. "Please, Master Ferres, when will the Sultan come to visit me?"

And blushed at the naïvety of it, the girlishness where she was so determined to assert her womanhood; and blushed again at his smile, and his words.

"My lady, you must learn to say His Magnificence," he said, gently chiding, as if to a very little girl.

I could learn to say "my husband," she thought, in a sudden fit of mulishness. But that was an easy mood to shrug away. "Of course," she whispered, "but . . . ?"

"But he will not come to you, my lady. He will send, and we will take you to him."

This was real isolation, then. Like a suspect ship she would be quarantined, stranded, waiting on his whim.

"And the other ladies of the harem," she said, as they stepped up into the long gallery, "may I visit them to make my curtsey, or must I wait till they also send for me?"

"Lady, I would not see you lonely for the world," which neatly turned away the question without offering the least hint of an answer. "But you are young, and this day has been a toil to you. You have been raised up higher than a woman of Maras dare dream; besides which, a great many priests have mumbled prayers over you today, and you have not eaten since the dawn. I think you are hungry and tired, uncomfortable in that dress and more than a little afraid. Go in and be quiet, rest, eat, be easy. No one will trouble you more today, unless His Magnificence send."

"Is he, might he . . . ?"

"His Magnificence follows his heart," Ferres said gravely.

"Of course. His heart must lead us all."

Another bow, a low bow; and then a swift and subtle gesture, a flick of the fingers that sent all his fellows tumbling down the steps behind him, bowing and mumming, aping their good-byes. His departure had more dignity, but was just as swift. She felt caught out, startled. Had they really finished speaking? Had he said more than she had understood? Oh, she was not clever enough for this life . . .

She stood there on the gallery for a minute longer, watching the little band of eunuchs go, seeing how their movement emphasised the stillness in the garden. Like a single boat on a lake, the ripples of its passing swiftly lost in all that weight of water.

Then she turned to where tall slender double doors stood open wide. She might be lonely here, but at least she should not be alone. She came into the cool shadows of a vestibule, and here waiting were what she most prized among the few possessions she'd thought worth the bringing. Here were her father's last and kindest gifts to her, that she had begged him for: *I know I cannot have Clerys,* she had said, *but give me Mirjana, and Teo too.*

It was strange and wonderful to find them here, like familiar plants up-rooted. They both rose, from where they had been sitting quietly in a corner. Mirjana kissed her, and was immediately at work to unfasten the headdress from her hair, where the tight weight of it was giving her a headache. She felt hands at her feet; that was Teo nudging them up one by one, to slide the cumbersome shoes away. Later, there could be slippers; for now, bare feet on cool tiles was sheer bliss.

Two sets of nimble fingers turned to the laces and fastenings of her dress. She heard the breath of a giggle from the boy, when his hands over-lapped Mirjana's; Jendre smiled, and that was like a little liberation. She couldn't remember the last time she had wanted to smile.

A greater liberation was in the sudden lift of her body as they eased the heavy, heavy robe from her shoulders. The bodice would have stood up by itself; she stepped over it, out of it, and wanted to laugh with relief, with stupidity, with despair. And felt her face crumple instead as her iron resolve crumpled, as her spine crumpled, as she dropped her head into her hands and wept.

———

SHE wept until her head ached worse than it had before, until she was tired of weeping. Then Mirjana spoke to Teo and the boy fetched a robe for her, light and silky and blessedly soft against her skin. With it he brought a bowl of water, sharp and fresh from the well, with rose-petals floating. Mirjana sat her in a chair and bathed her face and temples, while Teo bathed her feet; and she wanted to laugh again at the sheer absurdity.

"Enough," she said, "enough now. I'm sorry, I will try not to do that again. Teo, stop fussing over every separate toe or I'll make you kiss them dry," but her hand on his ever-hairless cheek spoke otherwise, while her sore eyes did the same for Mirjana. And then, something she could find words for, "Is there food in the house? Please, tell me there is food . . ."

———

THERE was, of course, food. There was a feast of food, a monument of food. It was laid out in another room, within easy reach of the couch where she stretched herself: cold meats and birds, smoked fish, cool drinks and sticky sweetmeats, rice and breads and cakes and nuts and grapes and persimmons. Mirjana and Teo would have served her, but she wouldn't let them.

"Not now," she said, "not today. You eat, too. There's too much here for all of us together."

"Only one plate," Mirjana murmured, "one spoon . . ."

"You take them, then, if you're too proud to eat with your fingers. That's what I'm going to do, and Teo too, aren't we? Here," and she tore a leg off a roasted grouse and passed it to the boy, took the other for her-self and bit into it joyously while her free hand scooped pistachio and raisin stuffing from the bird's cavity and worked it into a bite-size ball.

Mirjana shrugged and poured a goblet of fruit juice for her mistress. "Only one of these, too—and don't tell me you'll drink out of your cupped hands. You will not."

"All right, but we can share."

"I can fetch more."

"Don't go." *Send someone else,* she nearly said, but there was no one.

"Oh, don't be a child. One little minute," Mirjana said, sweeping out through a shadowy door behind the table.

Jendre grunted, fished wafer-thin slices of beef out of a marinade, rolled them up in a flat bread with radishes and pickled vegetables. "Teo, here, this is for you. Tell me, though, why aren't there any other servants in the house?"

He grinned around a mouthful. "Mirjana sent them away. There were so many, a slave for every little thing, one to fetch your slippers and one to hold your cup and one to cut all your food into dainties. I said you were not so dainty, and the stupid women would have seen me whipped. But Mirjana chased them all out. She said you would be tired and want only your own people about you."

"She was right, and I am so glad to have you here. But you be careful, Teo. My voice must be small for a while, until we have learned how to live here. They may keep a stricter discipline than my father. I think they must, there are so many of them; it may be that they do whip, if they think you disrespectful." And then, because she had chased his smile away and regretted the loss of it, "Were there boys, as well as the stupid women?"

"Of course, my lady," and he was all respect now, sitting back on his heels, anxious and alert and unfamiliar. She remembered his unaccustomed silence lately in her father's house and wanted to learn all his secrets.

Lacking the means, she fed him titbits with her fingers, the honey-soaked bakes he loved, that made him think of home; and she said, "I want you to mix with the boys, listen to them, learn from them; only gossip as they do, when they think it's safe. Tell me what you hear, be my spy—but Teo, first thing, most important, find yourself a friend." It was what he most needed, she was sure. Someone like himself, but who knew the rules and the habits of the house; someone who could lead him into trouble and keep him out of trouble, both at once. Someone to run with and to whisper with. They were a constant conspiracy, these eunuch boys, they did not thrive alone.

"Yes, my lady." He licked honey and nut-crumbs from her fingers like a puppy, deliberately like a puppy, to make her laugh. Then he reached for a napkin and wiped those fingers like the most delicate of body-slaves, while she lay languid and supine on the couch like the most indolent of odalisques.

AFTER she had satisfied her own appetite and was sure of her slaves' also, Jendre let Mirjana lead her to what was her own private bath, apparently, so long as this was her own house. Here there were sounds of others at work, water being raised and fires stoked, even a distant hint of voices in the flues, but she need see no one. She need do nothing, indeed, but lie and soak up heat and oils while Mirjana worked her stiff and aching muscles into pliable ease. And then she slept, she did sleep; and when she roused there was coffee to drink and nothing else to do, it seemed, but drowse a little longer.

And so she was entirely unprepared when Ferres came hustling into the bath with a train of subordinates behind him, eunuchs and women both.

"Good, good," he said, "you are clean and rested and ready."

"Ready for what, Master Ferres?"

"To be made ready," he said, to soft laughter and applause.

"For what occasion?"

"For the Sultan, of course, for your blessing in his bed. It is your wedding night, my lady; did you think to pass it lonely?"

"You said, you said he would send for me, but not, not necessarily . . ." What had he said? She was suddenly unsure, but not this, certainly, nothing he had said could lead to this invasion. The eunuchs lined the wall, sweating beneath their caps; the women were flurrying, fetching this and that, knowing exactly where to find it.

Ferres shrugged and spread his arms wide, a confession without guilt. "Lady, my words may have misled you; if they did, that was deliberate. Had you known that you must go to him tonight, I think you would not have eaten as well as you have, you would not have slept, you would have been anxious and fretful and your girl could not have made you easy. You would have gone to His Magnificence strained and peevish, which is no condition for any bride. Come now, unwrap that sheet and let these make you lovely . . ."

THERE was more massage then, and scrubbing after with a rice pack and oil. There were tweezers and pumice for her body hair, henna for her skin to stop her sweating. There were oil and perfume for her head hair and colour for her nails, kohl for her eyes; there was another fabulous robe to wear, though this at least was soft to the touch and easy to slip on. There was the humiliation of being preened and groomed under the eyes of strangers, without any voice in what was done. There was the silence of Mirjana and of Teo too, that might have felt like betrayal but was not, was strength and support and anger, all that they could give her. Above all there was Ferres, watchful, critical, demanding.

At last there was Ferres satisfied, smiling, making a deep obeisance and swearing that His Magnificence would be pleased, very pleased indeed, delighted with his new possession; Ferres offering his arm for the tricky walk in unaccustomed shoes, through the shadows of the darkling courts and gardens between her house and the Sultan's apartments.

Chapter Five

N a way, it was what he'd been hoping for, what he'd worked for in those early mornings, a private lesson with the master. Time to sit at Tel Ferin's feet, to learn from him undisturbed; perhaps even time to be honest, to show him truly what Issel could do.

In another way, it was the last thing that he wanted. Partly because the others had seen him do something spectacular—*spectacularly stupid* might be a better way to say it—and now saw him taken aside, given special treatment behind a closed door. They must be talking, muttering to each other, asking questions and making wild guesses. Only give them long enough, fuel enough to stoke that smouldering curiosity, and one of them might even divine the truth: *he's been out there all his life, roofrunner, strandfly, always in the Shine—I bet it's in his blood now, souring his water-magic. I never heard of a dogtooth with talent, but if there was one, wouldn't you just bet it'd be like that? We should throw him out, before he poisons the rest of us. Or better, give him to Baris to keep safe. It'll be in his bones too, he'll change soon enough, it'll start to show. He belongs out there with Baris, not with us . . .*

But that was still in Issel's head, however real the voices sounded. This was worse, this was actual: this was Tel Ferin giving him a lesson in humiliation.

"I blame myself," Tel Ferin said, "for being slow to find you. I should have reacted more swiftly to the rumours and sought harder than I did. There are always rumours, though, and most of them are nonsense; I grew tired of chasing shadows. In your case, the rumours were half nonsense and half true, and the nonsense dispirited me too soon, so that I didn't try hard enough to see the truth.

"You do have talent, and strength, but you've been alone too long. If I were to make anything of you, I should have had you at Ion's age, or sooner. Now—well, it may be that you cannot be taught. Leave a sapling untended and it grows in the wind's orchard, as rain and sun and stones dictate, a twisted thing, ill rooted and ill made.

"I can't prune a boy as I might a tree, but I would like to. I'd take off years of growth, all those years where you have used and misused and misunderstood the water-magic, to make this crude and clumsy weapon out of what is subtle and delicate and strong. Perhaps the most I can do now is to show you what you've lost. I'm afraid you would find that cruel."

"Master—"

"Hush. It may still not be too late. Perhaps I can teach you something. I have to keep you here regardless; you can't be let loose on the streets again, neither you nor we would be safe now. So you will go on sitting at the younglings' table, learning with Tulk and the children; but for you, there or elsewhere, the primary lesson is self-control. You have none. With no one to guide or to train you, you have become wilful, indulgent, vicious in your understanding and your use of what you have. It astonishes me that you have survived this long, let alone kept yourself out of Marasi hands.

"I will also give you lessons individually, in hopes of giving you some sight of what you've missed, how far you are away from where you ought to be. We'll begin this now, out of the others' hearing. They'd mock; this is a lesson for six-year-olds."

Issel hadn't been taken through into the master's private apartments to learn it. This was upstairs, where almost no one came. Even when he'd been searching for somewhere to sleep, he hadn't looked up here.

He sat in a room of shadows and uncomfort, sharp angles amid softness. The windows were shuttered and undiscoverable, hidden behind banks of furniture and boxes and bales of cloth, all stacked athwart each other in that kind of orderless complexity that takes decades to achieve.

Squinting into the dark of it with a thief's eyes, he thought this was heaven and hell both, and both together. Probably there were genuine treasures, jewels and gold and pieces of greater value long lost among the rags and ruin of a life packed up to moulder here. Certainly there were what counted for treasure in Sund, things he could sell tomorrow, today; there was enough to take something new to market every day for months. But how it was, all tangled and tied together so that nothing could be reached without first moving something else, and that sure to cause a collapse elsewhere—it would need a gang of thieves and a warehouse to handle this.

Beside, he was no longer thief. Nor waterseller; and Tel Ferin seemed to be telling him that he wasn't an adept-in-embryo either, and that was hard to hear. Nervous and noncommittal as he was, some deep part of him had been rejoicing since he found the school, or since the school found him. It was a place to practise what he'd never had the chance to learn, to explore the range and depths of what he could do with water. Tel Ferin was the man he wanted to follow in that exploration, his chosen guide; Tel Ferin was the man belittling him beyond measure, telling him that nothing he had done or could do was bold or truly Sundain or in any way worth the doing.

"This is simple well water, that you drew yourself this morning with the simplest of equipment, a bucket and a rope. You could say that those are the primary tools of the water-mage. There are other means to magic, rare drinks and oils, smokes and incense," *dust and mirrors, or whatever slick sick potency drove the bridge into being, whatever light it was that shone above the river every night,* "but we need no more than this. Or not so much: there have been adepts in history who would not stoop to draw water, who would work only in the rain or in the river, where the water came by nature."

Tel Ferin did not actually stoop to draw water himself, of course. He had his school to do that for him.

"Those were the greats, in the days of our ascendency, when men and women could work directly with the world's water, plunge a hand into the river and have it rise up in response. Not so today. I and my fellow adepts see only a shadow of that power, and understand it less; but we were apprentices when the Marasi came, and have worked in hiding since, so there is some excuse for us. Our masters, though, even they could only work the river at one remove, with purified water in their hands. Like bringing a flame to oil, to make it burn: the results were spectacular, but they had to have the flame. The famous men and women of our kind made their own flame, or else they were the flame. We do not know.

"From the stories I heard, I had thought that you were like that, a glance back in time, a natural revival of a talent lost. You never had purified water to work with, and yet the rumours said that you could do so much . . ."

And so he could, only Tel Ferin held it all in contempt, so why would he want to?

He touched the shallow rise of the bowl set before him and felt the water that it held, even through bone-dry porcelain. He used to flinch from such light contact, even while he sought it out. No longer. Now he knew how water could really hurt; this tingle was nothing, next to the bite that Tel Ferin gave it.

"Master, what do you do to the water, when you bless it?" That was never the word Tel Ferin used, but it was common through the school. Issel liked it, that suggestion that the virtue came from the man.

"Not for you to know." Not for any of them to know, seemingly. He had asked around, and no one did. "It is a skill reserved to the adepts, and rare among us; rare indeed, where there are so few of us surviving. I must purify for all the city," and distribute it in secret, in dribbles, as Issel had seen. What he had seen had been a play, a snare set for himself, to drive him off the strand and into his bad day that had ended here, where he was meant to be; but it had been true too. That strange selection of people taking water from Baris in the night, they were all adepts or their servants, trusted hands. More normally, the school spent much of its time running a flask here, a flagon there, delivering Tel Ferin's blessing all across the city.

The school did, but not Issel. Tel Ferin kept him close but did not use him; nor teach him, in the way that he yearned to be taught. Even now, this lesson was all about loss, whatever Tel Ferin could take away from him.

"You sense it, I know, without touching—and that's almost all you have that's clean and original and right. How much can you unlearn, Issel? I don't expect any delicacy in the younglings, children are loud and clumsy by nature, but they can be trained. You I'm not so sure of. It may be too late to do anything but contain you. Still, I'll try.

"Lay your hand flat on the surface of the water there. Yes, you feel it, of course; but can you feel it and not respond? Can you be quiet against the thrill, lie still beneath the needle, listen to the music and not sing? Think of a cat in sunshine, purely passive, drinking heat . . .

"Water hates stone, and stoneware too, the chilly stillness of it. Frost and ice will break stone, rainfall and current will erode it; these are the weapons of water. Water is patience, endurance, permeation. It need not do anything; its presence, its being is enough. We do well to hold water, and not to use it . . ."

COMING out dizzy after an hour of Tel Ferin's scalpel attention, feeling peeled, raw, holding on to the banister because he didn't trust his footing on the stairs, he found Rhoan waiting below. He wasn't sure quite whether he was acting like a man who stepped from sunlight into deep shadow or the other thing, a man in darkness dazzled by a sudden glare; either way, he wasn't seeing clearly. Nevertheless, even before she spoke, he just knew that she was smiling in that particular way she had, as though she saw more clearly than anyone and was constantly amused by what she saw, by him.

"Well, what?" he growled.

"Show me your hand."

"No, why?"

One or the other of those might have been defensible, the flat refusal or the answering demand; together, they were hopeless. She just tutted, reached out and took what she wanted. Gripped his wrist and turned the hand palm upward; looked once, and nodded.

"I thought so. You're as wrinkled as a laundry maid."

I know what he's had you doing—she didn't need to say it. Rather, she'd said it already, as clear as need be. Issel didn't know what came next; nor perhaps did she.

"I broke his bowl."

"Did you?" She looked impressed. "Deliberately?"

"No, of course not! Just, he had me sitting there with my hand on the water for so long, while he talked and told me to do nothing, and I did try, but . . ."

"But in the end it just burst out of you, all that power you'd been soaking up? Don't worry, it always does. I think that's the point of the lesson, how inadequate we are to control ourselves, how much we need him to control us. Most of us just spill the water, though. I never heard that any-one broke the bowl before. Is Tel Ferin still picking potsherds out of his beard?"

"No, no, it just split clean across. He wasn't happy, though. He said to-morrow I should do it again with a wooden bowl that mattered less."

Rhoan nodded. Her voice dropped suddenly into a mock-male register, no bad imitation of the master: " 'Water hates stone, but it fears wood, the dry death of it. Water and wood repel each other . . .' That's what he'll say. We all know that one, too. His pipe is sound, but he only plays the same few tunes, round and around again."

Issel frowned. "You shouldn't . . ."

"What shouldn't I?"

"Laugh at him."

"Oh. Right, I see. Issel, sweet boy," and she was laughing at him now, although there wasn't a hint of smile on her face, "Tel Ferin is many things, master and teacher and the man who saved our lives, for some of us at least, maybe for all of us in the end. He gives us a roof to sleep under and the means to eat, though sometimes we have to go out to earn that food, or to fetch it, and sometimes it seems like we are feeding him. He is not God. Do you understand that, are you listening? He is *not* God."

"I never said . . ."

"Your voice said, your eyes said. We are grateful to him; we learn from him, whatever he's prepared to teach us, not enough; we run his errands and scrub his floors and do him all the honour that he likes, but we do not worship him. We do *not*. And yes, sometimes we do laugh at him; some-times he is ridiculous. And maddening, and secretive, possessive, arrogant, mean . . ."

She might have gone on; he thought she meant to. He thought her list was longer, and she meant to recite it all. They were interrupted, though, before she could finish or he could find a way to make her stop. It was one of the older boys who came, Lamartine, who would count as a man in any other company, outside the walls of a school. Issel thought he should be outside, living as everyone lived in Sund, any way he could.

Perhaps Lamartine thought so too, and Tel Ferin wouldn't let him go. Perhaps that was why he seemed always so angry, so pent up. When Lamar-tine was loud, the younger ones trod carefully around him; when he was quiet, they took more care to keep entirely out of his way, out of his reach.

He was quiet now, and all the effort of it—the gritted teeth, the breathing through flared nostrils, the voice held back to a hoarse whisper—was aimed directly at Issel, who had never had a single spoken word from him before.

Never a word, never a touch, barely a glance in passing; and now all of that focus, and one vast meaty hand flat against his chest, shoving him back against the wall and pinning him there, and his face in Issel's and disregarding Rhoan altogether, and that tight hiss of a voice saying, "You, Issel, I heard what you did. You tell me about it. Now."

"What? I didn't mean to . . ." Nobody was hurt, were they, except for a few cuts and a lot of startlement? This fury baffled him.

"You've been hiding from us. I thought it was weird, all those stories we kept hearing about you and the way Tel Ferin lashed us on to find you, and then you came here and nothing, no power, you were just a bore. But that was a lie, wasn't it? You've been making fools of us all, laughing in the shadows—but we know you now, you gave yourself away."

"It just broke, is all. The flask broke, and people got splashed, and . . ."

And that hand shifted to get a grip of his shirt, it lifted him up onto tiptoe and slammed him against the wall again, and the voice said, "How stupid do you think I am? Tulk's people are all leatherworkers and he says a leather flask can't do that, it can't shatter like glass, but you made it happen and I want to know how . . ."

And Issel was frightened and angry both at being exposed this way, as both weak and wilful, and in front of Rhoan of all people; and he had hands too, and he couldn't fight Lamartine but one of his hands had spent the last hour in water, the skin was still wrinkled from soaking it up and he thought he'd soaked up power too and kept it in his hand there, far more than he'd need, he thought that was what the lesson was really about; and without really thinking about it he was reaching to grip Lamartine's wrist with those damp and dangerous fingers, and—

—AND suddenly it was a case of hands all round, because he felt Rhoan's grip around his own wrist, just in time, and it was strange because she might or might not be stronger than he was but she didn't seem to be trying very hard and yet there was something in the cool touch of her fingers that drained all the impulse out of his, he had no resistance at all.

He thought he might be grateful, later. For now he was only lost in the moment, the feel of her skin on his, the intensity in her voice and eyes as she stood that close to him and told him no—"Issel, no. Don't do that"—so he didn't.

He thought Lamartine probably ought to be grateful too, except that the other boy had no idea what Rhoan had saved him from.

She wasn't finished yet. She laid her long fingers over Lamartine's where they were bunched in Issel's shirt and somehow just unknotted them so that his hand fell away even before she told him what she'd told Issel, "Don't, Lamas. Not like this. No more bullying now, we've had enough of it. It won't fetch you anything you want in this house. He's right, though, Issel, you have been playing hiding games with us, trying to dress yourself as weaker than you are. Maybe you had reasons, but we've seen the truth now, some of it, so no more of that. We need to know what you are, and what you can do. Lamas, where is everybody?"

"In the bathhouse." He said that as though it was obvious; she nodded, as though he was right.

"Good. Go on, then. Tell them we're coming. And fetch water."

"It's fetched already."

"Better fetch more, then. We'll need plenty."

THERE were bathhouses in the city, grand survivors of a better world, used now by the Marasi and those Sundain they would allow to share, the wealthy and the cooperative. *The willing and the craven* was another way to say it, Issel had heard that on the streets. Like most such mottoes, it was said less fiercely than it sounded. Half of Sund had no memory of a time before the Marasi; those who did seemed mostly exhausted by the weight of what they carried, the burden of another life once lived. Treachery was not forgotten, ongoing collaboration was not ignored, but there was small heat now behind the hatred. It was banked up, perhaps, or simply weakening, failing year by year as the resistance failed, as the occupation's roots sank deep and ever deeper. Roots break stone, in time; they drink all the water from the earth, and all the goodness with it.

They had never quite been closed to Issel, those temples to an alien luxury. There were always back doors, cellar doors, windows inadequately latched. And there were lesser bathhouses too, that never had been grand in that exclusive way. Meant for the use of the common people, these days they were held in common by all the people. Issel had been in and out of those all his life, if seldom to wash. He would help unload the wagons of wood and dung cakes that fed the furnaces, of oil and cheap wine that fed the skins and bellies of the bathers; he would fetch individual favours, run messages, spread news for anyone who'd pay. As ever, he'd found it hard to be around so much water; as ever, he'd found it hard to keep away.

But there were the private bathhouses too, those belonging to houses like Tel Ferin's, where the real money used to live. These, Issel never had been in. There had been small point when he was a thief, always something better to steal elsewhere, and no opportunity else.

Till now, till he came to the school; and till now, he had kept away entirely.

Now, Rhoan held his hand and took him there.

———————

TEL Ferin's bathhouse—but no, not the master's now, not by usage. He went elsewhere and left this to the school.

Left it chilly, by and large, but they used it anyway as a place to meet, a place to talk and fight and be young together without disturbing him, without his disturbance.

Issel had never so much as walked down the covered passageway that led to it from the house. He went that way now, because Rhoan did; followed her sidlingly through the open leaf of the double doors at the end because she had still not let go of his hand; only blinked and raised his head and gazed about him then because suddenly—too soon!—she had.

Tiles cool underfoot, tiles of many colours brightly climbing all the curves of all the walls, high and higher until they swooped inward from every side to make a rising dome gored with glazed panels, dirty enough that even now at the sun's height the light they let through was pearly-grey like dawn, like a shadow of true light. Issel was used to this, the whole house lived in shadows, behind shutters, not to show how busy it was within. Here was light enough to see by: to see how many of the tiles were cracked, some missing altogether, most of them as grimy as the glass or grimier.

The chamber wasn't truly circular, although it tried to be. Issel counted the walls, and there were ten of them; each one had a curve to it, as though it were part of another circle not expressed, and all ten together made a roundness that was almost more than a circle, a deeper kind of circularity.

Most of those walls had a bench at the foot, and all of those benches were occupied. To avoid everything that came with that—the accusing, the questioning, the simple staring—Issel kept on looking at the bathhouse.

The floor sloped inward from all sides, to a central drain. Beyond that, opposite the door where he stood with Rhoan—no, where he stood alone now, Rhoan had left him—was a plunge pool, empty. To one side, a bank of stone cisterns by steps that led down to a low door. That must go through to the furnace, then. The cisterns there were full of water, and heaped about with buckets. It might be the only water in the house, he thought, that he'd never fetched himself.

Rhoan was going that way and looking back, beckoning him over with a gesture of her head. He went, reluctantly; if he couldn't be a secret anymore, he still didn't have to be a circus. He'd show them something, but as little as he could get away with, as dull as he could manage. He dreaded exposure and didn't understand other boys at all, those who vied for attention, who made an exhibition of what should have been most private, their bodies or their talents or—

Rhoan's fingers took his wrist, and some long-buried part of him wanted to shriek *look at me!* and impress her mightily, if it took some towering magic to do it; was already impressed with himself, indeed, and wanted to be sure that everyone could see them handfast together. *Look at me!* it urged, it impelled, even while Rhoan was saying, "Look," and nodding across the bathhouse.

He did look, because she told him to; and he saw where a boy and two girls had claimed one bench to themselves, and were being left to it. The boy, Rubin, lay all along the length of it, with his head in Sharra's lap. The other girl was Pipet, and she sat cross-legged on the floor. His hand was on her shoulder, and all their attention was inward; they were the only three in the room, Issel thought, who were not looking at him. Rubin's eyes were closed, Pipet's cheek was turned against his thigh, while Sharra just watched anxiously over both of them.

"They had a rough time this morning," Rhoan murmured. "Marasi stopped them, and wanted to . . . play with Pipet. Rubin got in their way, just for long enough to let her run."

Which meant by definition that he'd had no time to run himself. Issel could see too well what kind of time he'd had, at the soldiers' hands. Hands and boots, most likely. There were shadows of pain around his eyes and marks, dark swellings on his ribs and limbs, bruises forming like storm clouds all about them.

"What he needs is steam," Rhoan said, "there's nothing better when you're sore. I meant to ask you anyway, that's why I was waiting; I didn't mean for you to do it like this," with an audience, "but you've got to show them something now, so would you? Please?"

"Why ask me?"

"Because I think you can, and there's only Tel Ferin else. This isn't his blessed water, it's straight out of the well and we don't have the strength, unless it's the training we lack. We can't do it, that's all; we can't heat this much by water-magic, and we haven't the wood to work the furnace. If we ask the master, he might do it for us, but he'd ask a lot of questions too, and be angry . . ."

Rubin and Pipet had been somewhere they shouldn't go, then, or done something they shouldn't do. Trouble with the Marasi was never far to seek, but Tel Ferin was constantly warning against it: *don't take risks, don't chance your luck, keep safe. For the school's sake, if not your own skins', don't get yourselves noticed* . . . Yes, he would be angry if he heard about this; if they got their healing steam, they'd get it with a lecture and perhaps tighter bounds hereafter, fewer errands and less trust, less licence to roam across the city.

Issel reached to touch the stillness of the nearest cistern's water. With his free hand, his left; no need to break her grip on the other. Featherlight, his fingertips broke the surface, and all his body twitched in response.

Rhoan's fingers tightened suddenly, spasmodically on his wrist, and he wondered if she felt it too. Perhaps she'd only felt his twitch.

No matter. Where he touched it, a little steam was rising from the water; not enough, nothing to what was needed. They'd be laughing at him in a moment, Lamartine and his friends, those boys happy to follow where a bully led.

He stiffened against the burning that he knew would come, and thrust his hand entirely below the water.

Steam wreathed his arm, and stung him all the way. Steam writhed around him, reached up and out above him, rising high enough to mist the dirty glass; and then he pulled his arm out of the water, with a little sob that was half loss and half release.

He hugged that arm against his chest, where it was stinging still. Rhoan had let go his other hand, he'd been aware of that—half loss, and half release—when it happened; now she said, "Issel—that's good, more than we could all do together, but it's not enough to ease Rubin, or to calm Pipet. They need so much, you can't stop now . . ."

Nor had he stopped. He thrust his other, his right arm deep into the second cistern, as if he thought the vicious surge that rose in his skin would be enough to scour away the other burning shiver, that bracelet of surprise where her fingers had left their mark.

—————

THERE were four cisterns, and it must have been a labour just to fill them, one bucket at a time. He set them all to boil, till the air grew thick and warm and wet, so that what he breathed scalded him inside while every lick of steam against his skin was a tongue of flame. It wasn't even like pain anymore. He felt translated, shifted to a different state where no words matched the feelings, where nothing matched the world.

Until there were her fingers, round his wrist again and her skin was wet, of course, and so her grip burned like a fiery rope, but he would have followed her anyway; and she tugged him out of the steam, down steps he couldn't see and through a door that slammed behind them and out into a blessed chill, dry air where he could blink and rub his eyes and look around him.

Steps, a door—this was the furnace room, of course, and little to look at in the dim light bar the bricks and iron of the furnace itself, a few inadequate gleaned branches where there should have been a stack of cordwood, another door that must lead out into the garden . . .

Little to look at, then, except her; so he did that instead, until she smiled, uncertainly for her, and said, "What do you need, Issel? A drink, a meal, sleep? A towel . . . ?"

His skin shivered and his bones ached, but nothing tempted, other than that last; and, "No point in getting dry," he said. "I'll only need to get wet again, when I go back in."

"You let them be, you've done too much already. You've left a roomful of happy people in there," all the school stripped and oiled and pink like suckling pigs, "and that's more than any of us hoped for. Even Tel Ferin doesn't make that much steam, those times he's kind enough."

No. Issel couldn't see the master exhaust himself this way. He hadn't expected to do it himself, but she was an imperative. Her hands on his shoulders, they were another; they pressed him down till he was squatting with his back against the wall, shivering more simply now.

"Wait," she said, and he did that until she had gone and come back and brought a dry towel with her, a clean shirt, a bucket of water and a dipper. Briefly, he thought she meant to dry him, dress him, water him herself. She only handed him the towel, though, and waited in her turn. He made a scant job with it at first, earning himself a scowl and, "No, do it properly. I want to teach you something, and you can't learn wet."

When she was satisfied, he got the shirt; and then he got the lesson.

———

"WHAT you've just done in there, I couldn't come close to that. Well, none of us could, though some of them will be trying harder now. They'll ask you to teach them, and I think you should.

"This, now, this is from the well, untouched, unblessed: good to drink, good to wash in, and that's enough for me. What you need, you need to learn that it can be enough for you as well. It doesn't have to burn, every time you touch it. You can't control the water, Issel, any more than you can stop the rain or turn the river back against itself; you just have to control yourself instead. That's the lesson. Look." Her arm went into the bucket and stirred it around; his oversensitised skin shuddered inside the fresh rough linen of the shirt, and she sighed at him. "It's only water," she said, "unless you let it be the source of something more. Like a blade in the hand, it can just be a weight, a shape of steel, it doesn't have to cut."

He shook his head. "Like a fire in the hand, it always has to burn."

Her hand shot out to clip him on the ear, sharp and stinging. "No, listen to me. It does not. You let it, or you don't. It's in *you*, Issel, it isn't in the water."

"It is. Sundain water, from the rain to the river, it's always been blessed. It doesn't need Tel Ferin or anyone, it's the gods' gift to us in our need, because we have no strength else . . ."

"Tel Ferin says that's just superstition and lazy thinking. The gods didn't make us weak, and they didn't give us anything in compensation." Which was as good as saying *there are no gods*. Issel didn't know, and didn't worry about it, but he did most earnestly believe in the water.

"But he knows the power is in the water, he purifies it for more potency, he sells it to the people . . ." Or sent his dogtooth and his disciples out to sell it, rather, in secret and in tiny portions.

"Like any warrior, he knows how to sharpen a blade and how to use it. But he also knows that the strength, the means, the choice to use it all lie with him. No matter how sharp, it won't cut of its own accord."

She tipped a slow stream of water from the dipper, and even the sound of its falling into the bucket made him shudder.

"I don't," he said, watching his fingers knot themselves together, watching how they flinched away from a single drop falling from his hair, "I don't think that's what he's telling us."

"Perhaps he teaches older students differently. More deeply, because we understand him better. Anyway, he is not here to argue with me. Will you listen to what you think he said to you, or will you listen to me?"

And she swung the dipper in one hand so that its bowl tapped into the palm of the other, and he thought she was testing the weight of it, and measuring by eye the thickness of his skull.

"Tell me, then." It was a capitulation of sorts; he could stay without belonging, he could listen without believing. He could live all his life this way, he thought. Why would it matter?

"You put your hand in water, any water, you feel the bite of it. Maybe Sundain water has a quality, even a magic to it that's unique; who knows? I've never been outside the city to find out. Neither have you. Believe it when you touch Marasi-water, and find it empty. But I don't think it's in the city, I think it lies in us. I think we take it with us, where we go.

"If you grip a knife by the blade, of course it's going to cut. All your life you've taught yourself to do that, to bleed for the knife's sake, because there wasn't anyone there to teach you different. Now you've found Tel Ferin, or he's found you; but some of us have been learning from him for years. You'd do best to learn from us."

With his eyes on the dipper, he offered no argument; just a shrug, *convince me.*

She dropped the dipper back into the bucket, and used her hands. Scooped up as much water as her palms would hold, and let it dribble between her fingers. "It's in yourself, Issel. You choose. Now you use it, now you don't. Why is that so hard?"

"Fire," he said, stubborn in bewilderment. "It burns when I touch it, every time. It can't be anything else but hot."

"Like a candle, then. It burns when you light it; and then, yes, it's hot. And then when you're done, you blow it out. You saw. Do you think I was pretending?"

No, not that, she couldn't. But, "You're not like me," he muttered, the one thing he'd wanted not to say.

"No, I'm not. I'm smarter, and I'm better trained." *I don't have your strength, or your responses*—that was what she was really saying, and he heard her clearly. "You can learn this, though. If you try. If you want to try."

Was that it, did he not want to? What was he if the water didn't sting at every touch, if his skin didn't tingle under his own sweat?

He didn't know the answer, but he thought he had to learn. He lifted his head, and said, "Teach me."

"Good. Close your eyes, hold out your hands. I'm going to tip some water into one of them. Which one is it?"

"This. The left."

"Good. How do you know?"

"It's fizzing." She must be holding the dipper above his palm there. How far above, he wasn't sure; he'd never tested himself like this.

"Okay. Don't cup it up like that, I can see you flinch. I won't tip yet. Just focus on that fizzing. Feel it, think about it. Now think about stopping it, calming it down, relaxing. Just that hand, think about it one finger at a time if you need to . . ."

Chapter Six

ENDRE needn't have made this last short girlhood journey on foot. There had been a litter and bearers waiting, to carry her to her husband's apartments. Like an alabaster girl, poised and opalescent, too perfect to risk contact with the ground . . .

"Oh," she had murmured, "can't we walk? Won't you walk with me, Master Ferres, and instruct me as we go?"

Ferres had gazed at her, his placid face unreadable. It wasn't a hesitation, she thought he never was uncertain, but he wasn't to be hurried either.

At last, he had smiled that curious vagrant smile. "Of course. We will dismiss the bearers and all these other silly men, and I will walk you through the delights of His Magnificence's garden, and we will talk of what might bring him pleasure."

Her shoes were not designed for gravel, nor for flagstones, nor for grass. Not for walking at all, in honesty, only for showing an elegant ankle and a pretty painted toe. She was glad to cling to Ferres' arm, and she managed—just—not to suggest that she slip the shoes off and go barefoot.

It felt as though Ferres were leading her barefoot through the Sultan's

mind. He spoke with delicacy but no restraint. What His Magnificence enjoyed in a woman, what he disliked, what overmastered or revolted him:
it was laid out for her crisply and clearly, with an occasional sharp question to be sure that the virgin understood.

Never mind if the virgin was nervous or daunted or reluctant. Now if
ever was the time to be compliant.

". . . Your voice is excellent, but speak little unless he invites it, and
speak softly always. When he takes you, moan if you must, but never
screech. Some girls think a man likes to hear screaming as he rides, and I
suppose some men must; but His Magnificence cannot abide a shrieker.
Cry out if he hurts you, he will be sorry for that and more careful after;
but otherwise, softness and silence are your keys . . ."

———————

COURTS and pavilions, groves and glades and vistas. Sometimes Ferres
would murmur a word of explanation: this was the court where the barren wives lived, choosing not to be sent back in their disgrace, preferring
this strange and bitter exile, under their husband's eye but never in it; here
was the house for the eunuch schoolmasters, who taught the Sultan's
brood; here the house for new concubines, where they were kept in hope
of their master's later favour. Like herself, Jendre thought, but not so isolated. That was another lesson to be taken from this walk, how far she was
from the centre of things.

There was a growing shadow bulking against the dusky sky. That was
the harem proper, the harem-house where the other wives and favourites
lived with their children, where all their slaves and servants had their cells,
the eunuchs theirs, the Sultan his apartments. It was the house of desire,
where every woman yearned to be, the place of influence and power. So
long as she didn't displease the Sultan mightily, Ferres implied, Jendre
could expect rooms of her own within the year.

Before they could come to the harem, though, there was another,
darker shadow to be skirted: a high square block of a building, walls without windows, a single door barred and guarded, great men with weapons
drawn. They must be eunuchs, or they could not be here; they had the look
of warriors.

"Is that . . . ?"

"It is," and even Ferres seemed reduced, his high pride a helpless gesture and almost an insolence, like a candle lit against God's darkness.

"Come by, girl, and don't stare. It does not do, to seem too much interested in the *Kafes*."

No, she was sure not. She and all her new sisters, all the Sultan's women, must live within his walls, possessed and guarded; but there were walls within walls, and these were the highest and most closely watched. The *Kafes*, the Cage: confined in there were His Magnificence's three eldest sons, all those who had so far come to manhood, and his sole surviving brother. Heirs to the empire, blind to the world, they waited only for the Sultan's death. They had no hope of life else, and some perhaps no hope at all.

Man of Men, lord of life, his throne was no safe place to sit. Few sultans had died of age or lawful sickness. Most were poisoned, stabbed or strangled, most often by a brother or his men. It used to be that a new Sultan would dispatch his janizars with bowstrings on the night of his accession, to send every one of his brothers to carry the news to heaven. Jendre had heard the tales told: the procession of coffins next morning from the palace to the sepulchre, twelve or fifteen or twenty and some so small, boys and babies, and the people muttering, rebellious, shocked and chastened every time. And so this Sultan, coming to the throne in his youth, at his impetuous father's death in battle: sooner than upset the city more, he had sent two brothers to the war and kept the youngest at home, building this cage around him. Around him alone, when the other two came back in a catafalque, fallen at a failed siege. *He is the heir now,* rumour had him saying, *the Sultan-in-waiting; so let him wait. He need do nothing else.*

Then came his own procession of sons, and still he let his brother live, still heir, the nearest male of his line. As his sons came of age he'd had them circumcised with all the pomp that tradition demanded, and then he had them locked up with their uncle.

No one outside it knew the truth of life inside the *Kafes*. The only servants let pass in and out were mute from birth, or mute from instruments. The women were all elderly, or otherwise barren. If the next Sultan wanted heirs of his own making, he must begin their breeding once he sat the throne; till then, there would be no rival lines to challenge the Man of Men. Even so, the city was more curious than comfortable, uncertain why the brother had been let live so long, once there were sons enough.

Rumours abounded, of course. The enduring tale said that it was the Valide Sultan, the Sultan's mother, who had kept his hand from his brother's throat. The *Kafes* had been her idea, it was said, to save her younger son's life. The brothers who had gone to the war and died in the war were the sons of other women; there were rumours about that also. Whatever the truth—and truth is a stranger to the battlefield, as to politics, as to diplomacy—she had been left mother both to the Sultan and to his heir, and thirty years later she still was. She was hated, of course, within the palace and without. Jendre had stopped even listening to what rumour said about the Valide Sultan.

Rumour also said that her younger son was mad, within the *Kafes*. Now Jendre had seen, she could not doubt it. Thirty years, from boyhood, penned up in such a box? There must be a court at its heart, surely, there must be windows and sunlight, but even so. Whether the imprisoned heirs could talk and groan together, or must huddle apart and in silence, she still thought they must be mad and growing madder.

The empire kept its hopes, its future at its heart, as though it were ashamed. Perhaps it was. Jendre thought it ought to be. There were fruits, she knew, that were only ripe because they rotted; an empire perhaps was like a man, needing a seed of darkness to bring it to maturity.

"You need not come this way again," Ferres said quietly, "if it disturbs you. There are other paths, other ways in and out. His Magnificence made it so, that there should be more than one door to his favour, he said. His mother would have had it otherwise, so that all of us who live here should always see the *Kafes* and understand its meaning."

And new wives, it seemed, were still brought this way, at least the first time. *Did she tell you to be sure I saw, or did you not need to be told, Ferres? Whom do you serve here, the master or the mistress . . . ?*

She had seen, and she thought she did understand. She saw the Sultan's great hand closed around his heirs; she saw his mother's hands enclosing his. Cold and grey, she thought they were: a dead touch, ambition made flesh, silver without the shine.

STILL under the blank blind stare of the *Kafes*, they came to the harem proper and its garden door. The guards here showed no weapons and might have been simple servants, as they bowed Jendre through.

She tried to slip her hand free of Ferres' arm, but he trapped it between his ribs and elbow, her mind somewhere between his silky smile and his shallow, deceptive voice. "Lady, show me your favour, this little walk longer. I am sure your feet are impatient; mine are old, and must go slowly."

He was not old, she thought, except that eunuchs did not often live to grow old; he might be old for his kind. He did walk with the distinctive shuffle of his kind, like a man not used to slippers and trying to keep them on his feet. She thought they must be taught it, this oddity of walking. It wasn't native, nor natural; Teo had shown no signs of it even when he'd been fresh to her father's house, freshly cut and still sore.

Be it by age or training or some unfathomable guile, Ferres was slow. She was glad enough to go at his pace through the silk-hung corridors and the perfumed halls, past the busy women and the idle women, all making their obeisance to him while their eyes measured her and made a judgement. It was hateful, this processional, worse than being shown to the people—and yet she still wished no end to the procession.

"I know what you are thinking, little bird."

Her cheeks flamed; she stammered an incoherent rebuttal, but he went on, "You are thinking that the Sultan could have built a private entrance to his apartments, a solitary stair, to save you this parade. I am right, am I not? Well, he has done so; and if he sends for you again, you may use it. This first time, this one time you must be seen, by all who care to look. Tonight completes the wedding week; without it, no honest marriage and the city floods with rumour and insult, outrage and blood. If you are not reported in his rooms, plotters will say you never came there; they will say that the Sultan is a broken man and you should be sent back to your father, a mock-wife for a mock-man. You have seen blood, I think, a little; the streets would swim in it, if such a tale started. Be patient, then, and let the women stare. Having nothing else to do, they will gossip all night about your beauty, and the truth of that will wash all through the city like a flood."

———

THIS place was like a suq, she thought, as they went deeper into the harem, like a market except that whatever she saw here had already been bought and sold. The narrow passages and the many doors reminded her of booths and warerooms crammed closely in a market; the carpets and hangings and lamps and incense burners filled all her senses like the mazing, deceptive treasures of a market; the turns and stairs and winding ways were a plunge straight back into childhood, when the world was too big to be

contained or comprehended. A visit to the suq with Clerys had been an adventure into wonder, but a runaway visit with her wild friends was im-
mense, terrifying, an early understanding that freedom was all about loss.
No one watched her, no one was careful of her, she might be lost in truth
and never found again . . .

There could be no freedom in the Sultan's harem and she had nothing
much left to lose, but she did briefly taste that same clawing terror, that
she would never find her way out of here.

She was still being watched, still paraded. As they went further and
higher, so they climbed through the ranks of the women who observed
them: at first slaves, then concubines. Now, on these upper storeys, the
apartments were larger and more luxurious, the women a little more subtle in their examination, happening to be stood talking in a window bay
when Jendre came by, or else glancing up by chance through an open doorway as she passed. Fabulously dressed, idle, attended; she was among her
sister-wives at last.

And they all knew who she was, where she was being taken and to
what end. All she could do—the best, the least, the only thing—was keep
her head down and hope to look modest and shy, hope to hide the fierce
heat of her blushing.

Straighter and wider ways brought them to an antechamber with a
guarded door, and these must surely be the Sultan's rooms at last; those
surely were the Sultan's guards, looming and huge and hugely scowling.
But here too was one more woman, more elaborately dressed than any. A
dozen women, rather, but only one who counted.

One who sent Ferres immediately down onto his knees, onto his face;
and on his way down he gave just the tiniest hint of a tug to Jendre's skirts.

She would not grovel, nor abase herself like a eunuch. However high
his rank, Ferres was a slave of the harem; Jendre was a wife of the Sultan.

She knelt, slowly and gracefully, and folded her hands in her lap; murmured, "Valide Sultan," and waited for whatever might come next.

What came was a pause, so deep and long and complex it was a thing
in itself. Not a silence: she could hear her own breathing and Ferres' beside her; she thought she could hear all the separate breaths of all the old
lady's attendants; she thought she could hear the rustling of their dresses
and the creaking of their bones. She didn't think she could hear a sound,
not the least trace of a whisper of a sound from the old lady herself. It

would be an impertinence to suggest that the Valide Sultan might move enough to rustle a dress when she chose to stand still, or that her bones might creak at all, ever. It was almost an effrontery to wonder if she breathed.

This was the throne that stood before Jendre now, it was the empire, the Sultanate and all its lands and history. The Sultan might say, "I am Maras," and mean it; but all he truly said, all the court could ever hear was *I am my mother's son.*

She had been tall once, perhaps, but was no longer. The rigidity in her was pride, no doubt, and stubbornness, not to use a stick; but it was the rigidity of old joints also, that would not bend without pain. Her back had bent, and that would never straighten; half the courtiers around her were bent themselves, desperate not to stand above their mistress.

She was old, and her body gave her trouble; she would still trouble the world in return. There were no concessions here. And she would most certainly inspect her husband's new wife on their wedding night. She must have approved the marriage; now she wanted to approve the girl. Jendre supposed that a girl who failed this inspection could still be sent back to her father in humiliation. *The Sultan rules,* they said in the streets, *but his mother makes the laws.*

"Stand up, child."

She rose to her feet with all the grace that she could muster. She meant it as a reproof to ill manners, feared it would be read as an insult to stiff old age, and did it anyway. She might be afraid of this terrible old woman, but she would not let it show. Better to seem defiant, mocking, arrogant in her youth and health. Even a modest demeanour might seem insolence in dumb show; Jendre was at least half-minded to mean it so, as she folded her hands and kept her eyes low. She tried to fold her thoughts away also; old age was adept at reading minds, no matter how mute the body.

"Well, she holds herself fittingly, but what does that mean?" It was a mutter, aimed she knew not where: at the entourage, at herself or nowhere, heedlessly let fall for whoever was close enough to hear. "A jumped-up soldier's brat, no family, no breeding. Pretty enough, but that's nothing. Time was, when it was politic to marry princesses. It'll be the janizars' daughters next, no doubt, to keep them loyal; and then the priests'. Slaves and supplicants, he will marry them all. Ah, these are drab days. What will you say to me, girl?"

"Madam, what would you have me say? My father is a soldier, true, and risen through the ranks; he has served the Sultan and the empire with his blood and strength. There are those who would say he has earned his place at court, more than a man who was only born to it."

"Are there, indeed? They do not say so to me." She sounded not displeased, though. "Lift your chin, then, defiance; let me see your face."

Jendre did that, though her soul rebelled.

"As I said, pretty enough, and your father should be glad of it. There are other ambitious generals, and they have daughters too. When all else is equal, men are men and beauty wins the day." With a sniff, to say that her voice might have been given to a family with other assets, wealth or fame among the people or influence in foreign courts. There was beauty enough in the harem already, Jendre had seen that in her passage here; she might herself have agreed with the old woman.

But she was here, and the words had been said in the temple, in the eyes of God and the citizens of Maras, and it seemed that the Valide Sultan was not going to override them now. "Remember who you are, girl, and where you came from; remember where you go, and who he is that you go to. You are for him now, and no greater rise could you have dreamed of. All other loyalties fall away; in serving him you serve the empire itself."

"And you, madam? If I serve you also?" *And where are my loyalties then, to him still or to you? And where are yours, truly?*

"If you serve me, girl, you serve the Sultan. If ever you find a way to do so."

Just then the wall swung open—or no, not the wall, a door within the wall, silk-covered and half-hidden behind a splendid hanging; she might have walked past dozens such, missed evidence of another life that must be here somewhere. Kitchens and furnaces and storerooms, all the staff needed to serve this little city that was the harem. Hundreds, perhaps thousands of people. Women and eunuchs all, no whole men within the walls; and what a strange city it was, its people both pampered and beset, and could there be anyplace like it on the earth . . . ?

There was no man, surely, like the Man of Men. That was an article of faith. And no man could be better cared for. Here was a cook, one of his cooks, and a boy behind to carry a tray with a covered dish, another with a tiny charcoal brazier below an intricacy of gold and silver, worked in the shape of a bird with jewelled eyes; and a fat man, a glossy man with costly dress and wide and frightened eyes. Anyone might be frightened in the service of the Sultan, in the presence of his mother; Jendre was frightened herself. This man she thought had his own fear, another kind altogether.

He was almost perfunctory in his obeisance, as though there were no time for it. The boys knelt side by side, eyes down and the trays held high. The cook lifted the cover from its dish to show an array of little birds roasted gold and still sizzling, beaded with fat. The mistress of the empire chose one; the portly man, beaded with his own sweat now, cut it apart swiftly with knife and fingers. Then he lifted all the pieces in his palm, blew on them for a moment, and one by one he ate them, bones and all. All the time his fingers were delicate and careful to let her see that there was no subterfuge, no conjuring; his tongue came out to take each morsel, and he chewed with an open mouth.

She nodded, turned back to the dish and picked out another. This one the cook retrieved with silver tongs. He lifted the jewelled bird by its head to show that it was hollow, another dish lid, and it sat an empty nest of gold and silver grasses. The roasted bird spat as he set it there above the glowing coals of the brazier. The cover came down over, a napkin wiped a few stray spots of grease away, a bright and folded cloth was laid beside—and then the cook took the tray with all its contents and offered it to Jendre.

Thrust it at her, rather, with a look of desperate urgency. The food-taster was flapping his hands at her, *take it, carry it, go on;* even the Valide Sultan seemed infected.

"Swiftly now, girl," she snapped. "He must have it while it's perfect yet."

Suddenly unready, Jendre took the tray. The guards swung double doors open before her; she stiffened her spine, took a breath—and felt a hand between her shoulder-blades that sent her stumbling forward, and no, surely it couldn't have been the Mother of the World herself who pushed her . . . ?

She recovered in a step or two and reached deliberately for that same lithe grace that she had shown before. She tossed her hair back where it had been left to hang loose below her simple floral headdress; she let her hips sway as they wanted to, the only feasible way to walk in these ridiculous shoes; she thought there was nothing demure about her now. She felt menacing, predatory, a girl fit to tease and provoke her lord's every appetite . . .

Just for a moment she did, as she passed through the doorway into the Sultan's apartments. And then she could have laughed at herself—the timid virgin bride trying to play the lascivious courtesan, when she barely knew what it was that the courtesan should do—except that this was no game, and she was not playing now. Her throat closed over any hope of laughing, as the big doors swung silently closed at her back.

———————

LAMPLIGHT and opulence, soft carpetings that made her long for Ferres' arm as she teetered forward, a heavy incense that made her yearn for the fresh perfumed air of the gardens, everywhere the gleam of gold and jewels, the sheens of silk and velvet. She was in another place, she thought, the source of all wealth and comfort; what lay outside was only an echo, a shadow of what was within. The closer the richer, but still hollow, meaningless, unreal.

She might have thought more, she might have gazed more, she thought she might have lost all night in gazing, but that there was a man sitting on a couch—a long way ahead, it seemed, a room that stretched far into its own twilight—and beckoning urgently, both hands, *hurry, hurry* . . .

She couldn't hurry, on these carpets in these shoes. She stepped out of them, two swift little kicks, and scurried forward barefoot with the Sultan's titbit, this tiny bird in its mad elaborate service. As she came closer, she saw what she should have seen before, and never mind the dimness and the haze of scented smoke and her own nervousness making her stupid. This man, this urgent and impatient man was himself the Sultan.

Of course he was, now that she was looking. The size of him, the gorgeous robe, the way he wore his beard—especially that, cut as no man else would dare—all said that this was he, the man who had stood beside her on the altar steps, the man who owned the better half of the world and all of her.

And yet it was hard to see that majesty and pomp in his soft, swift gestures, harder to understand his childish importunity; hard to hear the voice that governed nations in his crooning, "Oh, hurry up, hurry up! Here, here, set it down . . ."

There was a table low beside the couch, where his flurried fingers showed her. It was natural to kneel, easier than stooping to lay the tray there; and once kneeling, and with nothing else seemingly to do, it was easiest and surely wisest to stay there, hands folded again in her lap.

No doubt she should have kept her eyes turned down, not to watch her sovereign lord in the press of his greed. But she was fascinated, bewildered, a little appalled; she did watch, from under lowered lids.

There was little enough to see. He lifted off the bird lid, and murmured blessings over the bird it sheltered; then he picked it up, that roasted morsel, exclaiming in whispers over the heat of it in his fingers.

He popped it whole into his mouth, so that only its bony head peeped out between his lips. She heard his gasp, saw how he panted at the scorch of it on his tongue, sucking air in and out around.

A delicate grip on the stub of its beak, a flash of white teeth to nip it off, and the head was dropped back onto the tray. Then he picked up the cloth that lay there; when he shook it out, she saw that it was fringed with gold and embroidered with a pattern of birds on branches. To her astonishment he cast it over his head like a veil, so that it covered his face entirely and hung halfway down his chest.

And then there was nothing but the movements of the cloth as he breathed. He sat quite still, his big hands on his broad thighs; only occasional muffled noises escaped. A gasp, a swallow, the faintest moan of pleasure: it must be pleasure, surely. It ought to be ecstasy, to justify this. She had seen a man taken in raptures once, at temple; but he had screamed and drooled and rolled on the ground, until priests hustled him away. This was an ecstasy of stillness, of hush, of concentration on the moment. That much, Jendre could understand. But for a bird, and such a tiny scrap of a thing, when he was Sultan and had the world and all its ministers to command . . . ?

Perhaps it was because he had the world, that he must take his pleasure in the little things. There was a waft of the cloth as though his head had shifted, an indistinct cracking noise, and she thought that he had chewed. Once.

Her turn to shift, then, to ease her body in its stiff anxiety, to turn her head and rise up on her knees and look around.

Lamps were set in niches, set in standards, hung from chains; scattered as they were, all through this long room, they seemed to do little more than underwrite the darkness, to let it weave garlands of shadow around the little pools and drifts of light.

It could weave other things within the shadow, from the shadow maybe. She saw something move and stretch, a shadow-figure reaching for a lamp, as though the darkness reached for light, to eat it. She had always thought that night came to eat the day, that in the end darkness would engulf the world, although the priests taught otherwise.

She didn't think it would start here, in the Sultan's apartments. Perhaps it should, they said he was the Heart of the World, and death should come from the heart—but she thought the end would come in desolation and despair, for all world and equally. It wouldn't come first to the Sultan, even in reverence. She didn't think that desolation did reverence.

She did think that they were not alone here, the Sultan and herself. It might be that he never was alone: another reason for that cloth over his head, perhaps, the closest he could ever come to solitude. She heard him chew again and might for a moment have pitied him, except that it would have been an outrage.

Instead she leaned forward, trying to see who stirred in the shadows. There could be guards, a little squad of deadly men; the figure moved again, this time deliberately setting her face in the light, and it was a woman. Jendre couldn't see her age or rank; it might be a slave attendant, a favoured concubine, it might be a senior wife. She could believe anything, after meeting the Valide Sultan herself in the antechamber.

Whoever she was, the woman had a single message for Jendre and relayed it in dumb show, large slow gestures: *be still!*

Jendre nodded and knelt back on her heels again, turned her eyes again back to her husband. This was a chance to stare, to learn what she could from his body while he couldn't see her staring.

He was a big man, a strong man; he had been a warrior. His robe hid the scars he carried from famous wounds taken in battle, but nothing could hide the bulk of him, chest and belly, where the young warrior was buried. Men grew heavy with wisdom, it was said. For herself, she thought that men were like women, that they grew heavy with food and idleness. The woman who lurked in the shadows had a round face, a fat arm, the suggestion of a hefty body; most of the women Jendre had seen in the rooms and passages had been plump, well-padded beauties. Only the Valide Sultan was as lean in her body as she was in her mind, lean and sharp like a blade.

Perhaps there were only the two of them in all the harem, the Valide Sultan and herself. Jendre had never felt so thin. They called her beautiful, but that was only form; she was the Sultan's wife, of course she must be beautiful, and never mind that she was scrawny and unappealing. No doubt she could be fattened up. Perhaps her husband would send her away, out of his sight and touch until she measured up. Perhaps the other woman waited to be her substitute, to warm his bed with her padded bones when Jendre was dismissed . . .

She heard him crunching beneath his cloth and wondered how long this could take, how long he could linger over a single mouthful, how long he would keep her kneeling, wondering, afraid.

———————

THE answer, of course, was that it took as long as he wanted it to. He lingered until he was quite finished, until the last shred of meat must have been long gone and the savour too, until he could be tasting nothing but the dust in the cloth where it covered his mouth, where it dimpled as he breathed.

At last, at long last his hand lifted, to pull that cloth from his head. He wiped his fingers on it, used it like a napkin to wipe his lips and beard, tossed it down on the tray, and all the time his eyes were fixed on her. Everything had changed, and nothing had; she was still on her knees, still wondering and still afraid.

"The ortolan," he said, and his voice matched his figure, strong but softened by age and good living. She knew that he could still make the echoes in the temple ring; she learned that he could also hold a girl in thrall with a silky murmur. "So small, God's whimsy, a nothing, no value that a man might measure. And yet so fine, so delightful a nothing, it is worth all the trouble that it takes.

"You do not know its troubles? Well, it is a royal bird, forbidden to the common; perhaps you should not, until now. Listen, then.

"The ortolan cannot be reared in my aviaries or it is dull and lifeless, flabby, a wretched thing. It must be taken alive, while it is young and tender. It will be bone-bare, so frail that too rough a net will break it; it would eat like a mouthful of quills.

"Then it must be kept in a lightless box, or else have its eyes put out with a hot needle. Some say the one is better, some say the other; I say it makes no difference, only that it must live in the dark. Then it will eat and eat, millet and grapes and figs, and never fly again; so it grows fat, four times its weight in a month.

"Then it must be drowned in good wicked brandy and swiftly plucked, roasted in its own fat and nothing more. And so fetched to me, and so eaten as you have seen, spitting hot and whole.

"The head belongs to God, and we do not eat it. It has been said that all the bird belongs to God, and so we hide our heads from him when we take ortolan; I think that is not true. I think that one of my forebears learned to cover his face with a napkin, the better to taste every moment of its eating.

"We hold it on our tongue, and the fat spills from the bird and runs down our throat like molten gold. We do not chew, we must not chew until that flood is past. Then—slowly, slowly!—we eat the breast, the legs, the wings, cracking every tiny bone. It is the bird's free life we eat now, the wheat and the sea's salt and the lavenders and herbs. At last the lungs, the heart— and here is the brandy in which it drowned, opening like a flower upon the tongue.

"It is a nothing, but there is nothing like the eating of it, my Jendre."

Well, he did remember her name, then. She was still wondering how much he had truly been talking about birds, or just how little, when his fingers touched his lips, then reached to hers. Startled, she managed not to move, except that there was a tremble in her skin that made him smile.

"Come," he said, and held his hand out to her as he rose. "We have had a long and a tedious day, and must help each other to a night of charms. I will drink a little naughty wine which God will not condemn in me on such a night, it is a nothing," another of his little nothings, like her-self. At least she was his own possession, and God had no voice to raise against her. "You will drink a little virtuous sherbet, to liven and refresh you; and then we shall enjoy what you have brought into my house, your body and your beauty and your wit."

———————

DID he really find her beautiful or was that meaningless, empty words from the man who need not care what he said or to whom? She dared not ask; she felt it should not matter, though it did.

He undressed her with his own hands, displaying easy familiarity with the ties and buttons of a woman's costume. Then he spent a long time just looking at her in the furtive lamplight, having her turn and pose for him, sparking a little defiance in her, a little humiliated anger that turned of its own accord into sudden giggles that she didn't understand, that turned into hiccups when she tried to suppress them, and those lasted until the moment when he reached a hand out to touch her.

Like a fire quenched, like a page turned, like a curtain drawn, like a glass bottle broken: so sudden and so thorough was the change in her, or in the world that held her.

———————

HE held her, and he was the world. That much she had always known, but now she knew it newly, otherly, like one who knew all the names and descriptions of food being suddenly fed, fed and fed again, who had always gone hungry before.

———————

HANDS, his hands were a revelation. They could be tender, curious or mocking; they could be satin-smooth and delicate, and then abruptly grip and bruise and compel. The hands of a warrior, only lightly disguised by the politic hands of the court. Like his voice, then, and like his body: the one thing, the original, perhaps the true thing yet, overlaid by the other; or else the one thing had grown out of the other, and sometimes it remembered yet what it used to be.

———————

HANDS, her hands were tentative: frightened first, then shy, never confident. He was patient with her, unexpectedly so. Her master, master of all, lord of the horizons—he shouldn't need to tutor a raw girl. She was afraid he might be angry, but he laid her palm on his great chest and held it there. Here was the Heart of the World and she felt the beat of it beneath his ribs, the slow commerce of his blood and bile. Then he set his palm in turn against her body, just below her breast. She felt the flurry and kick of her own heart against his solid strength, like a bird in cupped hands; she remembered the ortolan; she pulled the coverlet up over her head, over both of them, and let him guide her hands where he would have them.

———————

HANDS, someone else's hands: bringing fresh drinks to the bedside, lighting a censer to send drifts of sweet smoke through the room, snuffing all the lamps but one. She had forgotten that they were not alone, her husband and herself, that there was a woman who watched and waited in the growing dark.

It didn't seem to matter. Soon, all too soon she had forgotten it again.

SHE had been afraid of many things this night: pain, humiliation, failure, rejection, shame. She had given hope short rein and little nourishment. At most, at best she had hoped to satisfy him, not to let her name be a cloud to his mind or his mood in later days.

For herself, she had hoped nothing. She had not thought to find pleasure, or startlement, or release.

Above all, she had never imagined that she might find laughter in his bed.

NOR sleep, but she found that too, she did sleep and so did he.

Once she lay awake and listened to his snoring, nestled close into his heat and bulk. She thought that she had never felt so little. As a child, she had been her own size, and the world had been so big; recently she had been too big within the world, envious of Sidië and anyone let stay small. Suddenly she was small herself, and not only in her spirit. She felt diminished, overwhelmed, a zephyr in a storm of wind, a whisper in a yell; most of all, though, her body against his, she just felt small.

Once he woke her, those hands again, imperative, imperial, demanding.

SHE woke another time and there was light in the room, the dim grey of dawn before sunrise, too high up here for bridgelight to corrupt it. Any other morning of her life, awake at this hour, she'd have slipped out of bed and gone to the window to watch the daybreak.

Any other morning of her life she'd have woken alone, or else with Sidië.

This morning there was a weight across her belly, which was his arm laying claim to her even in his sleep; there was a tickle against her ear which was his whiskers, and the warm damp thrumming of his breath. She thought she could hear all the depth and distance of that breath's journey, through his mouth and down his throat and on into his lungs; so far away that sounded, she thought she'd like to follow. She thought that she was small enough.

And then breath turned to blow, a teasing greeting, soft huffing in her ear. She smiled, she couldn't help it; and at the second time of trying, once she'd found some dim husky remembrance of her voice, she said, "How did my lord's magnificence know that his servant was awake?"

"I could feel her thinking. There is a tenseness here, here," and his fingers showed her, lightly dancing on her skin. "Your body resists you, Jendre. There is a time for thinking, even perhaps for women's thoughts, but it is not now. What were you thinking?"

"Nothing that matters, my lord."

"Of course," he said, making her laugh again silently, internally, where she used to have secrets, no doubt where his fingers could find it, "but what?"

"Only that another day," *any other day, my lord,* "I might get out of bed and open the shutters, to see the sun come up."

"Another day," he said, "and I might do the same. Today your body holds you where your duty lies, here where I lie, where my pleasure lingers. This morning you are my pleasure, and so neither one of us will greet the sun today. No matter. The sun will wait."

A good girl, she thought, a well-trained girl would say *you are my sun,* and never mean it. Herself she could not say it, and wondered if that meant it might be true.

AND then there was no time, no space for wondering, no room for any thought at all. His body blotted out the world.

That did not last, he would not stay. He was Sultan of all the world that mattered; she was a wife, a new wife but still only one among dozens, one among hundreds of women who were his. Eunuchs came, and that was an end to his pleasure, to her revelation. They wrapped him in robes and took him away to his bathhouse, where men were waiting. Men of his household, men of the court and the army, men like her father, perhaps that man himself: they would soak and steam and discuss affairs of empire and importance, and none of them would ever mention her.

SHE stayed in bed, peeping over the covers while her husband was dressing, sliding beneath them once he was gone. She curled into a ball in the hollow warmth of his absence, and thought that she might cry now. She'd thought she might before, but somehow never found the breath or quite the reason for it. She was still short of reasons, except that she was alone, abandoned . . .

And was not, of course she wasn't, she'd forgotten again. A hand ripped back the coverlet, and a woman—the same woman, surely, somehow the spirit of this room—gazed down at her.

"Well now," she said, "and did my lord acquit himself well for you, was he all that you had dreamed over?"

Jendre gaped. "You can't," *whoever you are,* "you can't speak of him like that . . ."

"Can I not? If not I, then sure no one can; and you will find that they do. You're right, though," sitting down beside her on the bed, "you'll find that I do not, except to stir up little innocents in their morning. This is your morning; the women had a look at you last night, today they will talk about you, they will try to judge his mood and yours. Some will hate you, some will seek your favour, most will dismiss you as a meaningless little slip of a thing, which you are, but they will still be talking. Enjoy it if you can; you will never matter this much again."

She seemed as friendly as she seemed offhand. "I think he was pleased," Jendre said slowly, drawing her knees up, drawing the coverlet around her like a cape.

"Oh, he enjoyed himself. He does. If a woman does not weep or scream or scratch at him, he takes his pleasure as he finds it. Don't let that deceive you, little one. He has his fondness and his favourites, for a little time, a month, a year; they are wax women, he melts them in his gaze and then looks around and finds me, Theosa, always here."

"I would not melt, I think," said Jendre.

"Sweet, you will not have the chance. You are too late, too young; you have all your growing still to do. Look at you, half boy yet," pinching at her, breast and buttock: not unkindly, just to make the point, "and he has never shown an interest in his pages. And you are wife, not woman; he did not bring you here to warm his bed, beyond this night gone. Neither to bring him babies, he has sons enough. Too many, for the empire's comfort. The *Kafes* will be crowded when he goes, or else the graveyard will."

And then she was silent for a moment, as though she had given him sons and saw her sorrow building, either way. Jendre shook her head at ill news promised; the woman smiled grimly.

"He has wed you, girl; best be content with that, and take some other lover. You'll likely not see this bed again for a sixmonth, maybe longer. He has women, wives, he hasn't touched in years. If he sends for you again, it'll be a privilege, and set the others hissing."

And then perhaps she noticed the quality of Jendre's silence, or felt her stare. A check, a glance, a frown, and, "What did I . . . ? Oh, that. Child, did you think a thousand women could be caged and kept and no man ever climb the wall to steal something bolder than a kiss? Or did you think that His Magnificence would care? He is not an old man, sure, but he seldom looks beyond his favoured few, and he was never cruel. Nor unaccommodating. He made sure of his first few sons, but half his get resemble other men. The eunuchs are meant to keep records, which women in his bed and when—but the only men you cannot bribe in this house guard the *Kafes*. We know, it has been tried," with a twist to her face at the memory. "Otherwise—oh, there is traffic, in and out. There are lusties enough in this city, young men who think young girls are better, and those married to the Sultan best of all. Why do you think the new wife has a house so far from any guards, so near the wall? He knows his women, Jendre, and he is not unkind. Nor ungenerous. Come, see . . ."

And Jendre was gripped and pulled off the bed with the coverlet trailing behind her; and she was taken to a chest where the Sultan's clothes of yesterday had been gathered together. Not by him, nor her; the woman must have done it, sometime in the night.

"Here," she said, "this is a game we play, he and his wives and all his women. You go through his pockets now, and anything you find there, that is for you."

"I can't . . ."

"Don't be proud, girl, and don't be stupid. He'd be offended if he thought you took offence. This is his way of giving; he chooses, sometimes with great care. Feel, you, and see what he has left you."

So she did, and found a purse and a ring of gold and garnets that closed tight around her arm above the elbow, that fitted well and looked well, even though she was wearing nothing else.

"You see? With your hair, your colour, that is lovely. And here," she tipped coins from the purse, a thin stream of gold, "this you will need more. There are pretties to buy, and friendships, in here you can buy those too; and then there is the eunuchs' favour, and that will cost you more. You have a boy, don't you? He can run errands for you in the town, the eunuchs have their own ways in and out; and he can win you as much favour as your gold will buy, if he has a pretty smile and a wily tongue.

"I'll not ask questions, girl, nor should you answer any; but if you came in here with a fancy, some lad whose charms have caught you by the eye or by the heart, there are ways and ways to fetch him to your bed. You'll be lonely for your husband anyway, so why be proud, why live like a widow where you can be comforted?"

Part 3

Chapter One

YOU know your trouble? What it is, you're bored, that's all. Nothing happens in here, and Tel Ferin won't let you out. You miss your old life, all the excitements of living free. Classes must be dull as, dull as, dull as that sky up there, after what you had before. And out of class, what is there to do? I get bored, even, and I like things quiet. For you—well, no wonder if you're like a monkey in a cage . . ."

They were in the garden, up a tree. If Tel Ferin had seen them, he would have hailed them down, for fear of their being seen above the wall. Children could come and go and inspire no more interest than they deserved, cheap servants cheaply dressed; they had better not be spotted lounging, playing, behaving unlike any servants should.

But it was raining, as it had been all day, a cold grey drizzle from a lead-grey sky. There were few on the streets, and those few kept their heads down, their hoods up; Tel Ferin kept his own head very firmly withindoors. Even Baris must have crept into shelter somewhere, out of the relentless wet. Besides, the tree was in the garden's heart, masked from the street by its own heavy foliage and half a dozen others'. There was no risk worth troubling themselves over. And furthermore they were boys, and meant to be wilful. With the master's eyes not watching them and not his dog's either, there had been a gleeful pleasure in the scamper from house to tree, another in the swarm up rough bark into the sodden canopy. They had been all wet already, wet and hot after half the afternoon broiling themselves in the bathhouse; the rain was one more pleasure just for the shock and the chill of it against overheated skin, never mind what more it brought, Sundain water falling on Sundain watermages in the making.

For Issel, of course, nothing could ever be that simple. Even as he lay sprawled full-length on his branch like a cat in idleness, he was aware that Rhoan at least would know that he was here and doing this. She'd be pleased, satisfied, gratified; she'd believe that the weeks of training were having an effect at last, that Issel was learning to be easy with water in any form, if he deliberately went out in the rain.

That had been one more reason for doing it. Not a pleasure, just a use. He didn't like or want to deceive her, and was astonished that he could. That was one thing he had learned from her, that even clear-sighted Rhoan could be cozened, if she wouldn't be charmed.

Tulk had never needed cozening, he would yield every time to the charm. Even when Issel was being not in the least charming, when he had a resurgence of that early wish to keep Tulk at a distance; when his manner was spiky and his voice was unkind, generous and diplomatic Tulk would still find an excuse for him, and seek some way to cool him down.

As now, quite literally, when Issel had grown snappish and edgy in the bathhouse, and Tulk—not seeing what would have been obvious to Rhoan, how so much steam had left him skinless, how he had been overwrought by the constant demands to make more and more of it, hotter and hotter—had somehow seen instead how close an answer was, the sudden change from that to this, from scald to chill.

And the rain was still water, and it did still bite deep into Issel's bones, but he was grateful none the less; and he relished that hint of defiance, the certainty that Tel Ferin would forbid what they were doing; and he liked the opportunity to mislead Rhoan without the need to say a word to her; and he was amused too by how very thoroughly Tulk still managed to misunderstand him.

He reached out the length of his arm, and was surprised a little by how far he could reach. One finger hooked over a springy, slender branch; he drew it slowly down towards him, testing how far he could force it, just with the muscles of one arm; then he let it go. As it whipped away, all its leaves shed all their water at once, and much of that fell just where Issel had hoped, neatly onto Tulk where he sat propped in a cleft below.

He yelled, and threatened mayhem, and didn't move a muscle. Issel grinned. He had counted on that. There was an indolence built up by long hours in the steam, that even a sharp cold shower couldn't dispel.

Was he bored? He didn't think so. He wasn't sure what bored meant. What was he meant to be missing so much, from before—being hungry all day, every day? Being cold and wet and tired and having no way to get dry or warm, nowhere to sleep? Being frightened, just a little, all the time? Being out and exposed in the night, in the Shine . . . ?

He said, "It's not me that's so fretful, to get out beyond the wall." That was Tulk, caught between an unbidden loyalty and a romantic yearning. "I've been there; this is better. Never mind monkeys, I saw a lion in a cage once, down at the docks." Issel had been looking for something worth the stealing, while it was waiting to be taken over the river. There was a steady trade in animals to Maras, the fierce and the beautiful, to adorn the gardens of the great; some few still passed through Sund on the way, if they had been fetched up overland. "You'd think it would be pacing, wouldn't you, fighting the bars, wild to be free? You'd want it to." *You* meaning Tulk, very specifically here. "Well, it just lay there, scowling at the sunlight. What did it need to do, except eat and sleep? Eating's not so easy when you're free, you have to search or hunt or fight for food; and sleeping's not so safe, if freedom means no one to watch over you. I envied that lion in its cage, and I didn't think it envied me at all."

"Wanted to eat you, I expect. Lions do eat monkeys. Don't they?"

"I don't know." He'd barely known it was a lion. What he knew, everything he knew came from the city, from the streets, and was all about staying alive. Lions were alien. All he could do with a lion was set it free; the thought hadn't crossed his mind, at the time or since.

"WE could go in. If you wanted."

"Yes." The rain's needles were pricking him into foolishness, stinging sparks: half the leaves around his head were gleaming now, bright with an unnatural light in the gloom where he had brushed against them. He was afraid some luminescence might be dripping off his skin and down to where Tulk would be watching it, remembering, storing it up. Issel might be learning, slowly, how to live with friendship; he would still turn away from envy, every time; he had no idea what to do with awe.

Going in was like rising from a bed of broken glass. Towels were an uncomplicated pleasure. He was still rubbing at his hair—not for any abiding water, it was barely damp enough to tingle now, only because he liked the feel of it, coarse linen scratching at his scalp—when he heard her voice, and that was a tingle too, as though her fingernails were running slowly down his spine, featherlight, with just a hint of scratch.

"Issel, there you are."

"I'm here too," Tulk said, aggrieved.

"Of course you're here too, where else would you be? And just as well, as I have messages for each of you. Tulk," taking him first, as though it was a kindness, "the master wants to see you."

"The master? What does he want?"

"I don't know, he didn't confide. Issel, though, we need you in the kitchens."

"I've done my chores," first thing, as ever; his share and more, as ever.

"We all have." This wasn't about chores, he knew that already. "We want to talk to you, is all."

"Who's we?"

"Some of us. Seniors."

"What about me, then?" Tulk again, from the doorway and aggrieved again.

"Oh, what, are you still here? When Tel Ferin asks to see you, he doesn't mean when you're ready, he means now . . ."

Tulk knew that. It was why he was halfway through the door already. But he hated to miss out, he resented being excluded. He said, "What are you going to talk about?"

"The way the master hung you up by the ears and plucked out every single one of all the hairs you have, if you don't hurry. Go on, Tulk!"

"Wait for me, then. Just, just wait . . ."

"It can't be that urgent," Issel said, listening to the sounds of Tulk's hasty departure. "We were in the baths an hour ago, and no one said anything then."

"Half the younglings were in there too, and I don't want them getting caught up in this."

"We could have chased them out."

"Yes, but they'd have known something was up, and then they'd have been spying on us to find out what, and whispering in corners, and making everyone suspicious . . ."

Rightly so, by the sound of it. The more she said, the more reluctant Issel was, even to hear her out. More so yet, when she went on, "It wouldn't have been a good idea in there, anyway. All that steam and water, people get too excited."

She said "people," but she meant Issel. She knew exactly how overwrought he could be, none better; she had stood over him day after day, struggling to teach him detachment. She'd coaxed, lectured, bullied, battered at him with words and hands and occasionally implements; she'd seen him raw, shivering, weeping sometimes. She wanted him quiet, unstressed: amenable, perhaps?

"If it's something to get excited over," he said, anything but amenable, "we really ought to wait for Tulk."

"Can't. I'm sorry, but you'll have to tell him later. Tulk's all right, he'll sit and listen; if it's you, he won't argue. He won't want to, anyway. But how often do you think we can get Lamas and his friends to be still, to be interested, to give us a hearing? Right now they're curious, they're bored with being bored, the steam's left them softheaded and willing to be talked at. It won't last, they won't wait, and if we don't give them something worth listening to right now, we won't get the chance to try again. I'm sorry Tulk has to miss it, but better him than them. We need them."

We don't need Tulk, that seemed to say; unless she meant, *we've got Tulk already, because we've got you.* He wasn't sure that was true, either half of that. Something in him wanted to follow her, wherever and whenever she would lead him; something else—unless it was the same thing in reverse, the other side of the coin, the shadow to the sun—always wanted to resist her. If it was a battle, that side of him never won, but nor did it ever go away. It argued, niggled, irritated her almost past measure sometimes. He couldn't quiet it, or else he didn't want to, in the same way that he couldn't keep away from her, or else he didn't want to.

THE kitchen wasn't crowded, it was too big a room for that. All the school could have collected here together, if they'd been willing to crush up. Still, there were more than Issel was used to seeing together, except for busy times in the bathhouse. They were sitting on benches, sitting on tables, almost all the older pupils; someone had brewed a tea of lemon-scented leaves, and they were passing that around in beakers. They had been talking, twos and threes together, but fell quiet as Rhoan and Issel entered. Every head turned to look at them, at him: they all thought this was about him, he could sense that. He could have predicted it.

He shook his head, *not me, I'm not a leader, I haven't a clue what's going on here.* He wanted somewhere out of the way to hide himself, and couldn't find it, and had to squat in the warmth of the hearth, where the eternal cauldron steamed in the ashes. That set him next to Rhoan and right at the heart of the room, at the heart of the house. At the heart of the issue, in everyone's judgement but his own . . .

He looked to Rhoan automatically for an explanation, but she sat quiet beside him. It was Rubin who got to his feet, to pull the room's attention away from Issel at last.

"Listen," Rubin said, redundantly into the silence, "we were all children in the city and we've all spent time out there since, fetching food or fuel, trading, selling water for Tel Ferin." All except Issel: but Issel had lived out in the city all his life, that was understood and apparently that was what counted, because Rubin went on, "We know what life's like under the Marasi, we've all had a taste of it," the bruises and other hurts, the news they fetched back sometimes with the food or instead of the fuel, damage that the water couldn't heal. "We're protected here, Tel Ferin's name keeps us safe; the soldiers don't pass the gates. And we have shelter, those of us with sense enough to come in out of the rain"—a stabbing glance at Issel, who glared in his turn at Rhoan beside him, who just shrugged—"and what the master teaches us, we can use that to look after ourselves if we need to.

"Other people don't have any of that. Ordinary Sundain, the poor, the untalented. All they do is suffer, and wait.

"But what are they waiting for, if it isn't us? And what are we doing for them? Just a whisper here and a splash of water there, nothing public, nothing that matters. Nothing that hurts the Marasi, or helps anyone.

"Up till now, that's all we could do: sell the blessed water to anyone who could use it, keep the school going and not let people know that we exist. Keep them waiting. We couldn't give them anything else. We couldn't afford to give them hope.

"But we can now, that's what I'm saying. We've got Issel now. We can hit back at the Marasi for ourselves, we don't have to leave it to other people anymore. We know who to talk to, how to plan; we know all the water-secrets in Sund, who are the adepts and who are their pupils, who are the rebels and who are the spies. We can be a weapon for them now, all those people we've been running messages and water for . . ."

That seemed to be the limit of Rubin's eloquence. He ran dry, looked about him—for support, for argument, for opposition, anything at all—and seemed not to be certain what he saw. In the end, then, he just turned to Issel and waited, as it seemed the whole room was waiting.

Rhoan too, but she was impatient; she nudged him.

Until then, he hadn't had anything to say, his mind had been as empty as his mouth. Suddenly he was full, mind and mouth together, spilling over; he said, "I don't want to be anybody's weapon."

It wasn't the response they'd expected, any of them. He heard Rhoan's startlement, then he felt her glare. There was a rising hiss in the room, indrawn breath turning to murmurs of protest, muttered accusations; quickly, before it could become a gabble where everyone would be talking and so no one would be heard, she said, "No, let him speak. Why don't you want to be our weapon, Issel?"

That wasn't fair; she'd turned it, just a little, so that it seemed like he wasn't just rejecting their plan, he was rejecting them. Specifically rejecting her, indeed, and the rest of them her army. He scowled at her, then gave her an answer he could work with.

"Weapons get people killed."

"He's afraid."

That came from someone else, out of his view, as he was only looking at Rhoan. Lamartine, perhaps. It didn't matter. He could answer it without turning round to see.

"Not for me. I'm the weapon, remember? Weapons are what survives the war. But this isn't war, this is Sund; and none of you has lived in it the way I have. When you were out in the world you were children, people looked after you, they kept you away from the worst; now you're here and Tel Ferin keeps you under his eye, inside the wall when he can. How many of you have picked your way down a street full of corpses?"

That fetched him the silence that it deserved. They knew, but most of them had never seen; if they'd seen, it had always been at a distance and hurrying away. They'd never been close. It was a weakness in them, and he was ripe to exploit it.

"No one. That's what I thought. I have, more often than I remember." For a while he'd supported himself and his friends by gleaning what the Marasi left, picking his way literally from body to body. If there were obvious purses, jewellery, tradeable goods, the soldiers took those; they always left bodies where they fell, and the Sundain had taken to carrying their little wealth in hidden places, hems and hair-knots, where a boy's knowing fingers might find it.

"So?"

"So that's what happens, when someone attacks the Marasi. They kill everyone, all the witnesses, anyone they can find. And that's when they're attacked with ordinary things, knives and rocks. You want to attack them with the water-magic and see what they do? Or no, you don't—you want *me* to attack them with the water-magic. You want all those deaths on my hands, on my heart. I won't do it. That's not how we live in the real city, that's not how we survive." It was all about survival, always.

"You don't live in the real city anymore, if you want to call it that. You live with us." Definitely, that was Lamartine, and definitely threatening. Issel had a kettleful of water at his back and wasn't afraid of him, didn't need to be afraid of anybody; he was very afraid of consequences, though, in here as much as outside. "You should do what we tell you, we're senior."

"You should stop trying to make other people's choices for them, Lamartine." Rhoan, hot in his defence when he needed her; he was grateful, wary, silent. She had brought him here, he knew which way she wanted him to choose. Indeed, she turned to him and said, "There are plenty of people who do live out in the city there, Issel, who do fight back when they can. And they do use the water that we sell them, just that they do it discreetly. Lamas doesn't know what discreet means, but you do and so do I, we can learn from them, be careful . . ."

"So it's not us that gets killed, you mean? Well, maybe we can do that. We can try. But you can't stop the killing."

"Other people think it's worth it."

"They're not the ones who do the dying. Ask those. Or go and look at them, just once. And don't just look, touch them," *pick their pockets, check their teeth,* "get the feel of them, the smell of them into your head," where it would linger longer than any other memory. It lingered in the streets, Issel thought, the smell of terror: more acrid, more pungent than the old-meat smell of death, it caught the throat like smoke and twisted the belly like a rank latrine. "Then see who thinks it's worth it."

"That's not fair, Issel. How many people will die, how badly, if we just let the Marasi have the city and go on as we are? They kill us anyway. Not so many all at once, perhaps, but more and more every month, every year. You'd have to line them up and ask them too, whether it was worth our fighting back. It's not for us, it's for the city: for who we are, for what we are, the Sundain, the water-mages of Sund. If we don't fight, we die; that's certain. Tel Ferin can't protect us forever. It's a good secret well kept, this school—you didn't know about us, did you?—but sooner or later one of us will do something stupid and the word will leak out, probably in a Marasi interrogation room. Then the soldiers will come and kill us all, Tel Ferin too, all his contacts wouldn't save him then; and then the water-magic will die, and then the city really is dead."

If she'd stopped sooner, he might have lacked an argument; but she overreached in her urgency and offered him another place to stand.

"Sooner or later, maybe—but it'll be a lot sooner if the stupid thing you do is to start fighting the Marasi with water-magic. I've spent all my life trying not to use the water," and never mind why, let them think he was just afraid of getting caught, "and they still nearly had me the day I came here, and half a dozen times else. You stir them up, start them looking for us seriously, there'll be something that leads them here: one of us under the question, or a spy that follows the dogtooth home, an ear listening to Tel Ferin in the baths, something for sure. The way we are now, how long has he kept this place a secret—a dozen years? He can hope for a few more, at least. And by then all of you," the seniors, all but adult already, "you'll have gone somewhere else, spread yourselves around the city, you can start schools of your own before the Marasi find this place. That's the only way to keep the knowledge alive, is to protect it. Keep it secret, and pass it on."

"Not use it, you mean." That was Rubin, and he sounded disgusted. "Hoard it, like a miser with a jewel that could feed all his family. You sound like the master. No, worse. At least he sells his water, he lets other people fight . . ."

"He lets other people do the fighting for him," Lamartine grunted.

"That's right," Issel insisted, "that's what I'm saying. The people he sells his blessed water to, they can go out and use it against the Marasi if they dare to, but then it's the innocents who die," chance's hostages who just happened to be living in the street or passing by or selling fruit by the wayside when a patrol was attacked. "And it's the master who's at fault, twice as much at fault, because he keeps twice the distance between himself and the risk. Or three times, even, because he has you sell the water for him."

Was it heresy to accuse Tel Ferin this way, or was it simply betrayal? Issel wasn't sure. He had said it and he had meant it, but it felt strangely wrong in his mouth, words not meant for him to utter. It wasn't Tel Ferin he was angry with, anyway. It was these would-be conspirators, all of them, Rhoan included. They were trying to tug him, chivvy him, drive him somewhere he didn't want to go. Like the rush of water, like the suck of a current, it was hard to resist; in trying, he was flailing around, grabbing at any argument he could find.

Which made it worse than unfortunate, fatally unkind that he should find that argument at just that moment. He knew it from the silence that his words dropped into; from the way all their heads moved at the same moment, first to look over his shoulder and then down, away, out of the window, anywhere else at all; from the touch of Rhoan's fingers on his thigh, light and arresting and too late.

He stood up without looking round, wanting to meet this on his feet; and then at last he turned, and there of course was Tel Ferin, monumentally still in the doorway, monumentally angry.

Tulk was bobbing and weaving behind him, trying to see around the master's stiff figure without drawing any attention back to himself.

Issel felt very alone, even though Rhoan was rising too, to stand at his side. She couldn't share this; he couldn't let her share.

Into the silence, against that stillness, he said, "Master, I didn't—"

"But you did, Issel. I heard." It had been a mistake, to speak at all. That sudden desperate denial broke Tel Ferin's shell, as a hurled stone can break a dark and brooding vase. Detachment or disdain, it shattered in a moment and was gone, and here instead was this furious flood, this race of words he could not stand against: "What I heard, Issel—and never mind the rank ingratitude, I should have expected that, a boy with your background would have no notion of returning loyalty for kindness; and never mind the vitriol, I don't understand why you should want to spit in my face that way but let it go, the mind of boy is often inexplicable to adults, and street boy perhaps has no mind worth the naming—but what I heard was a direct accusation, except that you lacked the courage to accuse me to my face. You call me coward, you say that I employ others to run risks for me while I hold myself here in safety—"

"Master, no, it was—" The name "Lamas" was on Rhoan's tongue, Issel could hear it there in all its honesty and betrayal. She bit it back just in time, and stammered on, "I mean, it wasn't Issel who—"

"Be quiet, Rhoan. I heard what I heard. Oh, no doubt others among you were chiming in, I know how you mutter between yourselves that I keep you on too short a leash, I don't make best use of your abilities or my own; but muttering is one thing and open rebellion something else. Sheer wilful ignorance," the words snapped out one by one, to drive over Rhoan's renewed protests, "that is another thing altogether. You are not so new here, Issel, that you have not had it explained to you, by me and no doubt your schoolmates also, why we do not go out into the city and fight the Marasi face-to-face. Once more, then, in simple terms: this is a school, and not a rebel stronghold. You are children, however you dream of being warriors. The spirit of Sund lies in its water-magic, and we few are all the city has, to preserve it. My duty is to teach, and yours to learn; we serve Sund best by staying safe. I do not sell purified water for others to fight with, but to practise, to teach, to learn in their turn, as they will discover shortly. I have made my home over to this project, at the ultimate risk to myself. I sought you out and gave you shelter, you particularly, for very particular reasons; you know best where you would be, else."

At last there was a break, a pause, a moment in the flow; and Issel couldn't use it, couldn't defend himself even with the bluntest, truest, most hopeless plea, "But that's what I was *saying* . . . !" Where he would be if he had never come here, no one could say; he knew very well where he deserved to be now. Out in the garden, sharing a kennel with Baris the dog-tooth. Waiting for the poison in his bones to speak, beyond what it said already in his magic: waiting for his spine to twist and his teeth to grow, his face to change, his mind to dull and decay.

Meanwhile Tel Ferin had turned away from him and was berating the others even for listening, while he took not a moment to listen himself.

"No, I will not hear you! You were hearing him, and that is shame enough. Twice shame, for all of you, senior as you are: he is what he is, what the streets have made him," *the streets and the Shine,* Issel heard, "but you all, I had thought that you were at least in part what I have made of you. I thought you had accepted my rules, however much you like to kick against them. Now I find you giving a hearing to one who would tear them up and lead you into disaster. This is no random gathering. You sent the little ones away, which is to say you took him seriously. Boys will be stupid sometimes, boys like Rubin, like Lamartine, who think I don't notice when they come in with bruises, with blood on their clothes; but you, Rhoan, you disappoint me deeply. I had thought you cleverer than this, if not wiser . . ."

He still had it all the wrong way round, and no one could find a way to tell him. And it was strange, but while he'd been attacking Issel, even though he was so completely wrong, Issel had felt no anger, no resentment, only a kind of numb inevitability. Now that the master had turned on Rhoan, even though he was at least half-right, Issel was suddenly raging himself, furiously defensive. She shouldn't have to face this, she should *not*, not while he had any power to intervene . . .

He didn't try to speak. Instead, he spat: hard onto the collar of the ancient iron kettle, where it seethed in the ashes of the hearth.

The black metal rang dully, like a muffled bell; and then it split like an overripe apricot, it tore from rim to belly and its water came spurting out.

Spurting like a curtain between Tel Ferin and all his school, but most specifically between him and Rhoan. It was low, no more than ankle high and failing already as the kettle drained; but it was water, and steam rose and swirled above it, needle-sharp on Issel's skin, and this was Tel Ferin's school in Sund. That was enough.

That should have been enough. But because he was Issel, because he was angry, he reached into the steam and down through it to that long spill of water across the floor, where it was soaking through the cracks between the flagstones. He gripped all that water in his mind, and ripped at it.

Flags lifted, and shattered, and dropped away. The earth beneath rushed upward like a wall, a darkness between master and school before it all fell down again in a shower of mud and stones.

And then, because he couldn't stay without doing more damage, and because he didn't want to see what damage he had already done reflected in the master's eyes—or in Rhoan's—he turned and walked away. He walked out of the kitchen and out of the house, almost out of the school entirely. He might have let simple momentum carry him through the gate and away into the churn of the city, he might have put himself deliberately out of their reach, gone further, gone all the way out of Sund and into the world beyond.

BUT it had been raining and he'd forgotten that, he'd been so bound up in the moment and so overwrought by water. All of Rhoan's training, all his own discipline he'd let slip. So he came out into a garden where the stones sang like gravel, sharp beneath his bare feet; every wild untended flower kissed him as a rose kisses, with its thorns, where he brushed by. Shrubs lashed at him, every leaf barbed with drops of rain. Before he could find the wall, never mind the gate—and he did not like the gate—he found a little broken pavilion in a tree's shelter, where the roof was still sound and the floor was dry.

There were signs that someone else had found it before him, heaped cushions and blankets ragged in a corner, but Issel was a long way from wanting any kind of comfort. He sat huddled against the wall, listening to the unpatterned drip-drip of water above his head.

His eyes were stinging. He hated to cry, because the sparks could blind him. He tried to think instead, how he could recover what was his, his gaberdine and his little things. He was sure to be seen. So he must walk in boldly, claim his property and leave. Leave again, and properly. Not a gesture, just a departure, a denial, *I am not one of you* . . .

He waited too long, and heard footsteps come to find him. Not Tel Ferin, come to be sure of his expulsion; not the dogtooth Baris, even blinded Issel would know that creature by his sounds, his smell, the dreadful promise of him. Perhaps it was Rhoan in a last act of kindness, with his things; unless she'd come with her dipper to clout him about the head again. He wouldn't put it past her.

Tulk surprised him, clattering into the pavilion in shoes. "Well, at least it was only the floor you split, not somebody's head. Tel Ferin might have been angrier at that. Secretly, I think he's impressed. Rhoan's talking to him, telling him he was wrong to curse you out like he did, and maybe he believes her now. He says so, anyway; I reckon he just doesn't want to lose you, now that he's seen what you can do . . ."

Issel spread his hands helplessly, gazed into the palms as his sight came swimmingly back, as though there were some secret written there. Perhaps he needn't leave, but he still couldn't see how to go back. He still couldn't see much, just what lay close on the floor there, his bare feet next to Tulk's unexpected shoes . . .

"Where are you going?" They never did wear shoes around the house or garden; going out, sometimes it was insisted on.

"On an errand. D'you want to come? He hasn't said, but after that I reckon you're entitled . . ."

And at last, at long last there was a spark that was nothing to do with water.

IT felt good to be outside the wall, out in the city again; it felt better to be out without approval, without Tel Ferin's consent, without his knowledge. *Or Rhoan's.* That was a nonsense, he didn't need her say-so, but it was a truth too.

"Slow down, Issel! I don't know where you're going . . ."

"The Silkmart, you said."

"Yes, but this isn't the way. Not the quickest."

"If we run, it is."

"I can't, I've got a stitch."

Issel sighed and pulled the other boy down into the shadow of a cistern. "Listen," he said, "if we go the shortest way, it leads us through more of this," the wide tree-grown avenues, the high-walled houses, all the money that was left in Sund. "We will be seen and watched and wondered over, two cheap boys wandering where we should not be. We might be stopped." And they might be taken to the Marasi barracks that lay beyond the houses, if it were soldiers that stopped them. It had happened. Tel Ferin had bought others out of trouble, but he couldn't afford that often, neither the money nor the risk.

"Even so, the master said to go quickly, and I can't run the way you do . . ."

"You're too fat," but Issel said it smiling; Tulk could only look heavy next to himself, who was whip-thin. "I won't make you run, then," though his heart sighed for it. "But we'll still go my way. It's not so much further."

ISSEL'S way was the fly way, the high way, the roof-run through his city. There had always been a community up there, almost it seemed another city. Familiar faces, some near friends through one long summer when Issel had lived among them, aloft. He'd only moved on when they'd grown watchful, wary around him, disinclined to talk.

That was the end of his easiest time. He had been the lovers' darling, running messages for comfits, taking kisses as his due; the world had drawn in on him when he came back down to earth. The closer to water, the stronger its pull, and so he had ended up with the strand, the urn, the Shine.

He had seldom been up on the roofs in recent years. For flight, when he had to; not otherwise. The people he and Tulk saw that day were still watchful, still wary. He couldn't say if they were just resentful of strange boys in their territory, or if they remembered him from before. People change, and the young and the poor change most from year to year; he couldn't say if he remembered them.

It was said that the memory was the first intimate thing to be lost, as the teeth were the first visible change to come, when you had spent too long in the Shine. He clung to what he could, but it was hard; the name, the face, the boy he best remembered was the one he would be most glad to forget.

TULK might never have climbed anything higher or harder than a flight of steps. Issel had to help him with a strong pull here, a stirrup of his hands there, a bent back to scramble up or else a hard shove from below. Once there was a leap, no more than three paces but the other boy was afraid of it. Issel showed him, back and forth, encouraged him from this side and the other. The drop was in Tulk's eyes, though, it was all he saw and all he could imagine.

"I could leave you," Issel said, "but I don't think you could make your own way back, do you? And I don't think you could make your way down," three storeys, "except the straight way, which is what you're afraid of. But I've got a flask of water here—"

"Is it Tel Ferin's water, is it blessed?"

"What do you think?"

"A whole flask? How did you . . . ?"

"I was a thief first, Tulk, and a good one." Lying came later. He had the art of it now; there was only Armina he couldn't lie to. "But if I use the strength that is in this water, I think I could throw you over safely. Shall I do that?"

"No. No! You could not . . ."

"Remember the kitchen floor. You didn't know I could do that. Even Tel Ferin didn't know."

"I didn't say so. I'm not sure, maybe he knew and he just wasn't sure that you did."

"Well, then. He would know that I could do this. And you said his errand couldn't wait; it can't wait on your nerve."

He took the flask from his pocket, and uncorked it. Tulk shook his head wildly, reached almost to knock it away; said, "No, I'll do it. I'll jump. I can do this."

"I know you can. Do you want a sip of the water?"

"It doesn't work like that. Not for me, at least. Not for any of us, we don't drink it! And you, you didn't drink it either, when you split the floor like that . . ."

There was an edge of doubt in his voice suddenly, in his narrowed eyes. Issel just smiled at him, and raised the flask. Tulk's attention shifted swiftly to the leap. He backed up, took a run at it, longer than he needed; Issel thought he would falter again, but this time not. This time he made the jump, high and howling, and landed in a sprawl on the opposite roof.

Issel grinned, and jumped it again behind him.

"Good. You did that, you can do anything now. Quickly, though, we should go more quickly. Just don't think, Tulk. What's the point?"

You made the jump, or you didn't. The fall was always in your eyes.

—————

THE high road, the sky-roads ran quicker anyway in the lower city, where houses and streets were squeezed together. Here they were busiest; here ropes were slung across gaps and alleys to make precarious bridges for the bold. Not for Tulk. There was always another way, stairs down and up again or a courtyard wall to walk, not wide but wider than the footing of a rope.

They touched ground when they had to, when it was wise, stayed down when it was swifter going, and so came to the old bazaar, the Silkmart. All their lives they had called it that, and never seen a bolt of cloth or a needle's thread go near it. All the fine goods went to Maras, and so did the people from Sund's fine houses when they needed goods, crossing the water in hired boats or private galleys. *Except for us*, Issel thought, grinning without humour. *We live in a fine house and deal for what goods we need, water is our stock-in-trade and doesn't buy us silks.* They lived like beggars in a stolen house, except that the house truly was Tel Ferin's.

———————

THE Silkmart stood in its own wide square, declaring itself a place apart; Issel and Tulk could never have reached it by the roof-run. There was no other structure near enough to throw a rope from, and no firm footing on its roofs if they could get there.

Even without that isolation, it couldn't have looked less Sundain. The silk-traders had not been citizens themselves, nor made partners of any local merchants. A remote and foreign people, they had rented wharves and warehouses, and then this land at the city's centre to build their great bazaar.

To the eye it was more Marasi that it was of Sund, or so Issel had been told by people who, like him, had never seen Maras. Here they preferred plain stone walls and simple roofs, roofs a boy could run on; the Silkmart was domed and semidomed and tiled like a temple. Its doors and shuttered windows were narrow and complicated to a Sundain eye, arched and pierced behind covered galleries. It must have had an intricate beauty once, before the paint had peeled, before rain and neglect had dislodged so many tiles and streaked the rest with filth.

That beauty had masked an inner strength, iron gates behind the pretty doors and bars on every window. Guards too, there would have been guards in the galleries: giant black men with scimitars, Issel had heard, mutes or eunuchs or both. It was said that all the servants had been muted, to protect the secrets of the craft.

No guards now. If there were secrets still, they were kept as Tel Ferin's school kept his, behind the dirt and the shadows and the rust. In daylight this was still a marketplace; what traders were left in Sund would bring what goods they had, what they could make or grow or barter from the hinterland.

Before nightfall, though, all trading ceased. The less the people had, the more care they took; with the dusk, the Silkmart changed its nature. Now it was a shelter for the lost and crippled, the homeless and the hideaways, the beggars and the children of the street. More than one winter, Issel had made his bed within its walls. And fought with knife and teeth to protect his space, his blanket and his little things. Again he'd been chased out in the end, cold glances and hard hands, hard words, *you're a freak, a dan-*

ger, there's no place for you here. It was you and your kind fetched this trouble to us at the first, making play with water, making promises you couldn't keep . . .

It hadn't changed since then, unless the window bars were rustier and more were missing, more shutters hung rotting from a single hinge or else had been torn down and burned in smoky little fires against the rain of years. He'd seen men down on the strand with wrinkled eyes, scarred and ravaged skin, broken noses, blackened and missing teeth: old men but not so old as they seemed, taking more damage than the years owed to them. He looked at the Silkmart and thought of them. Not with pity: they were cold men and this was a cold place, hollow at its core since the silkmen left. Still, he thought he understood it.

What he didn't understand was Tulk, his sudden nervousness as they stood gazing at the Silkmart in the gloom, the slow press of figures making their way towards a night's chancy shelter.

"At least tell me who we're here to find. I know these people."

"I was told to ask for the widow Elmen, whose man used to fish the river."

Well, that was luck; Issel really did know her, and had known her husband. It was a deeper puzzle also, because he knew nothing good of her.

"What, is she here? She was living with her son's wife in a hull on the strand," the last he'd seen of her. She'd always been a stiff and unkindly woman, as hard with her daughter as with anyone. Perhaps that daughter had finally flung her out; perhaps her son had, if he'd finally come home.

But she was a sour and a stupid woman too, or so Issel had always thought her. What business Tel Ferin could have with her, he couldn't imagine.

"Come on, then. Let's seek out the widow Elmen, and you can whisper your precious errand in her ear while I whistle out of the window."

Tulk's feet, Tulk's shoes clattered on the broad flags at his back, and Issel didn't see the point when barefoot was quicker and quieter and safer too, but he was tired of asking questions and not being given answers. He could tread softly, if Tulk could not.

———

ACROSS the square and they were watched, they were noticed. No one spoke. Two steps up, from the square onto the gallery; out of the glow of the city sunset into a dimmer half-world, where the ironwork pillars behind them and the arching canopy above their heads cut them off from more than sky-light.

On this one side of the building a dozen doors let into what had been a dozen separate warerooms, where a dozen merchant families would have stored and sold their bolts of silk. Every room was different, designed and decorated according to the family's tastes and resources; every room had a ladder or a narrow stair, leading to an upper floor where the trader's sons could sleep, to guard the family's wealth-in-kind.

The traders were long gone. They had taken what they could, and left only their mart behind; that was wealth enough to the poor and desperate, but wealth was dangerous. The upper rooms were the most valued, being easiest defended. Already the tough, the vicious, the petty tribes of beggars would have colonised their preferred space, and pulled the ladder up behind them if they could. Below the less organised, the solitary, the more easily cowed would be shifting and shuffling, quarrelling over space and sleeping rights and food, if they had any food, if they let it be seen.

Small hope of a friendly welcome, for two stray boys. Less hope of a friendly answer if they started asking questions, naming names, *do you know the widow Elmen, where she is . . . ?* There was a shield of silence that the lost would draw around themselves and each other, all the defence they had. Issel knew.

Something more that Issel knew: each side of the mart held a passage, arched above and once gated at either end. The gates were long gone, cut or chiselled or—as this was Sund—water-torn from the walls to be reused or melted down for valuable, saleable iron, but the passages remained, like tunnels through the building. At its heart lay a wide court, open to the sky.

It had been a garden once, private to the traders. Nothing grew there now. Flowers and shrubs in pots and beds, lawns of herbs and grass, those were all long dead; baked mud made the ground, brick-hard and bound with ashes. Young trees had been cut down, their roots grubbed out, all burned, a generation of mean fires fed on gleaned scraps and rags. The fires were a constant yet, the only consolation of the court. This was the last refuge of the weakest, the smallest, the most hurt or vulnerable; this had been Issel's place until his fellow refugees had seen how he twitched and started in the rain, and how it made him stronger.

The passage was a darkness, leading to a bad time, memories of loss. It had been a small loss, though, a bad refuge, and all the city was like this.

His life had been lived in every quarter, and all his life was loss. He walked through with barely a shiver. At his back, he heard Tulk's anxious shoe-scuff on the cobbles.

The court was just as he remembered it, the same shadows punctured by the same dim lights, the red smoulder of half a dozen fires half-hidden, shrouded by the figures huddled round. Hunched shoulders, blanketed heads, barely a face to be seen or a whisper to be heard, no questions asked. All those backs said *we have fire-rights here and you do not*, and that was all they needed, all they could think of to say.

Except for one. As the sound of Tulk's shoes clattered out of the echoes in the passage, one shadow stirred; one head lifted; one face found the light.

Issel jerked back, would have run if he'd been alone.

The face had been shrouded in a hood, but she turned the rim of it back for their sakes, enough to show that she was a woman, that at least. At second glance, when he dared a second glance, he thought she was the woman that they sought. *You lingered too long on the strand, old woman*—and of course, the back of that thought was the mirror's metal, the turn of the coin, *did I linger too long on the strand? Is this waiting for me too, is it in my bones already, in my teeth and tongue?*

A sudden brief flare from the fire flung shadows across her face, showing all too clearly how her jaw thrust forward, almost to a muzzle. She opened her mouth to speak and her teeth shone strong and sharp and heavy; her words were slurred and difficult for her to make, difficult for them to understand.

"Who sent you?"

"Tel Ferin." It was Tulk who answered, seeming suddenly quite unafraid. Well, he was used to a dogtooth in his master's service, and here was just another—which only showed how ignorant he was, or else how far he'd always lived from the Shine.

The woman glanced at his shoes and grunted. That was it, Issel realised, that was why he wore the shoes, why messengers from the school often did wear shoes; they were a badge of office. Those and the name together made a guarantee. Dangerous to carry a ring, a seal, any token of value or significance; a pair of shoes was just happy going for a beggar brat.

"Who were you to ask for?"

"The widow Elmen."

Another grunt, a nod. He'd been sure already, but it was still a shock. It couldn't be so long since he'd seen her: just a year at most, and did the changes come so fast? Or had she been hiding what was true before? A stoop and a woman's shawl could disguise a lot, especially from a boy who was dodging hard hands and suspicious stares himself. She'd have found it harder to hide anything from her daughter, sharing an upturned hull. That must be why she'd left, or been driven out more like, the girl turning flint against corruption. Maybe that was why the son had run, because he saw what was happening to his mother. Or because he felt it happening also to himself . . . ?

Issel was not, was *not* going to touch cheek and jaw, run his tongue across his teeth, do anything so visible. All his doubts and fears were seething in him, like water under his hand, and he would not let them show.

He thought she could see them anyway. Oh, it was her, no question now; the old cold glare was in her eye and quite unchanged.

"Up there." She pointed to a stair that rose from the court to an upper gallery. That was all she said, but her eyes glittered, just as soft and yielding as the river-washed glass Issel used to find sometimes on the strand. Whatever they found up there, he thought, she wished them ill of it.

THERE was a run of six doors off the gallery. The families who owned these rooms must have been linked, by contract or marriage or blood. Perhaps all three, binding them close enough to join their stores this way, to keep one watch on all.

One door stood open, with a man outside. His stillness said that he was on watch; his folded arms said that he had blades to hand, and the swiftness and the skill to use them.

What Issel could read, he could also speak. He could lie with his body as swiftly as with his tongue, if there was need and opportunity. He let Tulk go first in those telltale shoes, with the name of Tel Ferin on his lips; he followed as if by right, as if he were part of the message sent.

The door was closed behind them, and a light flared ahead. Tulk shied; Issel grabbed his shoulders and pulled his back to the wall, already looking for another way out. It was over in the furthest corner, a hatch with a ladder going down, except that someone was drawing up the ladder now and dropping the hatch. That left the window and a wild leap out into the dark, onto the canopy and slide off if you didn't fall through, drop down to the public square and just run.

A fine plan, but there were bars on the window. Rusty they might be, but not rusty enough to break at a boy's weight hurled against them. Besides, even as he looked, a man was moving to close the shutters. No way out, until they were let out. Assume the best, then, assume that these were friends.

That was hard for Issel, always hard. Friends had been few in his life, and generally betrayed him. He wished bitterly that he'd stayed in the court and sent Tulk up alone. Or stayed in the garden and let Tulk come out alone. Or not stayed in the house at all, never gone to the house, never begun the trail that had brought him here . . .

Armina. She was here, at the back of the room, and somehow that was no surprise at all. His mind was on betrayal; of course he had thought of her. Besides, she had some link with Tel Ferin, or why would she have let Issel walk into his possession?

They might be friends, he thought sourly, distrustfully, and did not give her any sign of greeting.

"Which of you has what your master has sent?"

It was another woman who asked the question. In her middle years, short and thin and patchily dressed, she could have been any one of a thousand Sundain women, ten thousand, born to a better life than this but grimly determined to survive it.

"I do," Tulk said, when Issel nudged him.

"He usually sends the dogtooth."

"He does; but there is a message also, which Tel Ferin said was better given to me. He said it mattered more."

These people had been tense already; secret meetings in shuttered rooms were a means to death, swiftly at the sword's edge or slowly under question. Now there were sidelong glances, anxious shifts. A message unlooked-for was seldom good news.

The woman took a breath, and said, "Bring it here."

From inside his shirt, Tulk drew something wrapped in a piece of worn and faded leather. Something neither liquid nor solid, that moulded itself to the shape of his cupped hands as he held it in the lamplight, that flattened and spread a little when he laid it on the table beside her.

There was no great welcome in the room. A hiss of indrawn breath, rather, and a discontented muttering.

The woman said, "So little? Is this all he sends?"

"This, and the message." Tulk was stiffening himself to it, Issel saw. Just in case, he reached forward quietly and began to unwrap the water. It felt to his fingers like steak wrapped in muslin, cool and damp, firm but giving both at once. It made the hairs rise on his arms, just the touch of it, even through oiled leather.

The woman said, "You'd best tell us, then. What does Tel Ferin have to say?"

"He says . . ." Like a boat on a mudbank in the suck of the tide, Tulk's voice ran dry. *He needs a drink of water,* Issel thought. Slowly, trying to be inconspicuous, he peeled back one slick flap of leather, and then another. The jellied water seemed to stir a little, though Issel had been careful not to touch it. Perhaps it was only a flicker in the lamplight, a shadow that slid across that deceptive surface.

Tulk swallowed, a rattling sound like pebbles in a pipe. "Tel Ferin says that he sends this pure water as a sign of his good faith and trust in you, that you will use it rightly. But he says also that there will be no more, until he is sure that trust is well placed. He says that knowledge and power are the province of the wise, and that wisdom teaches caution. He says that his duty, ours, yours is all one duty, to preserve the heart of Sund. If you attack the Marasi while they are strong, you risk all, he says; and he will not supply what is most precious, to support your folly. This is what he said, he made me learn it . . ."

Tulk's voice trailed off into a heaviness that was more than silence and more than anger, some distillation of the two; the air was sticky with it, and vicious too. Issel's fingers were lightly on the table's edge, a short touch from the water. No one was watching him except Armina, who watched him always, present or absent. Tel Ferin had indeed done well, he thought, to send a boy with this. The dogtooth could not have managed that speech or any of its subtleties. He would have coarsened it, and likely not have lived to take an answer back.

Tulk might not have lived either, except that Issel was here to protect him and Armina was here to forestall that protection, that little further stretch of hand to water.

"Easy," she said, her voice as soft and heavy as her flesh. "The boy is not to be blamed for the message he carries."

"I see two boys," a voice came back at her, a lean dark whip of a man with a hand on the dagger in his belt. "We could send one back to Tel Ferin carrying the head of the other, our message to him to be more scrupulous with us."

"Issel, stand!" Her voice was a blade fine enough to slice between one moment and the next, the moment when he was not killing and the moment when he was, or would have been. He could feel the water, he could see it almost reach for him, a tightness, a stretching in the gel . . .

When she was sure of him, Armina went on, "What, then, Gilder, do you want war with the one man you think you need the most? Is that your best advice?"

"There are other adepts . . ."

"And they all listen to Tel Ferin, and this is a message from them all. They are one in this. You know it."

"Well then, we know it. So shall we be craven and dust our knuckles at their feet and do as they bid us, do nothing and nothing again? Is that your advice, Armina? And why should we listen to you, in any case? You have no power here; you should have no voice. You are slave, and not Sundain . . ."

". . . And so know more of freedom than any of you, because mine is lost entirely where yours is only stolen, and so you should listen to me. Water is nothing to me, except I drink it; but I have my own gifts, and so you should listen to me. The adepts hoard what you desire, what you believe you need; and you would bully and argue and fight for it, and so we would all lose, and so you should listen to me."

"Indeed." The woman at the table: she cut through Gilder's hot response, and her voice was ice by comparison but no less angry. "And what will you say to us, Armina, to set against Tel Ferin's contempt and his complacency and his oh-so-generous gesture, less water than we would need to tickle the feet of the newest recruit at the bridgehead?"

"That you are wrong, of course. That you only think you need him and his secrecy and all his company of adepts."

"This is nonsense. We have no useful weapon except the water," and her eyes were covetous when she glanced at it, "and we have no source but Tel Ferin."

"That is only true because you let yourselves believe it. Everything you need is in this room."

That was Armina's way, familiar from a lifetime's frustration: to make broad and emphatic statements and never to explain them, making it hard to tell what was wisdom, what was prophecy, what was faith or philosophy or just a different understanding of the world.

The woman at the front was used to this, as Issel was. She gazed at the boys in slow enlightenment. "Is it so?" she murmured. "Everything we need? That'll be you two, then. A pair of water-boys, Tel Ferin's brats . . . But what can we do with you? Should we keep you? No, I don't think so—and you can take your hand away from the table there, you don't want to fight your way out of here and I don't want you playing with what little you've brought us, no . . ."

She bundled the water-gel up in its wrapping again and slipped it into a satchel at her hip. Issel still had his flask, and wasn't going to say so.

"What I'm thinking," she went on, "you're with us, boys, aren't you, more than with Tel Ferin? You could sit at his feet and learn and keep him happy, never use what you have learned, preserve the knowledge to an utter pointlessness; or you could be one with us and join the fight, strike back against Marasi occupation, face pain and ruin and never rest until their foul bridge is broken and their army is destroyed, and Sund is free again."

Issel had heard these speeches before, whispered in corners or screamed in the public square. They were the words of dead men, a sure sign of coming death, like falling leaves in spring; those who listened, often they died too.

But Tulk was a boy yet and nothing could keep him wise, not all the time, not now. He had left home for the school, for the promise and the thrill of it; he would leave school for the rebellion if they asked it of him, here, now. His eyes shone, too bright for conspiracy, a danger in the shadows that he sought.

"What do you want us to do?"

"Tulk, no . . ."

"Tulk, yes," said Tulk. "And Issel, yes, why not? She's right, he keeps us the way he keeps his water, hoarded up, never to be used. You don't know, Issel, you're still new, but we talk about this all the time, how we see all the bad stuff happening and he won't ever let us help to put things right. Years he's kept me there, and others longer, while he's let these people fight and us not. Him not, when he's the one with all the power and the understanding. And now there's you, and he turned on you that way, and that just wasn't fair, and . . ."

And you're my friend, that was unspoken in the fierce undercurrents of Tulk's voice; and there was more to come, more that would be said, *you're as powerful as he is* perhaps or something like it, and Issel absolutely did not want these people to hear it, true or not. Nor did he want to turn on Tulk in his turn, in this place, under these eyes with an easy accusation, *what, will you let them turn you into a killer, then, is that how far your dream of freedom reaches?*

Instead, he said quite mildly, "Tel Ferin has given you a home, a life, a different kind of learning than you could ever have found with your father. He has been your father, for a long time now."

"I know," Tulk said, and his voice was soft and perhaps a little ashamed; but then he said it again, "I *know,*" and that swift fire was back and burning in his eyes and voice together, and he tossed his head and was a rebel entire as he said, "My father, my master, no difference. I wouldn't let my father treat me this way, either. Not now. I'm old enough to choose where I stand, who I stand beside. And that's you, Issel, and these," with a sudden open gesture to include all the room and all that that implied, Sund's cause allied to his own personal rebellion.

Issel's heart might have broken, except that he would not allow it. A year ago, last month, he might have walked away; there was nothing in this except sorrow and death, perhaps a great many deaths, and no purpose. He didn't want a champion; he didn't want to be a rebel on these terms or any. He was accustomed to making his own bad choices.

It seemed as though he didn't have a choice. Where Tulk was ready to betray his master for Issel's sake, Issel could not betray Tulk. Not yet, at least, not in the open. And besides, Armina was there and keeping quiet now, only waiting, she must be satisfied with how this went; so he just let it happen, he turned to the woman in authority and said what Tulk had said before, "What do you want us to do?"

That wasn't a commitment, only an opening. The woman smiled, though, more for herself than for him. "Nothing dreadful. Go back to the school, be quiet, learn your lessons. Say that Tel Ferin's message has been understood; I promise, we will do nothing that he might hear about. Try to be his regular messengers to us, his trusted runners. If he trusts you in this, he will trust you in other matters. All the time, come as close to him as you can, be useful."

"You want us to be spies." Issel said it flatly for Tulk's sake, to make her meaning clear. "He is our master, and you want us to betray him."

"He betrays his city and his strength, by never using it. Sund is your city also; will you let him betray your strength also? He will possess you, boy, and never use you. Sund deserves better than that."

Betrayal has its romance, hand in hand with its bitterness. Street boy and craftsman's son, they had both sat on pavements and listened to the storytellers; Tulk thought himself already caught up in a story, his city's story, dreams and tears that must come to triumph in the end. He didn't know it, Issel thought, but he had been hooked and netted.

Issel only bowed to the inevitable; he bowed to this. "What should we be looking for, in our master's house?"

"His secrets. No, his one secret, his little treasure by which he rules us all. Discover how he purifies Sund-water, lads, to make it so potent. That knowledge is not his to hide; and when we share it, when we can bless water by the barrel load, then all of Sund will rise and drive the Marasi into the river, and she will roll over in her bed to drown them all."

Chapter Two

IDLE days, empty days: Jendre thought that if she could cup time in her hands like sunlight, it would dribble between her fingers like honey-syrup, sweet and sticky and oh, so slow.

Idle nights, empty nights: even with others in the bed, warm bodies for company and soft warm voices for comfort in the dark when she most needed it, even so she felt alone, neglected, bereft. Teo and Mirjana were beloved, but not for this. She wondered what kind of wanton wife she was, that just one night with her husband could leave her so physically wanting, so hungry for another, more and more.

Sometimes she wondered what kind of unkind husband he was to make her want him so, to know it and yet to abandon her to all this want. That was a treason, though, stepping close to heresy, to think critically of His Magnificence. Besides, the answer was easy, obvious, fundamental: he was the Man of Men, and master of more than her slim body. He had a world to rule, and another world of women in his harem. She had seen him at his governance of them, distantly, a grand figure in a lake boat with eunuchs to guard and punt and half a dozen concubines to chirrup at him. Their voices had carried over the water like birdsong, fluting and meaningless; she had watched for a little while, admiring how hard they worked to please him, wondering which would be given the token of his handkerchief to say *this is my choice, I will have her tonight.*

She harboured no resentment. They did what they were here to do. Perhaps she did the same; perhaps a dutiful wife should ache so for her husband's touch, perhaps she and all his other wives were meant to live this desolate life as a service, an offering to him, proof that he was the great man that his life and rank asserted. How could he be less, where so many pined and craved what he so casually dispensed?

In fact she thought that he was bigger than that, genuinely great and kindly with it; but she'd been wrong before.

———————

NO matter. Whatever his motives or the manners of the harem, this was the case, that he had held her one long night and left her since; and left her hollow, helpless, unredeemed.

It had caught her all unawares, this yearning passion. Unprepared, she had no weapons to use against it. Simple endurance had seen her through most of the troubles of her youth, the endless quiet patience of a stone in a river, letting it all flow by. Now the flow was internal, a terrible churning of fierce waters that she could neither control nor ignore. Her wedding night had taught her a new definition of desire, for which her marriage offered her no satisfaction. It was a physical thing, a hunger that would hold her dry-mouthed and shivery half the night; it lay like a dull weight, cold iron in her bones, and yet it was in her mind too, in her eye and her imagination. At first it was her husband who walked there, he alone who claimed possession of her waking dreams. Time passed, though, and she despaired of him; and at the same time worried that he might feel the heat of her craving and be disturbed by it; and at the same time could not help but wonder about other men, other bodies doing what he had done to her, or else doing something else entirely.

Eventually her gaze would follow the soft shuffling walk of a eunuch in the gardens and gift him with the stride and all the body of a man, only to play with him in her head: to let him play with a play-Jendre in her bed or on the grass here or down by the lakeside in the curtained shadow of the willows. Never Teo, and—lord, no!—never Ferres, never anyone she could name. Just the anonymous pretty ones who came and went and never looked at her, to whom she could do no harm, from whom she could take none. Idle dreams, empty dreams . . .

THAT there was another dream that was neither idle nor empty, but stirring and hunting and full of threat and promise: that she would not admit, even to herself, even in the dullest, the bleakest, the most desperate dark hours.

No. That she would not. She would *not* . . . !

HER slaves gave her a companionship that only emphasised her solitude; her sister-wives—when they came, those rare times when they did venture as far as her pavilion—offered her a friendship that could not help but stress her isolation. They brought it with them like a packet of pleasure, a bright moment that they unwrapped and shared and took away as a matter of course when they left.

Lady Selena, Lady Rhus: Ferres had brought her to them one sunny morning in a meadow of flowers. To be examined, she thought, to be assessed for beauty and manner and comportment, for open-handedness and discretion, for likely influence and likely risk, all the ancient currencies of the harem. She had tried to be amused, and had struggled to keep that amusement private while she carried herself like the perfect new arrival, demure and shy and eager to please.

They were not so much older than she was, these junior wives, and not so much wiser, but she made believe that they were both. She gave them a respect they must have craved, to judge by how delightedly they took it. When Selena admired a bracelet she was wearing—not the Sultan's gift, no, never that, but a doubled loop of diamond-flecked silver that she'd had from her father years before, that he'd fetched home from one of his distant wars, that she had loved for its exotic design and its telling weight on her wrist and because it came from him—she gave that too, without hesitation, as clearly she was meant to. It would be a bauble to the other woman, nothing more: something not to wear but to keep a while as a trophy and then to pass on, a gift to a cherished slave perhaps or else trade goods, a debt settled or a pledge redeemed. Every harem was a marketplace. Jewels and trinkets passed constantly between women and eunuchs, and that was only the currency that could be counted. They would deal in favours too, in little kindnesses and cruelties, in gossip and support. She needed to learn what could be traded and how to reckon its value; until she was sure, she would pay whatever was asked and take whatever was offered in exchange. She might beggar herself before she was wise in her accounts, but she was practically a beggar anyway in this market. She had little enough to lose, and much to gain from others' good opinions.

Especially now, an inner voice had suggested dryly, *while you still stand close in the Sultan's shadow, under his eye, when he may yet notice who treats with you and how, or while they may still think he does . . .*

Influence was a creature of the shadows, never coming out into the light; it lived in the eyes of those who looked for it, and its strength lay in their estimation. In truth—at least in her own eyes, and in the Sultan's—she might have none, but if others thought she did, why then she did, at least in their eyes, where it mattered. Where it had effect, and for as long as that effect might last.

So she gave her bracelet, and hid the pang it cost her. *Here I am, who might for all you know turn out to be our master's new favourite, swift to rise; and see, I will play such an innocent, so grateful for your condescension, I will give you what I have loved simply because you desire it. And you who are so subtle and so aware, you will wonder what else I have to give in my naïvety, whether the Sultan's grace lies within my all-unknowing gift. And you will show me favour just in case, and bring me gifts of greater worth than my poor bangle; the two of you will compete, perhaps, in kindnesses, or else collaborate; and by the time it comes clear that the Sultan's eye has moved on, I will have my place in the market and the wherewithal to bargain with. So much, at least . . .*

So much, and perhaps more. There was always—she supposed—the chance of a genuine friendship, beyond what could be bought and paid for. If there was anything within these walls that could not be bought and paid for. She would learn.

A few days after that first encounter, boys came running to her pavilion as harbingers of a great event, a visit from those same two sister-wives. Teo knew the boys' names already, which pleased her mightily; his reward was to join them in their urgent work. While they raced to erect a canopy and screens out on the grass, to spread carpets in their shade, to fetch cushions and coffee and a hookah pipe for Rhus, who liked to smoke a little *khola* in the afternoons before she dozed, Jendre had to indulge Mirjana too for fairness's sake: which meant letting herself be hauled away to change her dress, to be swiftly perfumed and modestly painted, as befitted the new wife awaiting the kind attentions of her seniors.

"Like a horse being groomed for market," she grumbled. "I thought I was done with all of this."

"You did not. You know better than that. Every day is a market, here; and you, what do you have to sell, except yourself?"

I have you, she might have said, if she wanted to earn herself a slap. But in a way Mirjana was selling herself as well as her mistress, sending Jendre forth in a style and condition that would speak well of the skills of her slave-girl. It was all one; they both knew it; Jendre submitted with a surly grace.

And stepped out, adorned, into a sun that made the wet ground steam beneath her feet, beneath her silly silky slippers; and had only a moment to think *they'll be ruined, and those women will laugh at me behind their hands, them and their slaves too, and what was Mirjana thinking . . . ?* before Teo was abruptly there and hurling a bolt of cloth down at her feet, hand over hand, laying a path of crimson and gold for her to tread across the grass. And this wasn't simply silly, it was absurd, and she loved it, and loved him for it; and stepped graciously, gracefully along that gaudy way till she came to the shade, to the carpets, to the coffee.

And she lay there in her luxury, only in order to be able to rise at her sister-wives' approach, so that they might see her do them honour; and she teased their boys with pretty words and sweetmeats while she waited, so that they might give good reports of her later to their mistresses and perhaps be kinder to Teo for her sake. All three of the boys were talking around her, perhaps about her even now, with glances and subtle gestures and the fluttering finger-talk that all the eunuchs knew, that Teo had refused to teach her. She hoped that was another good sign, that he was not excluded from their talk, be it idle chatter or conspiracy; she yearned to know what it was that they were saying, and she was utterly certain that he would never tell her. Of course he must be allowed to have his secrets, but it infuriated her that he did.

And he knew that, and so he was blatant about it. Boys . . .

———

AT length they came, carried in swaying litters not to exhaust themselves unduly or soil their own delicate footwear, besieged fore and aft and on both flanks by a tremendous fuss of attendants wielding parasols and trays and boxes, more rugs, more cushions, more vivid colour. The Valide Sultan herself went about with less commotion. Perhaps the less you mattered in the hierarchy, the more noise you felt compelled to make? If that were true, Jendre ought to acquire a hubbub of her own in lieu of this quiet retinue, Mirjana at her side to help her to her feet, Teo barefoot in the grass with his new friends.

Lady Selena, Lady Rhus didn't share her peculiar reticence, in this or in much else. That came clear once her two guests were settled, served with dainties, arrayed to their own and their slaves' satisfaction. They started to talk between themselves, and suddenly it was like being back at home, in the baths with Ezerria and all her father's women, like all her long girlhood spent listening to women talk about their man. She felt younger, smaller, diminished: except that here she knew the same man in the same way, the intimate touches that had been a mystery to her before. Half of her wanted to blush and be angry for his sake, that he should be so discussed, so debased it seemed to her; the other half wanted to hear everything and store it up, to learn, to take gossip as part payment against the bracelet and whatever more they took from her.

She couldn't sustain the anger, she wasn't allowed to sustain her silence; Rhus turned to her and asked, "What, Lady Jendre, have we shocked you?"

"You must speak as you wish, of course."

"And yet you wish that we would not, at least where you must join us."

Well, if she wanted honesty, she could have it. "He is my husband, my master, and it would ill befit me—"

"He is everyone's husband and master here, and how else are we to understand him and his pleasures? We can help to teach you, as our seniors did us."

Ferres had had almost the same conversation with her, but that had been preparatory, truly a lesson to learn. This seemed different, salacious, almost desperate. It occurred to Jendre that she was not so alone as fancy painted. These women too had married her lord and had their wedding night, and perhaps not too many nights since. Perhaps their skin burned, their bones ached with his absence as hers did. If so, they had found an accommodation, a way to live with it. That she did most dearly want to learn.

"I'm afraid the lesson would be lost on me," she said. "His Magnificence has not seen me since our marriage night. He takes his pleasures elsewhere. I think he has wed me and forgotten me."

If they had wanted to measure her chances of advancement and so how far they should befriend her, they had their answer. But they must have known the fact of it already; now they had her reading of it, modesty and shame. They were quick to offer comforts, what they had:

"His Magnificence never forgets anything, or anyone. He has a thousand women, and he knows us all by name."

"He is a man of quick enthusiasms, and slow passions; he buys cheap pleasures and treats them cheaply, while he stores what matters more for taking when the time is right."

"You will see, Jendre sweet, he will come back to you as he does to us, in time, in tenderness. If God is kind, he will give you children. They can be a solace."

"A solace and a blessing too. If he gives you children, you will sit in his shadow all your life."

"If you give him children, is what my sister means . . ."

Jendre was confused already, not sure for a moment if they'd been talking about the Sultan or God. But then suddenly they were giggling together and the look they exchanged was nothing religious at all, nothing but lewd. It startled her, where they had been so formal and so dignified before; it made her uncomfortable. She didn't understand it, and almost didn't want to. Almost. But this was her husband they were speaking of, that at least was clear now; it was her duty to understand, and in her interests too.

She said, "I'm sorry, I don't think I see the difference. If he gives me children, if I give him . . ."

And then she did see the difference, bright and fierce, like something precious shattered at her feet. What these approached sideways, what they giggled over, Theosa had simply spelled out, blunt and honest. Half the Sultan's children resembled other men. The new wife had a house to herself, close to the wall, not closely watched. The eunuchs could be bribed, expected to be bribed, might be the more suspicious if they weren't.

And oh, she did ache with more than loneliness, with loss: a gateway opened and then slammed shut again, one night of dawning pleasure, not enough. If he did come to her, it would be rarely; if another came—these implied, Theosa had said, the easy manners of the harem all suggested— he would not care, so long as they were careful.

She could be careful. She could be very, very careful. And she knew, she thought she knew a man who would be careful of her, very, very . . .

Chapter Three

A SECRET shared is a secret broken. Issel had always known that. What he and Armina held privately between them, they cupped like shatters of glass in nervous hands, waiting for the blood to run. The only security was silence, bone-bare and absolute. If a man couldn't trust himself to say nothing, how could he trust whoever he told his secret to?

And now there was this new secret in Issel's life, and so many people knew about it, it barely qualified as a secret at all. Perhaps it was a conspiracy. Whatever the word, it was a whole different order of having things to hide, and he couldn't be comfortable.

Especially, he couldn't be comfortable with Tulk. The group they had met in the Silkmart, the people Tulk had so rashly sworn their loyalty to, the rebels had barely touched his life since, and then only through Armina. Nothing new in that: all his hidden life was held in her. Tulk was something other, more dangerous perhaps. Tulk was excited, scared, a little in love with his own daring and eager to share it all, delighted to have a companion in secrecy. He clung to Issel's company, and took every chance he could to whisper confidences; even during Tel Ferin's lessons, he would send meaningful glances down the table, perhaps nudge Issel with an elbow if they were sitting side by side as he preferred.

To Issel it was all folly, all risk. He blamed himself, for letting Tulk come so near. They had been almost friends already, before their expedition to the Silkmart; that was Issel's folly. Now they were abruptly bound much closer, and needed to disguise it under the cloak of an easy friendship, and Issel had no true idea of how to be a friend.

How little he really knew about other people, he was gradually coming to learn. He had lived his life in watching them, stealing from them, selling to them: the essence of his city in its survival, pure Sund. Living with them was something quite outside his experience, a constant challenge, and often just bewildering.

As today, this morning, now.

IT was raining in Sund, as so often. Sund welcomed the rain, perhaps more than ever, now that the fountains were broken and the river was poisoned in the Shine and the best wells of the city were all in Marasi hands.

Here in Tel Ferin's house they had their own well and did not need more water, but still welcomed the rain. Need was not the issue. Water was life, endurance, promise; water held their secrets and their power and their hope. Water at the last would lead them back to freedom, though that might yet be long delayed if Tel Ferin had his way. Rain or river, well or fountain, they celebrated source and substance.

But it was raining not only in the city, it was raining in the house itself. Tel Ferin's struggles to keep his school secret had their costs, and the most obvious was to be seen in the fabric of his home. His relative poverty had to seem absolute, his household reduced to a scratching of street children who came and went apparently as they pleased; to his own peers, to the Marasi, to anyone who cared he appeared to be a man who could afford no better servants. Certainly no workmen to come and mend the roof, where missing tiles were letting in the rain.

So the rain was still slipping insidiously into the house, soaking through cracks in the ceiling plaster and dripping into bowls and buckets, threatening worse, collapse; and so Issel and Rhoan found themselves in the roof space together this morning, on an unlikely errand.

"You two go up into the roof," Tel Ferin had said, "and do what you can to block the gaps from the inside. Use rags, timber, whatever you can find in the house. My father's life is in the rooms upstairs, in keeping; there aren't many treasures left, but you shouldn't want for material. Use anything, use it all; I don't care, if you can only find a way to keep the rain out."

Master of the house, not always master of his temper, he had woken with a sodden patch in his mattress and a steady drip to worsen it. When the rooms under threat had been empty, or those used by the school, he had preached long-suffering and equanimity; now his tune had altered. He wanted repair, immediate and reliable.

Issel thought he wanted the impossible. He had thought so when Tel Ferin asked for it, and he was twice as sure once they'd made the climb-and-wriggle up a ladder and through a narrow hatch into the roofing.

"Step careful," Rhoan warned him. "If your foot goes between the beams, all of you will go, all the way through. He won't be happy."

Issel grunted and stepped careful, more for his own sake than for his master's happiness. It would be a long fall through the plasterwork, and a hard landing. As Tel Ferin had promised, the rooms below were cluttered with relics of another life, which were few of them soft or tempting.

Neither Issel nor Rhoan had thought to bring a lamp. Thankfully, worryingly, it wasn't necessary; there were enough tiles gone to give them a dusky light to see by. If Issel had cared, he would have despaired. He might not know people, but he did know roofs, and he was also intimately acquainted with rain. Where tiles were lost—and he had shifted a few himself in his time, accidentally or deliberately, in secret or in mad scramble, in carelessness or in uttermost care and silence—they needed replacing, that was all. From out there. Once the rain found the gap and dribbled through, there was nothing to be done from inside. It couldn't be pushed back out again.

"Issel."

"What?"

"Oh, nothing. Only you hadn't actually moved for a couple of minutes, so I thought I'd best check if you were living."

"I was thinking."

"Well, while you think, why don't you take some of this," a handful of old and rotted velvet that must have been glorious once, still holding its vivid colours in its seams, "and work it into those gaps just by your head there?"

Like caulking, she meant, worked into a boat's seams. He knew all about caulking. But you used tarry old rope for caulking; the tar got under your fingernails and into all the creases of your skin even if you did it with an iron, and it took forever to be rid of it because you couldn't wash it off, tar resisted water. That was the point. Ancient fraying velvet, though . . .

"You're wasting your time," he said. "However tight you pack it, it'll just soak up water until it starts to drip itself."

"I know that. But at least it's something, we will have done something. And it might hold for a day or two, enough to calm him down and dry his mattress out. Next time he'll send someone else. Eventually, he'll send us all down to the cellars to hide while he gets people in to mend it properly. You can't fix a roof from the inside."

That was Issel's own thought, and he'd been sure of the truth of it until now, this moment, looking at how the rain ran in over the tiles' edges and thinking, thinking . . .

"Wait," he said, and was slithering through the hatch almost before he'd finished saying it, halfway down the ladder before her frustrated yell could follow him.

Into one of the abandoned rooms and ferreting through a tangle of heaped furniture to get at a shelf he'd seen, what stood on the shelf there under dust as thick as woven wool; slipping all the pile of it into his shirt regardless of dirt, he was filthy already and needed his hands for the climb back; and so up to face Rhoan in her wrath and simply grin at her.

"Well, what?" she demanded.

His hand ducked inside his shirt again, and came out with his treasure trove.

Rhoan blinked. "Tin plates?"

He nodded. Old, thin tin plates, scratched by knives and worn by washing, bent out of shape and roughly pounded back again. Rhoan was scowling at him.

"Explain. What manner of good can you do with those? If we had a fire hot enough to melt them, which we don't, we still couldn't seal gaps this wide. Nor do I want molten tin dripping back into my face, thank you . . ."

A shake of the head, and, "You don't understand." Of course she didn't. He barely understood himself. That didn't affect his sudden confidence. He took one plate and handed her the rest; then, stepping lightly from joist to joist and hunching crabwise under the angles of the roof, he made his way over to where a grey square of light marked the absence of a tile. Rain was spitting in directly through the hole and dripping more steadily from its upper edges.

Standing just a little to the side—Rhoan didn't want hot tin spattering her face, and he didn't want cold water—he held the plate out under the dribbles of rain. His fingers tingled, but he was ready for that. He rubbed the plate between them until it was wet all over, grinning faintly at the thought of what she must be seeing, his absurdly washing a filthy plate with filthy hands.

Then he stood quietly, focusing on what he did, only a little part of his mind slipping back just a short time to his urn, his broken urn and what he had done to mend it, what he had not felt capable of doing. He had learned a lot since then. That day he could seal a lead seam or shape a slug of lead and give it a brief glamour, a silver shine, a street boy's tricks; he'd taken the urn to a tinsmith for more intricate work.

Today—well, here was tin and water, and he ought to need no more. If the work called for a delicate touch, there was Rhoan at his back with her filigree skills, but he hoped not to need her. He'd always been a shameless beggar, but to ask in this new life, help between equals, that was another thing, and harder. He was still too good at being alone, which made him bad at company.

Wet tin in his hands, and his hands were fizzing. He felt the surface of the tin through that skin of water, like his own skin under a slick of sweat. The tin was warming, taking heat from his hands; he closed his eyes to understand it better. Just as wet lead would soften at his touch, so would tin. It needed only the training, the understanding, the certainty; and he had that now, he knew that he could do this and more than this. He thought perhaps that he could do it without the tin, even, that he could make a tile of water and slip it into place and leave it there, confident that it would still be there tomorrow and the day after and the weeks that followed that.

Better not, though. Better not to have the others talk about him too much. They did enough of that already.

So he held the tin plate on the flat of his palms and just let the tingle loose. He opened his eyes at Rhoan's little gasp, to see how the tin was soft and settled into the shape of his hands, drooping like a pancake where it overhung, even stretching under its own weight—not molten, but loose enough to lose itself in slow, dense dripping if he let it hang.

He did not. He lifted it quickly, rather, in his two hands, and brought it to the hole above his head. *You can't fix a roof from the inside,* no indeed—but you can slip something flexible through the gap and set it there like a tile, if you can only make it unfold and stiffen on the outside, if you can only make it cling. Issel thought he could do better than that. He thought he could seal soft wet tin to rough wet terracotta tile so that they became almost the same thing, like tar-soaked rope, so that when he took his touch away you could never unpick the one from the other, to say where the tin ended and the tile began.

Through the hole the tin went, then, bunched up like a leather purse, and he let it unfurl on the other side. He had just the lightest touch on it, but it still felt half-alive against his fingertips, responsive, as the clay responds to the potter. He stretched and flattened the upper edge and gave it back a measure of stiffness, then slid it up beneath the higher course of tiles, between them and the batten they rested on. The lower edge he let lie across the course below, like the tiles still in place on either side.

Then—was it his mind, or was it only his fingers stretching beyond themselves, through the water and through the soft and tingling tin, to the coarse damp tiling all around? Touch by extension: whether it was in his head or in his hands, he couldn't tell. He could feel the two surfaces seething together, though, the tin that was all his own and the terracotta that was almost not at all, that was cold and resistant and would yield only a little and only when he pushed. But it was wet, and the wet reached deeper than the surface, and anywhere that water went, so could he too go. He could reach through the tin and grip that little skin of damp, and he could meld the two, press and squeeze and feel how they mingled . . .

And then—slowly, carefully—he could come back. Let the terracotta be itself again, obdurate as rock; draw back through the tin and give it all its stiffness now, sheer metal reshaped, nothing more except perhaps at the edges, where plate met tile and gripped tightly and neither one was quite the thing it had been; let his fingers at last drop away and find himself standing, stooped and shaken, not quite sure that he himself was quite the thing he had been.

"Issel . . ."

"Unh?"

"What did you do?"

"You saw."

She must have done, she was standing right by his shoulder. Normally

she was that annoying little bit taller; now she was just that gratifying little bit more awkwardly hunched beneath the slope of the roof, so that they
could meet each other for once entirely eye to eye.

"I saw it, yes. What I mean is, I don't know how you did that."

"I'll teach you. You should learn. There's a lot of holes to patch here,
and just the once has made me tired."

"I can't learn that. You weren't even using purified water, just the
rain . . ."

"No, but I've got some," in the flask that never left his belt. "If you use
that, it'll help. Now . . ."

"The trouble with you, Issel," she said, not moving, taking her time,
"the trouble is, you have just no idea who you are. Or what you are. Are
you sleeping with Tulk yet?"

———————

AND that was it, that was the numbing moment, the stupefying question
that he had no answer to. He gaped at her, and she gazed back with a little half-smile that he understood no more than he understood her, which
meant not at all. And when she saw that she wasn't going to get a response, no matter how long she waited, she shrugged and turned a little
away from him, and said, "There's nothing that you can teach me, with or
without a blessing on the water."

And he didn't understand that either, but he saw this much at least, that
the time for magic was over. Already she had gone back to packing cracks
with rags of velvet. After a minute, after a long, long minute, he joined her.
It wouldn't work for long, they both knew that, and Tel Ferin would have
another soaking before anything more was done; but thinking about it—
thinking about anything, sooner than think about this girl at his side, the
stretch and reach and sway of her, the silence in her hips and her swinging
hair, the mute assessment of her eyes—he thought that perhaps there might
be some good to be found in that.

———————

THERE was rain and rain, days of rain, a tumult of water. Issel was glad of
a roof over his head, even if it did leak. It only leaked a little; their half-
measures were holding, better than he'd expected. That was a frustration.
They were all frustrated: confined and oppressed by the battering weather,
goaded by Tel Ferin's lingering ill temper and their own fierce untapped en-
ergy. Inevitably, there were fights. Word fights and fistfights and once a

water fight which mattered more, which might have made a dreadful end to that stormy time.

Might well have done, if Rhoan hadn't been there.

Issel was there too, but Issel didn't understand people; it was his fault that it started and then he only watched, waited too long, was too late even in thinking that someone ought to do something.

The only wonder, he thought later, was that it hadn't happened earlier. There was too much water everywhere, too many honed tempers and half-trained hands. Every creature in the house—he included Baris, and Tel Ferin too—was like a naked flame in an oil store. Except that fire was too hot and clean and dry a thing to fear, in this house where danger dripped from the ceilings and puddled on the floors, overflowed its gutters and soaked through wood and brick, bubbled and seethed suggestively in kitchen pots.

In kitchen pots and bathhouse cisterns too. These rainy, rainy days when Tel Ferin made few other calls on them, they spent much of their time in the bathhouse, lounging and soaking, talking and arguing and playing little games between themselves. Rhoan had quarrelled with them and with Issel, separately and together; she perhaps saw more clearly how it exhausted him, how it fevered him, both at once. They shrugged at her, jeered at her, "so long as he's willing, what's it to you?" while he only said stonily, "You taught me not to fear the baths. How to use the water and not be scalded by it."

"Not well enough," she retorted. "I can see your scalds, Issel. Inside and out. Just go careful, will you?"

But he thought going careful meant giving the others what they wanted, at least enough to satisfy. So he did that, he kept the bathhouse blind with steam and never mind what it did to him, he thought he was doing well. He didn't see the frictions building under the sheens of sweat and oil. What he did do, he took his flask of blessed water with him one day and played Tel Ferin, tipped a drop into each of the cisterns; but where the master would have touched the water then into seething life, Issel left it for his fellow students.

"I'm not touching that now," he said. "If you want to be warm in here, if you want to be clean, you'll have to do it yourselves."

He meant it for a demonstration, a challenge, a chance for them to stretch their skills further than Tel Ferin was inclined to stretch them: *see what you can do,* he wanted to say to them, *more than you think, more than the master wants you to think.* He was sure that Tel Ferin taught them less than he might, only to keep them quiet and biddable and under his control. They had had years of training, and they did so little with it . . .

Four cisterns, all in a row: four senior students stepped up, a little hesitantly. Nervous of what they meant to try, he thought, and nervous too of trying it in front of all the school. He ignored that last and gave them balm for the other: "It won't scald you," he said, "no matter how hot you make it. Water knows its master."

Rhoan was one of the four; she gave him an ironic look, *I can see your scalds, Issel,* but he ignored that too.

One by one they dipped their hands into the water. Steam wafted up from one cistern, from another. Rhoan's wasn't the first, nor the last. He didn't need to have noticed that, but he was sure that she had.

First a waft, then a rising column; four columns, then a thickening cloud where nothing was quite distinct or clear. The water seethed and bubbled, even after the students took their hands away. Touched into boiling, if it was left untouched it would boil until it had boiled all away. If they weren't cooked by then, Issel would spend a little more from his flask, to give the younger ones a chance. The younger the better, he thought; let them learn early, that they could inhabit what they had thought was the master's province.

The master's and his, but he was a freak. That was common knowledge. Even Tel Ferin needed a drop of the pure water to work with. Issel was unique, and still afraid; sooner or later, someone was going to work out why. Maybe Rhoan already had.

That day, no one else was worrying. They were cocky and curious and wanting to test themselves further, harder; they wanted more of Issel's blessed water, all the flaskful, and he wouldn't let them have it.

"Steal your own," he said.

"If I tell the master that you stole it . . ."

"Well, he wouldn't be at all surprised, would he? I'm a thief, he knows that. He'd just make it harder for me, for anyone to steal any more. For you. If you want some, take it. It's not that hard."

It had never occurred to Tel Ferin, seemingly, that his pupils might want more than he gave them. Until now, seemingly, it had never occurred to any of his pupils either. It made Issel wonder whether the master really

guarded his secrets as closely as the rebels claimed; it might never have occurred to him that others would want those either.

Well, they'd find out soon, Issel and Tulk. They had a plan.

In the meantime there was trouble flaring, but not for Issel. Cocky these
older boys might be, but boiling a cistern of water was nothing, next to
what they'd heard or seen or imagined that he could do. None of them
would confront him again, not even Lamartine. They turned their bore-
dom, their frustration, their aggression against each other in lieu, and of
course it wasn't long before mock-fighting turned into the real thing. Two
boys head to head, pushing became punching, and even then it might have
been nothing except that there was altogether too much water around.
Simple well water had its effect, though they could do little with it; today
there was the sting of pure water everywhere, in the steam they breathed
and the condensation, even in the sweat that slicked their skin. They rolled
in it, wrestled in it, across the tiled floor while the others lined the walls,
stood on the benches for a better view, hooted encouragement to one or
the other or to both impartially for their generous assault on the tedium of
the day.

Until one of them rolled free with blood running from his nose, rolled
into a blocked gutter, must have heard their laughter above his splashing
and so found just how far further he could go, when he was driven to it.
He came up with a double handful of that water, cloudy and a little pink-
stained, the power in it massively dilute but still enough to shape a blade,
bent and crude and lethal.

The other saw it and might have backed away, spoken softly, brought
an easy end to this. He didn't have to make a dive for a cistern, sink his
hand in and draw out something of his own, longer and heavier and half
a blade, half a club, an edged mace you might have called it.

There were gasps, there were mutters; no one moved except the two of
them in their slow and furious circle, weapons passing from hand to weaving hand, two boys remembering the street and the struggle and nothing
more now except that they had better weapons than they were used to.

Issel hadn't realised that they would learn so much, so quickly. He
watched. And perhaps, just perhaps, his eyes moved to find Rhoan before
she stepped onto that killing floor and said, very quietly, "That will be
enough now. Let it go."

The two boys stepped both the same way, to avoid her; otherwise they took no notice, until she made them do it. She dipped a bucket into a cistern and flung all its contents across the floor towards them, so that they briefly stood in the same wash of water; before it could find its way to the drains, she touched her hand to it.

Sparks fled from her fingers and flowed with the water, touching everything it touched, all the way. The watchers by the wall there had time to see it coming, and scrambled hastily up onto the crowded benches. The fighters were not so lucky.

The sparks found them and found how wet they were, and ran all up their bodies, climbing where the drips were running down. Issel thought it looked like nets of blue fire swathing their skin, living nets that wove and rewove themselves at every touch of fire to fire, seeking out new paths to water and suddenly blazing incandescent when they found the water-blades.

The boys had already been gasping, staring down at themselves, at how they burned. Now they screamed.

It was only for a moment, but a moment was enough. Their hands opened, they dropped what they held and it lost its shape, it fell and splashed and lost its fire too. All the sparks were gone; Issel watched the last of the water find the central drain and thought he saw a brief faint flicker of blue down deep below the grille, but he also thought that he'd imagined it. The rats would know, but who would ask the rats?

The two boys were standing all bereft of fight or purpose, rubbing at themselves one-handed, each of them holding out the other hand as though it were burned and blistered. Just sting and shock, Issel thought, he couldn't see any greater damage. The others would ask all the questions that mattered: what it had felt like, how she had done it, how she had kept it so controlled. He'd hear about it later. For now he didn't need to stay, no one was going to be yelling for more heat, more steam, more blessed water. They'd all be glad enough to let things cool.

He turned and left the bathhouse, walked out naked into the rain and felt the stinging lash of that on his own skin, like a fire that did not burn. Tulk came after him and he was sure, he was certain sure that he could feel Rhoan's eyes marking the two of them in their going.

———

ARE *You sleeping with Tulk yet?*

It was that *yet* that left him floundering. It was unanswerable; even the hottest denial would only reinforce her unspoken certainty, *you will,* while at the same time it would sound like a confession, *I'm not old enough* or *not bold enough,* either one a humiliation.

The school all slept together, except for him; that didn't mean that every pupil in the school slept every night in innocence, alone. He was sure that he was not the first to slip quietly out of the dormitory in darkness. The house was so big and so empty of people, so full of things upstairs, some old and soft, furnishings and fabrics; he was sure there were nests where eager or curious couples could slip off for an hour in the day or a long slow night together, deceiving themselves that they could keep it private. *A secret shared is a secret broken:* privacy was an illusion and so perhaps was love, thought Issel, who was as cynical as the streets. Sex was a whip, that drove to folly; love was a smoke behind the eyes, drugging, dreaming, deceptive.

He wondered which Rhoan thought of him and Tulk, whether they were driven or drugged. He understood how she could think it, either one. Tulk laid it bare, that something lay between them. The glances, the nudges, the whispered conversations broken off: they would be the signs of a weak and hopeless spy, if they were not so easy to see as the signs of a lover. He supposed he should be glad that Rhoan was so wrong, so deceived; he thought perhaps he should encourage her belief, except that it seemed he didn't need to. Whatever he did with Tulk, she would interpret.

As this, where they had run off together into the rain, snatched towels and dried off skimpily in the house, dressed in haste and were to be found in a private corner, wet heads together when she came looking.

She seemed not to be looking for them, but he at least didn't believe it.

Whatever she would have said, he forestalled her.

"And you're the one who couldn't bend a little tin, even when I offered you my flask to work with. I don't know what you did there; does anyone?"

She shrugged, a little awkwardly, not what she'd come to talk about. "The older boys, a couple—but they would have hurt those two idiots, they're not so delicate with it. All water has a sting; I only livened it up a little. I can show you how, if Tel Ferin won't. Do you want me to?"

"Yes. Yes, please," but that was Tulk and she hadn't been speaking to him, nor looking at him. She acknowledged him with a shrug, and it was still Issel she was watching.

"Show me sometime, yes," *show us* he should have said, to drive her suspicion deeper; but the more he encouraged Tulk, the more risks that boy would take with their true secret, and he felt as if he were dancing in the river and both his feet were burning, "but not now. We have chores."

"You do?"

"All those buckets upstairs," and the bowls and trays and planters, every possible receptacle for catching drips and dribbles of water, "someone has to empty them."

It was a blatant truth, she couldn't argue with it. And Tulk couldn't keep a happy, deceptive grin from his face as Issel pulled him to his feet; so there was no reason at all for her to think anything other than what she was undoubtedly thinking, as they trotted off.

He supposed he really should be glad.

————

UP the stairs they went and in and out of every door, looking and listening for any signs of water. On a dryer day Issel could find leaks if he was blind and deaf, just by the prickle in his skin; today, with his shirt damp and his hair still liable to drip, as well ask a drowning man where he thought the water was.

It was still not hard to find. There were paths cleared through the jumble, to where the bowls and buckets stood; there was the hard, flat sound of every separate drop where it hammered down.

No one had done this duty yet today, or else the leaks were getting worse again. All the vessels were heavy with water, some brimful and overflowing. Issel and Tulk emptied each with due care and the barest minimum of giggling anticipation. Back and forth, back and forth: they were so careful to miss none and to spill not a drop where it was not wanted, it took them half the afternoon. That only won Issel further arch glances from Rhoan when they came down at last.

He ignored her, as best he could. What he couldn't ignore was the way Tulk stuck to him afterwards, his face alive with secrets, breaking into constant glee at mischief done and undiscovered. He might have been a child, half his natural age; he might indeed have been a lover in his first passion, overmastered by the shivering delights of it all. Issel wanted to hit him.

What he did instead was to take Tulk aside and talk to him fiercely, edgily, every word a blade: "Keep control now, or you will betray us both. Tonight of all nights, you must hide what you're feeling and what you're waiting for. Don't spend so much time with me; talk to the others, or be alone as you used to be. Pretend we've quarrelled, if you like. Give me a bruise, a black eye, make it convincing . . ."

"I don't want to hit you."

"It's all right, I won't hit you back."

"I'm not scared of a fight!" protested Tulk, who should have been. "But you and me, we're together, we share . . ."

"We share too much, that's what I'm saying. We have our secret; we can't afford to share more. People are watching us already, talking, wondering."

"They only think we're friends." He was young enough to believe that; Issel tried, but he couldn't escape what Rhoan thought. Why should others see the same and think differently, if they thought at all?

"We can't afford to be friends," he said, feeling the brutality of it as he watched Tulk slump. "We mustn't be seen as friends," he amended hastily, weakly he thought. "Especially now, they mustn't see that we're both waiting for something to happen . . ."

Nothing could repress Tulk too deeply or for too long, but he did at least spend the evening away from Issel's side, and he did struggle to conceal his irregular rising bubbles of joy, his constant expectation, his sheer self-content. The price of that was Issel's to pay, Rhoan's to collect.

"Did you two argue, or are you only trying to kill the gossip?"

More unanswerable questions. He took the hot spiced drink she'd brought him, sipped at it and stared at her accusingly above the beaker's rim.

"Actually," she went on with a tight smile against his silence, "I don't think there is any gossip, if that makes you feel any better. I'm not hearing any. It's just me that knows what's going on. As usual," with a laughing snort to follow, to mock at her own pretensions.

"You don't know either," he said quietly. "Tulk and me are friends," *and we can't afford to be,* and she wasn't going to believe him anyway.

"Of course you are, that's why you're sitting against opposite walls and watching each other all the time, that's just what friends do when they're together."

"We're together a lot."

"I know, I've seen you."

"And I've never had a friend before, I'm not sure that Tulk's had many, maybe we don't know what friends are meant to do. Maybe we should ask you. How many friends do you have, Rhoan?"

That was a cruel cut, a wild savage slash at her, meant only to drive her off; it wasn't meant to make her bleed. She stayed quite still for a moment, then stood and walked away, and let her parting words fall back over her shoulder so that he barely heard them.

"I had been hoping for one or two more. Or just the one, even, that might have been enough."

————————

IT was the sound of rain that kept Issel awake all that night, hard against the shutters of the window bay. Hard against his ear was how it felt, striking like hail on a drum skin and stinging like water on his own skin, despite the wood and the cushions and the old folded curtains wedged between them. He might have moved his bed again if he hadn't been glad to have a reason for his wakefulness, glad to have something to blame.

For sure, he wasn't lying awake waiting for collapse, for calamity. Tulk might be doing that; not he. He'd almost forgotten that there was anything to be waited for.

He heard it, even so. The rain had eased at last in its pounding, there was a dim grey showing through the cracks in the shutters where he hadn't stuffed them tight with rags, he was beginning to feel that he might be better off out of bed and watching what dawn could manage. Sitting up in his embrasure with his blankets wrapped around him, he heard a soft and distant thudding, followed an instant after by a cry of furious indignity.

Despite himself and his long night, despite everything he'd said to Tulk about control, Issel couldn't keep from grinning as he scrambled out of his blankets and into his shirt, as he ran through the house towards Tel Ferin's apartments where all the noise was coming from, as he joined the rest of the school where it milled around Tel Ferin's door in various stages of undress and confusion.

None of them would go through uninvited, it was the strictest rule in the house. After a short time, though, the forbidden door opened and their master came out with a damp and somewhat slimy appearance to his hair and beard, flecks and clots caught in the grizzled hair.

"All here, are you? Well, I suppose that bespeaks a degree of loyalty, at least." He was snappish, impatient—embarrassed, Issel thought. "I thought I had asked, several times, that the leaks in the roof be attended to? It seemed a task simple enough to me, but apparently none of you was up to it. My bedroom ceiling has just fallen in. On me. As you seem to find this so amusing, Tulk"—and it was true, he was choking over a gale of swallowed laughter; thankfully, enough of the others were having trouble hiding theirs, he only stood out for his immaturity—"you can be the one who clears up the mess in there."

That was perfect, ideal, as good as it came. Issel slipped through to Tulk's side and said, "I'll help him, master; my fault, for not doing better work in the roof," and never mind what anyone might think.

THEY went in to see the damage, and all the others pressed in at their backs. Of course they did, how not? This was unknown territory, beyond Tel Ferin's door; and he was out, and for once could not lock up behind him. He was going for a bath, he'd said, and then a breakfast: that meant either a rendezvous with his old cohort, the friends of his youth, to show them—as he liked to do—the privations and poverty of a Sundain patrician who would not be a collaborator, or else a meeting of conspirators, he and his fellow adepts come together to sigh and whisper and make slow plans to wait. Either way, he wouldn't return before noon at the earliest. Plenty of time for the school to wander through his rooms and run collective hands across his things, to gaze and touch and gossip—

"Who cleans all this? I know we wash his clothes, but please don't tell me that he sweeps his own carpets, beats dust out of the hangings and makes his own bed up by himself."

"Not he. He has a woman, didn't you know?"

"No, does he? So where is she?"

"And why can't she clean up all that muck, why does it have to be Issel and me?"

"Hush, little Tulk. You should have learned by now, never to laugh at the master. He does have a woman, but he doesn't keep her here. Some of those nights when his cronies come, they bring her with them, and she stays. I suppose she tidies up next morning. I suppose she's not really his woman: just a loan from another house. Quiet to come and swift to go, she sounds ideal."

"You be quiet, you. Virgin boys, what do you know about women?"

"I know one when I see one."

"And you know enough to keep your distance, and that's about all you do know, so be quiet or I'll heave one of these, these sharp things at your head."

"You wouldn't dare."

"Rhoan would. Where's Rhoan?"

"Oh, can't you leave fighting, just for an hour? What are those things, anyway?"

"Sharp."

"Shouldn't have touched, then, should you? Here, let me, there's some water here, and we don't want you bleeding on Tel Ferin's things, not on top of all this sludge everywhere . . ."

—and time enough for them to lose interest at last, or else to realise that if they stayed much longer, they'd have to help with the cleaning.

And so there was time, more than time enough for Issel and Tulk between them to fill a chain of buckets with sodden plaster, to strip the bed and turn the mattress and put the covers out for washing and still to stand and gaze in a kind of contemplative awe at the underside of what they'd achieved, before they needed to give any time to why they'd done it.

The weight of the soaked plaster had brought half the ceiling-laths down with it, so that they could see the boards of the floor above. Issel thought he could make out even the particular board they'd levered up yesterday, to be sure that all the rainwater they collected went just where they wanted it, directly above Tel Ferin's bed. Tulk hugged himself in high delight as he looked up at the damage; even Issel allowed himself a smile as he imagined the cold shock of it, the moment's gasping, choking suffocation before a sudden flailing of hands and head together could shake off a thumb's thickness of cloying, clinging, half-dissolved plaster.

Then a punch on Tulk's arm, he allowed himself that too, to turn that boy's attention to the spying they were here for.

TEL Ferin had three rooms to his apartments. The bedroom was all comfort, the best of his family's furnishings gathered into a soft and spacious nest. While they were cleaning it, Issel had looked for any signs of a woman's presence. He had found none, but that meant little; he didn't really know what the signs would be. No female clothes in the closets, but she didn't live here. There were oils and unguents on a side table, but he recognised the perfumes as Tel Ferin's own.

He believed the story none the less, but shrugged it off, a privacy he was prepared to allow.

Beyond the bedroom was clearly where Tel Ferin entertained his guests, such few as came. It was a casual room, again a comfortable room, with low sofas against three walls and a table between, space to share food and pipes and bottles with their talk. The walls were tiled to the ceiling with bright and intricate designs, Marasi work. Issel had seen similar rooms before, once or twice, on this side of the river; once, in an abandoned house, he'd helped to chisel the tiles off the walls for whatever they would fetch at market.

There was little to the room, beyond its comforts. Little worth the searching. Just a token, then, a sop to patience: they bent double to squint beneath sofas, turned up the corners of rugs, tried the private garden door to find it locked, as it always had been locked the dozen times they'd tried it from the outside.

And then, finding nothing that could even pretend to hold their interest—no papers, no hidden hatches, nothing in the least indiscreet: a squad of Marasi soldiers could search this room and take no offence at all—Issel and Tulk moved on to where that was absolutely not the case, where a single soldier's single glance in through the doorway would be a sentence of death to everyone in the house.

This was Tel Ferin's workroom. The whispers of the school had made it into a sorcerer's cave, rich in arcane instruments and vivid potions that seethed and smoked behind glass. Never mind how ill that jarred with what he taught them, the simplicity and clarity of mind and water; they wanted him to have secrets, and a powerful magician's secrets ought to be abstruse, dramatic, a little frightening. At least a little frightening. Street conjurors and witch-women had frightened Issel when he was younger, Armina still could frighten him; he needed Tel Ferin's private quarters to offer depths of dark promise that would justify the dogtooth servant, the respect of the school, his own more tentative service.

They were setting themselves up for disappointment, he and Tulk both, and duly found it. Tel Ferin's workroom was more a scholar's study than a den of mystery. There was one long, scarred table that did hold an array of bottles and flasks, but all they held was water, purified or else waiting to be so.

Otherwise, the desks and shelves of the workroom were layered thick with books and unbound sheaves of paper. Issel gazed at them hopelessly and turned back to the table. Perhaps a second scouring look would turn up what the first had missed. If there were a knife, perhaps Tel Ferin added a drop of his own good Sundain blood to the water, to fire it with his strength? If there were a pot, a tin, a missing tin whose absence was shown up by a little pinch of spilled powder mapping its moon-crescent edge, that would be something at least, something to tell the plotters, *he mixes a powder into the water, look, we have a dusting of it but we don't know what it is . . .*

There was nothing: no knife, no nameless powder, no hint of any such. Just those containers brimful of well water, before and after blessing. There was the bucket on the floor beneath the table, that one or another of the school would fill for their master when he asked. Issel had done that in his turn, and so had Tulk. Indeed, they'd spent hours lingering outside these rooms quite out of turn, in hopes of that or other errands. They'd never been let in past the door before. It had been a frustration till now, a waste of time. Now Issel saw those hours as another kind of waste. Spying was thieving, and he was a good thief; but what use was a spy who couldn't read, when it was apparently paper knowledge they had come to steal?

Tulk could read. Tulk was reading, while Issel peered uselessly into shadowed corners in hopes of finding some hidden artefact that he might understand. Trying to see without lifting books, without touching paper at all; if there was magic in this room, it lay in words, in writing, and that was a mystery too far for his courage.

Tulk was the brave one. He picked up sheets of paper and ran his eyes over them swiftly, too swiftly, surely, for the words to speak to him. His lips barely moved and his reading-voice was a thread of air, no more; but he seemed confident, sure of what he had, the meaning squeezed from every sheet in moments. Then he laid them back again, as near as sight could say to where they were before. He took books, even, from the shelves and opened their covers, read from them with equal swiftness, put them back.

Only one book detained him, one which he had found half-hidden beneath a toppled sheaf of papers on the table. This one cost him more. His eye slowed and his voice grew stronger, murmuring individual words as he made them out; sometimes his finger came up to track his path along the page. Twice or three times he tried to set the book down, rebury it, dismiss it; he could not.

At last he said, "I think this may be what we're looking for. The writing is crabbed and strange, and changes hand a dozen times, but I think that's right. I think it's a book the adepts have made, one man after another setting down his wisdom. Lord knows how old it is, or when the last of it was written. Not recently. There are blank pages at the end but I know Tel Ferin's hand and this is not it, this last. Perhaps he had it from his master, and he from his and so on, back and back . . ."

"Does it say, about how to bless the water?" Issel was excited but impatient, anxious to be away. Disappointed too, if what they were looking for had to lie in a book.

"I don't know. I haven't found that yet, but if it's anywhere, it will be here. I need to read it."

"All of it?" To Issel that seemed a monumental undertaking, the work of heroes.

Tulk just smiled. "It won't take so long, once I'm used to the way they shape their letters."

"We can't wait in here all that time, while you read . . ."

"No, of course not." Already Tulk was slipping the book inside his shirt and turning for the door.

"He'll miss it. If it's what you say, he's sure to miss it."

"Perhaps—but in this?" With a wave of his arm at the chaos of the room, the cascades of books and papers on every surface, the piles slumping all over the floor. "He won't know where he's put it down or what put on top of it. It would take him days even to be sure that it was missing."

It was true. Issel—who couldn't imagine such a life, who always knew where each of his little things lay—looked at the mayhem of Tel Ferin's work and nodded slowly. "Well, then. But how will we return it, when you have read?"

"We'll worry about that after. When we have read it, both. I'll read it to you. It needs your ear too, to know whether this is for our friends, and how much, and how to tell it."

———

"FRIENDS" they called them, though Issel for one really doubted that. It was only that a name was needed, some way to talk about the people they were spying for, that wouldn't bring disaster if they were overheard.

One thing that was not in doubt—if Tulk was going to read to Issel from Tel Ferin's private book, it would have to be in secret, which meant at night, the only time they could be safely private. They went straight from Tel Ferin's apartments to Issel's bed space in the window; Tulk would have hidden the book there among the cushions, but Issel was too wary.

"If he does miss it, this will be his first place to look. Put it somewhere close, then, but somewhere that is not mine."

Not hard to find in this house, a place to hide a small, tight-written book. Inspired by yesterday's adventure, Tulk lifted a floorboard and stowed the book in the space beneath, once he'd checked that it was dry.

"There will be rats, but we won't keep it long." Even so, he took the book out again and wrapped it in his shirt before he put it back. They went together to the scullery to wash off the residues of filth and plaster-slime, and of course they met Rhoan on the way, and Tulk half-naked and Issel furiously blushing, and she said nothing and Tulk knew nothing and Issel could only wonder what she would say, what think when she realized—as she must, as he was sure she must—that Tulk was slipping out of the dormitory every night to spend hours with Issel in his bed.

Chapter Four

JENDRE was glad that she hadn't had to do the talking. Sorry for Teo, whose task it was, but mostly relieved that it was quite impossible for her. There were advantages to being a harem wife.

None that reached beyond the harem wall, though, and actually that was good too. Salem had grown up in the court, at the heart of power; his family had position and influence, where she had none. It wasn't the hope of imperial connections that fetched him to her. Teo's soft words, then, Salem's own memories of her—voice and touch and needing, in the blood and dust of the road—and whatever hot impulse it was that drew young men into danger for no tangible reward . . .

Her own task had still been difficult beyond measure: an afternoon across the chessboard from Ferres, playing more games than one. Trying to match subtlety with subtlety, and yet be sure that there was no misunderstanding. She had sweated that day, and her head had ached. It had proved expensive, too, to her heart and her purse both. The chess set had been a wedding gift from her old friend Tukus, and she was loth to lose it; the board was framed in gold and inlaid with rare and precious woods, while the pieces had been carved from white and green jades, smooth and heavy in the hands. She had owned little that was valuable, but that would always have been a treasure. Now she had spent her treasure, and owned less.

Now she found her reward, in the lithe bold boy who swung himself so carelessly over the harem wall. It was dark, of course; he had that much courtesy to the well-bribed, well-briefed guards, to come when they could pretend they had not seen him. It was dark, and he wore black clothes and was swift, and still she stood hand to mouth in an agony of doubt when she saw his slender shadow rise against the stars. She had done so the first time, she did so now, she thought she always would. He must be seen; once, surely, he would be challenged? Challenged and taken, and then no bribes could be enough. There would be the Sultan's rage and humiliation to face, his cruel public justice against Salem, more private and so more cruel against her . . .

They were the fears of a girl, fantastic. She knew this, and even so she worried herself into a fever every time. And every time he came and left again in perfect safety; and between his coming and his going, those hours were so jewelled that she betrayed her own determination every time, not to let him come again.

He smelled, she thought, of darkness when he came. Perhaps it was the particular confluence of black fabric and night skies and the lingering perfumes of the garden in the moment when she could press her face into his shoulder and breathe again at last, breathe him. Perhaps it was the memory they could neither of them shake, that dreadful day when they had first understood each other, like plants that grew in shadow; perhaps the scent of him would always carry its echoes of blood and terror, shrug off the bright hard sun of memory and paint it in darkness as it should have been.

She had been frightened then, she was frightened still, every time afraid when she was with him. The touch of him, though, that was an ebb of fear, what was cold and weak in her shivering away against his warmth and strength. Hands that felt big against her body, all-encompassing, though they were light and elegant to watch: they chased off that shuddering, chivvied it out of her with a slow, firm deliberation, as though they had patience but no interest. *As though I were a horse,* she thought, *high-strung, excitable, in need of calm and grooming . . .*

A hoarse, hissing whistle from the dark below the wall: that was Teo. What good his watching did, she was not clear, but she was grateful none the less. So many pairs of eyes in the darkness, it was good to know that one at least was friendly. If that was quite the word for Teo. Once, yes; now she was not so sure. The happy talking boy had grown wary and watchful. Body-slaves were not supposed to carry blades, but he had begged and she had given, if only to save him stealing some old hollow paring knife from the kitchen and thinking he could fight with it. His belt hid an ivory-handled blade against his belly, too pretty for a boy but forged for proper work. Whether he was a boy dreaming himself a warrior, or whether he nursed some darker purpose in secret, Jendre was inclined to let him run with it for now.

Besides, she owed him more gratitude than she could pay in goods or promises. She owed him this, Salem, summoned by proxy, her pleading in his voice.

His whistle wasn't truly a warning, only a nudge, *others walk this garden . . .*

It was as true as it was timely, as it was unwelcome. She peeled herself from Salem's wiry body, her weakness somehow overmastering his strength; she took his hand and tugged at him, to draw him out of the moonless dark and into the soft lights of her house, where he could be safe, where she could look at him.

Mirjana was another watcher, at the door. She would wait there in the vestibule, delicately out of earshot unless Jendre called, at which time she would find that it was within earshot after all. Teo wouldn't come into the house at all while Salem was here. Perhaps he needed the knife because it was the only thing that Salem lacked in this place? Free and whole, wealthy, beloved: she could see how a boy might be envious.

Teo's troubles could wait. Teo was a gift, her own, a constant possession; she had Salem for an hour, perhaps for half the night if he was generous, if God was kind. She would give not a minute more of it to Teo, nor to anyone outside the circle of his arms, where she was.

———

AT first it had all been for his beauty, for this perfect moment of his golden youth, glimpsed through a screen: a symbol, an idol, a cherished hope denied.

Then it was for his courage, for sweat and blood, for stories told and given: grief settling on him like a grim gift of age, anger like the flush of a new fire. A blade in his heart and a blade in his hand—how could she not bleed for him, burn for him, be a vessel both for his sorrow and his rage?

Now, though, now it was for himself, beyond all attributes. There was his body, ardent and slippery; there was his mind, with all its reach and depth; he brought them both to her and made her free of them. Sometimes they were hard to distinguish, in the dark where talking was touching, a kiss was a whisper, a hand or a word could be equally revealing. His body illuminated his mind, or else betrayed it. What she held—in her hands and eyes, on her breath, beneath her skin—she thought might be his soul. The priests said that belonged to God alone; if they were right, she had no word for what belonged to her.

———————

TONIGHT he was urgent, hustling her through to the bedroom and tugging at her clothes, tugging at his own, almost tearing.

"Easy, sweet my lord," she murmured, stilling those deceptive hands of his with the lightest touch of her fingers, knowing just where her strength was to be found. "If we are careful, we will be just as swift; and Mirjana won't need to spend an hour sewing before you are decently dressed to leave me."

"Don't speak of leaving," he pleaded. "Our time is too short already."

"There is no time in here, short or long. Only ourselves," and she closed the shutters over the window, not to let him see the moon in its dragging journey or feel himself caught in the skein it hauled behind. The moon was no friend to illicit lovers, cold and reproachful, counting hours as the sun did. "We will not let time in. Neither the world," though she was eager as ever to hear whatever he had brought besides himself. She missed the many little freedoms of her father's house, but mostly the sense of knowing what the city did, and what the empire. She lived here in the heart of all, and yet she had known far more of her husband's doings before she married him.

For now, the world's news could wait. They were here and alone, and this was world enough. Her mouth against his skin: perfumed oils and applesmoke and the scent of himself cutting through, entirely familiar already, a flood to her senses with her eyes closed and only his voice in her ears, his hands in her hair, his urgency pounding her heart now, invading, possessing . . .

She could be invaded, she could be possessed; she didn't have to surrender. She'd learned that much, at least. She need not be governed in her own house. She could draw back, take his hand, lead him to the bed, slowly, slowly. There was no one to see, no one to count their steps or breaths or heartbeats. This was an infinite moment, their own, forever; all clocks failed here, and God was not watching.

———————

TOUCHING was talking, indistinguishable.

She said, "Don't sigh so deep. Your breaths are my breaths, but I don't have that much air."

He said, "Your breaths are my breaths, but my father wants it otherwise."

"Your father doesn't . . . ?"

"No! No, no one knows but us, and your two. I come alone, on foot, so not even my horse can betray me. I meant, my father wants to see me married."

———————

TOUCHING was talking, but it could be silence too.

———————

SORROW was a pierce, at every point they touched.

———————

SHE said, "I could wish that he had wanted that before."

He said, "And I—although I never thought that I would say it. Mussun used to tease me because I would lose some part of my freedom soon, which he never would. Who would marry their daughters to a nameless man, even one so close to the pasha's son? But your father would never have given you to me, Jendre. He always had his eye on the Sultan's hand."

"Did he? I didn't know . . ." Neither had she known that it was Sidië for the bridge, and not herself. She was not impressed by the narrow limits of her understanding, or else it was the breadth and depth of her self-deception.

"My father says so. And now that is achieved, and the Sultan is pleased—with you, and so with both our fathers, who fetched you to him—and so mine wants to seize the hour to my benefit, he says. He means his own."

"Of course he does. All one." If touching was talking, why were words so hard? "It must be one of the Sultan's daughters, then."

"I'm sure so. I don't have a name."

No. That would be a matter for negotiation. Lucky if Salem was let see the girl before the wedding. He had seen Jendre, but she was a commoner's child, elevated beyond measure. The Sultan's daughters were born in the harem here and rarely left it, only to go veiled to the temple on religious holidays. Jendre had seen some at a distance, from little children to girls her own age and older, but she'd had no chance to learn their names or characters.

If they had characters. Harem-bred, eunuch-trained: she doubted it. And accused herself of spite, and couldn't be troubled to deny the accusation.

"Well. Your first wife: it is time. Past time, perhaps. And a daughter of the Sultan, that is flattering . . ."

His shrug tugged stickily at her skin. "The Sultan has many daughters. Not one of them that matters, much. It is a flattery, yes; no more than that. He spends his coin with a scattering hand."

He was saying that he might have wed a general's daughter, and not lost advantage. His father would not see it so, but they did, both of them. They had to. And could not say so directly, only in shrugs and twitches. Touching was talking; what need words?

"What will you do?"

"I will marry, Jendre. As you did."

"I meant . . ."

What will you do about me? was what she meant. All her body said so, where they were bonded together; he could not say he did not hear.

"I know what you meant. I wish I had an answer for you. For now, you are my fire in the night, the light that draws me close and the heat that holds me; but that must change. The Sultan lies with his wife one time, then dallies days with his concubines. How can I lie with my wife and then come to you, and not cheapen you?"

It was his honesty that would break them both; she had always known that. She could be as cheap as she needed to be, but he would not allow it.

And she could not argue, fight, chip at that honesty without cheapening him, which was the one thing she would not do. They deserved each other, she thought grimly, bitterly; each would struggle to defend the other's integrity, and so they would both lose and lose and be utterly lost, each to the other and her to the world. There could be no more Salems, no more bright loves; only the inward life of the harem where women grew fat on their sisters' troubles, which was her mother's particular genius. She could perhaps learn to play at being her mother, but not she thought without going mad first.

SHE would not beg, not plead, not weep. Let him keep himself as best he could, within his sense of honour. He had the world; he could recover, find other loves, even maybe love his wife if he was lucky. She would do nothing to bruise his hopes of that.

As ever, he was reluctant to leave, she to let him go. They chivvied each other, blamed each other for their own delays; at last she found herself at his feet and in trouble with the lacings of his boots, she who was rarely and barely allowed to knot her own.

And then she rose and kissed him, a final talking touch, before they stepped out into time again. Time took them past Mirjana and then past Teo, two wordless watchers; they slipped as secret as they could to the foot of the wall.

No kissing now. A whispered promise for tomorrow night—and what did his friends think, she wondered, seeing him so seldom, and how much did his father guess, could this be a reason to see his darling married?—and he was gone, shadow-quiet and shadow-swift as he scaled the wall, gone to her eyes before he reached the top, only an occlusion of starlight as he rolled over into the world beyond.

IF touching was talking, then separation must be silence: unique, unbreakable, eternal. Truly, quietly, she thought she would go mad.

SHE thought she would never sleep, but Mirjana brought her a warm drink, heavy with milk and spices. What else was in there, what flavour the spices disguised, she had sense enough not to ask. Only the ritual protest, "Did Clerys teach you this? I'm not a child now, to be drugged with milk," as though she hadn't even guessed at something stronger. She drank it down and then lay on the bed that still smelled of him, of them, while Mirjana rubbed her feet with slow, strong hands. Too weary to weep, Jendre gazed up at the bed's hangings and felt the weight of the night slip away from her: too heavy to be borne, so she just let it fall. And then drifted, and then floated, and then sank.

ONE unequivocal blessing, in this equivocal house: she could sleep as long and as late as she chose, all undisturbed. That was new, and welcome. Her father's was a soldier's house, disciplined and early-rising. Besides, she had been there much afflicted with a sister. Here no one called her, no one roused her, no one else's noise broke in to wake her. Her little household waited on her whims. Some part of her thought they ought not to indulge her, but that part was her father's daughter, the Jendre she should have left behind. Here she was mistress and could be as wilful or as idle as she chose. She could sleep late and wake late and stretch slowly within the warmth of the bed, relishing the sheer animal that her body had become, the reach and touch and ache of her, the soreness earned and the sharp little twinges to be treasured, reminders of how they were achieved.

Later, she thought that she should have risen up all full of portent, carrying foreboding as a boy fetches water from the well. She should have smelled disaster on the breeze.

But she had slept too deeply, roused too slowly; if she had dreamed at all, she could not remember it. Besides, she thought perhaps she didn't believe in fortune-telling. It was a virtuous position, approved by the priesthood; it was a position almost impossible to maintain in a harem. Here they would believe anything, everything, tell their futures from dreams and omens and cards and smoke. She saw no threat in scudding clouds, the flights of birds, the fall of shadow over water. She had her own shadow, and thought that was enough; all she carried in from so late sleeping was a headache and a temper.

STUBBORNNESS and fretfulness, distress she was too stubborn to show even to her slaves: they turned the frowst of her waking into a thudding head before she had been up one hour.

That was another advantage of her new position, though, that she could be dog-tempered and capricious in black safety. Her mother would have cuffed her, Clerys would have snorted and scathed and made her feel smaller than Sidië; there was no one here who could do that. She had to live with her own foul mood, and so did those around her.

She snapped at Mirjana over breakfast and pushed her food away; she kicked at Teo when he fumbled with her bootlaces. Much as she had fumbled Salem's last night, and the memory made her want to kick him again. And then she wanted to cry, but she wouldn't do that either. How could she be dignified and discreet among the women of the harem if she sobbed and wept and screamed among her own people?

Temper and a headache: her better remedy was balm rubbed into her temples with soothing fingers, but she despised that kind of monstrous mistress, who abused her slaves one minute and demanded intimate services the next. She would go out, she would walk; she could walk for miles if she needed to, until she had walked off her grim mood and the breezes and perfumes of the Sultan's gardens had soothed her head.

The pity was, she couldn't walk alone. Even a concubine would not go about unattended; for His Magnificence's new wife to be seen on her own would bring disgrace to her and punishment to those who had allowed it. They must come with her, therefore, dutifully in her train. Her troubles would come too, dogging her heels more closely than her companions, but at least she need not sit and stare at them, and be outfaced.

SPACE and sky and weather, the freedom of birds and clouds where they rode the wind, the touch of that same wind welcome in her hair and on her face. If her eyes felt wet, it was only dust in the wind there, stinging just a little. Unless she had stared too much at the sun, it might be that also. She liked the sun, was grateful for it after days and days of rain. Perversely she had liked the rain also, how it brought Salem to her wet, sodden, how they had made play with towels—but that was gone now, history like the rain, all soaked up and swallowed by thirsty time.

Perhaps she ought not to look so much at the sky, it did make her eyes sting so.

There was plenty here that was earthbound. Grass and flowers, shrubs, trees, water—a girl could spend hours just aimlessly following the paths where they meandered, no end in view except to see what aspect of beauty lay around this outcrop or beyond that pavilion.

If she went higher, if she let the paths and steps draw her up towards the summit of the great hill where the palace walls encircled it, she would see all of Maras spread below her and the river's dark, the sheen of the bridge and Sund beyond, a view to be lost in. But then she would turn her head a little to the side and see the Palace of Tears, and think of Sidië, and wish she had not come so high. She preferred to stay here and walk among the trees, and never mind far views and great horizons. She had no reach and no ambitions; she must learn to live in this shrunken world and learn to love it, because there would be little else given her to love.

Birds fluttered and sang in the branches, fell silent or fled at her approach. There were women, many women who celebrated their own cages by caging birds. Jendre had thought to join them once, but only for a gesture. Now she was glad to have birds share this freely. She didn't think they were attracted to its beauty, rather to its worms and flies and nesting places; she had her equivalents, food and friends and comfort. If they could make a life here, so could she. Use what she had, and not look beyond the wall for what had been lost or taken . . .

There was a little lake beyond this narrow belt of trees. And fish in the lake, penned in as she was, not free to come or go. It was a made thing, not natural: cut from the rock and restocked with hatchlings every spring, she'd been told, to counter the depredations of the heron she'd seen stalking its banks. At high summer, His Magnificence would eat the heron that had eaten so many of his fish; but always there would be another come.

Thinking about that, she was startled by movement in the trees, in the undergrowth. Too great for birds. A first glimpse showed her a rounded, muddied mass heaving upward out of ground, and because she was still thinking about birds, because her mind's eye was focused to that scale, for a moment it seemed enormous, cataclysmic, some underworld demon breaking through.

Half a shriek broke out of her, before she could bite it off. Then an arm caught her round the waist and pulled at her; she staggered and was gripped, held upright. For one blind, mad moment she thought herself taken, seized, stolen by fiends. But this was Mirjana who held her, watchful and protective. That was Teo who had jerked her to safety and thrust himself forward, to stand between her and the creature in the trees with his blade in his hand, and she wondered if he had any notion how to use it.

Not that there was any need. What they faced was no demon, though he had come from underground. Just a boy: a scrawny, filthy, frightened boy, naked but for a twist of greasy cloth around his hips. He fell to his knees, pushing his face into the mould of mud and roots and rotting leaves; now she could see the hole he had come up from, and how she had misunderstood the hunch of his slime-smeared back and shoulders as he heaved himself out.

What was he, then, a thief tunnelling his way into the palace gardens to raid the rich pavilions? If so, he deserved his terror; but she didn't believe it for a moment. She thought that he was frightened just at being seen, and doubly frightened for having frightened her; she thought that he belonged here, as much as the fish and the water and the birds belonged. As much as she did herself. They all belonged to the Sultan.

"Teo, put your knife away and stop scaring the poor thing. Talk to him for me, ask him who he is, and what's down there."

She walked a little way away towards the glimmer of water beyond the trees and gestured Mirjana to join her, to give the boys space to whisper privately.

There was more movement here, another kind of movement, glimpsed through branches: a party in a hurry, a litter carried shoulder-high and a dozen men trying to turn that awkward eunuch shuffle into an awkward run. This time she didn't startle, but she might have done. No more than invasions from the underworld did this happen, people running in the harem gardens. A languid grace was prerequisite; it spoke of the security of the Sultan's rule, the eternity of empire. To be caught in haste was to admit that the perfect power could fall short, that something had not been seen or done at its proper moment.

This had the haste of desperation. Jendre hurried herself, through that belt of trees to see more clearly. She needed only one clean sight to be certain. That was the Valide Sultan's litter, with all her train ensuing. And what cause, whatever cause could she have for such a hectic scramble, the bearers stumbling all out of step with each other, down the slope towards the harem proper . . . ?

"Lady?"

That was Teo, calling her back from her confusion. Very well; one answer at a time. She turned and tried to smile, tried to look as though this still mattered.

"Teo. Tell me what you've learned."

"His name is Panis, lady, and he is a water-rat."

"A water-rat?"

"He cleans the sewers, lady."

Funny: she had never thought of sewers, not up here. The city had vast cisterns underground; of course the Sultan must have more. Cisterns and sewers and water-pipes, and his own small army to serve them. Boys thin enough to squirm through narrow channels, boys safe to use within the harem, eunuchs all . . .

"Did you ask him what he was doing there in the trees?"

"Of course, lady. He is very sorry to have frightened you, he begs a thousand pardons . . ."

"Never mind that. I was not frightened, only surprised; you must tell him that," even if it wasn't true. Teo knew it wasn't true; he nodded with the air of a conspirator. "But what was he doing?"

"There is a pipe that feeds the lake, and one that drains it. There is a blockage, and the water overflows. There is a hatch here in the wood, where he went down to find the blockage."

"Alone?" It seemed dreadful to Jendre, even in her distraction: the mud and the foul air and the darkness, and somewhere a deadly weight of water pent up, waiting to be freed . . .

Teo's look said *of course, alone; that is the life of a slave,* but his voice said something more. "His foreman was here and should have waited, but he has gone. Panis thought he heard us come, and ran away. The water-rats are not meant to be seen by the ladies."

She was sure not, it was all one with the seamless dream that was life in the palace, untouched by rough reality. But she didn't think that the foreman had run from fear of being seen. People were running, today; it was the mood of the moment.

"Something is happening," she said, "and I think not a good thing. Teo, you see your little friend back to his quarters and learn what you can there." The slaves always had the gossip first; that was inherent. "Mirjana, you and I will go down to the harem," following the litter, "and see who we can find to tell us news."

If they hadn't been so isolated in her little house, they might have heard already. News overspilled like rainwater, soaking everything, but there were always blockages. *The new wife, why should we hasten to tell her? Let her learn . . .*

Out onto the path, then, where it was little more than trodden mud. Wet mud, deeply marked by running feet, bare and slippered. She and Mirjana clung to each other, trying to step both quick and safe, and missing both. They didn't fall, but a dozen times they might have; they found a skidding streak in the mud where surely one of the eunuchs had, as he followed his mistress in her urgency.

They were as reckless as they dared to be, if recklessness and caution can go hand in hand. Perhaps she was as reckless as she was allowed to be, hand in hand with Mirjana. They came down with sodden shoes and mud on their dresses, no worse; and saw the looming bulk of the harem ahead, but the dark block of the *Kafes* first.

And the litter set down before its narrow entrance, and the bearers resting on their heels, and the eunuchs stood in a group beside.

"She, has she . . . ?" Jendre was gasping for breath and for words too, as the enormity sunk in. "Has she really gone in there? Alone?"

"She would have to be alone," Mirjana murmured, ever the sensible one. "The Sultan's word forbids the others; his guards there would enforce it."

Would they? She wasn't so sure. She thought that woman's word had built this edifice. Speaking her eunuchs past the guards ought not to delay her a little minute.

But she was inside, and they clearly were not. And one among the eunuchs was Ferres, who had his own significance here; but so did Jendre, and she was bold today. Or else she was only desperate in her heart and saw no point in playing games of subtlety and patience.

She left Mirjana with a word, two words, "Stay here," and walked forward to where the eunuchs huddled. They really were huddling: frightened, distressed, pressing together for comfort. Even Ferres, who was her monument, whose fingers responded to every tremor in the harem's intricate web, even he seemed broken.

He acknowledged her coming, understood her to be coming to him, took a step or two to meet her on the path. His companions only turned away, which was great disrespect in them but somehow fitting to the day. Too late, far too late, she was starting to feel that deep foreboding that had eluded her before. Nothing to do with dreams or omens, it was all in the people, there to be read in faces, hands, in movements.

"Ferres? What is it, what has happened here?"

A direct question, such as it was not done to ask; but today it won her a direct answer, blunt and brutal. His soft voice could not soften it.

"His Magnificence has been hurt, terribly hurt. His horse fell, and it rolled on him. He is being fetched home now, but the doctors do not think that he will live."

Chapter Five

THEY should, he thought, not be doing this. Almost certainly, they should not.

Tel Ferin would say so, absolutely, but they didn't seem to listen to Tel Ferin anymore. The rebels would most likely say the same, if for very different reasons. Palace spies, hidden hands at the heart of power: he and Tulk were invaluable to their cause, and so they would speak against the risk of this. If they knew. Armina must know; it was some surprise, some reassurance to Issel that she had not come barrelling through the night to chase him off, *Tulk is a child in this, but you, Issel, you know your value to us, to your city, and yet we cannot trust you to be careful . . .*

It was true, they could not. He was not given to them or to their cause. It was Tulk who wanted to do this, who had agitated for it. To Tulk it was glass-clear: their friends fought the Marasi occupation, by virtue of Tel Ferin's precious water; Tel Ferin denied them the water that they needed, so that they could no longer fight; Issel could fight with any water, rain or well or fountain water, river water even, if he must. It was Issel's duty, then, to fight where their friends could not, and Tulk's to urge him on.

Issel could have broken that chain of argument at any point, with a few scathing words. He could simply have shrugged and said no, he would not fight. He had said no, more than once.

And yet he was here. Cold, afraid, but here none the less, and not entirely reluctant. It was faith that drove Tulk, belief in a cause; for Issel, tonight, it was a fierce anger that had undone all his determination and overcome his wiser soul. That soul still murmured caution, retreat, but he ignored it. Besides, he had another. His wilder soul that used to run rooftops and messages, steal for a living, that felt eager and alive, glad simply for something to do that was not studying or washing—there did seem to be an interminable deal of washing in the school, clothes and skin and floors and all, and the water still scalded him at every touch, despite Rhoan's best lessons and Issel's best pretence—or listening to Tulk as he read in a whisper in the light of a stolen candle.

IT had been that same wild soul that had led to this. Yesterday, in the last of the light, with the rain blown away at last, he and Tulk had walked in the garden, walked to the gate—and just on a whim, on a sudden urgent impulse, Issel had pulled that gate open and said, "Coming?"

"Where?"

"Nowhere. Just out. Out for an hour, till supper. Just to run, to breathe, to look at something that isn't inside this wall. We could go see your family . . . ?"

"No. Not that." Tulk's family was a story that was told and over, not to be revisited. But he stepped through the gate and Issel followed, and only remembered to look down at the stain on the wood as he drew it closed behind them. A stir in the dark of his mind, a brief shudder; he turned his back to gate and school and all, turned his face to his city and rejoiced.

In that hour, he showed Tulk places and people that the other boy had never seen and never thought to see: the undercity, shadow-Sund in its hidden economy. Not the bridge, that was a brand burned behind every Sundain eye; not the strand, that would be folly; but where the beggars gathered for their parliament, where the thieves traded, where you could buy a girl's body or a boy's for silver if you had any or for favours if you did not. This was Issel's city, his life in Sund; he meant to show it proudly, *see how we can make a life, a thousand lives, with nothing?*

Tulk saw it differently, took it differently. He was angry. Not with Issel, and not with any of those he saw, even the whoremasters, even the fathers who sold their children on the streets. He blamed it all on the Marasi, on the occupation, fuel to his fire.

That was how they were talking about resistance, revolution, making war—how Tulk was once more urging Issel to use his talents, how Issel was once more saying no—as they walked through Daries. The sun was sinking, and they needed to get back before dark; already Issel could see a strange cast to the sky's light, where it glimmered on water tanks and puddles. If they hurried, if they ran all the way, they might stay safe; they'd still be too late for supper.

"No matter," Issel said cheerfully. "I've shown you where I lived, before; now I'll show you how."

This was the hour when everyone cooked, in Daries: out on their doorsteps, before the light was gone. It was the hour when a hungry boy with a light tongue, a swift smile and a flattering charm might beg a meal for himself and his friend too, if he hadn't lost all his skills for lack of using them.

He begged a flatbread here and a dip of pickle there, never too greedy, only something to munch on as they hustled homeward; and all the time his thoughts were ranging ahead to the next bite and the one after, to show Tulk how easily Issel could make his way in this other city. How he needed no family, no school, no master and no rebels either. *No Armina*, but that was blowing into the wind, pointless. Unimaginable, even.

And so round a corner with an aim in mind, the same widow-woman who had scolded and derided and given him breakfast on his last day as a waterseller, who could always be relied on for a handful of rice or a stew of lentils in a folded leaf. If it came with insults added, that was only spice to the meal. He took the corner confidently, already telling Tulk what they would find—and came to a sudden halt, staring in the street, as they found something entirely other.

The widow's life had been makeshift, perhaps, as everyone's was in Daries; her house at least had been strong enough, or seemed so. All these streets were long survivors, stone-built, patched with mud and brick and timber maybe but still solid, ancient craft.

Except that the widow's house was fallen, gone, a pile of rubble now between its neighbours. The widow herself was there, scrambling over the stones, gleaning scraps where she could: rags and splinters, the ripped and useless remnants of what life she'd had. She moaned as she gleaned, too dry to weep. Three times Issel had to call before she heard above her own lament.

"Old mother, what has happened here?"

"The Marasi came," and her voice was all defeat, dull and lightless with no edge to it. She would be dead soon, Issel thought; no one could survive long in Daries without the will to do it. "Someone sold me to them," one of her near neighbours most likely, trading an information for a coin, "they said I had more food than an honest woman ought."

That had always been true, or Issel could never have begged so much from her. If she fed him, she fed a dozen others too.

"Did they say you were stealing?"

"I never stole! What extra I had, I had from them, from soldiers, for their fortunes told. They knew. They said it was heretical, forbidden. And so this." They had destroyed her home in punishment, as warning. Her home, her life: she would sleep in the open now, and drift down towards the Shine. *Old woman, you should have told your own future*—but Armina always said that was not possible. It needed another voice to tell it truly.

Issel would have stayed to help, but what could he do? Only give her words of sorrow and sympathy, that did no good at all, and carry away a slow-smouldering fury that outmatched Tulk's and outlasted it too; that had led him finally to say yes instead of no, and so brought them out of the house again in the dead of night, and so here.

———————

THE Shine cast its sickly glow across the sky: perhaps not bright enough to poison at this distance, but enough to drown the stars and make a feeble marsh light of the moon. The stars held command of the future, Armina said; so long as Maras could smother its stars, Sund had no hope of freedom.

If she was right, the rebels' hopes would have to reach sky-high. Issel's were simpler, and more easily satisfied. All night, he had only really hoped to see the morning.

———————

SOON now, soon . . .

Down here in Daries, it was hard to spot the dawn's coming. The press of crowded housing blocked any horizon, and the bridge fouled all the sky.

He had the wind, though, that breeze off the Insea that always came before the sun; and he had his own senses too well trained, too many nights awake and waiting for the light. He knew. The sun in an hour, at most. By then, he hoped to have struck and gone, run home and left his spoils in the street.

He and Tulk together, run and gone. There was little Tulk could do but slow him down; the other boy was here, though, because he chose to be, because he insisted, because it had begun as his idea. He was in position on a rooftop, watching; Issel had had to help him up and find him a place to squat where he could feel secure first and then useful.

Issel himself was crouched against the chilly stone of a water tank in all the shadow that there was—Shine-shadow, moon-shadow and the shadows that his own mind could draw, dark thoughts in a narrow street. Tanks like this were common in the lower town, where wells were few. The Marasi had broken many, for punishment or from spite; this one was cracked, and a mighty blow that must have been to crack it, stone-walled as thick as his forearm. It leaked continuously, a thin skin of water on the slabs beneath that went on to make a muddy marsh of the roadway before it dribbled into a gutter on the further side. Days of rain had filled the tank, though, filled it and filled it. This was all that Issel needed, all and more.

THE Shine was like its own dawn rising, like an oil-slick dawn with all the colours of disturbance washing at pale stars like surf on shingle, the suck of river water on the strand. Except that it was there all night, unshifting; all its movement was internal, smoke in a bowl, swirling and sliding and going nowhere.

He couldn't count the nights that he had waited this way, watching what frightened him most. A man waiting for death might do that, watch it and watch it—a lion pacing in its cage, a blade where it lay on a block, a pestilence erupting in his body—and measure his life in moments of survival, every one of them worth the wait if only because it let him go on waiting.

He waited, and here at last was Tulk's whistle, thin and shrill. He could pretend it aped exactly the call of a kite, but no kite would be flying in this eldritch light. The birds knew not to trespass in the Shine; it was a pity, he thought, that boys did not.

Boys and men together. The street led up from the docks, and here came what he was truly waiting for, what the whistle was meant to alert him to, what he could hear quite clearly for himself: the tramp of feet backed by the slow heavy bellows of oxen breath, the rumble of ironshod wheels, occasional voices, a grunt, a raucous laugh.

The Marasi—rightly, wisely—would eat nothing grown in Sund. All their army's food was fetched in from the wide reaches of the empire, far from the Shine. But no animal would cross the bridge, they couldn't be tempted or tricked or forced to it; only men were bold enough, foolish enough to walk anywhere so unnatural. So the soldiery must be supplied by boat, a regular ferry to and fro across the water, which meant a regular wagon from the wharfside warehouses to the barracks above. That was always early on the road, coming up through Daries before the city stirred, before it dared to. Better not to be blatant with such a wealth of food when the Shine gave them light enough to work by, when their conscripts had no opportunity to refuse.

Blatant or otherwise, all of Sund knew about the ferry, and the wagon. There had always been talk of raids on the warehouses, ambush on the roads. Issel could remember a few attempts, and once he'd seen the deaths that followed; the Marasi guarded their provisions as they did their barracks and their bridgehead, in strength.

Marasi strength lay in numbers, largely. Training and discipline too, but these were not front-rank troops. Conscript boys, rather, serving out their early years under a sergeant's whip till they were hard enough to be sent on to the empire's further wars. They had learned all the lessons of brutality, but they might never have been called on to stand in the face of terror. Issel thought that they might run instead.

Or Tulk thought it, and had nagged Issel into an uneasy acquiescence. Tulk thought Issel could work wonders, could lead a march that would break like a wave through all the city and sweep the Marasi out of every shadowed corner. In Tulk's mind, this was the first step in that march, a declaration, *the uprising starts here.*

In Issel's mind it was an act of folly that just might yield some good, food for the hungry of Daries. He had that one desperate widow in the front of his mind, but behind her stood the serried ranks of all the bone-thin women that he begged from, year after year; he had thought of their descent onto an unguarded wagon, locusts onto a field of grain, and said yes.

And regretted it now, of course. There was little he had done in his life that he had not regretted, then or later. He thought that regret was the human condition, or at least his own.

Still, he could be stubborn, he could justify his regrets. He crouched with his cheek against the stone chill of the water tank, and waited.

IT had been a while since anyone had dared attack the supply wagon. The guard had its usual numbers, but small watchfulness: just a troop of young men walking ahead of the oxen, sleepy and shambling and thinking of breakfast. Issel had counted on that. Their complacency was a weapon in his hand.

His hand, his empty hand reached down towards the water, where it seeped through the tank's crack and ran out across the road.

Not yet. Not quite yet.

The soldiers passed, and he let them go. None of them saw him in his shadows; none was looking left or right, only down at their feet in the mud or forward to the mess hall and the day's rising. Marasi or Sundain, it made no difference; people moved at night when they had to, but reluctantly. No one liked to use the Shine to see.

The soldiers, then the oxen, with men afoot at their heads: two teams of six, to pull this one great wagon. More and smaller would be practical in these narrow ways, but like everything that was Marasi in Sund, this was a statement. Power, scale, contempt. Where the street had turned too sharply, they had demolished houses and pounded the stone into the roadway, sooner than find another route or more manoeuvrable wagons.

The oxen passed, and Issel let them go.

Now came the wagon, with just a couple of men astride its shafts. They too must be in the Sultan's army, but like the men who walked beside the beasts, they had the look of drovers more than soldiers. Issel hoped that they would be quick to run.

He watched the vast slow wheels in their grind along ruts of their own making. Just here, those ruts were water-full. As soon as iron rims broke through the deepest puddles, Issel touched his hand to the trickle that fed them.

Just the lightest, slightest touch: he had learned the forms of delicacy, at least, if not the art of it.

There was nothing delicate in what he did. He'd always felt stronger or more dangerous at night, when the river was bright beneath the Shine; even here where he sat in shadow, there was a glimmer to the water where it reflected the shifting glow overhead. He could use that, or he thought he could.

His touch woke the water, unless it was that the touch of the water woke something in himself. He never could be sure of that. Rhoan's certainty was unreachable, unteachable, one of those things he ached for and could not have.

Ice had a grip like stone. Issel knew that, he had seen: down on the wharves in massive slabs, ice fetched in from distant lakes and packed in straw to keep the wealthy cool all summer long. He had seen weeds and stones and whole fish frozen inside ice; he'd thought himself brave just to touch the slick bite of it, steel-hard and steel-cold.

Ice was only water in another state. If water could grip like stone when it was cold, it could do the same here, now, for him. All he needed was to reach along the flow to where it broke in waves before the wheels, where it surged back to swamp their rims entirely; to clench it in his mind, to have it seize . . .

———————

HE could still be startled sometimes, by how much power there was in water, or in him.

Puddles and mud, no more: but that inexorable wagon with its dozen oxen hauling, that wagon whose demands had reshaped the city simply stopped, stopped dead in its own tracks. The street echoed to the sounds of great beasts bellowing in pain and terror as their harness broke or their bones broke or they fell. Men yelled too, slipping from the shafts or struck by snapping chains or caught beneath the bodies of their cattle.

Issel closed his mind to the chaos, closed his eyes to the Shine, focused it all through the water to where those wheels were gripped. One long slow pull, like a strong man focused on straightening a horseshoe; through all the screaming and confusion he could still hear the creaking and then the sharp, swift crack as the axle broke, the crash that followed as the wagon bed fell to ground.

That was it, that was all he wanted, except that now the soldiers had to run away. He opened his eyes and saw how they had huddled together beyond the line of struggling, kicking oxen; even their sergeants were gaping in bewilderment, robbed of voice and attitude, almost unmanned.

Issel was sorry for the oxen, but they were hurt already, hurt and doomed, those that had not broken their traces and fled. He was more sorry for their drovers, those who had not fled on their own account; some of those too were hurt, but some were only trying to tend their beasts. Too bad. He needed, he really needed those soldiers gone, or else he had done all this for nothing, for a stab of temper and the chance to kick back. That was nothing, futile, absurd. Absurd and deadly, both at once. Tulk might dream of revolution, but Issel would never be marching at its head.

His fingers dabbled in the dribble of water where it left the tank, and the road began to steam. Like a mist rising, a mist that scalded where it touched; one drover screamed and leaped away, another screamed and bucked helplessly beneath the weight of the animal slumped across him. The oxen's noise rose too. Again Issel tried to shut it out, but it was harder now.

He couldn't see well through the thickening steam, but he could still sense it like a wall, advancing. He could not see, not feel the agony of steam-seared flesh, but he heard it clearly in animal and man. What the soldiers were doing beyond that seething wall, he had no idea; he still hoped that they would run.

Tulk could see. Tulk was whistling again, loud and clear and nothing like a kite, only like a boy in warning. Issel turned, and saw the other squad of soldiers coming up behind the wagon.

These were no raw recruits. Older, harder, scarred and battlewise and wary: they had heard all the screaming, they could see the fallen wagon. Worse, they could see Issel where he squatted by the tank. Issel and his water-magic, which was a slow and cruel death if he were taken.

He ought to run, he should be running now, up to the roofs and gone; but then men would guard the wagon until its load could be hauled away, and all this night's work would just be waste.

Besides, he had been running all his life from men like this. Tonight, just for once, he had sworn to make them run from him.

———

BOTH hands in the water now, and the roadway seemed to erupt beneath the veterans' feet, hissing and crackling, billowing with steam.

Steam that engulfed them, that hid them one from another like the heaviest fog; steam that blinded and burned like vitriol, as if all the air had turned to acid. It was only water and the heat of Issel's hatred, unleashed at last; it ought to have scalded, surely, as it was meant to, nothing worse than that. But they stood in the Shine, these old soldiers, and they should have known better. So should Issel. The Shine poisoned everything, but water most of all. The Shine had poisoned Issel, and his gift. Anytime he worked with water, he left it strange, bitter, greasy. The school had learned that, not to touch what Issel touched before them. He could make steam in the bathhouse without harm, because his taint stayed in the cistern with the memory of his touch, until it was all boiled dry and gone. Here, though, under the Shine—well, he should have thought, and hadn't.

He was half its creature, stronger in its light. Its influence pervaded everything he did out here; that taint rose in the steam, vicious and unnatural. It was too late, it had always been too late for the soldiers to run. Issel listened to how they sucked in breath to scream with and then they couldn't scream, because that seething steam was coiling and twisting down into their lungs, blistering as it went and stealing all the breath they had.

There were other men shouting beyond where the steam could reach, beyond where the tank's leaking had turned the road to a weapon in Issel's hand. Now, though, like fire following a trail of oil to where it pooled in a sump, Issel's reach surged to the gutter on the opposite side of the street. He and Tulk had dammed the far end with mud and loose cobbles, just where it fed into a drain. They'd done that early, as soon as they came here, before they settled to their long watch. The constant little leak hadn't done much to empty the tank, but it had been plenty to fill the gutter.

Issel's power, his passion, his fear, all poured into that long shallow stretch of water. All that he had learned of control, he simply forgot. Other students, whatever they did with water, their work was always slow and careful, structured, focused, solid. His was thin and wild and bitter, leaving a taste of the Shine in what he touched. Tel Ferin mocked him for it— *all fury,* he said, *and no subtlety, a street boy's work, mean and without authority*—but Issel was glad of it now. Now was a time to be mean, and not at all subtle.

Everything he had, whatever he could use: it met the flooded gutter, found so much water, filled so much. Again that explosion of steam, all the pent-up violence of water released in a rush, in a moment; and the acrid colours of the Shine, the bone-deep sickness of it somehow mixed with the steam to make it bite and cling, sear through eyes and skin and leather, eat at steel even, like rain and time intermingled to make a rust as swift as fire and as deadly.

Issel couldn't see anything of what he did, except when blundering shadows loomed at him through the fog, and then he flung handfuls of wet at them. Mud, stones, it didn't matter, it was only the wet that counted, seething and spitting like fireballs.

Perhaps that was a mistake. At first it did drive them back, but it gave them a focus too, where to find their enemy. And they were brave men, trained men, veterans . . . There were more of those shadows abruptly, dark within the searing white, and they wouldn't stop for a handful of flung mud, no matter how it burned.

He hadn't wanted this—better to see only the blank wall of steam, better just to imagine what the screaming meant inside it—but he took his hands from the road as the first of those figures came stumbling and groping forward.

The soldier had his sword in his hand, but he was using it mostly to feel his way along the wall, except for those times when he roared wordlessly and swung at ghosts, at nothing that he could see because there was nothing there and he could see nothing anyway. Not with those eyes, as lost to light as his tongue was lost to words. All his face was liquid, a sheen like molten fat poured over bones.

Issel might have been kind then, with the knife in his belt. But there were more men coming behind, and they might be less hurt, less helpless, and he didn't have time for all of them, or any . . .

He stood up and thrust his bare arm shoulder-deep into the water tank.

Now he was screaming too. His pain was in his bones, in his blood, a fire beneath his skin. So much water and all of it gleaming under the Shine, and he was alive within it or else it was alive within him, and a salamander in the coals could not burn so fiercely.

He moved his arm through that great weight of water, and his open hand struck the stone face of the tank. It shattered into a thousand splinters, that shot like so many darts across the alley as all the tank's water erupted behind them; and those flinders drove themselves deep into brick and wood and mud and flesh and bone, and all the screaming stopped at this end of the street.

Issel too was quiet, now that the tank was broken and the water spilled and gone. The cruel killing cramp was ebbing from his arm, and there was only his own killing to be seen.

He didn't want to see that; he didn't want to be seen. The steam was dissipating slowly, drifting, settling. He could still hear noises among the oxen and their men, though he didn't want to call them voices. He could leave those for the people of Daries to attend to, along with whatever they could salvage from the wagon. Its greasecloth covers might have saved its load from the foul steam he'd made, though they had been shredded now by splinters from the tank.

He turned and hoisted himself up onto the sidewall of the ruined tank; from there it was a short stretch to an upper windowsill, and from there onto the roof. Tulk was standing, stupidly exposed at the corner, like a statue on a pedestal, in a city where all the statues had been broken or pulled down; he was staring stupidly down into the street, at the destruction Issel had wrought there, rather than watching for signs of other soldiers coming.

Issel sighed, whistled, beckoned. Tulk seemed reluctant to take his eyes off the horror below; Issel beckoned again, more urgently, and the other boy was still slow to come.

It had been his plan, his eagerness to do this thing. Issel might have resented the revulsion on Tulk's face, if he weren't so sickened himself.

"I didn't, I didn't know that it would be like that . . ."

"What, did you think it would be all clean, it wouldn't hurt? This is real, Tulk, it's not your dream of freedom," and the first rule of the real was that it did hurt: everybody, always. "Throw up if you want to, but do it now or save it, we've got to go."

He was amazed how matter-of-fact he could sound, how in control, as though he'd known from the start what it would be like down there. As though he'd done it all before. Something was making him dizzy, making him shake even as he urged Tulk away, leaving him uncertain on his legs and in his stomach. He had the better excuse for throwing up or passing out, all that power expended, all that terrible strength of water; all the more reason not to do it, then. He wanted stillness and shadow and silence, nothing more. He plunged on, the skid of his reckless feet and the nervous scutter of Tulk's behind him, the hard kick of every breath in his throat, the Shine bright overhead and ready to fade only easterly, where the first faint tint of dawn was showing.

From roof to roof, he brought them both safely to the sight of merchants' houses within their garden walls; and so down to ground, where they could hide in the half-dark, hugging those high walls as they trotted warily back to Tel Ferin and their daytime life.

———

TULK made straight for the narrow wooden gate, but Issel tugged him away. "It's almost sun-up. Baris will be sniffing around, and you know those hinges squeal. Do you want to be caught, just a minute from home?"

"Baris has nothing to say to us, he's just a servant. You give him too much respect."

It wasn't respect, it was fear, and not really fear of Baris. Issel said, "It doesn't matter what he says to us, it's what he might say to Tel Ferin. I'm not ready to be thrown out of the house, if you are."

He led Tulk around the corner to where a tree had grown just grand enough that a slim strong boy, an agile boy, could squirm out along a springy branch and swing from there to the top of the wall, and so down into the shadiest part of the garden, quiet and unremarked.

Issel could do it without thinking, except that he thought all the way about what might be waiting for them on the other side, hot breath and a dog's leer, clawed fingers clutching like a promise. Tulk's fears were more earthbound. He was afraid of the squirm, of the swing, of the wall's height and his own teetering balance—or he was afraid of the fall, rather, that underlay them all. Issel didn't understand that. He'd never been afraid of falling.

He went first, to show how easy it could be. He couldn't call encouragement back, he didn't dare; all he could do was crouch on the wall's coping and gesture hopefully, trying to be visible to Tulk and invisible to any other watcher, both at once.

Tulk took an age to work up nerve enough to inch out along the branch, to that point where it bucked and bent beneath his weight; longer yet to let his body dangle, hang from his arms and use the flexion to swing himself back and forth, far enough for Issel's reaching arms to grab him. A sharp hiss in his ear, "Let go!" before the tugging branch could pull them both off again on the wrong side of the wall; he did that just in time, the branch thrashed back and they slid down into the garden at no worse cost than a little skin off hands and knees.

Then a slow, careful slither through the bushes until they could sight Issel's window, just the way they'd left it: shutters pulled as close as they could manage from the outside, not quite tight. They'd thought that shouldn't matter, but apparently it did. Something was moving, a darkness in the near-dark just by the frame of the window there, stretching and sniffing at that betraying little gap. Its manner said *dog* while its shape said *man*, so it was easily named.

Issel sank back against the roots of a concealing tree, pulling Tulk down beside him. If they stayed put, Baris would come hunting—*sniffing*, which was worse—and find them out, and they would have to answer to Tel Ferin. They could sneak around to the house door, but there was small chance of finding it open this early. Nor any other window. Issel could climb to the upper storeys, try his luck on the roof, maybe wriggle in through an open skylight or one of the gaps in the tiling; Tulk could not. Issel might manage to get into the house and down and open the door to let his friend in before Tulk was discovered, but it seemed unlikely.

Lights were burning in Tel Ferin's own quarters, the man was up already; besides, his private door was always locked. Issel was running out of ideas too soon, and Tulk had none of his own to offer.

Then there was a double slam and a thin warm wash of light across the garden. Crouching deeper into cover, the boys stared out at where the shutters of Issel's window had been thrown back, where Tel Ferin himself stood aglare in the glow of a water bowl.

"Baris?" From the tone, he had been expecting a different face on the shadow he must have seen between the shutters. "What are you doing there?"

His answer was a grunting mumble, too indistinct to carry.

"Gone? I can see that, I know he's gone. Tulk, too. I want them found. They have a precious thing of mine. They are thieves, they have stolen from me who trusted them . . ."

Oh, but this was bad. Issel was bereft, void, seeing no escape except to go back over the wall if they could make it and then down, nowhere but down, to scrape a living in Daries or beyond, sleeping on the strand again, sleeping in the Shine. He couldn't even send Tulk back to his father; Tel Ferin would be sure to seek him there. A runaway apprentice faced an unkind fate, but a thief who stole from his master faced worse. They were a hard people, the Sundain, in their time of hardship.

Not confused for once, confounded rather, defeated, staring at a wall he couldn't breach, Issel was offered rescue all unexpectedly, from a source unlooked-for: a body coming loudly through the tangles of undergrowth and overgrowth, and a voice as loud or louder.

"Master, I can't find them, but I think they might be in the bathhouse."

"Why so?"

"Uh, they often are, when it's just the two of them," which was a direct lie, which was how Issel knew this was a rescue.

"At this hour?"

"This and other times, master. I think they go there to be alone. Issel's little window ledge there, it's probably not very comfortable."

"I'd have thought two skinny boys could sit here with room to spare, but that's hardly the issue now. In the bathhouse, you say?"

"Yes, master."

"Are you sure?"

"Not really, I didn't go in to check, but . . ."

"Why not?"

"Well, master, they'd be looking for privacy, and I didn't want to break in all unwelcome."

Master, will you please stop being dense? was what she was really saying; and now, finally, he did.

"Oh! Ah. I see. How long—? No, never mind. That's not the issue either. Nor is there any need for delicacy. They are under my authority, and I still mistrust them. Go, Rhoan. Fetch them to me, in my chambers. Now."

Issel and Tulk heard this only distantly; they were already crawling away, as silently as they could manage, while Rhoan went on making noise. Around to Tel Ferin's wing of the house, where they'd be under the gaze of his lit windows, but that didn't matter so long as he was here and the dogtooth too. There they'd be able to stand and run, and with luck they'd be at the bathhouse even before Rhoan, if she went round the house the other way.

Crawling backwards, almost, to keep his eye on the ill-lit figures for as long as he could, Issel saw the dogtooth's head turn and the eyes glitter, looking for movement. Looking straight at him, he thought. But there was no cry, no chase; after a moment, Baris turned his face back to his master.

ALL that crawling, through dew-sodden grass and under dripping branches: they were surely wet enough to be convincing. Issel was tingling all over, from scalp to bare feet. Even so, Rhoan had them wash quickly before they dressed in clean dry clothes, before she ushered them before Tel Ferin. She was quite straight-faced throughout: no suggestion of conspiracy, no hints as to what they needed to say and what not. Tulk seemed a little bewildered; Issel figured that he'd catch up, sooner or later. Perhaps later.

Tel Ferin was furious, but his anger seemed a little disconcerted. It cost him work, to keep a hold on it; he found it difficult to meet Issel's eye, or Tulk's; he would stutter suddenly and have to begin again.

"Listen, you two—I don't care what it is you've been up to just now," though he clearly did, "how you spend the night is up to you," though he wouldn't say so if he knew what they'd actually been doing. Or when he knew, that might be a wiser way to think of it. He was bound to hear what had happened; and such a vicious, acid steam raised from simple Sundain rainwater, it stank of the Shine, which meant—to Issel, at least—that it stank of Issel. If he had to answer for that, though, it would be later. For now, "A book, a priceless book of mine is missing, and there is only you two could have taken it, or one of you."

"A book, master?" That was Tulk, being deliberately obtuse; they were in the workroom, with all its disordered stacks and shelves of books, and he gazed around at them all so insolently that Issel was wincing even before Tel Ferin's hand began to move. It was only a reprimand, though, only a cuff on the ear, and Tulk had a well-fed sturdiness; he stood the blow with little more than a blink and a sudden stillness.

"A book, indeed—and books are of no immediate use to your friend here, who cannot read. I would blame you, Tulk, except that I think you tend to follow Issel, wherever he may lead you"—and Tel Ferin paused, as if he heard another meaning to his own words and had to shrug it off before he could continue—"and he would know the value of a book, and where to sell it."

"Master, we have stolen nothing," only borrowed it, and Tulk was good at injured innocence where he didn't truly have to lie, "sold nothing," which was simple truth and better still. Issel stood quiet, a little startled by the notion that it was he who led Tulk into mischief. That wasn't at all the way it seemed to him. Of course he led across the rooftops, coming and going, and of course the use of magic must be his—and the guilt, the hurt, the ice in the heart, all of that—but Tel Ferin knew nothing of that. Yet. It was Tulk who urged Issel on, always, Tulk who was the enthusiast. Issel only wanted to live quiet and unnoticed, survive this world and hope for better after.

Startlement, that abrupt revelation of how differently other people saw his life, had stopped him listening. Another kind of surprise snared his attention suddenly, when he saw a water pot on the table bubbling and steaming quietly, a long way from any source of heat. A long way from him also, but this morning all the steam in Sund seemed like his own work. Had he grown so powerful, that water would seethe simply in his presence? Perhaps it was Tel Ferin, or the two of them together; but it had never happened before, and he was the one who was changing, growing, testing the limits of his power. Tel Ferin had done nothing new for years.

"If you did not steal it, you threw it out, perhaps, with the mess when my ceiling fell. Carelessness is theft, when it takes from me something so precious."

"Master, I don't believe we did. We are always careful of your things. And everything we threw out came from your bedroom." Tulk was still being careful with the truth. Then he risked another blow to look around again and say, "And—well, have you searched in here, master? There is a terrible number of books," *and a terrible muddle,* which thankfully he really didn't need to say.

"Of course I have searched," and to be sure it was not the same muddle as before: wilder, more papers spilled and piles overturned. "But if what you say is true, if you have neither stolen nor lost it for me, I suppose the book must still be here. You two can find it for me, and bring these rooms to order at the same time. This time, though, you won't be left unsupervised."

He described the book, and then he turned and swept out of the apartments. When he was gone, there was a loom of movement in the inner room, his bedchamber.

Not the dogtooth. This was another figure altogether, shadow in bulk; and there was something breathlessly familiar about the way the figure moved and the noises that came with movement, faint bells like the chimes of water-flowers in a breeze. Issel had barely time to think, *they say he has a woman, a slave lent,* and barely time to think, *no, not her, she could not,* before she stepped out into the light and of course it was her, and apparently she could.

Tulk knew her now; it was he who gasped her name. "Armina! I don't understand, what are you doing here . . . ?"

"What Tel Ferin thinks you and I have been doing in the bathhouse," Issel snapped, "only with her he can be more certain."

She nodded briskly. "That was well thought of, as a story."

"Not me that thought of it," and Tulk still hadn't even thought his way through it, by the frowning look of him.

For a moment Armina seemed to be gazing past them all, but that was nothing new. Then she smiled—and not at them, so presumably at whatever she was seeing, in whatever world her foreign eyes had opened to her—and turned her head that fraction that brought her back to this world, to the boys.

"How did you mean to return the book," she asked, "without me?"

Tulk's mouth opened and closed; Issel took it for granted. Of course she knew.

"We didn't think that far. If we could get in once—"

"—the chance was that you would never get in a second time. Especially if he missed his book in the meantime, which he must; it is his precious little thing."

"Wait," scowling, working it out on his fingers, almost, "you knew that?"

"Of course."

"So why didn't you just read the book yourself, those times that you were here?"

"Do you imagine that I can read? After all these years, do you know so little?"

After all these years of her reading him, reading his doings and his futures—yes, of course he did. He imagined more than she knew, and knew less than she imagined. He thought she need only look at a book and all its meanings would open up for her. But, if she denied it, "Well, take it, then, take it back to your friends. Why wait for us?"

"Because if I gave it to them, they would not want to give it back; and meanwhile he would miss it, and know for certain that I had taken it, because he let no one else in here until you soaked his bed for him. Again, that was well thought of."

This time Issel would have been glad to take the credit, but she gave him no opportunity.

"Except, of course, for the need to mend what you have done, which was not thought of at all. So your master must sleep under a broken ceiling," and so must she, some nights, "with spiders falling on his head, and now we must fetch back his book while he is glowering and suspicious. Well, so be it. Where is the book?"

Surely she must know that, she knew so much. Tulk told her anyway. "Under a loose board, near where Issel sleeps at night."

"What, must every board be poked at, till one gives up its secrets? You cannot fetch it yourselves. Say more clearly, where it is."

"Well, but you can't fetch it either, you never go into the main house. If you think we'd be seen, you'd be stared at . . ."

"It's all right." The voice came from behind them, soft and low and pleased with itself. "I know where the loose board is. I would have looked there anyway. I'll just go now, shall I?"

It was shocking, that voice, it was impossible. They turned and stared, and Rhoan smiled back at them both impartially. She was standing in the corner, behind the table, where she could not have come without their seeing.

"How did you get there?" It was Tulk who voiced the question for them both; it was Armina who answered.

"She came in with you, do you not remember?"

That was right, she did, she fetched them here and brought them in; but then she'd gone, hadn't she? She must have gone. Issel hadn't seen her since . . .

Nor had Issel seen her leave. He had seen water stirring, steaming, by itself. He'd thought it was reacting to him; now he thought he'd been wrong. But—

"Are you saying you can make yourself invisible?"

She smiled and shook her head. "Not invisible. Just hard to see."

"How?"

"Well, standing behind you, that helps."

"Tel Ferin must have been looking straight at you. He thought you'd gone, the same as we did."

"Tel Ferin only ever sees what he wants to see. He's very manly. Issel, shall we talk about this later? I'd better go and fetch that book before he decides he has a task for me."

He watched her go, looked back at the corner she had come from and turned to Armina in defeat, in accusation: "You could see her all the time. Couldn't you?"

"Of course. I'm very womanly. And she's a girl worth looking at. Besides, I knew she was there. I wanted her to stay."

"Why?"

"Because you should work together, you need each other. She has skills that you should learn, Issel, and there is much that you can tell her in return."

"She is no part of our secret," Tulk muttered, as though he wanted to keep his revolution to himself.

"She is no part of anything as yet, but she will be. Rhoan has values that you cannot see."

Well, he'd seen that. "How do you know all this?" from him and, "Did you set her to spy on us?" from Tulk, sullen and angry at his side.

Armina's smile grew more self-satisfied, if that were possible. "No, no. She does that for herself. She knows me, of course; I come and go, she has been here a long time, and I am not invisible either."

"I've been in the house almost as long as she has, and I've never seen you here."

"No. You grow as manly as your master, but girls see the world differently. And the people in it. Never mind it, Tulk. There is value in you too, that she or we or all of us women could not achieve. Just now, there is this room to be set in order, so that you may find the book unsurprisingly buried beneath a fall of paper in one corner or another. That had best be you, Tulk, that should find it. We will have your master pleased with you again; he is suspicious anyway of Issel, and perhaps a little afraid."

"Then why did he bring me here, and why does he let me stay?"

"He brought you because no one counselled him not to. He was fed rumours for years," and her smile spoke loudly of who had done much of the feeding, "about the boy with the wild talent, his untrained skills, his uses. Tel Ferin has his curiosity, and his vanity also; he would like to be the man who tamed you."

"Is that why you let him bring me here, then, to be tamed?"

"If you must question," she said, "then work and question, both at once. There is much to do. But no, why would we want you tame? We have no vanity."

"So why, then—just to steal the book?" When she could have stolen it herself, whatever she said? He didn't believe that, or else he didn't want to believe it.

"Not the book, but what the book contains, the knowledge—that, perhaps, though not only that. You need to be here, Issel, as much as we need you to be. What you learn here, this will help to bring you where it is good for you to be. All other threads are broken."

Good for whom? he wondered, briefly. There was no point in asking; Armina didn't distinguish between his welfare and the welfare of the wider world. What she wanted, that was good for all. And *where will it bring me?*—he wouldn't ask that either, because she wouldn't say.

Tulk didn't know not to ask questions. He was staring, bewildered. "How can you know all this?"

"Ah, how? It's no good, little shoemaker, I don't know how to tell you. I come from far away; your language is thick in my mouth, wet and heavy on my tongue, and truth is a gossamer, too fine to be expressed."

"She means she doesn't know the words," Issel interpreted.

"I mean you do not have the words."

"That's nonsense," Tulk said hotly, as patriotic for his tongue as for his city. "If a thing exists, of course we have the words. We talk about magic all the time . . ."

"Ah, your water-magic, yes; that is as wet and heavy as your language. Mine is soft as a breath and dusty-dry, like sunlight through a window. Look, see, I cannot say it but I will show you, here . . ."

And she picked up an old and spotted mirror from a shelf, wiped it roughly clean on her sleeve and laid it flat on Tel Ferin's worktable, where Issel had just cleared away a sheaf of papers.

"My father said that fortune-telling was wickedness, against all justice . . ."

"Did he so? Well, and maybe he was right. It was your justice that slaved me here, and I stand against that; does that make me wicked? Or you, for listening to me?" When he had no answer, she went on, "Will I tell your fortune, then?"

Among the bells and shards of mirror braided in her hair, along with all the beads and shells and pretty strings, she had some little tins that flashed like mirrors in the sunlight and were very hard to see for what they were. She twisted open one of those and took a pinch of reddish powder with her nails, scattered that across the mirror's surface and closed the tin up carefully.

"Why do you keep it in your hair?"

She quirked an eyebrow; even so small a movement raised a faint bell's whisper.

"People generally ask me what it is."

She wasn't smiling. That most likely meant that she was pleased, this most perverse of women.

Tulk shrugged. "I can see what it is."

"Ah. So wise, so young? Well then, young master, what is it?"

"I don't know what you call it," with a sceptical hint to his voice, as though she would call it something mystical to deceive the credulous, "but we call it rust. We grind iron oxides to get it, and it's used to colour hides, that ox-liver red that people like in their belts and boots."

"Good. Very good. This is rust, of a sort, though you should not use it to colour hides. I carry it in my hair so that it is always with me, even when I go naked else, in the bathhouse or elsewhere; and so that if people ask about it—people with swords, say, and a nasty habit of questions; a Marasi priest, say, with soldiers at his back, who would cheerfully burn a poor slave woman for such a sin as this—I can always say that I use it to colour my hair, and so I wear it there, to have it with me in the baths. Blow it from the mirror now, blow my rust away."

"Softly, softly," Issel urged, all the help that he would give. All that he dared give, and that too much, to judge by the glare it won him.

"Blow as you will," she said, but at least she said it lightly, not to urge him on.

Tulk drew a breath and blew, slowly, carefully. Some of the powder rose up, swirling, but most seemed to cling to the glass.

"Again."

He drew a breath, and blew again. There was more red dust in the air now, hanging as it seemed in a cloud between the two of them, the woman and the boy.

"And once more."

A deeper breath this time, and Issel from his little distance could actually see how Tulk inhaled some of that fine powder as he drew the air in. Then he blew, harder now, a little frustrated. Issel remembered that frustration—the indignity of it, that dry powder should hold to dry glass and so defy the tornado of his breath!—and what happened after.

Tulk blew and then was breathless, had to snatch for air. It was this gasping in the rising cloud of dust that mattered most, Issel thought, that decided how much of the powder you breathed, how deep you went. Sometimes he thought that all the blowing was just to cause the breathlessness, the gasping. Once he'd dared to say so, to Armina. She'd struck him and he hadn't said it again, but he still did think it. Sometimes.

He remembered the acrid, bitter taste of rust on the tongue, the way it coated your teeth and the roof of your mouth, the softly choking sensation as it drifted down your throat—and how that made you cough, and so you breathed again, breathed more. And how your mouth felt so dry, although it flooded with saliva; and how you had to swallow that, and so the sour taste went biting down into your belly, where it might gripe in your guts for days. But that was nothing, nearly nothing. What mattered more was how the powder got into your head, and what it did there.

That never lasted long, a few minutes, but it lingered like a living scar in the mind. Issel had suffered the rust, survived the rust half a dozen times in his life, and every time sworn never to go there again. He lived still with each of those separate journeys, like rips in his soul, unrecoverable.

Tulk knew nothing. Issel should have stopped him, perhaps—except that Issel knew no way to stop Armina, so likely it would have been wasted effort. And she never did use the rust unless she needed to, unless she deemed it important. Mostly she read cards or the fall of yarrow-sticks, the roll of dice. She who could not read, apparently, something to learn after all these years of watching as she touched a finger to a word or an image, as she interpreted.

Now they were hunching, the two of them, heads together above the mirror, Tulk leaning into her shoulder while his hands clutched the edge of the table. Issel knew that hold, the fever of it, the imperative: let go and you would fall, you knew you would fall, all into the glass and be gone.

It could look like the Shine in there, the gleam and the slow swirl of it, if the Shine were ever only red. Patterns of dust on glass, that was all, and he wasn't even sure about the patterns; he thought they might be more in the head than on the mirror. She told you to look for patterns and so you saw them, because she was your only safety and your only sure way back so you did what she wanted, always . . .

She breathed shallowly, he saw, when she breathed at all. That must be why she seemed so solid, so strong, one reason why: she never went so deep, she stayed where she could be a bridge, even into dreaming.

"Look into the glass there, Tulk, and tell me what you see." Even her voice was slow and sonorous, beating to a different pulse.

"Red suns burning, and a great fall."

Issel knew that: the drifts of rust like smoke but huge, so huge that every speck was a fireball and you so small that you could speak only in a whisper, only in terror of waking the wind's thunder to lift you from your desperate perch and then let you fall and fall, burned and broken, ash in flame, forever.

"No. Don't let the rust deceive you. See it clearly and it will show you all your world and how that stands. Look again and see what there is, no more than rust in patterns on a mirror; tell me what shapes it makes."

Dust eddies on a breath, in or out—though never as it ought to, sometimes utterly against the flow of air—or sticks fall into their own shadow, soldiers die in a bright darkness and none of that is important. It's the patterns that count: what the eye sees through the rust, how the sticks lie where they have fallen, not how the soldiers lie but how their death is read by others, what it seems to mean.

"I see . . . I see flames. No, waves, they flow like waves, but high and hot, I don't know what they are . . ."

Issel did. He saw those same waves in the mirror every time, unless they were flames. Red like flame and running like water, but they were only a precursor; Tulk would see more pressing patterns soon. Issel didn't want to hear. He knew how frightening the rust could be, and how personal. He'd hate to know that Tulk or anyone had overheard his own stumbling visions. He owed his friend some privacy, that at least. And they had a room to tidy . . .

Thinking about what Tel Ferin might say or do if he came back now to discover his pupil and his woman deep in the rust, Issel found it suddenly easy to let the low murmur of Tulk's voice slip away as he scurried around heaping papers together, heaping books.

———————

WHEN he heard the door, he thought Tel Ferin had come back, just at the worst time.

He didn't dare look round. He went on working, on his knees and bent over a pile of papers that he was struggling to make neat, against their slippery intentions. He heard footsteps, coming to stand behind him; and what, was he to be blamed for Tulk's transgressions, and Armina's too?

He felt the loom of a tall figure, and he did—just—manage not to flinch; or he thought he did, but she must have been laughing at something when she laughed, so perhaps he was deceiving himself.

His head jerked up, and of course it was Rhoan, teasing him barefoot, poking a toe into his ribs to say how pleased she was to have him there, and kneeling. He might have blushed at that, he might have scrambled to his feet except that at the same time she was fishing one hand down inside her tunic; he discovered suddenly a whole new world of blushing, and decided to stay where he was, with his hands full of papers.

She pulled Tel Ferin's book out—well, of course she did, what else?—from where her belt had held it, tight against her belly it must have been. And passed it down to Issel, who took it without thinking and almost dropped it as his fingers found how warm the leather was from her skin, warm and a little softened, just a hint like living skin itself.

And then she glanced over to the table, where the two figures were slumped above the mirror and mumbling to each other, and she said, "What are they doing?"

"She's telling his fortune." In a way.

"This is hardly the place."

"I know that. If Tel Ferin comes back—"

"Not he. He's out for the morning now. Even so, she shouldn't be doing that here. Magics quarrel, one with another," and she gazed around as if she expected the books to spark into anger at this trespass, blessed water to bubble of its own accord.

The way she said that, it sounded like something learned, a proverb of the wise. Was it true? Issel didn't know; but he thought about himself sleeping in the Shine, and how his water-magic was not the same as Tulk's or hers or anyone's; and he shivered, seeing himself suddenly as ground to be fought over, one magic against another and only him to lose.

"Don't disturb them," he said hastily. Tulk needed to be drawn back safely, by one who was there with him, Armina, his bridge to the world. Otherwise he really might be falling, fall and fall forever in the rust inside his head, in a dizzy spin of mirrors, down and down.

"No. I won't do that. What have you got there?"

I'll tease you instead was what she seemed to mean, dropping down to squat beside him, taking the sheaf of papers from his hands and riffling through them, laughing again.

"Trust a boy who doesn't read to sort a study. Did Tel Ferin ever do anything so stupid, since the day he fetched you here? If you put these all together, he'll never find anything again. You do something useful, wipe up all the dirt and dust while we've got these shelves clear; I'll put the papers in order. And while we're working, you can tell me why you stole Tel Ferin's book."

"We didn't steal it. Look, we're giving it back."

"What did you do, then, copy it?"

"No, not that either." Tulk would have liked to, but they had no pen, no ink, no paper, no time and no place to do the work. "He read it to me, and I remembered."

"What, the whole book?"

"As much as I could," and yes, that did mean more or less the whole book.

"All right, but why?"

"Because Tel Ferin wants us to learn everything—everything except this—and do nothing. He wants to hoard knowledge like gold and us with it, burying us all away for better times to come, and never help to bring those better times." Were these his own opinions? He wasn't sure; perhaps he had only spent too long listening to people whose opinions they were, perhaps he mouthed them like a mynah-bird that never needed to believe what it was saying. "We will take what he gives us, and what he does not give us—has he ever shown you how to purify the water, as he does? no? I thought not—and we will use it, all of it, where we can."

"He'll throw you out."

A shrug, *I've lived alone before, unsheltered all my life*; he hoped it was convincing. He hoped that was the worst Tel Ferin could do. He wasn't sure of either. "Your turn now. Why are you helping us?"

"Because I can, because you so need help, because Armina is wiser than anyone here—including Tel Ferin, even including me—and she is helping you; how many more reasons would you like?"

One at least, but he wasn't going to ask for it. Instead he said, "Was it Tel Ferin who taught you how to stand unseen in a room full of people? He's not shown that to us."

She laughed. "Not he, he wouldn't know. Being Tel Ferin is all about being seen by roomfuls of people. I had to learn it for myself. Growing up in a house full of brothers, it was useful sometimes not to be noticed. I used just to keep very quiet and still, and hope that would be enough. Sometimes it was, but not often. Then I started to find that water did things to me that they didn't understand, that frightened them a little. Then I really needed a way to hide. I knew all the stories about water-mages, so I tried to work a magic. When it didn't work I tried again, and again. And nothing ever did work properly, but it was like the opposite of hiding. So I was lucky, Tel Ferin heard about me and fetched me here. And then I had his pure water to work with, and his teaching to help, to guide; so I went on trying in private, and . . ."

A gesture finished the story for her, *eventually I found a way that did work.* And she wasn't going to share unless he asked, so, "Tell me how you do it. Please?" He knew how to make a lead slug look like silver, but that was different, that was a solid thing given a brief deceptive glamour. This was something else entirely, a solid thing just gone.

She gazed at him for a moment with one of those unreadable smiles, and said, "I wonder why it is that people give you things?"

Then she got to her feet, went to the table and fetched a bowl and a flask of water.

"Look." She poured a little water into the bowl, and touched her fingers to it lightly. Wisps of steam rose up, and kept on rising even after she took her hand away. "You know how hard it is to see someone through a mist. Mist is like a curtain, but because you can see it, you do strain to see through it. You can make the mist thinner, so thin it can't be seen; but it's still there, it's still a curtain between you and whoever might be looking. And then—well, a drop of water can be like a mirror, it can reflect something back at you, it can turn your eye aside, it never wants to let you see straight through. Mist is only water, countless tiny drops of water—go stand in one if you don't believe me, feel how it tingles on your skin—and every one of those drops will work for you, if you encourage it. People can still see through it if they try, if they know to look; most people never realise it's there. Or me, behind it. Do you want to try?"

All the time she had been talking, he had been watching her. Even so, even knowing where she was and what she was doing, even having her voice to focus on as a reminder, *she is there, she is exactly there, where she has been since she started,* he found it almost impossibly hard to keep his eyes on her. They wanted to slide aside; every blink, he had to squint to be sure that she was still there, just an arm's reach in front of him. It wasn't invisibility, just a reluctance in his head somehow to accept the solid certain truth of her.

It was disturbing, disorienting to be on his side of what she did; he wondered how it felt for her, to have him peering, blinking, struggling to find her. Did she ever doubt that she was there?

"Issel? Try?"

"Oh—no. No, not now." Not when anyone he cared about was close enough to touch. He knew what sort of mists he made, when he touched his hand to water. He had left bodies in the street to confirm it. "They're coming back now, Tulk and Armina, see . . . ?"

"All the better time, to test on someone unprepared," but she didn't press him to it. Instead she rose neatly and stepped back, making room for his more ungainly scramble up. A houseful of brothers, and now a school with boys; she knew how much space they needed.

It was the silence that had tipped him off. Nothing left to say, once the rust had soaked it up. Armina was back already; she sat straight and solitary, hands flat on her knees, immutable. Tulk was slumped all across the table, just raising his head, shaking his head, drawing his arms up so that his head could drop down onto them. Issel remembered that well: the feeling ill, a little dizzy, a little sick, not quite attached to your body or the world. He drew a dipper of water from the bucket under the table— nothing pure, nothing blessed, just good well water that he might have drawn himself—and took it over.

"Slowly, slowly"—tipping the water to the boy's slack lips—"sip and swallow, that's the way. Don't splutter, it's a shame to waste good water . . ."

One dipper in sips, and then a second that Tulk was allowed to hold himself only so long as he promised not to gulp it. There was little danger of that; his hands were shaking so badly, half of it would be spilled anyway between the table and his mouth.

Still, he was enough himself to meet Armina's gaze, not flinch away; enough himself to ask, "What was that . . . ?"

"We call it rust," she said, straight-faced. "I will not tell you how we get it, but we use it to journey into truth."

"Is that where we've been?"

"Perhaps. It shifts, it's difficult to recognise. Don't you remember?"

"I don't remember much."

Nor did Issel, ever, except the strangeness and the sick wonder of it, the first sights of pattern. What followed, what actually he saw and what he said, what Armina said to encourage him or lead him further on, what she said to bring him back—all of that was gone by the time he got to drinking water and rediscovering the sense of body, having his mind and tongue his own again. Dreamlike, nothing stayed.

Tulk worked his hands on the table, making fists and stretching his fingers, working himself back inside his skin; then he said, "Why did you do that?"

"You asked me to tell your fortune."

"I don't think I did. And I don't think you would, anyway, not just for asking. Why did you?"

"Because Issel is an old road, too often travelled. All that he can tell me, I have heard already. But you, you travel with him for a while; you have fresh eyes. And hope, and at least a little faith. It makes a difference."

"What, will you use me to tell Issel's fortune?" Too weary to be outraged, he could barely manage indignation, though he was clearly trying.

"No, not that; but if you go together, I have an interest."

"So tell us, then, what did you see?"

"It is not my seeing, it is yours."

"Well, then, what did I see?"

"Dark waters, and a terrible deal of death," she said, and even that was more than usually she would say to Issel. "But there is more, and worse. One of your friends means to betray you."

"What? How can you know that?" Tulk demanded, when Issel would simply have asked who.

"I told you, we journeyed into truth. It has its place outside our days and years; this is a part of your truth, a moment on your road, and so you told me."

"How could I? Drugged or sober, I don't know what's going to happen . . ."

"What's going to happen," Rhoan said, a little breathless, "is that Tel Ferin is going to come back and find his apartments no more tidy than they were before, if we don't get on with your work. Not you, Tulk, you sit there. We'll do what's needed. Armina—"

"—is leaving," that woman said, heaving herself to her feet. "I have duties elsewhere. You may hold yourselves at Tel Ferin's bidding; I do not."

"No, but wait, you haven't told us . . . Who's going to betray us, and how?"

"If I knew so much," she said, "do you think I would not tell you?"

And yes, of course, that was exactly what Issel thought, although he did not say so. He watched her leave, through the garden door that the master of the house must have left open for her, because she used no key; and then he turned back to his friends, and saw the first doubting scowl on Tulk's face as he watched Rhoan at her tidying.

Chapter Six

THEY had brought the Sultan back to his mother and his wives, to his harem, though not to his own apartments.

Jendre thought that he had come back to die. That was why he was let lie here among his women, in this separated space, this island in the river of the city. She couldn't imagine what was happening out there, beyond the wall: what her father was doing and what the pasha, what the other great men of the world. Salem would have told her, but she hadn't seen him since the catastrophe. After two solitary and anxious nights, she had sent Teo to find a servant of his house, to carry a message without words: *there is a boy here, he says he has no message, only that he has come.* Teo had returned to her with more than that, a token, a single unset pearl the size of his thumbnail, quiet and subtle in its lustre; its message was *be patient, be secret, be safe.* Teo wore it in a silver clasp on his cap, so that she could see it every time she looked at him; see it and be warmed, be comforted, *he will come.* Pearls were always dived for, however deep they lay.

She worried, of course, she could not help but worry. If there wasn't fighting in the streets, there would be diplomacy in the court, and that was the more dangerous. Bargains and conspiracies, allegiances shifting at every turn, and Salem—son of the pasha, a prominent man—entangled in it all. If there was fighting—and likely there would be, a city so restless, so swift to turn, left now without a master—she was sure that Salem would be in the middle of it. She wanted to send his own pearl back to him, *be patient, be secret, be safe,* but he was a boy, he wouldn't understand the message.

So she had Teo wear the pearl, and she drew comfort and anxiety from it in equal measure; and in the meantime the cause of all this trouble, her husband the Sultan was here and Salem was not, so that she slept her nights alone and spent her days in grief and revelation.

If there was trouble and anxiety beyond the walls, there was plenty more of it in here, in the Sultan's city of women. The harem could be a mirror of Maras, with just as many reasons to fear change, a new master, uncertain times.

All her life the Sultan had been the unspoken rock, the fixed point, the man who was the mountain; like every citizen, she had understood that strength, security, contentment depended all on him. If her father were to rise, it would be on the Sultan's skirts; if she were to live unmolested in the heart of empire, it would be beneath his protective hand.

Now he had come back broken, and nothing could be trusted anymore.

———

THEY had set him in a small pavilion on a little hill, where he could overlook the palace walls and all his city, where he could see the river and Sund and the far horizons, even the gleam of the Insea under the rising sun. She thought it was a kindness, to let him spend his last days with a view of glory. Better this than pent up in his apartments, amid the smoke and the dust and the wailing of so many women.

They had wanted to come and wail on the hill, standing all around his bed and down the slope, so closely packed they would barely find the room to tear at hair or costume. His mother had forbidden them; bent and gaunt and savage, she had sent them all away, wives and concubines and slaves and all. Eunuchs too, all but her select few, and her doctors. She and they had been closeted with him for a day and a night, silent lights on the hill while all the harem else resounded to the cries of mourning and despair.

Then she had returned to her own quarters, leaving her son the Sultan in her eunuchs' care; and now Ferres—of course Ferres, whoever else?—had come to Jendre with an utterly unexpected summons.

"His Magnificence commands me to fetch you to his side, my lady. Will you come?"

Of course she would come, he wasn't offering her a choice; but she gaped, and stammered, "Does he, is he—?"

She hadn't seen him to speak to since their wedding night; she hadn't glimpsed him since they brought him back. She'd heard about the press of women round the hill, whom the Valide Sultan had driven back with whips and curses, and she had determinedly kept her privacy, her dignity, her house. If he was so sick as rumour painted, he probably would not remember that he had a new young wife; certainly he would not care.

Even now, she thought the summons had likely come from the Valide Sultan, usurping her son's voice to give it added weight. Why his mother should want to speak to her, she couldn't imagine. A power play, perhaps, some way to win one general's loyalty in what struggle might follow the Sultan's death . . . ?

Ferres only smiled—though it was a thin thing, that smile, unconfident and shaken—and said, "Come and see."

Come and be seen, he meant. He was looking older than before, and his bustling seemed an effort suddenly; he was pale, she thought, beneath the grease of his former contentment.

THROUGH the garden to the foot of that little hill, the knoll crowned by its pavilion, currently the highest point of empire by virtue of its guest; and there Ferres stopped.

"Will you not come with me, Master Ferres?" *Go first,* she meant, *be my voice, my strong support, my comfort.*

"No, no. I am not commanded." Besides, he was breathing heavily, and the way ahead was steep; he was content to shoo her on with hasty little flaps of the fingers.

Up at her best speed, then, despite uncertain footing, slippery grass and a slimy dampness striking through thin soles. She'd been so startled by Ferres' arrival, so beaten down by his urgency, she hadn't even had the wit to change out of these frail silk slippers.

And so wet-footed to the knoll's peak, and here was the pavilion, a simple structure honoured now above its deserving. A wooden roof, a wooden floor, and pillars on all sides; the walls were merely screens that could be moved to admit light and air, or close them out. It was meant as a summerhouse, surely, for picnics and parties, to sit on cushions and admire the views; or else for the powerful to meet in private, to plot or complot or betray in uttermost security, where they could be sure they were not overheard.

On three sides the wall-screens were folded back, to let in all the sunshine of the day. She could see a bed, a great bed that must have been fetched in sections and put together inside, because it could not have passed between the pillars. She could see one solitary eunuch standing in attendance; she could see a figure in the bed; she could see no one else, man or woman. Above all, no Valide Sultan, with or without her train.

Her first reaction was bubbling relief, not to have to face that terrible old woman. Bad at any time, it would be dreadful here, in this living tomb. That was how it felt to her; she had seen tombs very similar, a roof built on a rise to cover an effigy where it gazed out over lands its likeness used to rule, while the original rotted below the stone. The figure in the bed was as unmoving as any effigy, and as unlikely to rise again. His empire spread out behind him, for hundreds of miles north and west and east; the heart of that empire, his own beloved city lay before him, with his latest greatest conquest Sund beyond; his eyes might be open, but she had heard that he gazed without seeing, blind inside.

Her second reaction was bewilderment. Ferres had said "His Magnificence," and she had thought that meant his mother. Clearly, she was wrong. But who, then—who else would dare adopt the Sultan's title, while the Sultan lived? Not the heir his brother, certainly; that man was still locked in the *Kafes*, though he might be seeing freedom sometime soon. Perhaps Ferres had fetched her on his own initiative, for reasons of his own. *His Magnificence commands* might mean *His Magnificence would enjoy,* if you had served His Magnificence long enough to anticipate his whims; but what could she do, for a man who lay with Death as his companion?

Still, summoned or sent, she could do nothing outside. One deep breath, *go in now or you never will go in,* and she stepped up between two pillars into the bright cool air of the pavilion.

And into the dull, heavy gaze of the man in the bed, and her third reaction was a kind of revolted fury, because she thought she had been tricked, deceived, she and all the harem and the city and the world.

Perhaps it was a stratagem, to keep him safe elsewhere; this man was not the Sultan, not her husband, no.

His head was roughly shaven, and his chin likewise. Perhaps to disguise the substitution, he had been appallingly beaten about the head. His face was swollen, blackened and bloody, twisted all out of human. He was naked to the waist, with only a thin sheet to cover him below; he lay full in the sun's light, and his body too, she thought, was a poor pretence. She remembered her husband's form, intimately so, all the many touches of him beneath her fingers, where he was soft and oiled, where his muscles bunched unexpectedly bone-hard. One long night was not such short acquaintance. She was sure she would know him in the dark; equally sure that she would find no touch of her husband in this man. He was grey where he was not purple, flabby where he was not distended—*like wine-skins,* she thought, *flaccid or swollen,* only that the skins looked rancid and the wine sour—and his skin was slack on his flesh, where the Sultan had filled his own like a ripe fruit glistening with juice. This man had no sweetness in him, except where it was the sweetness of corruption.

She looked, she saw, she thought all of that—and then she saw one more attendant here, a woman, on her knees on the further side of the bed.

"You, Theosa?"

"Of course I, and who else? Where else should I be, who am his woman and no more?"

Jendre could barely see her face in the bed's shadow, but that was how she knew her best, as a figure half-glimpsed in darkness. There was an age of pain and loss in her voice.

Jendre turned back to the man in the bed. Look past the missing hair, the missing beard; that would be the doctors shaving him, to keep all his strength for where it was needed more. Look past the bloody crusts, the bruises; crushed and trampled, a man would look ill-used. Half his bones were broken, so the whispers said. A man's body would be swollen and misshapen after that. And he would lose that glossy well-fed look he'd had, he had likely not eaten for days and his belly would be feeding on itself; and he would look grey and parched and oh, so much reduced, by pain and all the dreadful journey home. And now they had laid him here, and he too would see it as a tomb in waiting, they had even raised up the head of the bed on blocks, and there could be no better way to say *this is your eternal view, look your last and bid the world farewell.*

And if there were anything left of the man himself, then likely the only place to seek it would be in the eyes, beneath their bruises. She had looked already, but surely the doctors would have fed him poppy juice against the pain; that could give a man dreams in daylight, so that he was slack and mindless in this world, dazed and numb in his thoughts as in his body. She had seen her father that way once, when he came home wounded from a war. She had expected to go herself into a perpetual dreaming, and had seen her sister taken instead . . .

And that was not a thing to be thinking now. Ferres had said *His Magnificence commands;* perhaps he had meant it after all. She looked again, into the man's eyes where he lay in the sun. And saw how low he held his lids against the light's glare, and how bloodshot they were; and then at last she saw a gleam of life, deep deep within, and that was matched by a twitch in the mouth, and,

"Magnificence? Are you, are you *laughing* at me . . . ?"

"Well," the word was a scratch in the air, dry twig on dry rock in a breathless desert, "a little. You are very young."

"Time will mend that in me, Magnificence. If it is a fault."

"Indeed. If it is allowed to. Alas, that I will not see the woman rise inside you, Jendre . . ."

"You do not know that, my lord. Even you should not anticipate God's choices."

"Why not, where everyone else has done so? My mother has abandoned me, along with all her eunuchs, whom I had thought my own. My wives are bewailing me already, while my generals are abandoning my borders and fetching my armies home, to seize their best advantage in the new dispensation. My doctors suggest that I should listen to my priests. Even my slave here is wondering how she shall live when I am gone."

There was a mutter of denial from the far side of the bed, but Jendre believed it.

Still, she said, "If you have strength enough to tease me, and spirit enough to feel sorry for yourself, we need not think of burying you yet." If he meant to treat her as a kitten, wide-eyed and idiotic, she would show him another Jendre: one who had learned much from her father, something in recent days from Salem, far more from Clerys and most—idiotically, eye-wideningly—from her mother. "How can I best make you comfortable, Magnificence? While we address those longer questions, how we shall confound your doctors, your generals, your *other* wives," with a careful, punctilious stress, "and even, we must hope, your mother and all her eunuchs too."

Theosa had risen up on her knees and was staring at her across the bed. The Sultan, she thought, would have been laughing if only he hadn't been so weak, so drugged, so hurt. Smiling he could do, and smiling he was. Again she thought *kitten,* fierce and sweet and ridiculous; and this was why he'd sent for her, no doubt, for entertainment's sake, because she was fresh, not old enough to be cynical, not yet soaked in the politics and power struggles of the harem. He wanted innocence; well, and he should have it, but he would learn that there was innocence and innocence, and sometimes the innocent would go to war and win it.

"You could close the screens there," he murmured, "so that the sun is not quite so much in my eyes, so that I might look on you in your fury and wonder at what happened to the child that I married."

"You married her, Magnificence." And then there was Salem, but him she would not share. And of course she could close the screens, but she shouldn't need to do that; he shouldn't have needed to ask. "Theosa, if you please. I don't understand why you have been let lie here squinnying into the glare, Magnificence, but . . ."

"Don't spit at her, little cat," he said, as though even his poor sore bloodshot eyes could still see well enough to read her mind. "The doctors decreed that sunlight would be healthful for me." Obviously Theosa believed them, or else Jendre simply lacked any authority in her eyes; either way, she showed no signs of moving from her place.

"I thought you said they recommended priests?"

"Healthful in the other world, I think they meant: that I should lie here naked in the gaze of God, so that he need not examine me further when I pass into his possession."

"Well. Perhaps he can peek in through the shutters. Now, Theosa," and she turned her own attention to folding her scarf and moistening it with rosewater from a bowl before she laid it lightly across his eyes. "This will ease the soreness," she said, as barred shadows closed over the bed like an abrupt twilight.

"Thank you. Twice, thank you. Perhaps a little of that water also to moisten my mouth, if you mean to make me talk so much?"

"Ohh—Theosa, what have you been thinking, to leave your master dry on such a day, in such a sun?"

"Oh, hush, little cat, little scorpion, don't sting my woman so."

"Don't *sting* her? My lord, I would whip her. Sell her. Both." Strangle her, perhaps, with these same hands that were wringing out another cloth before they held it to his lips. Cracked like mud under the sun, those lips. "Suck on this a little first, my lord. You should not take too much too quickly, and I would need to lift your head to help you swallow."

He sucked at the cloth—she would have said greedily, except that this was all need; no wonder his skin was so slack, if they had baked all the water out of him—and then, when she took it away to soak again, he said, "They have lifted my head already, did you not see? So that my poor women can see me the better as they trail past on the path below, to do their mourning here."

After he had died, he meant. Perhaps that truly had been in his mother's mind, that this would be the place and style in which to display his body within the harem. Or perhaps he was just being ghoulish at her expense. She was still too angry to be teased; she said, "That day would come the sooner, if your care was left to this woman of yours."

"It's true," he said mildly, "but don't be so angry at her, she means it for a kindness."

"A *kindness* . . . ? My lord—!"

"Truth." His voice seemed easier already. "Her people expose un-wanted infants on the hot rocks of their mountains, in full sun, to help them die the quicker. They do the same with the old who have no family, when they cannot feed themselves; and with the sick, when they have passed beyond the aid of medicine. They say it is more cruel to suffer less, but longer."

"Do they so? Well, you are not so old, and you have more family than you can count, and any one of us would feed you," *though I seem to be the one,* "and you are not so sick as that. You might want different doctors," if cutting his hair and leaving him in sunlight were all they had to offer.

"Ah. Well, they are my mother's men; and she has another son to follow me. A Sultan broken in his body, tied to his bed, victim to any rumour or revolt: such a man is a danger to the empire, a danger to herself . . ."

He made a gesture with his hand: small, but still the first movement she had seen in him. No matter that it was a gesture of dismissal, discarding, *such a man were better dead, the empire needs another, and so does the Valide Sultan.* It was at least a sign that he had his body at his command, although it hurt him.

Even so, he did require doctors. So much bruising, so much swelling and discolour to speak of bones broken and other damage, poison and infection and distress: she thought he needed herbs and grease and poultices, but she lacked the knowledge to prescribe.

"You," she said, with a glance at the mute eunuch standing watch over his master's bed, "fetch your brother Ferres here, swiftly. He may still be waiting below; he may have gone about other duties," though what his duties might be while his master died, she didn't want to consider; no doubt his mistress had instructed him. "If so, find him. Don't come back without."

The man bowed and was gone with gratifying speed.

"More water?" the Sultan suggested, just as she felt slightly at a loss what to do while she waited, how to speak to him. "Perhaps with a little wine in it, that would be strengthening. Theosa could fetch it to me."

"Magnificence," and bless him, he could still encourage her to smile, "will you come so close to God and sin so blatantly?"

"Oh, I have sinned so often, I don't think a little goodness now will help at all."

"Perhaps not, but a little goodness in the water will help a lot. You may have wine if the doctors allow it," she didn't know if that would be healthful or the opposite, "and in the meantime, take this," another dip of the cloth, "while Theosa fetches honey to stir into a drink." Honey at least she was sure of. Whenever she was sick as a little girl, Clerys would make her honey-water. "Honey and cinnamon and cloves, and we will warm the water. Heat is always healing."

"Child. That is a child's medicine; you are too late to make a child of me."

Nevertheless, she thought that he would drink it.

BY the time Ferres came, she knew what she wanted to say to him. It was a sudden inspiration, a reason to be glad of who she was, wife to her husband and her father's daughter too. How else should the Sultan survive?

"Ferres," crisply, as though there could be no questioning, "a message for my father the general: he is to send the best of his regiment's doctors here, to attend His Magnificence. Immediately, please." Who better to treat such dreadful hurts than men trained on the battlefield, who dealt every day with injuries as bad or worse? Oh, she was pleased with herself, for having thought of this.

Ferres blinked, slowly; she thought he was thinking fast. "Military doctors? My lady, I hardly think—"

"I am sure you do not forget that His Magnificence is a military man," while his mother's doctors were her servants first, and seemingly religious men, believing more in prayer than potions. Jendre doubted the power of sunlight to mend broken bones, even if the sun were the mirror of God's glory, as it was said.

"No, no, my lady, His Magnificence's prowess in war has been the rock on which the empire has stood, throughout all these years of triumph. But the general's doctors will be whole men, they may not come into the harem, and it would cost His Magnificence great pain to take him out again beyond the walls."

Ah. She had forgotten that. The reminder only made her angry, though, and more determined.

She couldn't say what she wanted to, *you all connive to let my Salem in, and other men, quite whole*—not in her husband's hearing, whether or not he knew. She could glare, she could glare a diatribe; and she could say, "There is no question of moving His Magnificence. I am sure that you can find a way to fetch the doctors in without disgracing the customs of the harem. If necessary you could bind their eyes between the gate and here, so that they see none of His Magnificence's privities." Except herself: she would veil if she must, but she would be here. She trusted no one, except herself and those she called her own.

"Doctors are proud men, my lady. I doubt they would consent to that."

"I think you would find them amenable, once it had been explained to them that the alternative was to keep them here and to cut them. To have them cut each other, indeed, military doctors are expert with their knives. Don't send a common messenger, Ferres, I want you to go yourself. My father will recognise your significance," as she was sure Ferres himself recognised the flattery she offered. *Honey in the water, honey and spice . . .*

"I think I would need His Magnificence's own voice, my lady, to send me on such an errand."

"I think you do not." The Sultan was there, of course, hearing it all, and he could give the order in a moment; but if she allowed that once, she must depend upon it every time, and she wanted her own significance to be recognised. "We are speaking of your master's life, eunuch." *Would you leave it in your mistress's care?* That was another of those suggestions that must remain unspoken but were there none the less, this one emphasised by a simple glance around the pavilion: the absence of doctors, treatments, attendants. His tomb, she thought, would show more care for him than this. "Just go. The need is urgent."

It was, all too obviously. Even so, she thought that he would go to the Valide Sultan first. Well, let him. The Sultan's mother couldn't countermand this order, given in the Sultan's presence. There might be trouble for Jendre, now and later; she didn't care about that. She told herself she didn't, very firmly. Her husband's life, that was all that mattered now.

———

HE said, "Still there, little cat?"

She said, "Of course, my lord."

He said, "Good. Sit close, on the bed here; I can barely hear myself, and I want you to hear me."

She said, "Your Magnificence should rest, and not speak . . ."

That won her another of those precious, twitching smiles. "What, will you order me as you order my slaves about? You will find me a stubborn creature, ill broken to the bridle. And my Magnificence has been resting too long, if resting means waiting to die. You almost persuade me that I have been wasting my time."

"If I am able to do that, my lord, then I will have done all and more than I ever hoped to do with all my life."

"Do you have lavender on your tongue, little cat? You flatter like a eunuch, all perfume and precision."

"No, my lord, not flatter. I will see you rise up, if I have to force you to it. You are the world's master; you dare not leave it yet."

"Well. I am your master, at any rate, and I will not brook disobedience in my chattels. Come, sit close."

"I am afraid to hurt you, my lord, if the bed shifts under me." He was lying spectacularly still, as though pain encased him on every side, and any touch would wake it.

"Oh, are you grown so heavy? I remember a slender little thing, a wand, supple beneath my hand . . ."

At least, beneath his blindfold, he could not see her blush. "No, my lord, but I think the smallest movement brings you pain."

"Child, I inhabit pain; my body is pain's house, and I come and go within it, visiting all its ways and chambers. Everywhere I go, my host is there before me. If you picked me up and shook me, you could not hurt me more."

Jendre was fairly sure that that was a lie, but she wouldn't argue more. She slid her feet out of her slippers and climbed up onto the stiff mattress. The bed in his chambers was softer, and strewn with many cushions, many covers, furs and silks and every touch of pleasure. Not this, not here. Again this was like a platform for display, for laying out: no indulgence, no luxury, only the simplicity of mattress, coverlet, canopy.

Still, she was here, on her husband's bed, where she had thought she might never find herself again. This time, no nestling close. This time, his hands were necessarily still; hers touched him only to check that the silk was still damp where it lay across his eyes, against his dry and fevered skin. Never mind the sunlight, an hour of him would bake out all the water.

Then she curled up, knees to chin, and said, "Well, my lord. If you will not rest, I suppose we must be talking. What will it please your Magnificence to talk about?"

He lay quietly for a little while, and she imagined his mind ranging far: reaching back through his long and potent life, stretching—as his life had stretched—from one end of his empire to the other. He had been soldier, diplomat and potentate, and that was only his public character. In private he was husband to many, lover to many more, father to dozens; and a man who loved beauty as much as he loved women, a man whose passions for art and music and poetry were as legendary as his other attributes.

And this man, this Man of Men, he pursed his lips thoughtfully and he said, "It would please my Magnificence very much indeed, Jendre, little cat, if we were to talk about you."

Chapter Seven

EL Ferin was raging, but his fury lacked a target. His hands were rough with everyone; his tongue was the same, entirely indiscriminate. Issel thought that his eyes, though, his glare, that was particular and aimed directly at himself.

No one knew for certain what had happened. Rumours were wild, and yes, it would be easy to listen to those and think *Issel*; but any fair man knew that rumours ran far ahead of truth. When rumour talked of magic, it lost any grip on what was real. Even Tel Ferin couldn't condemn a boy for what the street was saying, even if the street was speaking true.

He had kept them all close within the house for days, while rumours and counterrumours ran in and out; now he had called them into the formal audience chamber. The room was too big, or they were too few, or too young: they didn't know whether to spread out or to press together, so they did both and neither, scattering to the walls on either side in little clots of two and three. Tel Ferin stood on the dais at the room's end and gazed down at them with all the contempt of his age and class.

"Very well, then. Hide as you like, in what shadows you can find. We will all need to hide, for a while. This city does well to fear the Marasi, but there are fools abroad who do not think so. Fools whom I have dealt with, some whom I have trained, to my shame; and perhaps much of my anger is directed at myself," though it didn't seem likely, the way he scowled and thundered. "You have heard the whispers, and so have I. None of us knows the facts," *unless one of us was involved,* though he didn't say that, not quite, although his eyes did, "but it is clear that the water-magic has been used in a direct attack on Marasi soldiers, and maybe dozens have died. There will undoubtedly be reprisals. Those of you who go out, these next few days, you must be careful, be discreet, step softly and speak little. I need you to be my eyes and ears, only that, no voices in the city now. Baris, come forward."

The dogtooth came, carrying the urn he'd used the first time Issel had seen him, selling water on the strand, in the Shine.

"I need to hear what people are saying, and there could be no better spy than a waterseller. People gather where there is drink and talk while they are drinking. No better reason for a boy to be on the streets, in this heat. Baris cannot be seen about in daylight, so one of you must go."

Issel was surprised, he'd expected to be pent up. But he was ready, willing, relieved to have something to do, almost on the move already before Tel Ferin spoke again.

"Tulk, come forward. Go to the fountains to fill the urn, not to our well here; then make your way—"

Tulk was making his way nowhere yet, standing astonished, his head turning between Issel and Tel Ferin. Nor was he the only one. No one would say anything, though, if Issel didn't.

Issel did. He strode forward, aware of Tulk and Rhoan both starting after him, either in support or else to pull him back, he didn't know and didn't wait to learn; he cried out as he went, "Master, no! This is my work, send me. You must send me."

"I have chosen," Tel Ferin said softly, dangerously. "You will be sent nowhere; you will stay here and be glad that you are let do so."

Which was more or less what Issel had been expecting, but, "Tulk can't sell water, he can't even look like a waterseller. He doesn't know how to wear the urn, he doesn't know the proper way to use it," that particular twist of the wrist that was common to all the brotherhood, and would betray an imitation every time.

"He can be shown."

"Not in one day, master." Issel knew. He had had to learn it all for himself, while every waterseller in the city, it had seemed, had found him and beaten him and threatened him with worse. Fast feet and a sharp knife helped; better was a lifetime's watching, knowing just exactly who they were and how they lived. He doubted if Tulk had ever bought a cupful of water from a *saki*.

"It hardly seems difficult to me. All men are inclined to make a mystery of their trade. Tulk is better built than you, so he can certainly carry the urn when it is full. After that I care nothing how much he sells and how much he spills; I want information, not coppers. Enough."

"Not enough." That was Rhoan, at his side now. "Master, if Tulk doesn't look like a waterseller, he can only look like a spy. The Marasi will be watching, and they have their own spies. A boy not seen before, struggling to seem what he is not: he will attract attention. If they put him to the question, we are all dead. Everyone knows Issel, and they know him with an urn on his back. They may have missed him these last weeks, but they will not think twice if they see him out and selling water."

Tel Ferin hesitated; Issel said, "Tulk, make the cry of the waterseller."

Tulk blinked at him, blushed, then tipped his head back and tried. He did try.

That was Issel's victory, unanswerable proof; and his own sudden trilling ululation, "Suu-uu!" sang in the high ceiling of the hall like a triumph.

When he said, "Now you again, Tulk," it was Tel Ferin who stopped them.

"No. That really is enough. You've made your point, between you. I am still reluctant to let you leave the house alone, Issel, and you know why, but—"

Tel Ferin had said nothing, accused him of nothing. If he were innocent, he had no reason to understand that, but his conscience wouldn't let him dissemble. Instead he said, "I don't need to go alone, master. You have two urns in the house," this one and his own, that he hadn't seen since the day he came but it must be here somewhere, "so Tulk can come with me, if I do all the calling. Two boys working together, that is not so unusual on a hot day." It was a lie, but Tel Ferin was unlikely to recognise it, a man with his own well who again had probably never bought water in the street.

From his sour and doubtful look, Tel Ferin would have preferred to send any other boy with Issel. He had already suggested Tulk, though, and it would cost him face to change his mind a second time. He had lost enough already.

"Very well. Go. Don't go near the Marasi, this is not about baiting the enemy. I want the news and the gossip too, whatever people are saying. Back before sundown, please."

"Yes, master. As you say . . ."

———

EVEN without Tel Ferin's warning, Issel would not have cried his water anywhere near the Marasi barracks that day. Folly, to provoke a nest of wasps; all the city knew it.

Elsewhere, he would have cried in vain. The streets were eerily quiet, as though even the birds had found better business somewhere else. There seemed to be not a living soul out of doors.

The boys learned why when they came to the scene of their ambush. Shards of shattered stone littered the roadway; the bodies were gone, of course, men and beasts, and the wagon long gone too, but the air still reeked of blood and death and terror.

For one brief, blessed moment, Issel thought that was only in his head, his own guilty memories, something he would simply have to live with.

The stench was actual, though. Tulk was retching at his side. For one less lovely moment Issel thought about how air could hang unmoving in a hot summer, how it could seem to hang for days, thick and heavy and rank with all the smells of the city.

He didn't believe that any smell could linger so long or so foully. *There will undoubtedly be reprisals,* Tel Ferin had said; Issel thought he was smelling the first of them here. He thought that was why the streets were so empty, of Sundain and Marasi both. The soldiers didn't need to be out, if they could leave this message written so loudly on the wind.

He wanted to tell Tulk to go back, but it had been Tulk's idea, the thing they had done here; Issel couldn't take all the responsibility to himself, unless his friend allowed it.

Issel walked into the street, and Tulk came after.

———

NO dark today, no muddling Shine or sudden fog of steam, nothing to mediate. No mitigation. Only the high harsh sun laying a determined path for them like a river of light, a current they couldn't fight against, however much they'd like to.

The light and the heat and the smell closed over them, and Issel thought that this might be like immersion in water: anxiety and discomfort and a fear to breathe, a prickle all under his skin and an instinct to close his eyes and keep them closed. He thought that swimming might be like this, terrible and true.

He wouldn't let his eyes close, even when swarms of flies battered about his head and there was a dreadful temptation to duck down and run blind, all down the street to what must be clear air beyond. Somewhere beyond, there must be life again. Not here, unless you counted flies.

On either side, between the broken shutters and the gaping doorways, figures hung on the walls. They were colouring darkly in the sunlight, their skins as black as the stains that had run down the walls and puddled at their feet.

Issel left the bright path, the clean straight way; he stepped aside, to come closer to the nearest of the figures. It was small, so small. Its head was at his own height, but its feet dangled an arm's stretch above the roadway.

Its skin was shimmering, iridescent, liquid tar. As he reached to touch, it erupted outward, a cloud of flies; beneath it was a child, its eyes gone to the birds and the sockets weeping a liquor that was not tears, its own skin looking puffed and sticky, bad meat just begun to rot. Blood had caked its ragged clothes; there was an iron spike through its throat, to keep it hanging there.

The next was a child too, the next after that a woman.

Tulk stood in the middle of the street, as far as he could get from all of them, and made noises. He was being sick, Issel thought, and then he was whimpering in a way that asked please if they could get out of here now?

Issel wouldn't hurry. He crossed from one side to the other and looked at every distending face, met every one of those deaths eye to blank or absent bloody oozing eye. He didn't try to count. He thought there were too many, there were not enough numbers in the world to measure this much loss.

There were no men, in that long parade of the dead. There were old women and young women and children in plenty, and no men. He thought perhaps it was not over, then. These must be the families who had lived here: every house, every room in every house stripped of its people, all of them brought out here into the hard light. Perhaps to see what had been done, the brute bodies of the Marasi soldiers and their cattle before they were taken away; and then the punishment, the whole street condemned.

The men perhaps made to stand and watch while their women, their children were nailed to the walls one by one. And where now for the men, what more than this? He couldn't guess, he couldn't think like a Marasi. He had trouble sometimes thinking like a Sundain.

It was Marasi who had set these people here, but Sundain who had left them. No doubt that was the order, *leave them hanging, let them rot.* Even so, someone should have come for each of these, even if it had to be in the Shine. If no one else would do it, Armina's friends should have come, those who fought the occupation and brought this kind of slaughter down on innocents . . .

We should do it ourselves, but they could not. Two boys, what could they do? Witness, that at least, if nothing more. He went on brushing flies away, looking at deliquescent faces, breathing in corruption.

THE end of the street, the end of the gallery, not yet the end of the lesson. Issel still needed to know what had happened to the men.

His feet wanted to follow their own trail, his old familiar track to the fountains. He was content with that. He and Tulk both had urns on their backs, and where else should they be going? If there was news to be heard, that was where best to hear it: still the heart of the city, although the Marasi had first broken and then possessed it. He wondered if they had to break everything they owned, if anything whole was still reckoned to be dangerous.

He was sure the reverse was true, that anything broken was reckoned to be safe. That must be why they were so savage in Sund, because the constant sullen resistance was still a surprise to them, the sudden outbreaks of violence were still and always unexpected. They might occupy the ground, they might try even to possess the name—Maras-Sund, they said, as though their walls could stretch across the river as their bridge did—but they could never feel safe in their ownership, and so they tried again and again to break what seemed to Issel to be thoroughly broken already. He thought the Sundain could be broken but still deadly, shards from a snapping blade; he thought the Marasi would never understand.

Which was why they staged events like this. Here in the garden of the fountains, this was where they'd brought the missing men. The centre of the city, if no longer the beating heart, at least the place where people gathered: where else would they come, to do this thing? They had built a scaffold and penned the men within it, under guard; one by one they were taking those men out, and—

And Issel couldn't see, for the crush of his own people where they stood around the edges of the park, whispering and muttering and all bearing witness. That was his task more than theirs, and he couldn't do it, they were preventing him. He could hear screams, he could overhear what the people said one to another, and it wasn't enough.

He slipped his arms free of the urn's straps and left it with Tulk. "Stay here," right by the ruins of the eastern gate where the watersellers used to gather, "don't move or I'll lose you."

"I want to come with you."

"No, you don't," and Tulk manifestly didn't, still shaken by more deaths than he had seen in a lifetime, flinching at every hoarse sobbing cry from the scaffold. "You want to stay here and take care of what is ours," and Issel might have meant themselves and their urns, or he might have meant the watersellers and their place of right, or he might even have meant the Sundain and their freedoms. He didn't say, perhaps he didn't know; he left Tulk to chew it over.

And wriggled, squirmed, elbowed, fought his way through the crowd to the front, where even a short boy could see too much; and saw it all, watched it all, witnessed everything.

The scaffold was a cage and a platform and a frame for execution, all at once. From ground to shoulder-height, the props and struts served also as a prison, bars and bolts. Stripped naked, hunched over, bound or chained to the supports were the men who had lived in the street. Officially—it was announced from the platform above their heads, again and again as the crowd shifted, as people left and others came to see—they were condemned for not preventing what had happened below their windows. That weighed equal with collusion, a sergeant said who sweated in his uniform, who watched the crowd as coldly as his men did, their weapons drawn and ready. To do nothing, he said, was as wicked as to join in, and won an equal justice.

And here it was, that justice, Marasi justice: a man fetched up from the understage, already bruised and bloody, shrunken by days without water and more by what he had seen on the last true morning of his life, horror after horror, Marasi dead in an unnatural fog and then his own family nailed to his own wall.

He might think not to care, what happened now. He might expect his own death to be an easy thing, a grateful thing in contrast; who would want to live, who had seen such cruelties?

He might be surprised.

In the centre of the platform stood a frame, man-height and higher, higher than the tall Marasi soldiers in their hats. The man was strung by ropes to all four corners of the frame, spread-eagled; and then the men in bloody, filthy white stepped forward.

Their hands were slow and skilled; their flaying knives were slender, sharp and flexible.

They skinned the man alive, cutting and peeling, tearing off long strips and then cutting again, neatly and without hurry, unmoved by all the screaming, curious perhaps to see how far they could go before their subject died. It was said that the skinners of an earlier court could leave a man with no skin below his neck, and yet bring him live before the Sultan to make his last apology. These men had opportunities today to match that.

Again and again they tried. Some lived a long time under their ministrations, if never long enough to suit; lived and screamed and found new reasons to live, simply in the dreadful manner of their dying. They watched their own skins tossed into buckets, strip by bloody strip, chest-skin and belly-skin, while others flayed their backs. If they could live that far, then who could bear what worse was needed to leave them dead?

They did die, though they fought for life and air enough to go on screaming. Once they were slumped and silent and unequivocally dead, their bodies were flung into a wagon bed behind the stage; Issel couldn't see how many were there already, how many lives and deaths he'd missed. He stayed for all there were remaining, half a dozen wet red ruined things that had been men before. He stayed to see uncaring oxen haul the wagon off towards the strand, where the bodies would be tossed into the river, which was desecration to the Sundain, as the Marasi knew. He stayed to see one final act in the shattered gardens, when the Marasi soldiers emptied all their buckets of skin and blood into the great stone fountain-bowl that supplied all the water for half the city's use.

He watched them, and did nothing. He felt the stir and the sudden silence at his back, and that whole crowd of his people, they did nothing too. He wondered if he had done what the Marasi alone had never managed, in twenty years of occupation: if he had brought Sund to the point of despair, the utter failure of hope.

No need to fight his way back through the press. He stood numb and appalled for a long time, until he could no longer feel the weight of people at his back; he turned to find them leaving, those who had not already left. It was a slow and troubled walk back to where he had left Tulk, where broken stones and broken pipes showed where the water used to spout from long-lost lions' heads.

Where Tulk was waiting, somewhat to his surprise; but not alone.

THE rebel woman, Lenn, was standing with him. Holding his arm in a relentless grip, talking to him in a relentless mutter; as Issel drew close she glanced up and beckoned in a way that would also be relentless, that she would keep up until he joined them.

Stupid, he thought. No better way to draw attention, no more dangerous thing to do. People had died in Sund, for meeting together. In the streets or in back rooms, it didn't matter, if some soldier thought there were too many of you or your behaviour was suspicious. All conspiracy sprang from talking; it was folly at any time, doubly foolish to be doing it in the open. And here, now, with double the usual count of guards at the bridgehead, more at every corner, surely double the spies watching from windows. They would have been expecting trouble, probably hoping for it, at a brutal mass execution; contemptuous and disappointed, they would still all be watching, looking for excuses . . .

He tried to be swift without seeming to hurry, if only to stop the woman waving her arm at him. As he came up, she said, "Issel, I was telling your friend—"

"Not here. Have you no sense? Follow us. Not too closely."

And he scooped up his urn and slung it onto his back, gestured for Tulk to do the same, and led them out of the square. He tried to walk like a *saki* who had lost his source of water, but who knew where another could be found; he thought he was more likely walking like a Sundain boy who had seen horrors and wanted to take his friends away before more horrors could occur. Likely it didn't matter. Everyone who walked away from here today must be walking similarly: frantic, appalled, afraid.

"Don't be scared, little Issel," Lenn said—too close!—at his back. "No more deaths today, we've had enough."

He'd had enough, too much already. He wasn't at all sure about the Marasi. He said, "How can you tell, have you been counting?"

She said, "Yes. But I meant, they will not attack the crowd. Why do this so publicly, and then slay the witnesses? They would lose the lesson."

"Oh, were we being lessoned here? I thought we were being punished."

"The same. The punishment, the lesson: how would you distinguish? You and Tulk must carry the punishment; the whole city is meant to learn the lesson, that it is better to betray an ambush than to see it happen. Every street will be watching for its own sake now, every unfamiliar shadow will be reported, we will all be spying on each other."

"So what we did, Tulk and I, it turns us all against ourselves, more than we were already. Who were we working for, Sund or the Marasi?"

"Issel, you know the answer to that. Every such death benefits Sund."

He had brought them to a cloister, the fallen ruin of an ancient chapel. Who might have worshipped here, he didn't know; there were words on some of the tumbled stones, but of course he couldn't read them. Some foreign people, coming to trade and staying, building a community and a place to worship. What still stood, walls and angular arches in a square around a tangled garden, there was nothing Sundain to it, except that Sund was full of such strangeness, signs of strangers stopping, lingering, moving on.

In one corner of the garden was a stone-rimmed pool. The water was clean enough, this little distance from the bridge; he had filled his urn here more than once, when there were too many Marasi at the fountain. He laid it now in the depression that he'd dug himself, so that its mouth lay close to the pool's wall; he worked a loose stone free with his fingernails, so that water spurted out. Enough of it struck the mouth and ran inside. The rest might not be wasted, not today. He squatted on his heels and let one hand fall loosely into the spitting, spilling rush. He was not sure after all that there had been enough deaths today.

Tulk dropped down beside him; Lenn stood, perhaps a little warily, a little distance off.

He said, "You were here. Good, but not good enough. Have you been there also, have you seen their children?"

"And their wives, their mothers, sisters, yes. Issel, I have their names, every one of them. They have all been counted, and none will be forgotten. But the city needs these cruelties, or it will forget, it will learn to live with occupation. Today wins more to our cause than we have lost on the scaffold there; the Marasi act against themselves. This is what your master refuses to understand, that reprisals work for us. He only sees the loss. We count the dead and the gain together."

Spitting is a Marasi heresy, a sign of contempt for water and all that that implies. To the Sundain it is a shocking gesture, savage, repugnant. The Sundain do not spit, ever, unless to use the water.

Issel spat, and did nothing at all.

LATE that night, there was a light above the city to challenge the Shine. Pure, clean, thin and citrus-sharp, it welled up like water, like a spring, bubbling above the rooftops. In the house, they sneaked into upper rooms and worked the shutters open to look, to speculate. Tel Ferin said nothing, and would not answer questions.

"Either he's afraid, or else he doesn't know," Rhoan said.

"He doesn't know," Issel said, "and therefore he is afraid."

Eventually, Rhoan went to bed, for what patches of sleep she could tack together from the remnants of the night. Tulk watched her go, as he always did watch her, clouded, untrusting.

Issel said, "What?"

Tulk said, "Armina says that someone will betray us . . ."

". . . And you think it will be Rhoan. I know. She knows too, and yet she stays with us. Is that the way of the spy?"

"Well, but who else is there? All our other friends believe, and want to fight; Rhoan—"

"What of Rhoan? She's with us because she found out about us, is that what you mean, she's not committed so of course she must be a spy?"

"No, that's not what I was going to say."

He'd been afraid not, which was why he'd interrupted. "Well, what, then? Rhoan is with us why?"

"Because of you."

A silence, a shrug, and then, "All the more reason, surely, why she would not betray me."

"Perhaps she only wants to betray me," Tulk said, and to that Issel could find no answer.

IN the morning, early, it was Rhoan whom Tel Ferin sent to learn what had caused that curious flaring light. Tulk looked meanings at Issel, all manner of meanings, and stayed close by his side, *we stand or fall together, you and I.*

When Rhoan came back, she came with a tale of wonder.

"The fountain-bowl, that the Marasi—polluted—yesterday: that's where the light was, in the water there. People say that the water boiled or burned all night, until the bowl was dry and, and all the stuff that was in there was just ashes and grease on the stone. The water's coming back now, and people are in there scrubbing, getting rid of the stains. The Marasi aren't doing anything to stop them. They're keeping their distance. As if it had scared them, a little."

"Maybe it was the water," someone said, "cleansing itself."

"As the city will," Tel Ferin said, "in time."

"The water didn't wait," another voice, not Issel's nor Tulk's nor Rhoan's either. They glanced at each other, said nothing, tried to be sure who had spoken.

WHEN they were alone again, Issel said to Tulk, "You still think she will betray us?"

He shrugged. "Someone will, if you believe Armina. Perhaps it's not worth it for us alone, she wants the whole group; or perhaps she wants to betray the rest of us and protect you, and is still waiting for her chance."

"Which I will not give her."

"Which you cannot help but give her. You are too used to being alone; you have no idea how to be one among others, together. You will go off on some solitary fury," *as you did last night,* except that he had sense enough not to say that, even here, "you will leave all the rest of us waiting to see what you do; and we will hear Marasi footsteps and a girl's voice at the door, instead of yours."

Chapter Eight

LITTLE cat, will you slay me a little bird?"

"Magnificence?"

"I think I would like to eat an ortolan."

It was unlikely, it should have been impossible, it had surely needed heaven's help as well as all the doctors', but he was definitely, emphatically mending. She couldn't deny it any longer, however hard she tried. Hope was a serpent, writhing and sly and difficult to crush. As was the Sultan, clearly. His bones were knitting more or less straightly inside that great strong body; his flesh, the massive meat and fat of him, was fighting back against the poisons of infection; his spirit had never been overmastered even by the pain at its extremity, and now it was resurgent.

Even so, after days and days of coaxing him to eat the broths and gruels prescribed, she was startled to hear him express an appetite, and moved almost to tears.

"Oh, my lord, of course . . ."

There was a guilty flush on her face, she could feel it. No one to see, except her own companions; he had sent everyone else away, perhaps for just this reason, to have the chance to eat an ortolan. Jendre was sure the doctors would forbid it. By the smugly conspiratorial look he wore, she was equally sure that he agreed with her.

She didn't know what harm good food could do. There must be a reason, surely, why the doctors risked the Sultan's wrath on a daily basis by insisting on his diet of slops. Pap, he called it, fit for mewling boys with belly cuts, and whose idea was it to give him over to these army butchers? But one small bird, there could be small danger in that; and the benefits—the appetite restored, an eagerness for life and pleasure and flavour—those must outweigh whatever little risk there was. In her mind, absolutely, they did.

"Teo, will you run to the Sultan's kitchens and have them roast an ortolan for His Magnificence? Wait there to bring it back with you," or they would send it in procession and everyone would see. Everyone would learn anyway, soon enough; the Sultan's recovery was all that anyone talked about, and every detail was common knowledge. She could face whatever trouble came, she just didn't want his treat intercepted on its way.

"Of course, mistress." Teo was punctilious in his manners, here in the Sultan's pavilion; he was still overawed, she thought, at being so close to the Man of Men.

She watched the boy run off, and then turned back to the service that she and Mirjana were performing for the world's master, massaging his feet with sweet oils. The army doctors had reversed the way the bed was set, raising it at the foot, but his legs still tended to swell. Puddling of the blood, the doctors said, and prescribed a daily massage. That was another reason, Jendre thought, for this private hour; careful as they were, healing though he was, their ministrations still jarred his broken body, and he preferred not to have his people watching him in pain.

And there might have been a touch of vanity in it, too; he did look ridiculous from where she sat, with his good leg lifted up onto her shoulder now while she rubbed her hands all down the length and breadth of it, working her fingers into that great weight of flesh. He would not like his people to laugh at him behind their hands. Even the mutes could still snigger, though it was a strange sound they made, honking in their noses.

He groaned gently, sometimes he gasped a little; she thought that was Mirjana's work beside her, where the woman was bent over the leg that was broken. That did hurt, but every day she thought it hurt him less; she said that often, daily.

His mother came to see him daily, but did not stay. She was busy, she said, with her hands on every cord and string of empire, knotting what broke to hold his Sultanate together until he could resume his rightful place, however long that took. All the rest of the harem said that she had simply come out of the shadows, where she had always done this work before. Jendre wasn't sure. She found it hard to see the Man of Men as any woman's puppet, even his formidable mother's. He had fought wars to maintain his empire in all its reaches; he had fetched magicians from the far north to expand it, with the bridge into Sund; he had crushed revolts in the army and uprisings among the people. She thought he had never been the weakling that the harem wanted to paint him.

His other wives and women were predictably keen to ingratiate themselves these days, after their earlier neglect. They might also fancy that his incapacity and his mother's busyness would between them leave a space, where a determined woman could win more than favour. They came in flocks, mostly, cooing and fluttering throughout the pavilion, bringing inappropriate gifts and exhausting first his patience, then his temper, at last his mind. That was when Jendre needed the doctors most; they had saved his life, she told them, now they must help to save his sanity.

They had a tent, pitched on the grass at the foot of the knoll. Eunuchs guarded it with swords and trumpets, an island of the outside world within this island world. When the doctors rested, when they ate, when they spoke—to each other, for there was no one else—they did those things within the walls of their little private luxury, their tent. When any woman ventured too close, she would be waved away. Thus was the Sultan's monopoly preserved. When the doctors came forth to tend him, the trumpets sounded in warning and all the women were chivvied out of sight, out of temptation's way. That included not only Jendre, of course, but also Mirjana; those poor doctors weren't allowed even the glimpse of a slave-woman's ankle. When they came first, Jendre had talked to them from behind a screen, so that neither party could be teased into sin; once the tent was pitched, she had held conversations with them through its walls, but even then she'd needed Ferres with her as a chaperone; these days Teo carried messages between them, more fitting to her dignity.

There was an established routine now, when His Magnificence was overplagued with wives. Jendre would glance at Teo, it needed no more than that. He would slip away down the hill and a minute later there would be trumpets sounding, and she and all the women else would be chased off the knoll as the doctors issued forth.

Today had been different. It had been the Sultan himself who sent the women away, in a sudden access of authority; he had sent word downhill to the doctors, not to come till summoned. Jendre could reason it half a dozen different ways, and none of her reasoning mattered. She was here by his choice, he who was lord of the horizons, who was not supposed to notice her amid his throng of women. It shook her to her soul, she was as awed as Teo, still and always. Only when she was away from here, alone at night in her own little house could she think about Salem. Then she was racked: with guilt at betraying her husband, now that she did indeed feel married; with another kind of guilt at her tempting Salem into a fatal liaison that she might now want to turn away from; with a yearning, belly-deep hunger that lingered yet and went unsatisfied. Perhaps he wanted to turn from her, now that he was to be married. It was the wise course for both of them, she should be glad for his sake and yet, and yet . . .

But that was for the dark times. Restless, sleepless nights were for her miseries, all her unforgotten loss. Daylight was for her husband; his needs could push everything else away.

His needs, or now his wants. She watched the pathway and saw the trotting figure come, urgent but careful with his tray, and thought how different this was from the last time she had seen the Sultan eat an ortolan.

No parade here, no hierarchy, no real anxiety but still the same frenetic pace, he had to have it hot. That must have been impressed on Teo in the kitchens, while the bird was roasting; the boy almost sprinted up the slope. *In God's name, don't drop it now . . .*

Light-footed as a thief on a rooftop, Teo didn't so much as slip on a greasy step. He fetched his tray to her, breathless but smiling, excited; no choice today, no little flock of roasts, only the single jewelled bird on its gleaming nest above the tiny brazier, with the cloth beside. She set it all on the bed, close to where the Sultan had already hauled himself—sweating and shaking, but see, how much better he is already!—onto a stack of cushions. His hand reached towards the dish, but it was trembling; she said, "No, no, Your Magnificence, you have done too much. Let me . . ."

And she lifted the sizzling bird out of its nest, both hands to be sure of it, and raised it to where his mouth was stretching open; and she slipped that scorching morsel inside, remembered to leave the head hanging out between his lips, held that lightly between finger and thumb while his teeth nipped down through its neck, dropped the bony little thing onto the tray and then snatched up the cloth, shook it out and draped it lightly, teasingly over her master's head.

"Farewell for now, Magnificence. Speak, when you are ready to be un-veiled; I will be waiting for your word."

Only then, when she knew he could not see her, when she thought he would not be listening or paying any attention to anything beyond what lay inside his mouth, only then did she slip off the bed and cram all her fingers into her own mouth and dance a silent little jig of pain. Teo all but imitated her, trying to gag himself with both hands, smothering his giggles; Mirjana, ever the dignified one, fetched a bowl of water and offered it silently, but Jendre shook her head. Once the burn had cooled—though she thought all her fingertips would be pink tonight, if they didn't blister—she sucked at her fingers more thoughtfully, one by one, where the grease of the ortolan was clinging.

Then she did consent to wash her hands, and wipe them on a towel. She smiled at Mirjana, tugged gently at Teo's ear to win a smile back, and perched herself on the bed beside her lord, content in the silence of her friends to listen to all the soft noises of his pleasure, the chewing and the sucking and the almost voiceless grunts.

———————

SO focused she was on his little sounds and movements, she knew just when he was done. But waited yet, waited till he spoke; and the first word he said was her name, which thrilled her almost as much as Teo when it was his.

"Jendre, little cat."

She was ready on the word, lifting the cloth from his head, wiping his mouth and growing beard with it, trying to seem only practical and not fussy or teasing or maternal. Any of those might irritate a man so used to controlling his own body as he controlled his empire, loose and ruthless and delighted.

He hummed lightly, which she took to be a sign of contentment; then he said, "Do you have that little bird's head?"

"Of course, my lord, here on the tray . . ."

"Good. See that it is sent to my soothsayer. She likes to have a token sometimes, when a thing might matter. I think she wears all my significant moments in her hair."

He smiled then and lay back on his pillows, closing his eyes as though he rested. She could see his tongue working slowly into all the corners of his mouth; sometimes it poked briefly between his lips, and she thought that his closed eyes acted like his cloth of concealment, while he went on savouring what still lingered of the ortolan.

———————

SHE rested on her own account, there at his side, oddly able to drowse easy here where she could not in her own bed. Even without touching, for fear of touching any of his many pains into life again, she was aware of his bulk so close to her, and felt herself protected in his shadow.

So she dozed on the very edge of dreaming, and knew it as she did it, self-aware; and so was immediately awake again when she felt him shift, hurriedly and unexpectedly.

She opened her eyes and saw him sitting quite upright, bloodless and sweating. She thought of the effort of that rise, the pain it must have cost him; and she was rising herself and saying, "My lord, what is it? You should not—" when he cut clean across her as though she had not spoken.

Staring straight ahead across his city, across the river, across his conquest Sund to the land or the sky beyond, he said, "I need—"

And then he was sick, convulsively, agonisingly to a man whose bones were half-unknit and grinding edge to edge.

Jendre gasped and flung to her feet, helpless for a moment, ripped utterly by whatever ripped at him. It was her attendants who moved first, her blessed friends: Teo to pull away the fouled coverlet, to be rid of the stench of it, while Mirjana fetched a bowl, a cloth and water.

"Good, thank you, Mirjana," Jendre said faintly, trying to recover. "Teo, never mind that, drop it somewhere—or, no, take it with you. Down to the doctors' tent, quickly, let them see what he has done. And tell them to hurry . . ."

She wetted the cloth and wiped her husband's face, where he was still sitting up and staring. He sucked at the drip of it, and whispered, "Thirsty," so she asked Mirjana for a goblet. "Only water, nothing more. I think that bird was bad, my lord," *or I was bad to let you eat it, and how far will God punish me, and how far will the Valide Sultan . . . ?*

The doctors came in a rush, in a panic, as they should; but when they saw her they crowded back in another kind of panic altogether, hiding their faces or turning their heads. There were just the three of them; there had been more, all the best men her father had at his command. That some had gone back to the regiment was another sign of the Sultan's recovery, and to be rejoiced at. Now, though, she could wish to have them all again; what if the one she needed, the one who could cure this spasm, was one of those gone?

She, they, the world would never know, if these didn't so much as approach their patient. A fat man, a tall man and a man so scarred that she could see the mutilation even from the back of his head, below his turban; a sabre cut must have done that, and she wondered if he had any face at all.

"Quickly," she cried, "His Magnificence is terribly sick," *and you stand and dither, while the whole world teeters.*

"My lady, we may not, while you are there," and indeed a thin trumpeting from below reminded her; they had outrun their trumpeters, which was commendable, but—

"Don't be absurd. I will excuse the formalities. *Hurry!*"

"You might excuse us, lady, but would your lady mistress? Or your master? It could mean our lives," and they were grovelling now, down on their faces like eunuchs in salute, and she couldn't help the thought that crossed her mind, *or your stones . . .*

"If my master His Magnificence dies, and I am able to blame your neglect of him, then be sure it will mean your lives," she said. "See, though, I will sit behind the bed-board here, where you cannot see me, and my woman Mirjana will run to fetch the Valide Sultan, swiftly now, so that there is not a female in your sight until she come, and then you can do as you will so long as you tend my lord now."

As soon as they were sure she was safely out of sight, there was a rush of feet to the bedside. She heard medical murmurs, the Sultan's answers in groans, one clear sentence from him, "I am thirsty, and so dizzy, sitting up or lying down," and she didn't know whether or not they gave him water, but she heard him being sick again.

After a little, "My lady?" The voice was quiet, and came it seemed from just beyond the bed-board.

"Well?"

"We have some questions for you, if we may . . ."

"Ask."

"His vomitus, that the boy showed us—that was no food that we approved for His Magnificence."

"No, it was not."

"Will you tell us, then, what it was that he ate?"

"Have you not asked himself?"

"He is not in a condition to be much questioned."

No, she was sure not. Neither was she, trembling and self-accusing, having to bite her lip bloody before she could be sensible. "It was an ortolan, roasted, as he liked it. He asked for it, and I sent my boy to fetch . . . Oh, was it a terrible thing that I did?"

"Foolish, surely, to give an invalid such rich food—but that alone should not be causing this. Was there nothing more?"

"Nothing, except from the list that you allow," and most of that the doctors mixed up themselves.

"Strange," the voice said, in that tone that struggles not to say *disturbing* and gives itself away altogether, sounds strained and frightened and alarmed.

Then the Sultan spoke clearly again. "My head aches, and the pain is ebbing in my legs—did you give me poppy? I don't remember any poppy. Bring me drink, there, I am so thirsty . . ."

"Magnificence, can you feel what I'm doing now?"

"What? No. What are you doing? Is that my feet you're at? I can't feel anything in my feet. Why didn't you give me this before? So much pain, so many days of pain and now nothing, except in my head . . ."

"Sire, when you ate the ortolan, did it taste quite as it ought?"

"Mmm? Oh, God's curse on the ortolan, I need that bowl . . ."

Jendre understood the tenor of the question, if the sick man did not; her skin was chilly with a sudden sweat. *I gave it to him, I, with my own hands, after it must have been watched in the kitchens from pluck to pot . . .*

And there was nothing she could do but sit, sit and listen as her husband's sickness worsened, as the doctors grew more frantic: "Is the numbness spreading, Magnificence? Can you feel this, here, if I touch your calf? Behind your knee? No? If you must vomit again, the bowl is ready . . ."

But it was too late to save himself by vomiting, that was clear. She could hear, there was nothing coming up now except the pain of its bringing, and what had come up already must already have done what harm it could, great and terrible harm, to him and all of his.

She had small hope now, for him or for herself and hers—Teo had fetched the bird she ordered, Mirjana had witnessed it, they must all stand condemned—and that was before the Valide Sultan came.

HER coming sounded like a wind, a soft rush of footsteps and whispers; Jendre knew without seeing how her attendants would be fussing around her, *take my arm, madam, lean on me, these steps may be slippery, we should have had the bearers carry you all the way,* while their mistress would be stiff and grim and the last to falter on the climb. Bent as she was, Jendre thought she would stand in the face of the world's ending.

Not so her son's physicians. Jendre heard them fall down on their faces. She had thought that army men would have been braver, or simply more proud than this.

The Valide Sultan gave them no consideration. "What, do you take me for one of my son's women? I live in no man's shadow here. Stand up, all, and show me how the Sultan does."

She didn't speak to him herself, nor he to her. Perhaps their eyes said all that was needed.

"Well."

It was a short word from a mother, to greet her first son's ruin. She had seen it once already, of course, and seen his reprieve. Now she must be gazing down on the death of hope; it was a long time before she spoke again.

When she did, it was to establish facts. "What is happening here? Explain this to me. I saw him this morning, and he was weak but well."

"Madam, he has eaten, and was sick within the hour; and now he has dizziness and pain in his head and a numbness in his extremities, a creeping paralysis rising from his feet and now his fingers. We are in great anxiety for him."

"I am sure that you are. All this has come about because he ate unwisely, I am told? An ortolan, which a foolish wife allowed him, and that has so disordered his internal workings that this dreadful thing has come upon him? The violence of the vomiting, no doubt, has disrupted what was not yet healed, and so we see him in his relapse and slipping from us while we watch."

A wise man might have kept silent there, to let her tell him the tale of his patient's death. Two of the doctors did indeed keep silent; but the third said, "Madam, no. I fear there is more to this." His voice was slurred; Jendre thought she could hear the scarring, all the damage to his jaw. She supposed that a man who had felt steel bite so deep into his head, such a man might have as intimate a relationship with truth as he did with injury.

"Indeed?"

"Madam, too-solid food would upset his stomach and his recovery, but not to this degree. There is some agency at work here that has not yet been discovered."

"Is this certain?"

"I am certain of it. Madam." His colleagues grunted an unhappy confirmation.

"And will he die?"

"That is, ah, less clear. We have induced him to swallow a bezoar stone, which will absorb any residue of poison; there is nothing further that we can do, but wait and watch."

"Well, then." It was time for another story, and she spelled it out. "Poison, you said, and I am sure that you are right. This excuses you, if it was no part of your medicines; that waits to be determined. They will all be tested on yourselves. But I found his guards and attendants all at the foot of the hill there, while he was tended only by his new wife and her own slaves, these here; and the boy runs to the kitchens and comes back with this ortolan, at his mistress's order; and I believe in simple tales swiftly told. If anyone has poisoned the Man of Men, who more likely than one of these, the boy who fetched the food, the girl who gave it?"

"No!" That was Jendre, speaking before she was aware that she could speak, on her feet before she knew that she could stand, striding around from the back of the bed to protect her own and face down her accuser. "Madam, that is not true! I saved his life, I, when all the palace else had set him here in this, this catafalque to die; why would I poison him now? Or my people, after we have spent all these days in serving him, helping him to heal? I, I had my father send these doctors—"

"Who overruled mine, and now he is dead," the Valide Sultan observed, acidly.

"Not yet," *oh, not yet!* But she stole the swiftest glance aside to see, and his legs looked dead already, mottled and waxy. His body trembled in a sudden fit, but the legs did not, they might have been marble; if she had reached out in horror, she was sure that they would have been cold to her touch. She kept her hands folded, and said, "And you cannot blame the doctors, madam, if there has been a foul deed here. They have brought him nothing but good, you know this . . ."

"It waits to be seen," the Valide Sultan said calmly, chillingly. Already there were guards behind each doctor, keeping them apart. "We will medicine these doctors, and watch the results. But if I cannot blame them, child, I can most certainly blame you. You sent his people away, who should have watched over his protection. You sent your own creature to bring food, untasted, untested. If the bird was poisoned, how can we know when? It must be guessed at, if it cannot be shown; and there are many people in the kitchens, watching each other all the time, for fear of just this. We do not know the bird was safe when it left the cooks, but we can assume it. That leaves you or the boy, or you and the boy, and the girl complicit. My questioners will have the truth of that, from one or another of you before this day is out."

Jendre shook her head, wordless, helpless. She didn't look back, but was sure one of those guards had moved into place behind her also.

Startlingly, it was Teo who spoke, from where he was kneeling prostrate beside Mirjana. He lifted his head and said, "Great madam, if you please . . ."

The Valide Sultan glanced not at him, but at one of her guards. That man moved to stand above Teo, and for a moment Jendre thought he might die there and then; but the old woman made a gesture with her hand, *wait,* and said, "Well, boy? What can you say to save your life, and your mistress too?"

"Only this, great madam, that there was another bird cooked with this one. If this was poisoned, then perhaps that also . . . ?"

"Perhaps so. Perhaps I'll have you eat it, to find out."

"I think, I think it has been ate already. By the food-taster, great madam."

"What, was that man at his work after all? He should have been here, though. Why was he not here?"

"I believe that was your order, madam," Jendre said, to spare Teo a little of this interrogation, or at least to share it. "So long as everything His Magnificence ate came from the doctors, I understood you to have said that the food-taster was not obliged to test his medicine. What is healthgiving to a sick man might be dangerous to a healthy one."

"Did I say so? Well, perhaps I did. This did not come from the doctors, though, this bird—but we will consider that later. Continue, boy. Swiftly."

"Great madam, I went to the kitchen and said to the cook that His Magnificence had asked for an ortolan. He sent a kitchen boy to kill and pluck a pair: one for His Magnificence, he said, and one for the taster, who has a taste for them, he said . . ."

"Indeed. And well he might acquire one, keeping pace always with my son's appetites. The cook may have saved himself, by sending a bird to his friend; you should have ordered it, girl, but it happened, and so he may have saved you too. We will go to see the food-taster."

"Madam," one of her eunuchs, murmuring, "we could have him fetched . . ."

"Undoubtedly we could, but I think we will not do that." She glanced briefly at the Sultan, and in a moment's weakness, Jendre thought it was a kindness in her, not to send for a man who might be this sick. But this was the Valide Sultan, and kindness in her would be a weakness; she went on, "I am curious to see how a man lives when he should be attending to his master's needs, and is not."

"Madam, your word was that he need not . . ."

"This order did not come from the doctors. He knew that my son was recovering, all the palace knew; he should have been ready in the kitchens, if he was not here. You will not argue with me, girl. Your life is a thread, and mine to snap."

"Yes, madam."

WHEREVER the Valide Sultan went, she went in a procession. This was the first time Jendre had been a part of it: on foot behind her palanquin, behind her senior eunuchs in their dark robes and caps, followed by her own attendants, surrounded by guards. Not quite a prisoner, perhaps, not being paraded in her guilt and on her way to death—but not far from that, not far at all. What they found, what they came to at the end of this procession would determine whether she lived or not, and her friends with her.

Teo had known his way to the Sultan's kitchens—of course he had, he was a boy and into everything, getting everywhere—but this was all new to her, and she thought perhaps to the Valide Sultan also. She thought that one could live a long lifetime in the palace and never know where the food was cooked or how the servants lived. Their way led them round behind a

stand of trees and here suddenly was an outcrop of the main harem building, a run of structures that billowed smoke and scented steam, kitchens
and laundry too.

The Valide Sultan left her palanquin, gazing about her with a stifling
lack of interest, while the courtyard that had been so busy moments earlier became suddenly and entirely still, every idling cook or scurrying servant suddenly prostrate as they realised who had broken into the ordered
routines of their day.

A word with her own people, and she was led into the sprawl of buildings. Jendre followed swiftly, with a beckon to Mirjana and Teo to keep
up.

On foot, this was still a procession. It stretched out longer, here where
the corridors were narrow and the room to move between counters and
ovens and racks of meat was narrower still. Jendre was too far back to
hear what was said at the front, she could barely see who spoke to whom,
only the one glimpse of a terrified cook falling to his knees, to his face if
he were wise. He must have been picked up again and brought along, as
guide or sacrifice; he was not there when the procession moved on, when
Jendre passed the place where he had been.

Through kitchens and past cold rooms and stillrooms, into a warren of
stores and sleeping quarters. The food-taster—she didn't know his name,
and felt that she should; she thought that no one in this whole parade would
know his name except the cook who might be leading it, and she thought
that that was wrong—apparently rated a room of his own, where most
slept two or three to a pallet and wherever they could find the space to
spread it.

Perhaps she should call it a cell, rather than a room. It was small and
cramped and windowless, and she had to elbow her way between the press
of eunuchs before she could win through to the doorway, where she found
herself shoulder to shoulder with the Valide Sultan, except that Jendre's
shoulder stood so much higher and straighter.

Even so, it was the bent old woman who mattered, here as everywhere,
her word that carried weight. They stood there in the doorway and gazed
inside, and the Valide Sultan said, "It seems that you might survive the day
after all, girl—though that matter is still mine to decide."

"Yes, madam."

One thing was certain sure, the food-taster would not survive the day.

Like his master, he lay desperate and helpless in his bed, though his was a mean cot with no light except what fell in at the doorway.

Jendre wouldn't have recognised in him the sleek, glossy figure she had seen before. His hair was wild and matted with sweat, his eyes were wide and staring, unnaturally black; as they watched he was taken with a fit that shook his head and body violently but somehow not his limbs. It was as though the inner cords were cut, so that he had no means to move them.

"A creeping paralysis, the doctors said." The Valide Sultan tapped her stick thoughtfully on the slab tiles and went on, "I would not move this creature now, but we should have brought one of those doctors, one at least."

"I don't think any doctor could do him any good now, madam."

A snort. "Neither do I, but he is in advance of my son, if only a little. A treatment could be tried on him, likely too late, but if it showed any signs of efficacy, it could then be tried again on His Magnificence, and perhaps be in time."

Jendre thought these were the counsels of despair. She thought both men were equally advanced in their decay, and neither could be saved. She understood how it would make sense to the Valide Sultan to sacrifice the food-taster in experiment; indeed it was his task, his role in life to take the trial on His Magnificence's behalf, with every mouthful that he tested.

And what a failed test it was, that had resulted in two men poisoned where there should only have been one, one at most. Foolishly, she opened her mouth and said so.

"Indeed. One could blame your husband's impatience for that, or his greed, which is the same thing; but how long should the great wait for their dinners, while they watch to see if their food-tasters die of it? This took a while to set on. I do not know what poison acts so slowly; let us discover. And let us leave this building, it is malodorous."

Her son was dying, and she complained about the smell. It was true, though, that the taster's cell was stinking. It was too dark to see clearly, but she thought he had spewed up onto the floor, having no one to fetch or hold or empty a bowl for him.

THE interrogation of the cook was brief and merciless. It took place in the courtyard behind the kitchens, where he was flung on the cobbles at the feet of his cold mistress.

He had seen his friend the food-taster, in his death throes; he understood what that sight portended, both for the Sultan and for himself.

He gabbled, without waiting to be questioned. He had done nothing, nothing wrong, nothing unusual. He had cooked two birds, yes, instead of one; that was good, wasn't it, that was cautious? Usually he cooked a dozen and someone chose, sometimes even Her Magnificence—usurping his master's title in his terror, ascribing it to her who had brought this terror to him—would do the choosing. This time no one offered, no one proposed, so there were only two birds and he chose himself, which for the taster and which for his lord. But he had had them fetched and killed, drowned in the forbidden brandy and then plucked by the boy who kept them, he had seen it freshly done, there in the corner, Her Magnificence could see the feathers still, waiting to be gathered up. The birds had not been sick then, fine healthy birds, all of them, and eating well in their cage there.

Still warm they were when they came to him, as they ought to be, fat and fine; and he had set them in the tray, yes, and put them in the oven, and taken them out just when they were gleaming gold and perfect. And so divided them, one for the Sultan and one for his friend, and that was all that he had done and all that he had ever done and there had never been any harm in it, no poison, he didn't understand how poison could ever have come to them but not by him, not that, for sure not that . . .

Jendre believed him; why would he poison his friend and the Sultan both, knowing that it would be brought back to him?

Even so, she thought that he would die for it. Here and now, she thought, by a eunuch's a bowstring. She turned her head aside, not to watch; and saw how Teo had drifted away from this intense group and over to where the feathers were, and a wooden crate with a barred top.

She saw him bend, she saw him reach a slender arm down through the bars—and then she saw someone hit him from the side, a diving, frantic figure. She cried out, she couldn't help herself, as they rolled in the dust like dogs; skullcaps went flying and bare-shaven skulls gleamed in the hot light, bare feet kicked, Teo's voice was shrill and savage against the other's grunting wordlessness.

Not so little now, her little Teo, he overtopped her by a thumb's width; but the other was older, bigger, more used to brawling. Unobserved, left alone, Teo would have come back to her bruised and bleeding, if he came back to her at all. Likely he would not, the way the other boy's hands were digging at his throat . . .

But they were not unobserved, nor left alone. Jendre's cry attracted attention, even if the tumbling boys had not. Men hissed and ran, leaped on them, pulled them apart and then dragged them both forward to face the Valide Sultan's instant sentence, *oh, Teo* . . .

Jendre thought she would lose him, there and then; but before the old woman could pronounce an unkind judgement, Teo lifted a clenched hand and opened it, showed them all a scrap of green.

"Great madam, my lady," an appeal to Jendre, as if she could have any weight in this, "see, the birds were feeding on this, and they never should . . ."

The Valide Sultan's face twitched. Whatever doom she had been about to utter, she postponed. "What is it?"

"Hemlock, great madam. It is a poison, but it does not kill the little birds. We were always warned to beware of it, in my master's house; the birds feast on it, and if men net and eat the birds . . ."

They knew what happened if men ate the birds, they had seen it twice today.

Jendre said, "He has worked all these years in my father's gardens, madam; he knows plants, and their abilities."

"No doubt. But how did these birds come to be fed on hemlock, if its appearance is so well-known that he could see it in a pecked shred?"

Silence. Teo had done what he meant to do, offered his evidence in defence of his mistress and himself; he had nothing more to offer, and the other, the one who had attacked him was mute.

Literally mute, the cook said. "That is the boy who feeds and kills the birds, great madam. He knows his guilt, he would confess it sure, but he cannot speak, nor write . . ."

He could understand, clearly; his eyes stood out in his skull, and he struggled against the arms that held him. Struggled to lift a hand—to point, Jendre thought, at someone in the old woman's entourage—and to mouth words hopelessly into shape, to make himself somehow understood.

But the Valide Sultan made a gesture, two fingers tapped against her throat, and one of her people dropped a fine waxy cord around the young man's neck, pulling it tight with a swift and casual expertise, the efficiency of practice.

After that, he didn't hurry. It was a slow and cruel strangulation, scrabbling fingers and kicking legs, all useless; a darkening face to foreshadow a darkening vision; the mouth desperately working but not for words, only for a breath of air. Even so, Jendre was surprised that he was allowed so immediate a death, so easily achieved. Days of public torture she would have foreseen, for the man who poisoned the Sultan.

When the body slumped at last, the Valide Sultan turned to the cook, still on his knees, still grovelling. "He fed the birds on hemlock," she said, "by what folly or for what vengeful reason we cannot know," *and it is too late to learn*; "but he was yours to train and yours to watch. Besides, you cooked the birds. I cannot let it be said that the man who fed death to the Sultan was suffered to live."

She tapped her throat again, the same quiet gesture. Another bowstring, another brutal loop; soon—not soon enough for Jendre, who was shaking now—another body on the cobbles.

Mirjana was at her side, holding her hand, but it didn't help. *That one fed the birds, that one cooked them; this one,* her Teo, *fetched death to the Sultan, and not the cook but I fed it to him, I . . .*

The same thought might have been in the old woman's head, or else she read it in Jendre's stiff silence. She turned to find her, all unsmiling, and said, "The boy lives, because he discovered the hemlock to us; no reason else. And you—you live because my son was fond of you. No reason else."

Jendre dropped to her knees in acknowledgement, in relief. There were noises and movement all around her, but her mind was swimming, she couldn't follow them. By the time she lifted her head, the courtyard was empty except for herself, her slaves, two bodies and the distant rustlings of caged and blinded birds.

BY the time she came back to the pavilion of his sickness, her husband the Sultan was dead, the Man of Men, and bare blades stood guard above his body.

Part 4

Chapter One

RUMOUR, Issel thought, was like the Shine, whatever way you looked at it.

It was hard to catch in daylight, but in the dark it over-arched the city.

On the upper side of town it didn't count for much, people hardly knew it, but down near the river it filled the night, it pooled in the poorer quarters, inherent and inescapable.

Soft, liquid, insubstantial, it had a power and a presence that far outweighed its worth.

It was deceptive, it was dangerous, it carried a poison at its heart—and yet people used it, because they had to, because there was nothing else. People who went out at night on secret errands, they used the Shine to find their way because they dared not show a better light; people who plotted against the Marasi occupation, they listened to rumour because that was all the news they had.

———

RUMOUR said that the Sultan of Maras had died in an accident, come home dead from his wars, been slaughtered in a sudden rebellion of palace eunuchs.

Rumour said that the Sultan was sick of love, that he had taken yet another wife and exhausted himself on her. It said the old man was prostrate in his bed, and his doctors held out little hope for him.

Rumour said that there was nothing amiss with the Sultan, only that he was indulging all his appetites as he always had behind the high walls of his harem, while his generals plotted against him.

Whatever rumour said, something was amiss with the Marasi, and it was more than petty resistance could explain. There seemed suddenly to be both more and fewer of them; whole battalions had been seen marching back across the bridge, but at the same time there were more patrols in the streets and extra men on guard at the bridgehead and the barracks. Wherever you saw Marasi troops, where you used to see half a dozen, there were a dozen now. They went nowhere except in packs, but they did go everywhere. Rumour said or tried to say that they were pulling back, abandoning Sund, retreating to their own bank of the river, driven out by the fever of resistance. Sometimes rumour deserved nothing but scorn, and received it in due measure.

They were nervous, the more sensible said; some kind of political or military upset in Maras had set them on edge. They needed more soldiers there, which meant that those left behind needed to be more watchful. To the Marasi, watchful meant heavy-handed, assertive, brutal. There was no need now for the rebels to be provoking a reaction, to keep Sundain hatred on the simmer. The scaffold still stood in the fountain gardens; people died there every day. They died more simply too, in the streets and in their own houses, wherever Sundain stubbornness met with Marasi temper. Either the officers were no longer in control of their troops, or else no longer trying to control them, or else an order had been given to let the yoke lie more heavily on the city for this time, to keep the Sundain crushed.

It would not, could not work. Lenn had said it already, privately to Issel and Tulk by the chapel pool, probably to others, perhaps time and time again. Now she said it once more, with gentler words but just the same meaning and just the same intent. Just the same truth, too: Issel hated it, hated her for saying it, believed it utterly, all three.

"Every death brings more resentment," she said, "more whispering, more stone-throwing from the children, more sabotage, more plots."

"More deaths."

"Yes, Issel, more deaths—and too many of them ours, and too few

Marasi. Every death of ours brings us fresh support, but suffering alone is not enough; we must fight back, and be seen to do it. Not a leader—figureheads are too easily cut off—but the people need a lead, a voice to urge them on, a purpose they can understand."

They were back in the Silkmart, in the upper room, and Issel would never have known it just by looking. Not everything had changed, but everything he'd noticed or remembered from before. It was full daylight, for a start; and river or road or market, inside or out, daylight changes a place as well as its uses.

Even in the Terror—as they'd started to call these days of occupation, not between themselves but in public, whenever they could and whoever they were talking to—the people needed places to trade, to buy and sell, if what they bought was far less than they needed and what they sold was fundamentally themselves, far more than they could afford.

That was how Issel and his friends had contrived to come here, because the school too needed to trade. Tel Ferin gave out coins reluctantly, and those who cultivated the fields and farms outside the city were seldom interested in coppers. Issel at least knew enough not to buy anything grown down by the strand, in the Shine; nor would he let his schoolmates do it. Which meant hard bargaining, with people who valued money little and treasures less; what use was silk to a farmer, or an ivory carving to a peasant in his hut? What they valued was more immediate, the kind of service that Tel Ferin was loth to allow. Young people are hungry people, though, and none of their gifts would turn water into bread.

By his reluctant dispensation, then, Rhoan and Tulk and Issel had come armed with flasks of purified water, to offer what they could do in exchange for whatever they could get. They weren't expected back much before sunset; it might easily have taken them all day to find people with food to spare, who stood in need of their particular talents.

That was their excuse, persuasively provided in advance. In fact—because everyone knew Issel, and because the rebel chapter was striving to spread word about the water-magic as much as Tel Ferin was striving to suppress it—they had been busy all morning straightening a bent axle without need of blacksmith's tools or forge, putting a lethal edge on knives and hatchets and a rusted sickle, mending broken pins and breaking old iron brackets into useful and tradeable sections.

Nor were all their skills watery, or physical. Tulk and Rhoan could read letters and write replies; they could all take messages and promise their delivery, even in these difficult and dangerous times. They could do this, they could do that; they could fill their bags and baskets with flour and greens and oil, with rabbits in their skins and partridges in feather. Not with fish. From the river or from the Insea, they might still have swum in the Shine, and Issel would not have them.

A morning's work, then, had brought them what they needed, and bought them all the afternoon; and so they were in the upper room again.

Daylight changed a room. It made this one smaller and less threatening, less broody, more solid and reliable and square.

So too did company change a room. Last time it had been filled with strangers, wary and angry and afraid by turns. That gave the room a shape in Issel's head, a looming darkness, made it a place not to come back to. Now he was here regardless, with his friends and in the light; and here too were Lenn and the man Gilder, who had wanted to send a wet and heavy message back to Tel Ferin, Issel's head or Tulk's. He was not so fierce today. Issel thought that he was trying to be grateful, all begrudging and unpractised.

The five of them were all. *No more than we need*, Lenn had said, *this first time.*

In case we fail, Issel thought that she had meant; or else, perhaps, *in case we succeed*. She wouldn't want the rebel chapter to see her fail. If she succeeded, though, if it came easily to her hand, she would dearly like to be the only one who knew how it was done; and so Gilder was there, to be sure that she was not. The two of them thought they could hold a secret together, cupped in their mutual distrust. Issel didn't understand people, but he did know what they wanted. These two, they wanted to keep a grip on what they had: the leadership, the power, the ears and obedience of their people.

That much Issel really didn't understand. He thought he might need to undermine it later, teach some of the others what these two had already learned.

If they were able to learn it, or if he was, or his friends.

———

DAYLIGHT and company changed a room, and so too did furnishings. Before, there had been a table and a lamp, and he remembered nothing else;

people sat on the floor, or else they stood around the walls, and so they filled the space. Dark and crowded, that was how it was in his head. And possessive, retentive, reluctant to let leave even that little that it had, a little light, a little water, a pair of frightened boys.

Now, in so much light, with so few people, it had another focus. It was a room with purpose, a practical space. You could come here with questions and work to find the answers.

There was a long table set along one wall, a small one to the side with a chair tucked in. The shutters stood open to the sun; secrecy was a thin white muslin curtain, as innocent as hope. An open door looked out onto the gallery and down to the inner courtyard. That ought to be empty at this hour, its nightly circles out begging or thieving or scavenging as they could. But the streets were not safe now for scavengers, for anyone without an errand and a home; the courtyard was crowded with its own people and more, refugees and the bereaved. Armina stood guard on the gallery, to keep them from pressing up the stairs.

On the table was a bowl of water, freshly drawn from the fountain, where it rose clear and clean again at the heart of the city. There was a bucket more below the table.

There was another bowl, a dry bowl to work in. This should have been a kitchen, Issel thought, with a fire and ingredients and spices, spoons; except that there needed no ingredients beyond the water, a fire would help not at all, and all the work would be done with hands and words and power.

Or else they would only get their fingers burned and the table wet, while they embarrassed themselves and each other. Issel was ready for that. He knew little of his own abilities, less of his friends', but one thing he was sure of, his gift was stronger than theirs. Corrupted by the Shine, grown twisted and tainted beyond measure, but still stronger. If he couldn't do what the book had said, then no one here could do it.

Lenn clearly believed that too. Tulk she would accept, the two boys came together, but Rhoan was twice unwelcome: once because she was new, and that meant the boys had been talking where talking was always dangerous; and twice because she was unnecessary, bringing nothing to the table that Issel could not bring alone.

Issel had had to argue for her, where Tulk was conspicuously silent. He had argued lightly, casually: "She worked it out, we didn't tell her about you. And she wants to be here, she is Sundain too and we might need her yet. She has a delicacy of touch that I can't match, that rivals Tel Ferin's own, and if delicacy should be crucial, then who better . . . ?"

He had not shown to either one of them what he understood, that he was arguing for her life. Nor that he was speaking nonsense, driven by fear for her, while his own confidence crowed unspoken.

"Besides," he had added, "she is here with me. We came together, and we will leave together. Now or later." *Alive or dead*, but he was saying that the quiet way, the confident way, to these people who knew what he had done in the street in Daries. They had power too, but not like his; Gilder had a long knife at his belt and a willingness to use it, but Issel could not be afraid of that, with so much water in the room. "If you want my help, you must also accept Rhoan's."

She had smiled at him, half-amused to find herself so defended, as though she had no idea of the stakes. Perhaps she hadn't. She hadn't been in Daries, she hadn't seen what the Marasi had done in revenge; she'd been told, but this was fundamental to Issel. What you hadn't seen, touched, smelled, felt, you couldn't truly know. Rhoan was still playing power games with Tel Ferin, working behind his back, trespassing on his hidden knowledge; she might not have realised, she might not be able to understand that her life was forfeit here.

He thought he could protect her, or he would never have let her come. He still preferred not to put it to the test. It should be easy to make her seem useful and Tulk with her, to make himself the awkward one who was no good without his friends. It only meant that he couldn't be first to try the purifying spell, although he was their best hope.

On the smaller table were pen and ink and a thin sheaf of paper. It was dangerous, he thought, to write this recipe down. Dangerous to write anything and be caught with it when the Marasi were so mistrustful; half their soldiery couldn't read, and would take anything on paper to be seditious. In this instance, it wouldn't matter if they could read or not, they'd still be right.

But all these people, friends and rebels, they were the reading kind. They weren't sure a thing was real or true unless it was written down, they couldn't keep a hold on it. Lenn and Gilder wanted to have the secret safe, which meant having it in their hands; they didn't worry about keeping themselves safe, which meant having their hands open and empty as Issel did, and rarely even wet.

Tulk at the table, then, to write down what Issel recited; and at the same time—because time was precious, betrayal was common, lingering was dangerous and hadn't they been warned to beware of treachery?—it was only good sense to have Rhoan act on Issel's words.

Lenn and Gilder would have liked to try themselves, but they were untrained and out of their depths. They had talent enough to use the purified water for simple things, violent things; so much was in the blood. *Anyone can set a fire,* Tel Ferin was fond of saying, *but how many are there who can make it dance?*

Not these two, that was certain. They meant to learn, though, this trick at least; so they would watch and watch again, try and fail and try again until they mastered it. They had an avid, hungry look about them, pressing close against the table where Rhoan stood ready. Even so, she who thought sideways, who never trusted the simple course, Lenn was frowning, glancing from the girl to one boy, to the other.

She said, "Why must Tulk write to Issel's dictation? It was Tulk who read the book you took this from. Tulk could write it, while Issel makes the working."

She meant, *we do not need the girl.* Which was true, Issel could talk and work at the same time, but he wanted them not to think of that. He said, "Tulk can't remember everything that was in the book."

"Oh, and you can? You, who couldn't even read it?"

He shrugged. "Of course."

"It's a street trick," Rhoan said, just when she should and with just the right mocking in her voice. "These beggar boys can't read, so they learn to memorise. They sell gossip as news, and run messages all across the city, and never understand the half of what they carry. Like pet birds, chanting phrases without ever learning what they mean. Issel knows all the words for what we have to do today; but I don't suppose he could do it, any more than you can, until one of us shows him how."

She did it perfectly, as if they'd thought to practise on the way. It was just what he wanted, more than he'd hoped for; she was so convincing that he flushed, and that was perfect too, because Lenn for sure had seen it.

"It's a circus," she grunted, with a degree of contempt that clearly made her feel better. "Get on with it, then, the three of you."

Issel had never seen a circus, they no longer came over the river to Sund; but of course he'd heard stories, and he thought that Lenn was right. A circus was a performance, a team working to bedazzle the gullible with tricks not so clever as they appear. He felt back in his mind for those long nights and early mornings, when Tulk had read the book to him; he recalled the voice, the words, just as they had come to him. He didn't understand about forgetting. If you had a thing, you held it. His little things were precious to him, and so were words worth keeping. That was one more reason to dread the poison of the Shine, that it taught you to forget.

"Issel?"

That was Tulk, with ink in his pen and ready to scratch. Issel thought that was why people who relied on books and paper did forget what they claimed to value; he thought they never really had a hold on the words at all, they let them run out through their pens onto the paper and then the paper had all the wisdom and they had none, and if they lost the paper . . .

Well. He could share what he had, and lose nothing. Rhoan thought the opposite was true, that he was just a gutter for the words to run through, with their meaning never touching him at all. She was wrong; she would learn.

He opened his mouth and began.

"*There is a sense in water, like the shadow behind the gleam of silver, and those whose minds are tender to that sense can find it out and harness what is most potent. In crude water, from rain or well or river, it is sparse and fugitive, and few can use it to any good, though there is always harm to be done by the ignorant. Even the crudest water, however, may be brought perfect by an adept; and perfect water may be tested drop by drop against a bucket, a barrel, a cistern of its simplex source and be found not wanting.*

"*To Perfect a Quantity of Water:*"

And now they were listening, now they were attentive; only Tulk's rapid scratching worked on their silence, and that only to emphasise how deep it was.

"*It is needed only wisdom and ability, nothing more. No source of heat, no herbs, as the ignorant will have it; no moonlight, no chanting, as the superstitious do. The adept takes a bowl of good clean water, and lays his hand upon it. With his inner eye, he seeks within the water, to where he may find that dark sense, or the shadow of its lurking; and then he turns it to the light. Then will all the water look that way, and be fit use for the clumsiest of hands, the most stumbling will."*

Issel paused. He had closed his eyes, the easier to bring the words up from where they had been kept; now he opened them to find Lenn scowling at him.

"Is that all?"

She always did sound snappish, but now she seemed to feel personally affronted, as though *clumsiest* and *stumbling* had been spoken straight to her. In a way, they were. Issel was not above playing side games where he could, to hit back for himself or for his friends.

"No," he said now. "There is more, much more, we read through all the book together; but we thought that was clearest. If you can work with anything, you had best work with that. Afterwards, it gets harder."

"No one could learn anything from that," she said, "it's meaningless. High words and hollow, the same empty rhetoric that the adepts have always used to convince us of their art's great mystery."

"We are not so easily persuaded," and for once Gilder stood on the same ground, and they spoke for each other. "If you can't bring us better than this, boy, you were better not to come."

For answer, Issel only nodded. Towards Rhoan, where she stood with her hand spread out across the bowl, just to touch the surface of the water, so light as not to raise a ripple. He was surprised to find how much faith he had in her; so much that it was a jar, a wrench, something more than disappointment when she twisted away and shook her head, and said, "I'm sorry, Issel, I can't find it," for all the world as though it was himself that she was letting down.

"Try again," he said urgently, feeling the weight of Lenn's glare, *you see? I said, there's nothing there to use . . .*

Rhoan did try again, and fail again. Issel didn't understand it, the words in the book seemed so clear to him, so obvious that they didn't really need saying; surely not to someone so long learning at Tel Ferin's hand. It seemed to him that what the words said was no more than what he did daily when he worked with water, whether what he was using was blessed by Tel Ferin's touch or drawn pure from the well or taken from a cistern after sitting in the Shine.

But Rhoan wasn't doing herself any good here. She said, "I don't think I have an inner eye," mock-deflated and making to pout. Issel could have stepped forward, put her out of the way and set his own hand to the water; but he didn't like Gilder's look, nor trust his temper.

He said, "Wait, the book has other ways to talk about it. Tulk, write this: *When the water be opened to the light, it is as when words are joined to music to make song. The whole lies in both together, and each is weak without the other. That which must be found in base water sleeps like an animal in shadow, and must be woken lightly. There is peril here. If your soul seek the peril, where it lurks, there you will find the power resting. Touch it only, and it turns to life. It is like to your own spirit, in a glass; if you are swift and brutal, so will it be. Beware.*"

"Oh, I can go gentle," Rhoan muttered, "but I don't know where to go. Issel, you're the one for peril, you come look . . ."

She couldn't see the peril where it stood, close beside her, with its knives. Issel tried to believe that he was being fanciful; would they really kill her, because she couldn't work the trick they wanted? No, surely not. But they could certainly kill her because she knew their faces and their names and meeting place, because she was no use to them alive and might be dangerous. He'd seen death come for less than that. Fear and a harsh life had not made the Sundain a kinder people; and rebels must always be wary of betrayal.

Tulk thought that she would betray them anyway. He was saying nothing at his table, scratch, scratch.

"I don't understand gentle," Issel said, "that's why we need you. Listen: *Water holds its secret power as a seed its strength, enfolded, within every commingled droplet. Warmth will reach it, as the sun's warmth wakens seed: the warmth of spirit, blood and thought. As the dark of still water acts as a glass to show yourself and act on you, so you can act on power, to stir it into wakefulness. You bring the light, you are the light it seeks and hungers for; it is only dark in waiting. It will reach, where you offer. All a myriad droplets reach as one, to where your hand shines in summoning.*"

Even Tulk seemed defeated suddenly, letting his pen drop from his fingers, muttering, "Are you sure you're remembering it right? It didn't seem so vague in the book, I was sure I understood it there, it was in my hands ready, there to do. Now . . ."

"Perhaps the magic is in the book," Lenn said, with all the certainty of one who did not understand. "Whether he remembers the words or not, it may be a spell bound up in ink and paper, needing to be read out from the page, fresh every time. Fetch us that book, it's what you should have done before, sooner than try to be clever."

"No," Rhoan said, "wait. I think perhaps I do hear what it's saying now. It's a man's voice and I was trying to do it manly, seeking out the darkness to confront it; but it doesn't really say that. What I need isn't in the water, it's in me. It always is. I taught you that, Issel, remember? Of course that's what the book forgot to say; or else he didn't realise, the man who wrote it down. Men do a lot without knowing."

That was a saying, or half a saying; *women know a lot without doing* was the other half, and Issel had heard it often and often in his life.

This woman, though, this girl, she reached her hand out again, very much doing; and if that hand was tremulous, there was no blame there, with so much hanging on the moment.

She stretched out her hand, and laid it like a blessing on the water. Her turn to close her eyes, to turn inward. Tulk laid his pen down and came away from the table to stand with Issel, no more circus.

Issel saw a shy little shimmer in the water under Rhoan's hand, although she had not touched it. He heard gasps from Lenn and Gilder both, and thought it was half greed, half disappointment. They fought each other, constantly; now perhaps they had more to fight for. *One of your friends means to betray you*—if one of these lost that fight, might they not hit back by telling what they knew? The tale of the city was scarred with petty rebellions; half had failed, and the other half had been betrayed. A secret shared is a secret broken. Bitterness, the loss of what little respect or power or authority you had scraped to yourself from the thin pickings of Sund in its occupation, that might sour a man to turn against his own people. Or a woman. It had happened, time and again. He could be watching the seeds of it here and now. Too potent a gift, this might prove to be . . .

Too late to take it back. There was more than a shimmer in the water now. It didn't seethe or boil, there was no steam and almost no agitation, but something stirred it none the less. It seemed to move internally, as though every smallest droplet in the bowl was turning independently.

For a moment the surface seemed black and reflective, Rhoan's hand in a thousand broken shards; then it was silver, and it burned like shattered light.

Then it was still again, and water, and it seemed like nothing more.

"Don't touch it now, girl," Gilder said. "Lenn, you are the stronger of the two of us," and what had it cost him to admit that, in front of witnesses? "You see if you can do anything with that."

"Better to see if the weaker can. We all march at the pace of the slowest." But she didn't press the point; indeed she was already stretching her own hand out, her fingers thin and nervous and determined. Her lips moved—again thin, nervous, determined, like all her body and her spirit too—and her fingers touched the water. A little steam arose to twine about them. She spoke a word aloud, and dipped them in; made a spoon of her hand and scooped out a palmful, worked it with her other hand and showed them the result, a soft quivering ball of water wreathed in mistiness.

"It is exact," she said, "I can feel it. Just as it comes from Tel Ferin. With this I could break a door, or kill a man, or . . ."

Her shrug said that she knew how weak those acts were, how far they fell short of what was needed; and they were as much as she could do, and as much as she would ever be able to do, and so she would do them regardless.

"Now is the time," Gilder said. "Now, while the Marasi are fewer in number and distracted. Now is our chance to strike, and strike hard; we may not have Tel Ferin, but we can make more of this than ever he would sell us, even if we could afford—"

"I don't know how often I can do that, actually," Rhoan interrupted. She did look tired, she did sound shaken. There was a set look to her face, though, that said more; to Issel it said, *I don't know how often I am prepared to do that for you, for your war.*

She hadn't been with the boys in Daries, nor gone with them to the fountain, but she was Sundain; she knew.

"Well," Lenn said, "there is more than one of you; and we will try ourselves. Perhaps anyone can do it, when they know the way of it."

Perhaps so, but Issel was going to see his friends in favour first. He pushed Tulk forward, while Gilder was pouring off Rhoan's water into a flask and refilling the bowl with fresh.

Tulk was anxious and purposeful, both together. He wanted to be a part of this, to matter; Issel had left him behind, and now Rhoan was threatening to do the same.

He spread his hand wide over the water, as Rhoan had done before him; his lips seemed to move, and for a moment Issel thought he was going to mutter something aloud, as Lenn had. That would have won him a cuff from Tel Ferin; it might win him teasing from his friends later. It would do him no good else, magic didn't lie in the voice and it wasn't subject to command.

Tulk wasn't quite so graceless as to talk to the water. He did scowl, in a way that would have brought giggles in the school. His fingers trembled, his tendons stood out like tight-strung wires; Issel was as tense himself, willing him not to fail.

Rhoan had made the water shimmer; Tulk made it steam. Only lightly, a slow vapour rising, that had nothing to do with heat. Through that mist, they could see it suffer the same changes: from clear to black, and so to silver, and so home. It was Gilder this time who confirmed the change in it.

"Perfect," Tulk breathed, obviously liking the word as much as he liked his own part in making it so.

Rhoan applauded at his side. "You did that very manly," she said.

Sharper than Issel, always ahead of him: he thought that she was right, that this had been a different road to the same end. She had had to go against the sense of the writing; Tulk would have gone with it all the way. There was a lesson in that.

Issel had his own way, in any case. A lifetime's working with water, with only instinct to follow, learning through play and through need, through fear: if he could work with unperfected water, as he could—and like Tulk he liked the word, was happy to use it, found it better than blessed or purified or any other—then he thought it was because he did this every time, perfected it at a touch before he used it.

Easy, then. Another fresh bowlful ready; he stepped up before he could be asked, before he could be displaced by Lenn's eagerness. His friends had shown their usefulness to the rebellion, and he'd best confirm his own.

So he reached his hand across the bowl as the others had, although his instinct as always was to dip his fingers in. He'd never done this, to try to change water but not to use it; he'd never seen a need. Nor had he ever seen it behave that way under his touch, go to shadow and then to light . . .

Still, he'd listened to his own voice reciting, he'd seen it twice done differently; he still thought he knew how to do it himself.

He gazed at the surface of the water, and it seemed to rise up a little towards his palm. That must be illusion, surely; water didn't behave that way, even around him. *It isn't in the water, Issel, it's in you*—well, but he didn't behave that way, even around water.

All a myriad droplets reach as one, to where your hand shines in summoning. They hadn't reached this way towards the others, not that he had seen; but he was stronger than the others. He saw no shining in his hand, but there was something, as always around water, a prickling beneath his skin before it was even wet. Despite all Rhoan's tuition and his own ardent practice, he still hadn't learned to subdue the pain of contact, only to conceal it. He lied to her, and she pretended to believe him.

The warmth of spirit, blood and thought—the water was sensing something of that already, and responding to it. Not his imagination, he wasn't the only one to see it; at his elbow, Rhoan murmured, "Careful, Issel. There is peril here."

Don't be manly, she meant, go quietly in and out, just the lightest of touches to find the dark heart of the water and rouse it, turn it to the light. Every day, he thought, that was what he did. It was the others, all the school else who were mysterious to him suddenly, who must work in some other way altogether; see, all he needed to do was to reach his mind through that misshapen image of his own hand reaching, let his thoughts slide down into the receptive water and just nudge it, lightly as you like, so . . .

ISSEL screamed, but he wasn't the only one, nor he thought the first. He thought he had woken suddenly into a world of screaming, and been slow to add his own voice to that chorus.

He didn't know why the others were screaming, or why they'd started before him. Himself, he was screaming because his arm was ablaze.

When he looked, the first time he managed to see through the pain of it, it seemed not to be true. Something had engulfed his hand and was creeping up towards his elbow, but it wasn't flame.

It had come out of the bowl—the broken bowl, the bowl that lay scattered in flinders across the table there—so he supposed it must be water. It didn't look like water. It looked like what he had seen in the bowl for that little moment when Rhoan had turned it: a shatter like fragments of glass all cupped together. Except that hers had been first black and then silver, a sucking dark and a flare of light, and perilous either way. His was not so clean, nor so definite: neither black nor silver, but only shadow-grey and then glitter-grey, and shifting from one to the other like the shift of light and shadow over water, indeterminate, unfixed. There were colours too, thin washes of colour that he didn't have a name for; and whatever it was now, it didn't lie quiet under his hand as Rhoan's water had. It was eating him, climbing him, burning as it came . . .

He tried to drop it like a red-hot coal, he tried to shake it off like a biting rat; his arm swung, hard and hot and heavy, and the table shattered at the strike of it.

He screamed again and swivelled round, looking for something, anything, surcease; and couldn't see it in the room or in his friends or anywhere. Despairing, desperate, he slammed the agony of his arm against the wall, and the wall cracked. Tiles and plaster fell around him, and a billow of dust.

"Issel . . . !"

That was Rhoan, screaming more usefully now, screaming his name to draw him. He blundered towards her, towards the sound of her because his eyes were blinded by the pain again; he felt other hands catch him and guide him and he thought they were Tulk's, he didn't think the adults were coming anywhere near.

He was bellowing, he could hear it in himself, like a bull in a slaughterhouse. When he stopped—gasping, sobbing for relief or just for air enough to shriek again as the burning edged higher, drawing up his arm like a long, long glove—he could hear other voices, strangers'; they must be out on the gallery there and encountering Armina.

No matter. Here was Rhoan, her hands on his face as cool as her voice: "Issel, be strong, be still. Stand still . . ."

And then those same hands clamped themselves around his arm, below the line of fire where it was creeping upward. She screamed before he did, before he could, but she did something even while she was screaming; he felt a sudden cooling. Not that the fires went out but they were banked, not flaring, not running free: *there to be used* his treacher mind thought, although it would cost all this pain to use them.

And then something more, she pulled his arm down and it was deep in water, normal water, water untouched till now, unmagic'd. *Bucket*, his mind said; his eyes weren't looking, they were slammed shut against whatever horror his arm had become. He welcomed the common touch of common water, that usually he shied away from when she wasn't looking. He still didn't think a bucket of water could touch these fires, unless to feed them; but Rhoan said, "Stay," and he stayed. He couldn't see, and there was nothing to hear, but he felt another kind of cool, a fierce and greedy stillness reach out to claim those fires, to draw them down into itself to make it all the more still, the more strong, the more ready.

———————

"ISSEL . . . ? Issel, it's all right. You can open your eyes now, it's over . . ."

He was on his knees, he found, and wasn't sure quite how that had happened, or when. The bucket had been on the floor, of course; apparently it still was, and so was he. And someone else, one at least, the one with the arm round his shoulders and the voice in his ear.

That one wasn't Rhoan, it was Tulk. He didn't know where Rhoan was, or what she had done exactly, or how much too late she had been; he wasn't going to find out, until he looked. Tulk said it was all right, but he didn't believe that for a moment.

Even so, he did it. He cracked his eyes open and blinked about him at the damage, taking in everything he'd done, the best way not to look at what had been done to him. There was the shattered table, but he knew about that. There was the wall, and he'd almost smashed a hole clean through; he could see daylight in the cracks. There were Lenn and Gilder, in the doorway, looking on; if he was quiet, if he held his breath—great loud croaking things, his breaths, like a crow's voice calling—he could still hear Armina beyond. She hadn't come in; that might mean something. It might not.

There was Rhoan, also on her knees but solitary, bent over so that her hair fell down to cover her, face and hands and all. If he was really quiet, he could hear her crying.

Here was Tulk, on his left side, doing a friend's duty; and down there cradled in his lap was his right arm, and he had looked all the way around the room to save himself from looking down at that, and now he had to do it.

When he did, he thought his eyes were lying to him. Perhaps it was the water in them, deceptive and untrue.

What he saw was a normal human arm, a boy's arm, his own, thin and strong, with all his own old scars and pocks and freckles.

He wasn't sure what he'd been expecting—something black and withered, perhaps? or something flayed, torn open to the bone?—but not this.

He was used to pain without damage, water did that to him all the time; but not to make him scream, not to grind up his arm with teeth like broken glass and spit it out unharmed . . .

He lifted his arm and gazed at it, touched it wonderingly and wanted to sing in exultation, at being nothing more nor less than himself. And then he looked around for Rhoan, to share the abundance of what he was feeling because it was just too much for one boy alone.

She wasn't even watching. She was still hunched over, turned inward, behind her curtain of hair.

He said her name, and that brought no response. He touched her shoulder, and felt her trembling; he had to part her hair with both his hands and tuck it back, like the beaded curtains of Daries, before she would lift her head and look at him.

She had been crying, but he knew that already. What shook him more was the stricken look on her face, how pale she was, how deep her eyes were sunken.

"Rhoan, what happened? What did you do . . . ?"

"It's what you did that matters." Her voice was thin, hollow, frail, unidentifiable; not that she was whispering, rather that she found it almost impossibly hard to speak. "I don't know what that was, where you turned that water, what you woke it to; only that it was wrong, so wrong, and it was hurting you so much . . . I couldn't think of anything to do, except to turn it back. Like I did before, like you said, turn it to the light. If I could find it. But I, when I tried it was so unquiet, just touching it with my mind wasn't enough, I couldn't find the heart of it. It wasn't the same, it was hardly like water at all. Something with its own life, and so dark, so twisted, I think you put the Shine into that water . . .

"So I had to touch it," she said, "with my hands. I had to fight it. I had to be all manly," with a sobbing laugh, a weak try at being Rhoan, which only showed how far she was from herself. "And, look . . ."

She'd been holding her hands crossed across her body, like a carving of the dead on ancient tombs; now she held them out and turned them palm upward to show him.

His own arm had burned and burned, and had no mark to show it. Her hands were red-raw and blistering as he watched, bubbling from beneath to show how deep her pain had reached, how far the damage ran.

"Quick," he said, "put them in the water, it's good for burns . . ."

She was shaking her head. "I'm afraid of that, what's in the bucket there. I don't think it's water anymore. I don't want to touch it. You did something, I did something else, and it ran off your arm and mixed with what was in there; but it wasn't right, and I don't know what we've got . . ."

No more did he; nor did he want to find out. He wanted to cradle her injured hands, but the lightest contact hurt her unbearably. There was no gift of healing that he knew of in all the water-magic. The best he could do was to hold her wrists while Tulk poured pure well water over her palms, for what good that could do, which was little enough. Even a dribble made her gasp just from the touch, the weight of its falling, and the water tingle provoked the hurt, she said, rather than soothing it. She tugged against his grip, and if there was one thing Issel understood, it was pain; he let her go.

"Water's good for burns," he said again, scolding mildly.

"Maybe not for these burns. Maybe nothing is, or will be . . ."

Maybe so. He looked for Armina anyway, with all her eerie skills, but there was still no sign of her. Only Lenn and Gilder coming in, now that the shock was over, now that the danger was past.

Gilder gazed down into the bucket a little warily, as though he expected to see something live stir within it; he said, "Have you achieved this water also, girl? After the boy's catastrophe?"

"I've done what I can," Rhoan said flatly, ambiguously, her patent dislike riding even over her pain.

Neither of the others thought—or perhaps sought—to warn him. He dipped his hand in and drew out water, rolling it into a ball between finger and thumb as a woman might roll tamasseh. Rhoan shuddered, Tulk hissed softly under his breath; Issel only watched.

Nothing happened, or seemed to happen. Gilder was no magician, as weak with water as he was strong in his hatred of the Marasi. Tulk's mouth twitched; it seemed to say, *he is too dull to harm himself.* That might be true, but Issel wasn't persuaded. If there was harm in the water, he thought the slightest work would waken it; even as little as Gilder was using now, just to gel it, to play it between his fingers . . .

Except that he wasn't playing suddenly, he was gazing down at the little shimmering ball where it lay on his palm, and the expression on his face was like nothing they had seen before, expressive of nothing they had ever imagined that he could feel.

He said, "Lenn, this is different. Look . . ."

And he pinched off a fragment of that water-gel, pea-sized, and threw it at the wall, where Issel had already wrecked it.

There was an explosion—of steam, of smoke, of dust? Issel didn't know, only that a cloud billowed back at them with all the proper noises of a storm, the lightning and the thunder, sharp cracks and slow, threatening rumbles; and then the room collapsed.

The wall must have gone first, but that they couldn't see. It was the ceiling Issel saw, where it tipped suddenly down into the cloud, great beams breaking through the plaster as it went, with the chaotic sound of a thousand tiles sliding off the half-dome overhead to shatter in the square below.

He felt the floor shift beneath his feet, felt it heave up like a stray whale in the river, beneath a fishing boat; but by then he was already moving, seizing Rhoan—by the arms, a safer distance from her ruined hands—and pulling her after him, urging her towards the door, offering what thin shelter his body could afford as the first of the dislodged beams came crashing down at his back.

Tulk was right behind them, croaking and coughing in the dust. Lenn was quicker, first out onto the gallery; Gilder was last. Issel looked round to see the little man burdened with the bucket, carrying it clutched against his chest. His hair and clothes were filthy with plaster and the muck from the roof space; he was hunched over the open mouth of the bucket, to shield the water from the fall. Issel couldn't see the point.

No time to think about it. The gallery felt little safer or more stable with this many on it, but the stairs down were blocked, crowded with people drawn by Issel's noise. Armina was waving her arms at them to drive them back. It takes time to turn a herd, especially on a narrow iron stair that felt none too securely anchored to the wall; Issel thought they might shake it loose altogether, bring them all crashing down into the court.

He held Rhoan from behind, his arms loose around her waist, comfort and support for a girl who couldn't use her hands, whose feet were stumbling from shock and pain. Issel's mind was stumbling too; he couldn't understand how Gilder had wreaked so much damage with so little water, when he had so little talent in the art. They must have done something new between them, he and Rhoan, to make that bucketful so potent. Which might be why Gilder was hoarding it so carefully, strength to the weak; perhaps he thought that possession would give him a new voice in the rebels' counsels. If he did, Issel thought that he was wrong. Lenn wouldn't be cowed by a borrowed power that could be measured out in spoonfuls. Simple quarrels and infighting broke up rebellions as easily and as often as betrayal; Issel doubted now that this little group could ever hold together long enough to achieve anything worthwhile. There was only the one thing that was worthwhile anyway, to drive the Marasi entirely out of Sund, and that lay far beyond the reach of these. They could prick, they could annoy, they could tease others—like Tulk, like Issel—into violence; they could watch the repercussions and ride on the waves of hatred and feel that they did good work, but they could never achieve the aim that they preached and dreamed of. Maras could swallow hatred, swallow and swallow and never sicken.

Much more immediate was to help Rhoan down from the shaky gallery. Armina was wading into the crowd, bellowing like a cattleherd. They were retreating before her as any sensible creature would, woman or bull or boy. He followed gratefully—followed Lenn, rather, who nipped down in Armina's shadow—easing Rhoan down before him within the circle of his arms, "Here's the first step now, down you go, that's the way, don't worry about holding on, I'm holding you; and the next one now . . ."

And so at last to ground, among the burned circles of the inner court; and a press of sullen, hostile people all around them, demanding to know who they were and what they had done up there; and Armina lifting her voice to carry all through the crowd, to say, "What, and will you stay to argue what it was, and whether it should have been? Do you think the Marasi have no eyes here, no ears in the city anywhere? Do you not think that they will be hurrying here now, to ask the same foolish questions— and will you wait for them to question you? Out of our road, all you; and pick up your little things and away, swift now, or some of you will likely die under the question. Would you die for our sakes, when you don't know who we are . . . ?"

It was more than she needed to say; they were moving already, fraying from the back of the crowd till only the stubborn stupid few were left, who always are left, who do wait too long and so suffer for it. Armina pushed between them, with the others following; Issel walked beside Rhoan, still with his hands at her waist, while she held hers out before her like a supplicant. She couldn't lift her eyes, it seemed, from the wreckage; he had to steer as much as support her.

Out through the narrow passage into the open square, and swift away: not pausing even to see how much damage they had done to the Silkmart, but hastily down towards the strand, where they could lose themselves, where the Marasi seldom ventured.

At last they stopped by a long-abandoned warehouse, dank wooden walls and a fallen roof, the timbers too wet and rotten to salvage even here in a city that ate itself constantly, surviving on old substance reused.

Gilder set his bucket down with care, then looked around. He had their eyes and their attention, he knew that; he met their doubts full-face.

"Listen," he said, "don't you see? Lenn, we've always said, we need two miracles to defeat the Marasi. We need to be able to fight them here, without a proper army; and we need to break their bridge, to stop another army marching over. Anything else, everything we've done so far is just gnat bites, irritants, nothing.

"Well, we can do it now. We can. We've got a chance, at least. This," the water in his bucket, "you saw how potent this is. Tel Ferin won't help, we know that, but if the children can understand how they did this and make more," *much more* was what he meant, and Rhoan shuddered at the thought, Issel felt it against his fingers and then somehow all through his body, her distress like water down his back, a shivering stinging touch, "then we could fight a battalion each. There are enough of us already; and when the people saw, they would flock to join us. This is victory, what we have here."

"And the bridge?" Lenn was struggling to sound cynical, against the birth of hope; she believed him, although she didn't want to.

"For the bridge, they will need to go themselves," Gilder said. "When the girl's hands have healed, when she and the boy have learned how much they can do together, his strength with her understanding. We know what supports the bridge; magic, sure, but we have magic here, enough to meet theirs and overwhelm it. One house in a park, the story is, and guarded by old men. These two between them have the power to destroy that." And then, when no one cheered, no one spoke, no one moved at all: "We have to try, at least. It is a chance; we've never had a chance before."

"Oh, I agree. I only don't like depending on children."

Issel didn't like being called a child, and was inclined to refuse their dependence. He was waiting for Rhoan to say no, though, and she was still wrapped in her own pain, not saying anything. He thought her silence ought to carry weight, only that it was outweighed by Armina's. She ought to be forbidding this, and she was not; she was only standing, arms folded and watching him, as though she had at last brought him to where he belonged.

Chapter Two

ALF the harem had closed itself in behind doors and screens and shutters, and was wailing yet. Jendre had lost count of the black days, but there had still not been enough to satisfy some women's need to mourn, or at least to wail. Or at least to be heard wailing.

The other half of the harem—the quiet half, those who truly grieved their lost dead lord, and those who truly did not care—seemed all to have gathered out here in the gardens, along the path that ran from the main block to the *Kafes*. It went on further, to Jendre's house eventually, although that would be Jendre's house no longer. Even now, Mirjana and Teo were packing up the last of her small property, in hopes that they would be allowed to take it with them when they left. The fear and sorrow and confusion of this day would bring ripe pickings to the palace eunuchs; every pretty thing misplaced meant more profit for their deep pockets, and she trusted none of them, not even Ferres. Especially not Ferres, perhaps. She had bribed him, of course, to see that her possessions would be conducted safely to their new home; she still thought she would be lucky to end the day with her two friends around her and a second dress to wear.

The day's end could bring what troubles it chose. For now she was here and so were many of her sister-wives, all along this short stretch of the path. Behind and around them were packed dozens and dozens, hundreds of the dead Sultan's concubines and slaves. Not his favourites, Theosa and her close sisters, they were still attendant on his body; Jendre didn't know what would be done with them, when once he was buried. She barely understood what would be done with her, and that was grim enough. All the rest, though, those who were not wailing were gathered here, to catch whatever fleeting glimpse they could of the new Sultan in his first progress under the free light of the sun, in all his rank and substance.

She supposed it was a privilege.

———————

THE Valide Sultan's palanquin rested empty outside the door of the *Kafes*. Jendre had seen that before, but this time the door stood open. It was still guarded, huge men with unsheathed blades; the women could do no more than peep within. Jendre had snatched her own peep, while she struggled not to be seen peeping. She thought it was undignified in a wife, however young and foolish she was allowed to be; it was certainly disappointing. She'd seen shadows, an unlit corridor, no more than that.

She had a good view, though, a fine view—one of the advantages of height, and bony elbows—when there was finally movement in the doorway. Out of that dimness came a parade of guards and eunuchs in their highest degree of dress and pomp; and then the Valide Sultan and her attendants; and then, at last, flanked by more guards and more eunuchs, out squeezed the new Sultan, only surviving brother of the Man of Men.

That was one title, Jendre thought, that he would not inherit. Much else came with the triple crown of city, state and empire; respect did not. This was a fat man, the fattest of men, they could call him that and welcome. He could probably not keep saddle on a horse, if ever they could find a horse to bear him. His flesh—and so much of it, such an abundance of flesh, she had thought her own lord wonderfully fat, but this was monstrous—all his flesh was slack and white and heavy. There was no strength in that vast body, beyond what it needed to hold itself upright, to breathe, to walk. Rumour had said nothing of that, too busy painting him mad, but who could trust rumour? She doubted that anything true had ever come out of the *Kafes*. All she thought was that he had gone in there as a young man, a boy yet, and now he had grey in his beard and perhaps in his mind also. He'd had no chance to build strength or win respect, no chance to be a prince or to deserve an empire. She could feel sorry for him, so much was easy. She couldn't imagine how he or anyone would live now, how he would be Sultan or how the state would thrive beneath his rule.

Perhaps it would be the Valide Sultan who ruled, through him. They had said that of her other son, and Jendre had never believed it; now, watching this vast man blink in the sun as he waddled behind his mother, it seemed far more likely. Those who hemmed him in with their bright swords, they were her men, not his; Jendre thought they frightened him. Perhaps that was the point. He must have spent all his adult life frightened of men with swords, who might have come on any day to kill him. The Valide Sultan would know that. This was an assertion, Jendre thought: *you be the shadow of God on earth, my son, but I will be the light that casts that shadow.*

AT noon, trumpets and drums called them to the great high gate of the harem. The Sultan's body had gone out this way already, with his mother and brother, to begin a last slow procession through the city. For a while his women could be a part of that great cortège, although they had no hope of the last least sight of him who led it. Generals and nobles and judges, soldiers and artisans, all the men of Maras would be marching behind their master's catafalque. His wives must follow them, and not to the wonderful tomb that he had constructed for himself, not to see him buried and to hear the prayers for his swift accession into paradise. His mother would go that way, of course, with her son his heir, and then they would return to the palace. She at least would come back to the harem. It would be a strange place, Jendre thought, stripped of so many women: strange and silent, hollow, sad.

Not so sad as this, their slow procession, who had lost lord and home and life all in a day. Hedged about by guards, they were only to be let trail their master for one short mile. They were a sacrifice, perhaps, paraded like beasts on their way to the knife. Also it was convenient, the simplest way to move hundreds of women from one place to another, when all the city was parading or else watching the parade.

There was more drumming in the distance, a rough salute, and she guessed that the head of the procession, the Sultan's body, was passing one of the janizar compounds. The drumming was followed by shouts; that would be the men there crying for their dole, that a new Sultan always paid to keep them loyal. It was traditional, this shouting, but in deadly earnest too. Jendre had seen the janizars in a small rebellion, a single squad in riot, and she trusted that the fat man would find his coffers equally fat. She hoped his hands were generous, and not constrained by any meanness of his mother's. His brother had been a soldier first and foremost, he had earned all his loyalty on horseback in the wars, and men had loved him for it. This one would need to buy all his allegiance, and she thought it would cost him dear.

Well, it was no concern of hers. Properly, nothing in the city now was any concern of hers. Her true concern was dead, and she should be concerned only with mourning him.

She doubted that she could learn, though, not to think, not to wonder and worry. She was sure that she could not learn to wail.

One thing she could always do was walk. That was not so true of those about her. While none of them could rival His new Magnificence, many of the late Sultan's women were magnificent themselves; years might have passed since some of them had tackled the stairs down from their quarters. It seemed a petty cruelty to have them walk now, this distance in this heat, where they could have gone in litters.

Some of the heavier wives—widows, she supposed they were now, widows all—had thought to keep attendants with them, and they leaned heavily on younger women's shoulders. Others had to make shift for themselves, grunting and sweating as they shuffled forward. Passing by, Jendre felt spasms of guilt. But she had no friends here, she knew none of these women, and the way to meet them was not to make a servant of herself; do that and she would never rise above it, never be more than a servant in their eyes.

———

"YOU were his pet. His latest pet, his last."

The voice all but stopped her in her tracks. Not quite, she did keep moving; but she stumbled, and was angry, and was talking even as she turned, before she had seen who spoke.

"I was his *wife*! And I tried to save him, where all the rest of you had shut yourselves away to mourn his death already . . ."

"Not by choice, girl. Not all of us."

She was a big woman next to Jendre but not mountain-massive, not grotesque. She was a senior wife but not an ancient, not even so old as their husband had been. She must have had some reason for speaking as she did, but Jendre couldn't see it. Any harem was rich in spite, and it oozed like oil from the ground at times of crisis and fear, times like this, but the woman she was looking at would be better than that. Surely, she would be better . . .

"How, not by choice? He was the Man of Men, the Shadow of God: what was your choice, and whose will could override it? I chose for him, and no one tried to shift me."

"You have no children."

Oh, and what use are your children now, where they have no father? What value was there, in a dead Sultan's get? Or what danger? The girls might find husbands, but she couldn't imagine where; not in the capital, surely, and not abroad. The boys might be allowed to join the army, perhaps, be let die for their uncle in the empire's everlasting wars. Jendre said, "No, I only had a husband, and a lord. Was that such an advantage?"

She was not being kind, but the other woman seemed almost to welcome this harshness. "Girl, I loved that man before you were born; I bore him my son before you were born. Do not seek to teach me about duty. But she came to me and said that he could die, as God surely meant him to, or else it could be my son who died, as God so surely wanted a death from the throne's line; and she had the means to do it, she owns them in the *Kafes* there, so what could I do? Should I spend my own boy's life in vain, while I failed to save my man's?"

Only one woman in the palace, in the city, in the world could say such things. And there was probably only one woman in the world against whom they could be truly effective. "Your son—he was the eldest, then?"

"He is. He *is* the eldest, and the heir now, and I am his mother." The next male in the line: he would still be that, even if the new Sultan produced healthy children of his own. So long as he lived, he was the heir, and the *Kafes* was supposed to keep him safe, but . . .

"How will you know that he is well," still living, still heir, "from where we are going?"

Not a shrug, not a surrender; an aggressive act, rather, that shake of her head, defiance personified. "I will not. Until they send for me, to say that I am Valide Sultan."

Jendre could admire her stubborn optimism, if not quite understand it. It had still meant leaving the Sultan their husband to die, a certain loss against a most uncertain future.

"If I had kept him alive without you," as she so nearly had, or thought she had, "if he had not eaten the ortolan—what of your boy then?"

"I could not know. It seemed a fair chance that he would live if I was not to blame, if I did nothing. That is why you survived even the first night of your nursing. If my boy had died because of it, you would not have out-lived him by a day."

No, she was sure not. No matter. They were together now, their lord was dead, mother and son were parted by more than one guarded door; she said, "How may I serve you?"

"Child, there is no way you may serve me. We can no longer serve our-selves. We are outside the wall."

———

EVERY journey has its end, or else no journey ever ends, until with death. Jendre could believe one, she could believe the other; sometimes she could be two people inside her head, she could believe both at once.

This journey, this walk had its end: not far for her, too far for some of her companions, and yet it brought them no relief. They had wailed their husband to his last home, and now they wailed themselves, each other to what should be their own.

All through the city, it was known as the Palace of Tears. Jendre gazed up at the implacable gate and would not weep. She felt more angry than despairing, she felt robbed, robbed again; it was too soon in her life's jour-ney, she was too young to come to this.

Someone blew a trumpet call and the gate swung open, inward, like a summons. Lost to the world, more truly lost than in the harem; almost as truly lost as in the grave. This was death in life, and a silence welcomed them to it.

A high plain gate in a high wall, promising nothing; nothing was what she could see, a bare court, stone enclosed by dusty stone. It would be bet-ter than this beyond. It was better, she knew that, she had seen. As a child she had hung from trees and cliffs and overlooked the park with its pavil-ions, not so different from the new palace they had come from. This too was a palace once, and the home of great men. The entrance was built to be secure, severe, forbidding; beyond were trees and birds and water, com-fort, friends. She knew all this, but still felt the bleak and empty promise of that gateway, speaking of a bleak and empty life to come.

Well, perhaps. There would, there must be compensations; she meant to find them.

All through the city it was known as the Palace of Tears, and naughty children were threatened with it. *If you don't learn to behave, I'll send you there; men will come to take you, and you will weep away.*

These days it meant more than it used to; it was almost true.

As Jendre walked beneath the arch of the gateway, under the eyes of unseen guards, she had one word, one name resounding in her head, so loud she was astonished that no one stared at her, as though she had shouted it aloud and the echo was calling back from every wall around her. *Sidië . . . !*

———————

NO luxury now for anyone, no privacy for her, no separate house. But there was comfort, yes, and there were friends.

After the barren court and its narrow egress, the several doors with heavy bars set to drop behind them, here were long corridors so like the house they'd left; and winding stairs and windows like glimpses of a wider world locked out by iron bars.

This was a great house, a palace, and no one would ever live here now except them and their kind, and yet they were still kept to the women's quarters, the harem. Presumably the men who watched the walls must have the run of all the house else. Still, there was room enough, rooms to spare; they passed many empty doors before they came to those where their servants were waiting.

Mirjana, Teo: they stood against the doorposts, one each side to watch for her coming. They greeted her with smiles, Mirjana with a kiss, Teo with a little sigh. She couldn't see herself, but all her life she'd known how far she gave herself away to those who loved her. Did she look determined, furious, haunted? She felt all of those, and more. Mostly, though, she was only riven with urgency. She wanted to be here with her own, she wanted to have them feel welcome and beloved, as they had made her feel; she wanted to be out there in the gardens, in the park, finding the pavilion where the old men worked their magic, where the children slept, where the bridge lay in their dreaming, where her sister was.

"Lady, will you lie down? I will make tea, while Teo rubs your feet. You must be tired."

"After such a little walk? Hardly, Mirjana." In truth, she was ex-hausted by her emotions, the weight of them, the potency. This was no time to be running round the gardens anyway; she would have time enough for that, too much time, there was no hurry now and never would be. Her life had been shorn of hurry as of husband, as of so much else.

They held her hands and took her through the doorway into a suite of rooms that must have been lovely once. To be fair it was lovely still, in a weary kind of way: tiled and carpeted and comfortable. There were tiles missing from every wall, the rugs were worn through to ragged holes, one shutter hung crooked by a single hinge and there was rust on the iron that barred the window. Nothing mattered. There was a couch, and the mo-ment she lay down on its soft crimson coverings she never wanted to rise again. Teo knelt at her feet and slipped her shoes off; she felt his thumbs and fingers working deep into her arches, and she wriggled a little lower on the couch, a little further into the pressure of his hands where they tres-passed on the borders of pain, where the heart of pleasure lay.

"You, boy," she murmured, "master of my feet—can we be happy here?" Meaning *can you be happy here?* as she thought he had not been happy for a while.

"If you can, lady." Which was honestly not the answer that she wanted, but the one she should have expected none the less; and it was too much, far too much trouble to lift her head to scowl at him. The best she could manage was to wriggle her toes scoldingly, a signal that he clearly and—she was sure—deliberately misunderstood. His fingers tugged at them slowly, one by one. It felt wonderful.

So there was tea, and there was talking; there was Mirjana, who rubbed her head as Teo rubbed her feet, and between them they stole all her de-termination and all her anger too, and her courage somehow went with them, so that she was crying again before she slept, and she had been so determined to do neither.

———————

SHE woke confused and they laughed at her, these two possessive slaves of hers. Teo was still sniggering as she cuffed at him, as she demanded slip-pers and good sense, more tea, something to eat, some little touch of wis-dom. He went to fetch which of those he could, the tea and food; the wisdom was beyond him, and she told him so. Mirjana showed her what she had not seen, the inner room where a fine big bed waited, soft with pillows and covers, hung with curtains of elderly velvet silk. There were pallets on the floor for the humble; she thought that the humble would sleep with her, more nights than not. She thought that she would have no one else to sleep with.

It was good, she thought, to have Sidië so strongly in her mind, and somewhere in the gardens, within these walls and reachable. She could turn her mind from Salem as from the Sultan, from all her many losses; she could have someone at least to look for, one beacon burning.

LATER, in the day's last light, she and Teo went exploring like children, hand in hand. She had her sole objective, sun-bright in the shadows; he had a world to learn, to master in his quiet way.

They found women everywhere, all through the house and gardens: shrill and agitated like birds in flocks together, or else round and still like stones. No matter. They could slip by quickly, out of the shadow of the palace, out of the formal gardens and into the parks beyond, trees and walks and quiet pools between far-flung pavilions.

Teo tugged her up a mound, a hill in miniature crowned by a miniature temple. It was too reminiscent of her husband's last lying-place, she didn't want to go there, but the view from the top would be too useful to refuse; she distracted herself by grumbling and scolding at him, "You're like a puppy today, all bounce. If there's a stick up there, I swear, if it's not big enough to beat you with, I'm going to throw it down and make you chase."

"I would do that. If you sent me to."

"I know you would."

She pushed him in front of her, gripped both his hands and had him tow her to the top. Even so, the climb had her sweating in the warm air, head down and breathing hard, seeing nothing. It was his sudden check and her walking into him that told her they'd found trouble waiting.

Or perhaps it wasn't trouble after all. It was people: a person old and stiff-backed where she sat on a wooden bench before the temple, disturbed by their sudden irruption into her peace, her attendant at her feet and scowling. Jendre could be proud too, and stubborn in pursuit of her rights; and gracious enough to set all that aside, young enough to avert trouble with a little conspicuous charm.

She nudged Teo to one side and dropped into the courtliest of curtseys.

334 ep Chaz Brenchley

"Madam, you were enjoying the sunset, and my fool and I have shattered all your pleasure with our noise. How may I make amends?"

It was a question meant to be ignored, and duly was. The old lady—and she truly was old, old as the Valide Sultan and maybe older, wonderfully withered in her age—barely moved a finger to dismiss it. Perhaps to dismiss her also, the most abrupt of hints, *leave us as you found us, go away*; but the man at her feet jutted his beard towards Teo and barked, "Do you call that a fool?"

Ah, they were all dogs today. She said, "He is a boy, and that is fool enough," though thankfully he was quick enough to be on his knees with his head in the dirt.

"Is it so?"

The man scrabbled to his feet, and Jendre understood the oddity of him all in a rush. He was a dwarf, manly in his head and chest and stunted else, he waddled as he walked; and he was old too, albeit younger than his mistress, there was white amid the iron-grey of his beard; and he would be a fool for sure, his dress proclaimed it.

Dwarves and fools had been the pleasure of her husband's father's court, so long ago; she had heard that there were dozens, hundreds, bred like hounds or horses to scamper like wise and mocking children between the legs of the empire's great men. And to amuse its great women, of course; and the males cut to allow that, but never till after they had bred, which would account for the beard.

An old fool, then, a survivor of the last great reign; he must have left the palace forty years ago. His mistress likewise. No slave herself, no concubine if he sat at her feet long after his lord was dead. Fools were famous for their haughtiness, and also for their loyalty. A wife, then, she must be, a sister-wife to the Valide Sultan. If one old woman could endure all those years amid the poisons and pleasures of the court, surely another could come through them here, quietly ignored by all the world that mattered.

"Boy? What is your foolery?"

Teo could be quick, he could be clear; he lifted his head and said, "To love my mistress."

"Is it so? Aye, you'll be a fool, then, if one overtopping most. Mistress, will you lend him to me some days?"

"For what, lessons in foolery?"

"Those, and other adventures."

"Well, he does not noticeably need the lessons; I said, he is all boy already—but yes, if you are kindly with him. And if he's willing." Finding her head more or less on a level with the dwarf's, she rose from her curtsey, as swiftly as grace would suffer or else as gracefully as swiftness would allow. Then she poked her toe into Teo's ribs, to bring him up onto his knees; let the fool and him be eye to eye, if they could never be equal.

The look he gave her was equivocal, but not unwilling. He bowed to the little man, before settling back on his heels. Perhaps he did smell adventure in this, more than a boy might find in serving one redundant wife in a palace full of the same.

Perhaps so did she. She said, "He is yours, then, some days if not today. I should name him to you; we call him Teo," and she genuinely couldn't remember if he had brought the name with him to her father's house, or whether he had been given it there, and whether it had been her own suggestion. She went on, "I am myself called Jendre, and was wife lately to the Man of Men," *his latest pet, his last*, but they were all dogs here.

"My lady Jendre, we were sure of it already. Your beauty's fame has marched ahead of you, and the tale of your courage also."

"How is that, where you are so isolated?" The junior should always name herself, but she was entitled to a response, and not from the slave; it was his mistress's silence that made her flush, it was anger that stuttered her tongue. If he chose to believe that his florid compliments embarrassed her, if she chose to leave him believing it, that was just politic in both of them.

"Lady, news crosses these walls on the wind; it soaks the earth like water. You were a woman among women, the wife of wives. Of course we knew of you, and the service you did your lord. And how that ended." For a moment he was in utter earnest, and she could have laid her soul in his knobbly, misshapen hands. "I, Djago, told it to my lovely mistress, and so she heard it too. May I name her? My lady Jendre, this is Tirrhana, she who possesses my soul, she who did possess the heart and hand of the great Sultan, your husband's father . . ."

And she still wasn't ready to speak, it seemed, but she gestured again at the sound of her name; the same gesture, a finger's twitch, only this time it seemed to be an acknowledgement of her visitor and encouragement to her fool.

Jendre was reeling anyway. This was Tirrhana, still living? There could not be more than one of that name, the city would not bear it; Tirrhana really was famous. Little girls grew up among her legends. Only child of a great father—and that was a strangeness, a wonder in itself, that a great man could have but the one child, a girl, and be content—she had seized his army and his country at his death and ruled it like a man, its generalissima. Until the Sultan of Maras brought war and devastation, and fetched her home his captive. He could have kept her, concubine or slave; he chose to marry her.

And that was the last of her legends, of course, because she went into the harem and no more stories came out. And he died, and she came to the Palace of Tears as women must. And here she was, still here, still—if barely—in the flesh. Jendre was forming an idea, about where her spirit might be. Silence and stillness and the stare of her, wide-eyed and unblinking and so little like her legends . . .

Jendre stepped closer, and the dwarf Djago made no move to prevent her. He sighed, rather, and scurried ahead; and drew a handkerchief from his sleeve pocket to wipe a little spit bubble tenderly from the corner of his mistress's mouth, and then she knew.

"How long has she been like this?"

"All your long life, my lady, and more besides. Lives grow shorter, you know, as we grow older. Yours has been a tremendous time in the living of it; mine feels as little as I am myself, a tale told in a day; hers has become a moment, no more, and she is entirely caught within it."

She was. Jendre could see now how vacant her mind lay behind those eyes. And how baby-soft the face was in its wrinkles, lacking any severity of spirit to stiffen it.

The bench she sat on was all too evidently made for her. It had straps to hold her gently where she was, and wheels below, with shafts and a harness behind; it was a cart made small, made to be drawn by someone smaller.

"She likes it here. I think she likes it here. She seems more restful. We watch the clouds, and the sun's descent. The colours can be striking; she was always fond of fierce colours."

That might explain her dress, in its shades of bitter orange. It might explain his own, lemon-yellow and berry-red, if he dressed to please his mistress. Jendre felt sometimes that she was dressed to please Mirjana. Teo she thought might dress to please himself soon, any day now, if he found himself less watched, less disciplined. If he found less to be afraid of, as she hoped. Djago might help him there. Or, of course, Djago might do the other thing. She had no idea actually what Djago wanted, with Teo or otherwise. His care for his mistress was quite touching, but had nothing to say to the other habits of his life.

Well, Teo would babble to her, if he was happy; his silence would be just as eloquent if he was not. If Djago or anyone sought to harm her own, they would learn that a Sultan's widow, even his youngest, was not toothless even here, in this palace of discards.

No point in hunting trouble; better to trust, and hope not to be betrayed. She needed friends, as much as her boy did. More, she needed information . . .

She turned her eyes outward, trying to look as guileless as she tried to sound. "It is a fine prospect, Djago." The vast and lurid sky, and the great stretch of world reaching out to meet it; more nearly, the fall of the city towards the river, and the bridge that spanned it, gleaming sickly, lending its own eldritch colours to the view; and then more nearly still, the parkland within the palace wall, the scattered pavilions . . . "Can you tell which of these pretty houses is in use, and for what?"

"We have that one in the trees there, my lady," his stubby arm pointing. "She was never happy in the harem, even as it emptied through the years; those who are left now all seem like strangers to her, and she frightens easily. Alone is better, with the few of us who serve her. Most of the others stand empty. They were built for fêtes, and this is no house now for parties."

"No," though she would be stubborn here, grieve for her husband but not for her own life, and not lifelong. She would find a way to live contented, somehow. She looked for where the thrust of the hill rose up beyond the wall, where the cliff overhung it, where she and her little friends had dangled their feet and spat apple pips into the garden and whispered horrors about what went on in that building, there, she had it . . .

"There," she said, "that long pavilion up below the wall there, that's higher even than we are, the view must be even better. Does nothing happen there? Such a fine position, it would be a shame to let it stand empty all the year. When they are done with weeping, perhaps I can inspire my elder sisters to a music party there?"

"Not there, by your grace, my lady."

"Oh, solemn music, I mean, nothing inappropriate."

"Even so, my lady, not there."

"I'm sure you will say why," and she could still sound every bone the Sultan's wife and chilly in her dignity, just as she could still sound heedless girl in desperate search of something to amuse.

"I would prefer not. We do not speak of that place."

"Nevertheless, I hope that you will speak to me. No one hears us," except his dreamlost lady and her Teo, who was crouching in the temple's shade and pretending to be out of earshot.

"Lady, I think you know. I think you must."

Not highborn but risen high, and her father risen first: she could not be here if there had not been a brother or a sister given to the bridge. It was her husband's law, and she ought to hate him for it, who had done that to Sidië. But how could he be mighty over others if he could not be ruthless with his own? How hold the terrible weight of empire together, without cruelty for nails?

She understood it all, and still she hated it; and still he was her lord, to be remembered fondly; and still Djago had not said what she wanted to hear, and she was still determined to force him to it.

"All I hear is the hiss of street rumours boiled over, and the giggles of harem servants. How can I know anything? You can tell me true, and I wish you would."

"I am a harem servant too."

"But not, I think, a giggler. Master Djago, you have lived all your life in this world, and forty years within these particular walls; there is nothing here that could be hidden from you."

"Except inside that pavilion, where we do not go." He sighed and glanced at his mistress, almost seemed to be looking for her consent before he went on, "Lady, that is where the old men brew their magic, on our children's dreams."

"Not yours, surely . . . ?"

"No." Her husband had had no interest in his father's dwarves and fools. He must have sold or sent them all away long since, except those who were let retire here, companions-in-grief to mourning widows. If Djago had any children, he would not know where they were. "Nor yours, neither; but they are all our children, in that place. Our city's children."

He was a slave, a mock-man bred for ribald pleasures; was this his city too? It was, surely, if he thought it was. To challenge that would be an impertinence.

"It was a sweet house once," he went on, "all light and air, and my ladies played there often. When we first came here, when there were ladies enough and some of them still young enough to play. All gone now: light and air and ladies, youth and play."

Was he being sincere, or was this clever foolery, games with words and memory and touching him nowhere, carrying no weight? She couldn't tell.

"The youth is not all gone," she said, "not from there." And not from her either; she was determined still to be young. She could feel already how this place might make her ancient in a year, in an hour if she allowed it. The gardens had been as rough and untended as the house, the trees out here looked almost wild; if the harem in the new palace had been a city within a city, this was a forgotten city, a secret left to dust and rot.

She would not rot. Djago had not rotted, though his mistress had.

"Ah," he said, "their youth is the first that they lose, lady. I lied, when I called them children. Not no more."

"You said you had not seen."

"No more I have. The shutters do not open, and there is no passing through the door. But children run and laugh, they fall and cry and squabble. Children learn and grow. None of that for them. They go in; they do not come out, or never as themselves. We do not speak of them."

"Nor of their keepers?"

"The wizards? No." He shuddered, on the word.

It was enough. She knew where her feet should take her, but not tonight. Sun was setting, and she needed to see the place in day.

She said, "Tell me of your mistress, then, tell me of Tirrhana. Tell me the true tales and the fables both, and don't say which is which."

"I can do that, lady. And what will you tell me in return?"

He had been locked in here for forty years; of course he was hungry, he must be desperate for new stories. Truth and fables, he no more than she would care to cut a knife between them.

"I can tell you how the Sultan died," *who killed him, which was not that poor mute fool so swiftly dispatched in the kitchen yard, before he could point at who suborned him, and on whose behalf . . .*

She had had days and nights to think about it, and she was sure in her own mind. That knowledge, that certainty was currency; it was rash, it was reckless to spend it here, so soon, on him. Or else it was a gesture of faith. It was a gesture she chose to make, or else a folly she would regret more soon than late. Either way, he nodded, and the choice was made.

———

"NO need to hurry home," he said, "the breeze is warm, and she likes to look at the stars."

So too did Jendre like to look at the stars, how they were flung like shards of shattered glass across the blue-black silk of the sky. No treacher moon tonight, betraying lovers, betraying thieves and dreamers; only the broken crag of the hill like a shadow against the sky, something already alien to her, outside the wall. She wondered how her father did, out there in the new dispensation. A new Sultan might prefer new generals . . .

They sat on the hill, then, under the stars and close by Tirrhana in her cart, and told stories loud enough for her to hear, if she had mind enough to understand. Teo sneaked closer, at last lying happy with his head in her lap, augmenting all her truths with his fantastical fictions, which Djago affected entirely to believe.

When the wind shifted, when it came in damp across the river and the dew rose to meet it, then they moved. Djago hitched himself into the cart's harness and towed his mistress carefully down the steepness of the hill, back and forth along a winding path half-lost in the long grasses, while Teo held to one wheel, hand over hand to make a brake. Jendre followed, smiling into the emptiness of the old woman's eyes, just in case there was someone still trapped in there, someone who could see. There were many ways a woman could be locked away for life; not all of them demanded a harem.

Or a pretty pavilion watched over by ancient and malevolent foreigners, unkindly mystics, men . . .

———

SHE thought they were men, those old wizards, as she watched them come and go. Full men, intact. There was something in the way they held themselves, the way they moved, the way they spoke to servants and to each other. They didn't walk with the eunuch's classic shuffle, but it was more than that. Nor did they wear a eunuch's proper dress. They were strangers who kept to their own robes and customs; she could understand that.

That they should have kept their stones, and yet been placed in the harem—that was extraordinary, beyond rumour, beyond belief.

It wasn't their self-content or their assertiveness that persuaded her. Both those attitudes belonged just as easily to the smug and senior eunuchs that she knew. It wasn't any single attribute that she could isolate from distance. Only an air, a sense in her responding to some quality in them, something compounded from stance and manner that could speak of deeper truths.

She watched from a little white belvedere beside a pond. Framed by trees, with its back to the cliff of the hilltop and its feet lapped by water, it had been set there to overlook the city, the river, Sund and all its hinterland, the heart of the empire and all its southern reaches. Seeming to survey all that, Jendre could actually look slantwise across the pool and have a clear sight of the pavilion where her sister lay and slept, if you could call it sleeping; lay and dreamed, if you could call it dreaming.

All she wanted was to sneak inside, to find her sister and discover how she was. It wasn't much, but even that little looked impossible. There was no conspicuous guard on the pavilion, this wasn't the *Kafes* with its bared blades and blank walls, but there was still only the one door, and it seemed as though only the magicians ever used it. They had their own servants in the palace who fetched food daily, pots and baskets and buckets of food; even those servants never passed the doorway, they only handed their burdens through into the shadows within, where other hands waited to receive them.

Whose hands, Jendre couldn't see. Not the magicians', they were too proud to carry; they stood aside in twos and threes to supervise. They must have other servants whom they kept withindoors, hidden with their other charges, shadowed from the day.

Jendre did not like those shadows. She glimpsed them only when the door was open, and from this distance, and still she shuddered every time. They seemed to drift like smoke within the compass of the doorway, they seemed to shine just a little with their own light, and that seemed to have colours in it that she couldn't name. Yet she did still think that they were shadows, only shadows from a different source of light.

Very strongly, very clearly, they reminded her of the bridge. Which was only sense, of course, that was a fruit that had its seed in here; but she hadn't expected it, she didn't know how to meet it, and it frightened her.

No, it terrified her.

Only the thought of her little sister's worse terror was strong enough to keep her at her spying. She feared that she might not have the nerve to venture further, that she would spy and spy and never act at all.

At least she could do her spying undisturbed. Her sister-wives walked in the gardens, some ventured out into the park, but none of them came this far, up so steep a rise to so little purpose. Even Djago must balk at dragging his mistress's cart all this way upslope, even for the peace and beauty of the sun on dark water and the far views beyond. Jendre was glad of that; the fool's sharp eyes would not have missed her interest in the dreamers' pavilion. He might be curious anyway, seeing her ascend every day at first light and not return till dark; he might deduce her interest anyway, from their conversation on the hillock and where the belvedere lay, so close to the pavilion; at least he wasn't close enough to question her.

He might be questioning Teo, behind her back. The boy wouldn't say. Every other night or so he would be whistled out of her rooms, late, to go off somewhere with the dwarf. And would come back so late it was almost early; the first time trying to clamber into that big bed until Mirjana kicked him out with a hissing whisper, "A fool's pleasure earns a fool's reward," and he had giggled off to a lonely pallet on the floor, for what little sleep he could snatch before she was kicking him again, kicking him up at dawn's light. Jendre had viewed it all with a quiet satisfaction, asked a few gentle questions and taken his rebuffs in good part. He would not talk about where Djago took him, or what to do. She made guesses, of course, she couldn't not; Mirjana murmured other suggestions as they nestled into the bed without him, one night and another, yet one more. But whatever they were up to, he and the dwarf, Teo was happy about it: slow and yawning and pleased with himself, apt to doze in the sunshine, apt to glance sidelong at Jendre and hide a knowing smile.

IF the gardens were a little wild, the parks were wilder. There was a line of shrubs along the back wall of the sleepers' pavilion which was very wild indeed. Untouched, unpruned she would guess for twenty years, since the magicians came . . .

"Teo," she said one morning while she sat on the bench in her little belvedere, while he drowsed in the sun at her feet, "you make a better gardener than you do a footstool, and idleness is reprehensible in a boy."

"Lady?"

"Go and find where they keep the garden tools; there must be tools,

even if no one ever uses them. Fetch a pair of shears, and start to trim those shrubs into shape. You see how they march in file up the slope there, towards the pavilion? Start from that grove of trees below," *out in the light, where everyone can see you.*

"Lady, no . . ."

A sharp toe in the ribs, and, "Go. Go now. Take your time, there's no hurry. Snip-snip. I'll be watching."

So too would others be watching. They would see a young eunuch at work in the garden, and it would be such a rare sight, they might well watch it for a while.

For a while, for a day or two. It would take him that long, longer; that was a long line of shrubs, and the work was slow, as dull to watch as to do. Before two days were out, Teo should just be a part of the landscape, the clipping of his shears as natural as the birdsong and the scrape of crickets in the morning.

Before two days were out, she was sure, her clever friends would know what she was planning. She was counting on that, to push her into it. Teo could clip twigs forever, and no one suffer for it; but once he and Mirjana understood, once they started watching her and waiting for the day when she would move—well, then she would have to move.

———————

IT came too soon, of course, as such days always do. Teo had made his way all up the slope to the corner of the pavilion, and so it had to be today; the two of them were eyeing her askance, understanding her all too well, and so she dared not let the moment slip.

While Mirjana laid out breakfast in the belvedere, fruit and sweet breads and sherbet, Jendre took Teo into the little room behind the gallery. "Quickly now, off with those robes," his traditional eunuch's dress, sombre and discreet, a badge of invisibility, "and change with me," where she was already fumbling with the ties of her robe.

"Lady," he said, "I'm barely at the corner yet, let me go on one little day longer and see if they make trouble for me, working at their windows . . ."

"Oh, what, did you think I'd let you take the risk of that?" She'd use him as bluff, but not as bait. "You've done enough. Today you get to sit here and play mistress all day long. Mirjana has almond cakes in her basket and a bottle of palm tea."

"I know. I told her it might be today. And I did promise to share."

She had deliberately chosen one of her simplest robes, but even so she was muddling her task here, she couldn't even manage to undress herself; he had to help her, swift familiar fingers at her laces.

As he worked, he said, "Shall I shave your head for you, before you dress? I have the shears here, and my own knife to make you pretty after."

He thought he was being clever, flourishing his own shaved head and the little stiff cap that did not hide it, that could only perch helplessly atop her sea of hair; but if he had thought of his stomach, she had thought of this. Those who worked outside commonly wore a soft hood with a long loose flap at the back to cover their necks from the sun and save their precious skins from burning. She produced one from her bodice and flapped it at him.

"How did you come by that, lady?"

"I stole it," pleased with herself, light-fingered lady, "from a sleeve in the washing rooms," from the chaos in the servants' quarters. Far too few were trying to serve this influx of far too many, which was why there was only bread and fruit for breakfast, and why a wise girl supervised her own laundry.

He nodded, equally pleased with her; but, "You should have had me wear it, all these days."

"I know it. I didn't think, until yesterday. Today will be hot, though, maybe hotter, don't you think? You might have changed your cap."

Not he, he loved the sun; but he shrugged and smiled and helped her into his own robe. She'd thought to bring a scarf too, to wind about his head, that way she sometimes wore it. He would fool no one close-to, but no one would be coming close; if anyone looked likely to, she told him to retreat into the back room, where Mirjana could claim that her mistress was sleeping.

Jendre would fool no one either, if they came close. Young and beardless she was, but that was all, not enough. She felt exposed already, not knowing how to move in these strange clothes. If she could watch the magicians from so far away and see—or think she saw—that they were no eunuchs, anyone watching her would know the same. Perhaps she should try to imitate that shuffle that they had, that she'd been seeing all her life and used to play at as a child, copying her friends or mocking the older men, the ones she didn't like.

She tried it, to and fro across the belvedere's floor. Mirjana shook her head; Teo just curled up in a spasm, choking on a plum stone.

Irritated, with her dignity piqued, she kicked at him. "Rolling around like that, you no more resemble me than I do you."

He blinked up at her, his eyes wet and his mouth smeared. "Lady, do you think you never laugh?"

"No, but—not like that," boyishly, convulsively, all consumed by his own magnificent amusement.

"Really not?" That was Mirjana, unfairly stabbing at her even while she went towards Teo with a napkin. He fended her off, wiping his own face on his sleeve—no, on Jendre's sleeve, and knowing just what he was doing, by the gleam in his glance as he did it. "There have been times I thought I would bury you for laughing."

It was true, she remembered kicking, biting, howling till it hurt, till her belly cramped; but, "I was younger then. And I had my sister with me." Indeed it was often Sidië she laughed at, to that little girl's scowling fury, which only provoked the laughter more.

"True. And he is far from home," Mirjana speaking more softly now, "and has no one with him at all. Let him laugh, you. And don't try to walk like a eunuch, anywhere that anyone may see you."

SHE settled then for walking like herself, or stalking rather, in high indignation. Teo never had affected that shuffle anyway; why should she? With the shearing blades heavy in one hand, she skirted the pool and dropped swiftly down the bank behind it, then made her way over to the spinney where the shrubs began their march uphill.

From here, from the shadow of the trees she could be a gardener. People would see the costume, see the work, dismiss it. A boy trimming the shrubbery? They wouldn't even see it. Out of the shade, then, and into the light, out where anyone, everyone might see her; assume that everyone was watching, then try to forget it, try to be who she pretended to be. Just another boy, sent to carry on Teo's work. Which meant that she could inspect his work, dawdle over these early bushes, take the shears to a twig or two just to get used to the feel of them in her hands, their weight, the way they cut . . .

And so up the hill as though there were no hurry in the world, and none in her. A snip here, a clip there, a fragrant blossom tucked into a knot at her waist because these boys did decorate themselves with beads and flowers and trinkets. She tried not even to look at the pavilion, as though she were only concerned with her work, and doing as little of it as any boy might. As if to guide her, Teo had done a boy's job, a sullen job, skimping where he could; she skimped too, more and more as she came closer and closer to the pavilion.

She had thought it dark, sunk in its own shadows, but that wasn't true. Not on this side, at least, south-facing. The wooden frame was black and the roof tiles were river clay, blue-grey with their own inherent shadow; between the posts, though, the walls were white beneath the dirt of years, and busy with windows and screens that ought to slide aside to let the sun walk in, no need to climb across a sill.

Those screens had been fixed shut with nails, and blocks of wood to break the tracks they ought to slide along. The windows were all close-shuttered, as Djago had said, and overgrown by a tangle of climbing plants.

Those were her legitimate interest. If someone came to send her away, they would only find her clipping, trimming, as a good boy ought. She could scuttle off before they came too close, act scared because she would be scared, she was scared already. Small harm.

She snipped and clipped, pulled down the growth of years and no one came. At last she was tired, sweating, her hands were filthy and starting to blister, but she had all the windows clear, only those shutters left between her and whatever, whoever waited inside with her sister Sidië. No need for iron bars and bolts in what had been the Sultan's harem in ancient days, a house for lamentation since; now as then, there were other stronger walls to keep the world at bay. Who was outside these windows? Women and eunuchs: none who mattered. No man kept a watch, because no one cared.

The shutters were tied with cord, old cord, and she had shears in her hands.

Her breath came short and shallow; she was scared, more scared than the first night Salem came over the harem wall, which meant more scared than ever in her life. But she was here, she had come this far to do this thing; she had never been closer to Sidië, even in bed together she'd never felt closer than this, and she wouldn't turn back now.

She lifted the shears, worked the point of one blade under the cord that closed the shutters at the building's corner, the furthest window from the door, what might—please!—be the safest, the least watched; and gasped another breath, just one more living moment, and then snipped.

The cord parted, and fell away. Nothing more happened.

Slowly, she lifted the flat of her hand to one shutter and leaned against it.

GENTLY, gently. She felt resistance, and told herself—anxiously, fretfully, dishonestly—that it was just age and disuse working against her here, nothing mystical. After a little while she found the courage to try again, to push a little harder.

The shutter creaked, and she snatched her hand back.

Took a breath, looked about her, steadied herself; set her feet in the grass and her hands on the shutter's frame, and shoved from the shoulders.

It moved, it swung inward. It might have gone too far, slammed back and pulled her half in after it, if she hadn't kept grip and balance both, if she hadn't been so careful not to put all her weight behind the effort.

As soon as it shifted, she was drawing it back, pulling it closed again. Any bright shaft of sunlight driving into shadow could betray her. It was shadowy in there, she knew that, she had seen: sickly-shadowy, shadows with their own bad spirit that might shriek at a sudden fall of light, might spew out at her, might do anything.

Shadows in there, and silence too. This was a building full of children, and she could hear not a voice, not a cry coming from it. At least that wasn't the silence of alarm, where birds fall still and frightened people hold their breaths. It had been quiet already, quiet all the time. That was bad for the children, what it said about them; it was bad for her too, if she made any noise at all . . .

Well, but she had to look. Cautiously she worked the shutter open again, just a finger's breadth. She could see those shadows again, roiling like smoke in the sun; not spilling out as smoke would, but neither falling back as shadows ought. Another moment, then, before she stepped up to the gap and peered in. Nothing struck at her, out of that swirling; no insidious tendrils reached to insinuate themselves into her eye, her mind, her soul.

Nor could she see anything at first, except the swirling and the colours that it held, pale and searing, nameless shades. She blinked, she squinted, she waited as a wise girl does in the dark, until the eye adjusts; and at last she began to make out shapes behind the endless movement, the slow, chaotic, meaningless ebb and flow. She could see no patterns in it, no steady currents, but she could see what it moved around.

At first they were only square and boxy outlines, shadows within shadow, but at least they held still amid the drifts and eddies of the stained air. With those to focus on, she could make out more; there were other shadows, equally solid, except that these moved between the first. Not many and not often, but they did move.

Gradually, her mind made sense of what her eye was finding. Those were beds, those boxes, simple wooden cots, except that they were so high-sided you might as easily call them pens. The women who moved between them had to bend almost double as they reached down to do whatever it was that they did to whomever they had caged within those beds.

Whatever, whomever?

Sidië . . .

———————

FROM where she stood, at the corner and leaning in at the window now, heedless of alarm, Jendre could see into three or four of the cots. Each one held a child, curled on its side and sleeping, naked on a web of woven cord.

Sleeping, yes, but not restfully: they moved constantly in their sleep, twitches and shudders shook them, soft grunts escaped them. They looked healthy enough, if fat were healthy; well fed, at least. Not well. They sweated in their sleep, their long hair was matted and there was a rank smell rising. There were other smells in the air, smoke and incense, not heavy enough to disguise the corrupt and fleshy odours of the cots.

Three boys, and one more where the angle of her view was cut by the high side of the cot; she thought that might be a girl. She couldn't see the face, but the head was dark and a long arm stretched across the webbing. Not Sidië.

One of the shadowy women was making her way along the line of cots, with a whisper of bells to announce her. Jendre withdrew and pulled the shutter closed.

Breathing deeply, taking her time, fighting down a sudden dizziness, she took her shears and moved along the wall.

———————

AT the fourth window, at last, she found her sister.

———

HOW did she know her?

By her hair, initially. Long distinctive yellow twists: tangled though they were, sweat-sodden and foul, they still proclaimed themselves and Sidië.

Then by her attitude, that familiar sprawling skew; night after night she had slept that way in Jendre's big bed, and she still would sleep that way, however much the cot's sides might confine her. There were sores on her elbows, Jendre could see, where she must have knocked and ground them against the unrelenting wood, where she used to knock and grind them against Jendre's ribs.

Then—somehow, reluctantly—by her body. Sidië was still there, the bones of her, compact and strong; only that she had not grown but fattened up, not bloated yet but taken the first slow heavy steps towards it. It was like seeing her sister bundled in fat, still showing obscurely through a curtain. A sticky, slimy curtain: whatever it was those women did, it had little to do with keeping their charges clean.

Nor had it much to do with keeping watch. Four times now Jendre had put her head in, at four different windows, and still not been spotted. The women kept their heads down; they seemed all to have bells in their hair, to help her hear them coming. The sounds like the shadows were pent within the building; there was no sign of any magician, but the place reeked of magic.

She gazed down through the thick air at her sister's face, where it twisted against her dreams; she made a vow to come back, to fetch Sidië out of there, whatever bad place it was her dreams had sent her.

———

CAUTION was second nature once she'd seen, although she'd seen so little. Just as well. She had almost no thought in her head, certainly no thought of herself as she drew that last shutter closed, as she snipped vaguely at shrubbery for a few minutes longer, as she made her slow way back down the slope and through the copse and out of sight and so at last up again to the pool and the belvedere where her friends were waiting.

Sidië was all she saw, all she touched and smelled and held: Sidië like a picked fruit ill stored, sweet and sticky and starting to rot. She should not be left so, in the hands of the thieves of dreams. She should *not* . . .

———

JENDRE changed clothes again with Teo, and barely said a word. Her silence, her focus, her almost-absence affected even his frivolous mood; she only noticed him because he fell so swiftly quiet himself, under Mirjana's glare.

Dressed again, like herself again and yet not truly so, feeling oddly changed inside as though no one who knew her would recognise her now, as though she found it hard herself to recognise this spirit as her own, she said, "I have found Sidië. She is—not well. We will need to think, how best to fetch her out of there, and where we can house her after."

No question about it, no *if we can*, no admission of any doubt. It had to be.

After a minute—a thoughtful minute, or a respectful, or a fearful, a desperate, despairing: she wasn't sure whether these two thought her bold or mad or stupid—Teo said, "Lady, perhaps I can fetch someone who will help."

"Who is that?" She assumed that he meant Djago, that he would go trotting off to come back with the dwarf, the voice of experience, of understanding, who would know what could and what could not be done in here.

He only shook his head, though. "Not now. Later. Tomorrow night, perhaps. By your leave, lady."

A little later, he was a grinning idiot again, behind his hand or when he thought she wasn't looking. She loved him, but she couldn't depend on him, on his treasured mystery, his swelling secrets. She had only herself to trust in this, and she was afraid even to trust herself; she thought she would only be let down.

———

THAT night, Teo was gone again. She had expected it. This time there wasn't even the whistle from the passage, Djago come to fetch him; this time he went on his own initiative.

She didn't mind. There was the chance to think, deeply and undisturbed. She had found her sister; she didn't know how to save her. She couldn't think how to fetch her out of the pavilion, nor where to hide her after. The park was rich in empty buildings, the harem rich in empty rooms; none of them was safe ground to hold a hideaway. Nor could Sidië safely be smuggled into Jendre's own suite. The little girl would be missed, she would be hunted for; where else would they seek her first than in her sister's care?

Jendre puzzled and twisted in the bed all night, till Mirjana left her, to search for peace on a pallet. She drowsed and scowled and snapped all the following morning, while Teo sprawled across the bed at her feet and yawned and rubbed his eyes and watched her, smiling privately, a boy with a hidden triumph.

In the afternoon, she thought they ought to go back to the belvedere, where she could watch the pavilion and hope for inspiration, or else sleep in the sun. Even from a distance, though, they could see activity in what she thought of as her own place, as private as her rooms. Long before they reached it, they knew who was so busy there.

Tirrhana was not in her cart; Djago had hauled it up without her. Instead his load was cushions and furs and soft padded quilts in vivid colours, with which he was cloaking the bench and making a nest in the shady room behind.

"Teo reminded me," he said, after he had greeted her with all his courtier's charm, or else with a mockery too deep to fathom, "how lovely it was up here. I had forgotten, all these years below, since my mistress could not make the climb. She can, though, if I bring her; and she shall. With these comforts, we can stay all day, if she likes it."

Jendre couldn't fault him, he was right entirely. Nor could she blame Teo for spilling her secrets; as well blame the birds for singing, as that boy for babbling when he was content. She still felt robbed. This was her peace and her spy hole both, and it had been plundered from her. Djago bustled about like a magpie with stolen treasures, talking all the while; she was as polite as she could manage, and she came away as quickly as good manners would allow.

DISPLACED and angry, helpless and frustrated, she could feel the loom of failure building. She tried to imagine, to understand how she could live years and decades, a lifetime here, knowing how her sister's life had ebbed away in dreams and drugs just there, in daily sight of her, and she had found no way to save her. She couldn't do that, it was unimaginable. She would die, she thought, of sheer fury at herself. Jendre would wither and fail, at Jendre's own glare in the mirror. She would force herself to face that, and to visit the pavilion too, daily, hourly, so that she might die in her shame the quicker . . .

Or, better, she would fight her way into the pavilion with knives, and be cut down by guards with scimitars, or else blasted to death by strange magics. Die trying; that had to be preferable, where her life had no point else.

Certainly today had no point now, and she couldn't think what to do with it. Mirjana pressed food on her, but she didn't want to eat; nor to talk, nor bathe, nor walk in the gardens, nor play games. Nor feel Teo's eyes always on her in his smug self-content, but she couldn't avoid that, short of sending him away. She nearly did that, time and again, and only held back because it would feel like another kind of failure, if she couldn't bear even the company of her friends. Besides, this was still strange ground; he was better under her eye, out of other trouble. If Djago whistled for him tonight, he'd whistle in vain. She was suddenly resolved on that, and not sure where the resolution had come from, only that it felt right.

They endured the day, all of them, though it was difficult for all. Came the evening at last, came the night like a blessing, and she could start to think about bed as a place to hide, the dark like a blanket wrapped around her sorrow, her anger and her self-contempt.

Before she could seek it out, though, Teo said, "Please, my lady—a walk in the night air, before we sleep? It will soothe your head . . ."

"My head does not need soothing," she snarled. And heard how he struggled to choke back a snigger, and saw how even Mirjana was working to hide her smile, and—curse it!—she couldn't fight back a wry smile of her own. "Well, perhaps it does. But—"

"Oh, let him walk you," Mirjana sighed, as though her mistress were a dog or a bear, to be led about on a chain. "I'll have no peace else, from either of you. Go and walk off all your temper, go . . ."

_____

ASTONISHING to herself, but she did go. And she did let Teo take her arm and hustle her; and she was slow, so slow, she took so long to understand that he had some purpose else, other than her soothing. At last she remembered, *perhaps I can fetch someone who will help,* and she still thought that he must mean Djago; whom else did the boy know in here?

She thought this was to be a private meeting, then, with the dwarf in darkness. Teo might be right, after all. Djago must know all the intimacies of the palace here, after forty years within its walls. If there was a way to hide Sidië, he could show it to her; if there was a way to take her out of the pavilion, he could perhaps instruct her.

So she went without a struggle, without a question even, where Teo was guiding her. She didn't need to question, she knew the answers already and she saw no need to feed his manifest conceit. If she did have cause to thank him, it would keep.

And of course he led her through the gardens to the park, and then all through the park to where it climbed towards the wall below the cliff, and of course he was taking her to the belvedere. It was a surprise, but only a small one, when Teo checked a little way below, when he urged her forward with gentle hands but was clearly coming no further himself. Djago must have told him to wait apart, to let the dwarf and Jendre speak in private . . .

So she finished the climb alone, only a little hopeful, not at all concerned; and the greater surprise, far greater, was when she stepped up into the belvedere and saw the figure waiting in the moon-shadow, and it had twice the height of Djago.

Then she was afraid, just for a moment, until he moved. Until he stepped forward into moonlight, until he spoke her name.

She knew his body intimately, by the way his spirit wore it; she knew the whispers in the shadows of his voice. She gasped, soft as a fish biting at the air at the pool's surface at her back; she said his name, to complete the spell and make him real, have him here to the touch, solid and unsafe and her own.

"Salem . . ."

Chapter Three

AGIC never makes anything better. It never makes anything good."

It was Rhoan, of course, who said it: Rhoan who sat hurt and helpless, hunched over, staring at her hands; Rhoan the regretful, wishing she could walk away from all rebellions, though Issel thought she'd insist on taking her friends with her, and Tulk for one wouldn't go; Rhoan who did not want to make any more of what she called the vicious water, even if she were brave enough to try.

"We need magic to fight magic," and that was Tulk the believer, still passionate for his city.

"Do we?"

"Well, how else? Twenty years they've had their bridge, and we've never had an answer. There is no answer, except to bring it down."

"Or to let it stand, not fight, not have a war at all."

"Don't you want to be free?" Tulk was incredulous. "I know you were hurt, Rhoan, but . . ." But he was prepared to sacrifice more and far more than his friends' hands, that was obvious. Her surrender left him stuttering for words and finding none.

If it was a surrender. Issel wasn't sure.

"I don't think I believe in freedom. Will Lenn and Gilder give us freedom? It's all the same, Tulk. Them, the Marasi, Tel Ferin—they tell us what to do, and we suffer for it. Whether or not we do it, whether or not we can, we still suffer. Sund suffers, but so does Maras. They send their boys over the bridge here, and we kill some of them, and then they kill more of us, and so it goes on. Maybe the Marasi are right, maybe we are all one city, Maras-Sund. Maybe we deserve to be."

"Those aren't Marasi boys; only the officers. The rest are slaves," Tulk said. "They take them as tribute from all over the empire and make armies of them."

"So they have us kill each other. All the worse."

"Well, what would you do? What do you want to *do*, Rhoan?"

"I don't know. Nothing, maybe. Live with it. Sund is no use to Maras, they take no profit from us. No soldiers, either. How could they trust a Sundain? Eventually they'll leave, surely they will. We're not even a route to better places. And they've killed all the trade we used to have, or stolen it to themselves. Why stay?"

"They stay because they can, because they're strong, because they're greedy just for land, for subjects, they don't care how poor we are." It might have been Lenn talking, it might have been Gilder, any of the rebels; it might have been Tel Ferin, if that man ever voiced his thoughts. Tulk had done a lot of listening, and he'd swallowed what he heard, whole and undigested, to puke it up as needed.

"If that's true, they won't care how much we hurt them, either."

"Which is why we have to catch them now, while they're weak, while they're troubled, while they can be defeated . . ."

Rhoan shook her head, and dropped her gaze to her hands again.

They'd told Tel Ferin that she had stumbled and tried to save herself the fall, put her hands straight down onto a street-seller's iron cooking plate, and so burned herself so badly. He'd barely looked at the weeping, blistered palms, certainly not long enough to see what nonsense the story was: how that skin wasn't scorched so much as boiled, how such damage could never have come from hot iron.

He had said, "I can heal this," and fetched his book, and water. He had read, and furrowed his brow over the words, and then shaped the water stiff but soft, a glistening cushion; he'd told her to rest her palms on it, press them into it, as hard and as long as she could bear.

They had seen her cry, when she did that. He told her to keep at it, the healing process would take time, and the more she used the water-cushion the more benefit she would derive. That was all he had to offer; which had led, now, to this.

"Magic only hurts us," she said, "us and them too. What's the point? Nobody gains."

Her hands did look better, new pink skin growing in as the old peeled away like bark from a birch tree. Tel Ferin had claimed it as a healing triumph for his water, his knowledge, his skill. Issel thought that time was passing, and hurts did heal. Rhoan said not inside, under the skin they were no better, but in her current mood she would have denied the comfort of a cold drink on a hot day.

Tulk was impatient with her, with Tel Ferin, with Issel and all of them. "She's afraid," he said privately to Issel, meaning *she's a girl, she can't deal with pain, she isn't manly.* "The master's only trying to seem more impressive than he is. He thinks he's losing our respect. He's right, but this won't help him. There's nothing in that book of his that talks about how to heal. I'd remember that."

If Tel Ferin had brought out any other book from his hoard, they couldn't have been certain; but this one, they had its contents intimately. His supposed healing had been mummery, no more. A cushion of cool water might be good for a regular burn, but Rhoan claimed that it made her hurts worse. Like the extra sting of a burn in steam or sunlight, she said, all her flesh seared when it touched the tingle of perfect water. She had tried, just to hold their secret safe; now she wouldn't go near the water-cushion, and only lied to him daily to say that she was using it.

"We can't help her," Tulk said, "and if we could, she wouldn't let us try. Whatever happened to that water at the Silkmart, it was her work as much as yours, only she won't do it again. Even when her hands have healed, she still won't. You know that's true."

Issel didn't know that at all. Rhoan was a mystery to him. It could be true; she did say it, and he didn't know what there was in the world that could change her mind. He was only sure that there must be something. There was always something. He'd made promises all his life, and meant them sincerely, and broken them just as sincerely. Or broken them casually, unheedingly, carelessly. Or simply forgotten them, or seen them die with the man he made them to, or . . .

"So I want to try it now," Tulk said, following the relentless logic of the situation. "What she did, how she turned the water that you made."

"Tulk, no. You've seen what it did to her, and it hasn't finished yet."

"Only because she tried to stop it hurting you. She interfered, and she got burned. I won't do that."

Issel blinked. "No? What will you do?"

"I'll wait. Not touch it, just wait till you've done whatever it is that you do. You're strong, Issel, you're stubborn as the river rising, you just keep on to where you're going and never mind the damage on the way. I know it hurt you, the last time; I expect it'll hurt again, but you can endure that, and then you can learn to control it, not let it run wild that way. We'll have the water somewhere it can't break the bowl, and if it climbs up your arm again, you can push it back. Somehow. And when you've done, then I'll turn it like we do, the master and Rhoan and me, and we'll see what we've got. It may not be the same; maybe it'll be stronger. I think it'll be stronger. Come on, I want to do this. I want to do it now."

Oh, he was ruthless, with other people's pain. If either one of them was like the river, Issel thought it was not actually himself. He found his left hand stroking his right arm, where the flesh remembered. "We'll need more privacy than this," he murmured. "We'll have to go somewhere I can scream."

SO they came to a place that Issel knew, behind the high wall of the Marasi barracks: a marshy waste where nothing palatable grew, where the cries of gulls mingled with the cries of prisoners inside the wall, the cries of strange creatures hunching up from the strand and hiding in the high rank grasses. Anyone's screaming here would always be taken for something else.

With a flask of well water and an empty bucket, they might just be two idiot boys hunting marsh crabs and freshwater mussels, far too close to the Shine. Issel had done that, in his time; he had been that much of an idiot, that hungry. Today, it was Tulk that was hungry. Issel thought they were both idiots.

Tulk dug a hole with his hands in the wet, sandy soil at the foot of the wall. He lined that with greasecloth, to make a bowl that could not leak or break; then he looked up at Issel.

"Ready?"

No, but Issel nodded.

Tulk poured water into the hollow. Then he stood back: not far, just far enough to respect the risks, to have the chance to run if Issel's screaming did after all attract unwelcome attention.

Issel hoped to surprise him. He wouldn't scream unless he must. Street pride is fierce, and it was only pride that had brought him here, onto his knees beside that little glimmer of water where it ruffled gently in the breeze.

Even pride couldn't keep his fingers from trembling, as he spread his hand above. He scowled at them, one last prideful gesture before he noticed how the water was already rising, yearning towards his palm. He yearned too, he wanted to touch it, to feel its tingle and do no more, no worse, no further damage to himself.

And held his hand where it was, out of the water's reach as it seemed to strain and pulse; and then—swiftly, swiftly, for pride's sake, because Tulk was watching—he let his thoughts run down, as though they slid out of his fingers to jump that tentative gap.

And tried to turn it, sweet and easy as Rhoan did, through dark to light, black to silver and so to water once again; and watched it grey and glitter, watched it leap back against the touch of his mind, watched it reach up and grip his fingers.

And felt it like fire again, as though his hand clenched around hot coals, except that these coals were lithe and slippery, climbing as they burned.

Actually, he couldn't scream. All his body was clenched around the pain of it; he had no air to scream with.

Nor any air to breathe, but he could welcome fainting, even if he fell down into nightmare. Better a dream of horror than the thing itself.

Except that Tulk was watching, waiting, expectant.

Issel still had a finger's grip on himself, his pride, his desires. And this time he could think, he could focus through the pain; he could even use the pain to focus, to crush out any thoughts else. He turned all the force of his will—a little, little force it felt, not adequate, but all he had—onto the creeping, shimmering mass as it oozed up his arm. It had colour, it had motion, it had life of a sort; he could sense an urgency, an intent. Tainted, corrupt but purposeful: if he or anyone lacked evidence that he had stayed too long in the Shine, here it was. He did this, he made good water into this, because of what he was and what he had, a natural gift twisted into perversity.

And he hated it, but it was his, it reeked of him and belonged with him, belonged to him as much as his pain did, as much as it wanted to possess him. So he could turn it back, he could send it down his arm and into the bucket, there where Tulk had left it ready. He could drive it off with a final bludgeoning blow of his mind and a desperate cry, his last gasp of dead air released at last; and then he could fall back against the wall, sodden and sobbing and ashudder, twisting in the memory of pain like hooks left in his flesh, barely aware of Tulk as that boy cautiously approached the bucket.

"It looks, it looks like frogspawn. If frogs spawned ground glass, if ground glass could squirm . . ."

Issel shook his head, uncaring. He opened his mouth to say *be careful, don't touch*—and closed it again around the words unuttered. He didn't have the breath to spare, and Tulk didn't need the warning.

Tulk didn't even reach down inside the bucket's mouth. He spread his palm above, and Issel saw the play of shadow, of darkness, an inverse of the play of light: a sudden black within the bucket, and then a sudden shine that gleamed off pale skin in a way that still implied the shadow behind the light, what made shine into silver.

And then it was only the dappled sunlight reflecting from a bucketful of water; and then, finally, Tulk was ready to look around, to find Issel. Perhaps to see how he was, perhaps to show his triumph in his face. Perhaps both.

He said, "It's done. I think it's done. It feels . . . strange."

Issel said, "It frightened Rhoan, the way it felt, after she had done it."

Tulk shrugged, dismissing her girlishness, not being afraid. Determinedly, not being afraid. "How are you, was it very bad?"

"Oh, yes," Issel said. No need to be manly here, pride or not. Perhaps pride flourished on confession, *see how much pain I can take?* "That was bad."

"Can you stand up yet, can you walk?"

"If I have to."

"I think you should. I think we ought to get away from here."

He seemed urgent, overkeen; Issel thought this might be another part of the test, to see how quickly he could recover, to know how soon they could do it all again.

Not soon was the answer to that, not half so soon as Tulk would no doubt like. Some things grew easier with practice, some things grew less painful; he didn't believe that this was one of those. He might learn to bear it better. It did seem that he was learning not to scream. Even so, he still felt as though his arm had been enfolded in flame. Every little hair was there, unharmed, but it burned in the sunlight and he couldn't bear to move it; the bones of it felt charcoal-light, as though they would snap or crumble at the least effort.

Slowly, slowly he levered himself to his feet, not looking to Tulk for help, using his other arm and the wall at his back. Once he was up, it took a minute to be steady on his feet, a minute more to find that he could walk, totteringly up and down.

Tulk watched him with a kind of amused impatience. "Tell me when you can run. We'll need to run."

"Why? No one's coming."

"I think we should test this," and Tulk hefted the bucket cautiously. "Don't you? Before we go telling anyone what we've got here, I think we ought to find out what we can do."

And his eyes moved to that high and solid wall, and Issel just knew that he was thinking about the Silkmart, how easily its roof had been brought down.

The Silkmart was old and not built for strength, not like this; this was built to repel armies, or at least a city, rebellious citizens, themselves. Tulk was right, of course, they should know what they had. Issel was just afraid that this might be overreaching.

If it was, then what they had might not be worth the having. Best to find out now; Tulk was flighty with success, and wanted to proclaim it.

Issel nodded, trying not to sigh at the same time. "All right. You do it, whatever you want to do."

Tulk cocked his head. "What, are you afraid?"

"No, I'm not afraid. But that's what we need to know, whether it works for you; what I set my hand to comes out twisted. You know that, or we wouldn't be here."

A grunt, and, "You might as well start walking, then. If running would be hard for you. I'll wait till you're at the corner there," where the wall turned away from the marshland, back towards the city proper, "and then I'll come after you. Wait, though, I don't want to use all we've got . . ."

Of course he didn't, he wanted some to show off to the rebels, win their applause, their respect, hold their hopes in his hands. So he tipped the bucket carefully over the little lined hollow in the ground, and poured out a dribble. It looked like water, but Issel didn't want to touch it, any more than Rhoan had at the mart.

"There," Tulk said, not a doubt or a hesitation in him. "This'll be plenty." Or it would do nothing, and hence no harm; Issel could almost hope for that, hope to be the only one harmed today. "You take the bucket; hard for me to run without spilling. This is better."

———

FROM the great masonry blocks where the wall turned, Issel could still see Tulk, small and stocky and very much alone. He could see a few men up on the wall's height, leaning against the parapet, too bored to watch the swamp. He was surprised they kept a guard at all out here, where nothing threatened bar the odd Shine perversion flapping over in search of a hot blood supper. Perhaps it was good for discipline to set a watch, or else— more likely—bad for discipline not to.

The guards would need to lean over and look straight down to see Tulk below them. They could glance this way and see Issel, as easily as he saw them; but that would show them only a boy with a bucket, no threat at all. The threat was too close, and too immediate. If Tulk called up to them directly, it could not save them now.

Tulk didn't call up, nothing so foolish. He just raised his hand and threw, and turned in the same moment to run towards Issel.

He didn't run far. From where Issel stood, Tulk's figure was a sudden silhouette, against a flare of greasy grey light. Then it was consumed in a boil of dust that swept along the wall to overtake him at the same time as it rose to envelop the guards and suck them down into itself.

That was how it seemed to Issel, dust like a live thing, smoke that struck. He thought he saw shapes falling into the murk, stones from the wall and the men who had stood on top of it; he thought he saw Tulk knocked off his feet just before the dust could reach him. He might have tripped, but Issel didn't think so. He'd have said there was a wind, rather, that outran the dust to hammer Tulk flat into the wet ground.

He heard the rumble of the falling wall, a moment after seeing it come down. Dimly, he heard shrieks of dismay, of terror; then a silence from the barracks and the marsh birds both, followed by a rising babble of men's voices from behind the wall. Issel watched the dust cloud rise and spread, his own anxiety rising to meet it. If Tulk didn't emerge, he'd have to go back. Armed with the bucket that he did not want to use, to face an army of Marasi conscripts erupting like ants from their broken nest, vicious and afraid.

He pressed himself against the solidity of unshaken stone and waited, watched, prayed almost despite his cynical Sundain blood; and saw a figure come blundering out of the dust, wet and filthy and half-blind, it seemed, staggering through the margins of the marsh.

He left the bucket and ran back to find Tulk more bewildered than hurt, reeling the way someone does after a blow on the head. Issel dragged him away just that little time before men could appear warily at the breach, scrambling over shifting rubble and calling to each other through the dust haze, seeing nothing, particularly seeing nothing of a couple of boys who might be retrieving a bucket and sliding away around the corner and so away from the compound and strangely into the broad streets of the wealthy merchant quarter, when anyone with the least understanding of how the city worked would have expected two such shabby creatures to run to the rat-alleys of the lower town.

ISSEL meant to leave Tulk in possession of his precious bucket, in the secluded safety of the bathhouse furnace room, while he went to find Rhoan. Coming into the bathhouse, though, they heard two women murmuring, and he knew them both at once, just by the hidden timbres of their voices.

Instead of the furnace room, then, he led Tulk to the main chamber; and there was Rhoan, and there was Armina with her.

They were crouched over a bowl of water, the two of them, heads together. Rhoan had her hands held out above the water, palms upward, which looked strange; but she was peering down between them into the bowl or onto the surface of the water, rather, and that was not so strange at all. Armina used mirrors often to scry her visions of the future. She liked images without substance, because her little gift could support nothing weighty; if she had no glass and no bronze to hand, why should she not use the reflections in a bowl of water?

This was Rhoan's future, then, or some shadow of it, some aspect glimpsed. They would both have the rust in their lungs, in their blood, in their eyes and minds; there was no disturbing them now. Nor any point listening in. He could see a reddish cast to the water, where a drift of rust had settled on the surface, to cloud whatever images they saw. Nothing could ever be clear or clean or straightforward. Listening made it doubly muddled, someone else's fortune when they were seeing through the rust and you were looking at it. He could see it on her hands too, like brick dust clinging damply; Armina must have sprinkled it on her palms, he thought, above the water, and had her blow it off. Maybe she had asked for reassurance, *tell me my hands will heal,* and Armina was looking specifically to see.

Issel sighed, and signed to Tulk to set the bucket down. And settled down himself on his haunches, and thought how much of rebellion was simply waiting. Like being a student, learning in a school, living with other people. He had been busier, much busier when he had nothing to do all day but stay alive.

ARMINA roused first, and then Rhoan. She blinked and gazed about her, worked her shoulders uncomfortably, went to rub at her eyes. Armina gripped her wrists to prevent it; Issel gulped back what had been a yell building, *no, don't do that!* She had rust powder on her fingers; he couldn't imagine what that stuff would do in her eyes.

Besides, rubbing anything would hurt her hands. Would have hurt her hands last night, at least, should still have done this morning; but Armina rinsed them quite roughly in the water, and Rhoan didn't protest. Then the older woman lifted them out and took a towel to them, and was rougher still, and Rhoan only sat there flexing her fingers against the linen, as though she were waiting for, feeling for the pain and not finding it yet, somehow not finding it at all.

"Well, child?"

"They don't hurt. Not like before . . ."

"No. You will still have trouble with them, and you must work them until they do hurt. Like this," gripping one of Rhoan's hands and bending the fingers back until she yelped. "Do that, as often as you can. And stretch them wide, so," demonstrating again, pulling all the fingers apart as far as they would go. "All the cords have been trying to shrink and tighten, like catgut in the cold; you must pull on them again and again, until they are loose again as they ought to be."

"Ouch! I will, I will . . ."

"Do so, or they will shrivel into claws, like old women's with the knuckle disease, and you will have no use of them."

Rhoan nodded, earnestly working one hand against the other; then she looked around, scowling. "What are you two doing here?"

For once, Issel did have an answer. He knew exactly why he had brought Tulk, brought the bucket, come in search of her. It was important; she needed to be the first to know, the first to see what they had done. It was why he had fallen in with Tulk to do this thing, for her sake, and he wanted to tell her so.

Except that she and Armina had entirely thrown him out now, so that he had to meet her question with one of his own: "How has Armina made your hands better, how is that possible?" She told futures, and sometimes maybe gave the chance to change them; her magic had no power else.

"I don't know," Rhoan said as she gazed down into her palms, rubbing at one with her thumb, as though she rubbed dead skin away. "I know why, she did it to prove me wrong, but I don't know how . . ."

"She said to me what she said to you," Armina said, "that magic can bring no good to anyone. I showed her that it can. Magic is a tool, no more, in my hands or in yours. Different tools for different tasks, but none of them are weapons, unless you choose to use them so. You can do bad things with magic, you especially, little Issel, and sometimes those things must be done. Even you will learn to use it otherwise, if I can keep you alive long enough for the lesson. Today I have shown your friend that what I do is good for more than spying out her secrets."

Good for that too, though; Rhoan's blush was fierce. That was a pleasure to savour later, when he was private. For now he swallowed a grin, and said, "That doesn't tell us how."

Armina shrugged massively. "Rust is the bloom of time; it carries the perfume. It can throw your spirit forward, show your road ahead, where it runs straight and where it divides, where there are choices to be taken. It can also draw back a little of its source, like a rock from the sea that still holds water; it can spill time where it touches. I have given Rhoan's hands the time they needed, and not made her live the weariness of it. No more than that. It is your task now to tell her that she need not hurt them again."

Tulk stared, stammered, "How, how did you . . . ?"

Issel ignored him and Armina both; he was long used to this, having his secrets punctured in public. He said to Rhoan, "It's true. You were scared that we'd ask you to do what Gilder wants, to make more of that water.

Now you don't have to." This wasn't triumph he was feeling, it was deeper and warmer and far less brittle. He thought it might be satisfaction. "We've learned how to do it ourselves, Tulk and me. And he doesn't have to get hurt either." *Only I need to hurt*, and she didn't need to know that.

By the way she looked at him, he thought she knew it already. She didn't say so, though. She only nodded, glanced at the bucket with a shivery distaste, and thanked him as distantly as a mistress might thank a servant for some attention she had not asked for. Then her eyes dropped back to her hands, and her thumb went back to its rubbing. He thought she was rubbing harder, digging deeper, still searching for the pain that she thought must be lurking somewhere.

She was wasting her time, but she'd have to learn that for herself. He wasn't going to tell her. He hadn't understood Armina at all, but he knew this much at least, that when she spoke directly, what she said was true. There would be pain for Rhoan in the days to come, but it would be the pain of use, working against the stiffness of healed hands, nothing worse than that.

And no doubt Tel Ferin will claim it as his own achievement, even while he wonders how it happened—but that was a fugitive thought, his turn to waste his time. Strange how scared he had been of Tel Ferin such a short time ago and then how worshipful, how dismissive he felt now; like Rhoan in pursuit of her vanished pain, he probed for either fear or wonder and could not find them. He felt it as a loss, a part of himself somehow stripped away. That was strange too, how people could be possessive of their weaknesses, their damage, whatever they had that was theirs. Some things they should be glad to lose, and were not. He still kept all his little things, despite the memories they fed.

Gesturing at the bucket, not quite wanting to touch it, he said, "What shall we do with this now?"

"Give it to me," promptly. Indeed, Armina came to take it, against a swallowed protest from Tulk, who wanted to be possessive of his own achievement. She poured her rust-tainted water carefully into the drain in the tiled floor, "Let the fishes see for a moment, where their wet roads will take them," set the empty bowl atop the bucket like a hollow lid, and spread a folded cloth over both of them together. "No one will notice a slave woman with her slops. Some of us are invisible by nature," with a glance at clever Rhoan, who could be invisible by artifice.

Tulk snorted. "You don't look invisible to me. Very solid, I'd have said."

"That's why they won't see me. A pretty girl with a bucket," and another glance at Rhoan, "she might be stopped, and dallied with. Then a suspicious man might question what she carried; they are not all fools, these Marasi. Me, though, they will look straight through me; I am too solid, as you say, to catch their eye."

Tulk didn't like his own words being played with, any more than he liked to see her take away his water. He said, "What will you do with it?"

"I will take it to Lenn and Gilder, and they will call a meeting to decide what's best. Soon, today; there is just time, and they will not want to wait. Come to the chapel ruins, where you took Lenn once before. All three of you, come an hour before sunset and see what results. Come carefully, and watch behind; remember, there is a betrayal waiting for you somewhere. Tulk has shown me that."

TO Issel, going carefully meant going high. They found the roof-roads busy that afternoon, though, and unwelcoming, and somehow not so safe. Thin children huddled in corners, watching silently as they passed. Adults too, perhaps rediscovering their old refuge as they looked to escape the tensions and dangers of the city in its stress. If they had once been roof-rats like himself, they had mostly lost the way of it, seeming awkward and ill at ease, just too big for this.

As he led his friends from parapet to pitch, even as he smiled at the way Tulk so determinedly hid his nervousness from Rhoan, Issel was feeling obscurely threatened by all these people. So many, they were a threat in themselves; they would attract Marasi attention in a way that a few wild children never had.

Those who belonged here, the real roof-rats watched him with a blank hostility. He might not know them, but they must surely know him. Everyone knew Issel, who had been a thief and a runner before he was a waterseller, long before he was a magician's apprentice. Seeing him for what he was, fearing him for what he might do, these were too young to be rebels and too hungry to be patriots; perhaps he should be fearing them, what they might do.

Betrayal is waiting—Issel gazed into hollow, shadowed eyes and wondered. And on the heels of the thought, a ragged figure dropped suddenly down from a high gable, to land barefoot and balanced directly in his path.

This one, at least, he did know.

"Joss." A boy his own age, one he had run with for a while, before Armina had sent him to claim a waterseller's urn. Issel and Joss had been a famous, fierce pair of rogues, at least in their own telling. They had probably never been friends. He signed now quickly, quietly to those who were, Tulk and Rhoan behind him: *be still, be easy, I can handle this.*

"You should not be here."

It was what Armina had said to him in the Street of Smiths, what the dogtooth had said later the same day; it had a terrible echo to it.

"What, have I grown too big? You're the bigger." Taller, at any rate. They were both whip-thin, but Issel had surely been the better fed, these last weeks and months. It didn't matter, this wasn't about weight. Joss wasn't stupid enough to fight him. Not up here—roof-fights did happen, and usually ended with a fall—and certainly not now.

It wasn't about height either, and Joss was in no mood to play. "You're not one of us now, little frog. These roads are closed to you."

"Are they so?" Issel heard the lash of pride in his own voice, and hoped that he too was not stupid enough to fight. "Is it carrying an urn that made me a stranger here, or living as I do now, with others?" *Is it because I moved on and left you behind, Joss, or is it because I have talents that you lack?*

Goading was almost as stupid as fighting; Joss was wiser, saying nothing at all. Issel went on, trying to be calmer: "Let be. I see many people up here who do not belong—"

"And they are up here because of you, because you made the Marasi mad."

So he had been seen, attacking the Marasi wagon. Of course he had; they saw everything, these children. He knew. He had seen everything when he lived on the roofs, with his own eyes or through others'. The city was a net to snare stories; nothing happened, nothing could happen without its news running swift and far. Not always running true, but true enough. All stories have a truth that underruns the facts, like a pipe of water under dry, dry ground.

And because that was true—because both those things were true, that everything was seen and everything was heard—this little story of his meeting with Joss on the roof here could go the way it did, the way that no doubt Armina had foreseen it. He could say, "Not only me," and Joss,

"You mainly, you with your water-tricks," and then he could just shrug, because that was true, or he thought it was.

And then he could say, "I want to pass," and Joss, "No. We keep these roads, and not for you. There are too many up here already, and most of them are strangers, but you—you're deadly. If the Marasi came hunting, if they thought you were here, if they thought you'd ever been here, they would kill us all."

"They could hunt me anyway, whether I'm here or not. Half an hour, Joss, no longer."

"Not a minute. You go down now, and your friends too."

"We're in a hurry."

"You always were. A hurry to win your place with us, and a hurry to move on after. How much hurry did it take to claim your urn the way you did it, and be a waterseller?" And then, "The man you took it from, was he in such a hurry, that you had to help him as you did?" And then, "What will you do, Issel, if I still bar your way? Will you hurry me too, as you did him?"

That was one goad, one brutality too far. Issel shivered, *does he know that too?* and *yes, of course, everything,* and said, "Only if you begged me," which was also true. And then he turned to his friends, and said, "We go down. Joss has closed the roofs to us. Remember that."

"He's only one—"

And a scrawny one too, but Issel glared at Tulk, and said it again. "We go down."

———————

THEY went down. Issel glanced back up at the silhouette that watched them from the roof's edge, as it seemed that someone always had been watching, even when he'd thought himself alone; and he thought, *betrayal is waiting,* and wondered if he'd met it now, or renewed its acquaintance, or maybe given birth to the seeds of it in Joss's mind.

He didn't know what to do, except go on.

They went on.

———————

THE going was slower now, and more wary. No one was moving on the streets, even in the shadier streets where the Marasi seldom ventured. Issel could have led them straight and true, directly to their meeting. They could have run it, more swiftly even than the roof-run. But this was Issel, who had no faith in straight or true; he took them by a broken way, watchful at every corner, every doorway, wherever men might linger.

They were slow, then, and they were careful; and even so they were nearly at the rendezvous before they were overtaken, and they were nearly caught and taken when they were.

———————

NO one would encroach on the old chapel's ground, no one now would lift so much as a fallen stone for their own walls, for fear of letting superstition back into rational, unworshipful Sund. Who knew what foreign spirits might not be lurking in some stony void, waiting to be loosed into the world, vengeful after centuries of being unsoothed by prayer?

The local people had built their houses and run their streets right to the edges of the site, sometimes to the very walls of the cloister, so that the chapel lay nested in the quarter's heart. Issel would have to bring them close, very close, before they could see or be seen by anyone waiting there, rebels or Marasi, either one. He ached, he burned for the perspective and safety of the roofs, but he wouldn't go up.

Cautiously then and indirectly, he worked his friends towards the chapel; and they were almost, almost there, just one more corner and he thought he could hear voices already, which must mean the rebels because a Marasi trap would be silent; and then he heard something else, feet in pursuit, many feet behind them trying to be quiet as they marched. That many men, quiet was beyond them; their boots were heavy and their buckles jingled, their swords scraped in their scabbards and even their breath was loud.

Issel had time enough to grab at his friends and drag them into a doorway, time enough to realise that wasn't shelter enough, and then—just—time enough to be clever, just for once: to snatch his little flask of water from his belt, to thrust it into Rhoan's hands, to hiss, "Don't let them see us . . ."

But even while he was being clever, he was being stupid too. He had to let go of his friends' sleeves, to reach for the flask; and Tulk—urgent, determined, Tulk the rebel, all sworn to the brotherhood—he was away, the moment he felt Issel's grip loosen.

"Not me," in a fading whisper, all but lost in the scuff of his feet in the dust as he scurried off ahead, "I'll warn our friends . . ."

———————

AND then it was too late, because there were shadows in the alley and no time at all to follow Tulk or else to fetch him back. All Rhoan could do was bite out the cork of the little flask and tip that perfected water into her cupped hand, letting it spill out over her fingers; all Issel could do was keep very still and very quiet. He watched her sooner than watch the street, in case whoever came might feel his stare and look clean through her spell to find him.

There was little enough to see, just a gentle steam arising, dissipating. Hanging in the air, he hoped, to make a mist around them, an eye-deceiving veil. He didn't want to look for it, because he knew he would see nothing; he was afraid that belief might be important, and he wasn't good at faith.

Two reasons, then, to keep his eyes on her. But because he did that, he saw how suddenly she stiffened, how her own eyes widened, how her mouth trembled against whatever word was building behind her locked jaw; and then he did slide his gaze out of the doorway, he had to do that, just to know whatever dreadful thing it was that she was seeing.

BETRAYAL is waiting, she had said, she had seen it in the line of Tulk's future; if she saw it clearly, she must have seen herself, and did not say.

It was Armina who led this line of soldiers, quiet as they could come; Armina who took them past the doorway and so to the corner; Armina who held them there briefly, with her arm upraised, before she let it fall and let them loose, let them slip like hunting dogs ahowl.

Armina who stood for a moment and looked back, looked through the shadows and the mist and straight at Issel. She had bound her hair up tightly in a cloth, presumably to muffle all her bells, but it was still Armina.

Then she followed the soldiers around the corner and into the abandoned chapel, where all the screaming was.

"WHAT shall we do?"

It was Rhoan who asked it, and not Issel who replied; he had no answers, only a dizzy bewilderment, a whirl of contradiction.

Nevertheless, she was answered. A voice spoke, behind and above them; it said, "Up here, swiftly."

And that was Gilder in the doorway, in the house behind them; or not a house, no, a workshop. Empty now except for him, themselves. They followed him up creaking wooden stairs to a higher floor, to a window that looked over the ruin of the cloister walls and down into what had been the chapel's heart, its garden.

"What are you doing here?"

That was Rhoan again, asking questions to avoid all the answers that mattered, which were out there where they could watch. Issel was all eyes, all horror, bereft of words entirely.

"Someone always has to stand apart."

"What, to keep guard? Some guard you are . . ."

"Not to guard. To witness. In case of betrayal."

In case of this, he meant. It was certain now. Issel had hugged the least heart of hope on his way up the stairs, that perhaps Armina was playing a double game, leading the soldiers into a rebel ambush; they did have that bad water, after all, they could have annihilated this whole squad . . .

Except that there were more squads than one, he saw now, soldiers at every gap in the walls; and clearly, all too obviously, the rebels did not have that bad water. Armina might have given it to the Marasi, she might have tipped it away, she might have kept it for herself; it didn't matter. Betrayal is never mitigated, never measured by degrees. Like life, like death, it is the one thing, indivisible.

Very like death, except that only a few of the rebels were actually dying. Those who had blades, largely, and seemed inclined to use them.

"Why don't they fight?" Rhoan groaned at his back, her fingers digging into his shoulder.

"With what?"

"Oh, anything. Stones. But there's a pool, isn't there? You told me there was a pool. They may not have your vicious water," and at least she was starting to think, she'd got that far, "but Tulk could perfect all the pool, that would give them water enough to fight their way out of there. That's why he went, isn't it? Surely, that must be why . . ."

Surely, that had to be why: to give the warning, and then to help the fight. But the warning had been of little use, a few moments' grace to fear, and to find all the ways of retreat blocked already; and then, "There was a pool. Do you see it now? I don't."

He didn't see it, and neither did she, because it wasn't there.

"How . . . ?"

"Nothing magic," he said, sighing. He had his voice back, but there was no benefit in it, only further cost. "The Marasi must have come and drained the pool, broken the pipe that filled it."

"But, but that would mean . . ."

"Yes." It meant that they knew in advance, where to come and what to do. This wasn't a last-minute treachery, some spontaneous folly. It had been planned and prepared for, and Armina stood at the heart of it all.

For now she stood at the side, watching what the soldiers did, and Issel wished above all that he still had his little flask with him. He did ask Gilder, "Is there any water in the house?" but he knew the answer already, he could feel it, the building was dust-dry. He could spit, but that would do little more than sting her, even if he could spit so far. On the track of his thought, Armina turned her head to look directly at them—though she'd done that before at the corner and not betrayed them there, and he really didn't understand—and it was shared instincts or good training that had him and Rhoan each seizing one of Gilder's arms and pulling him back with them into the shadows of the room.

They could still see from there, if not so well; and they could hear, too. Especially Issel could see and hear Tulk, sobbing and screaming. He was throwing stones, and trying to threaten soldiers with his pocketknife. Almost, Issel wanted them to stab him, swift and easy. Better dead than in the hands of the Marasi: that was a given, a universal truth.

They didn't do it, though. They just overran him. Knocked down, beaten and bound, he went on cursing them until they kicked him into silence like Lenn and most of the others, those who were not dead or keening beyond any control.

———

THEY heard the cart coming before they saw it, wheels rumbling on the broken stone of the roadway. It was an unusual sound in this quarter but no Sundain would be coming out to stare, nor to laugh at the soldiers who pulled it in lieu of horses, through these narrow and difficult alleys. Mockers were liable to be roped to the shafts in lieu of soldiers, to learn their folly under the sergeants' whips; that would be light punishment this evening. Where there was death and screaming, Sund had learned long since not to watch, not to gather, not to speak.

Issel saw how the dead were let lie but the living loaded into the cart, tossed up like trussed meat. He couldn't see Armina anymore, but he

cursed her anyway, with all the livid liquid fluency of his youth and experience. Then he watched the Marasi retreat, and the first tentative figures sidle
into the chapel to run sharp knives and sharper fingers through the clothing
of the dead, taking belts and boots and picking open all their seams.

"Don't you want to go down?" he asked Gilder, goaded by the sight of
it, by the certainty that a few short months before he'd have been there
himself: quicker to the bodies, less tentative, more thorough. "Those are
your friends, and they'll be robbed of everything they have."

"They're dead," Gilder said dully. "What do they have, that matters?
To them, to me . . . ? Let the scum take what it wants, let the city have
them, body and breath."

Their money might have been useful to you, to all of us, but he didn't
say so. Despair was a gesture, a fling to the fates; let Gilder make it, if he
was moved that way. Instead, "We should get back, then."

"Back?" That was Rhoan: not challenging, just not understanding.
How could he think of such things, of anything, when disaster lay spread
before and below them like a tapestry fallen to the ground, sprawled figures and broken hopes?

"Back to the school." And, in the face of her continuing bafflement,
"We've got to tell Tel Ferin." *Tulk was one of his, as much as you are, more
than me. Tel Ferin has a right to know; and he has to learn tonight, from
us, before tomorrow comes . . .*

GILDER came with them. They didn't ask, and he didn't insist; he simply
came. It was all unspoken, as though there were no words left or else no
need to use them.

Through the streets, then, and not so cautiously; when the worst has
happened, what is there to fear? *The next worst, and the next worst after
that,* those were Issel's answers, but no one asked it aloud and Rhoan was
leading, so he simply followed along. After this—well, she clearly wasn't
thinking past the one terrible task, telling their master. *He went to help, and
we just watched while he was taken . . .* And she might not yet have realized why Tulk was still alive, but Issel had, so that would be for him to tell.

THE rain started as the sun went down, swift storm clouds and a down-
pour that made Rhoan yelp at the lash of it, that had Issel sobbing, every
nerve alive as he scrambled for shelter under a wagon. Gilder might have

laughed at him, he thought, any other day, any other time. He himself might have teased Rhoan, who always boasted her strong control, how simple water couldn't hurt her anymore. As it was they shivered mutely together, even Gilder rubbing uselessly at the sting on his wet skin, until the cloudburst ebbed to a constant drizzle; then they went on regardless, the news they bore a worse whip than the rain.

There were no scavengers in these merchants' streets, no bone-pickers or the house would have been stripped already, as thoroughly as the rebels' bodies in the chapel ruins. When they came to the little gate they always used, the door that Issel dreaded, they found it standing wide.

"Why is this not locked?" Gilder asked.

"The lock's been broken years." Issel knew.

"We never leave it open, though," Rhoan said. "Someone struck this, look, the hinge is bent . . ."

Gilder nodded, and pulled a knife from his belt. "We'll go in carefully. I wish the rain was heavier."

Rhoan laughed shortly. "What, for the water? In this house? If the Marasi came, if there's been a fight, we lost it. The school lost it, the whole school, fighting together. What could three of us do? Even with Issel, even in the rain?"

"I meant that it would hide us better," Gilder said imperturbably. "I'm not looking for a fight. Maybe the bones of one. Do you see, do you hear anything? Neither do I. Noise of a battle would reach this far. It's wise to be careful, though. Issel, you lead."

THROUGH the wilds of the garden, then, avoiding all the paths, the well, anywhere that trouble might linger. Pushing between shrubs, they grew even wetter than they were, and Issel thought he didn't need rain. He could make a weapon of his shirt; his own skin would be a shield to protect him.

Then they came through the overgrowth to their first clear sight of the house, and that quenched his foolishness entirely.

He'd never seen a house look so purposely abandoned. All the shutters on all the windows stood wide open to the weather; one or two hung crooked or had been ripped off altogether, but the damage was almost incidental. This was a statement, surely, and not addressed to them.

Its answer, perhaps, was the sluggish smoke that leaked out through a few of those windows.

Not trusting the silence, the stillness, that avowal of absence, they re-treated into the shrubs again to make their way around to the main door. Peering between branches, they saw that it too stood open and unguarded. Again there were signs of damage, axe hacks in the woodwork, but nothing significant, just done in passing.

"Well?" Gilder murmured. "Do we go in?"

"I think we have to, don't we?" That was Rhoan, trying to stifle her fear.

"There may be bodies," Issel said, thinking of children nailed by the throat. "And there is fire, we can see that . . ."

"Which is why it should be safe, soldiers wouldn't stay in a building they've set light to." She was stubbornly determined to be brave; there was nothing that Issel could do but acquiesce.

"Not this way, though. Not the front door. Round the back."

Round to the well first, he meant, and in through the kitchen: for fa-miliarity's sake, to come in as they always did, not to feel strangers in their own catastrophe.

———

THE back of the house was as deserted as the front. No guards, no bodies; Gilder said, "I don't think there's been a fight here."

"At the chapel, the Marasi took everyone away," *including Tulk, and what are they doing to him now, what will they do tomorrow . . . ?*

"They left the dead. But if they'd attacked a school for adepts, even if it was a houseful of children—well, your people would have defended themselves, wouldn't they? There'd be signs."

Blood and worse, he meant, more than stains on planking and far more than the rain could hide: splintered stone and trees uprooted, violence and terror, the story of the battle written in the ground.

Issel shrugged, and went to draw a bucket of water from the well. He found the well rope cut and the bucket gone, and so carried a plant pot full of rainwater in his hand as he led them into the house.

———

MUD and harm together were the tale of the house, so far as they could tell it through the smoke.

Blood seemed to be no part of the story.

Many men had tramped filth in from the garden, and some of that had to be deliberate, as the damage was, the mindless hacks and gouges at walls and doors and floors. In several rooms, wall hangings had been ripped down and heaped with rugs and broken furniture and set alight. None of the fires was burning well; smoke was the major threat, stinging their eyes and throats, leaving them choking and blundering half-blind towards the windows, seeking relief in the drifts of rain.

Once sure that the house was empty, Rhoan took the water pot from Issel and dipped her fingers in to make another mist: this one not to hide them, only to wash the air around them, to keep the smoke at bay. She didn't perfect the water first, but she still made it work far better than Issel had expected. He watched billows of grey seem to fail as they came, and what he breathed was damp and fresh, with only a taint of burning.

"I used to do this with rose petals in the water," Rhoan murmured at his side, "when I was at home. It's what my parents noticed first, what made them anxious, what drove them to find Tel Ferin in the end. I did it here too, those days when the house smelled particularly rank."

"Did it? I never noticed."

"You never would. It was boy it smelled of."

Now it was all smoke, but little fire. Wet floors and rain in the air, damp in all the fabrics, even so much water should not have been enough to choke the fires so badly. It was a soldier's talent to make fire in the rain and in a hurry, and Issel thought the house ought to have been ablaze, spitting sparks to rival the rising stars. Even the chairs and cabinets smashed into firewood, though, even those were barely smouldering. If Tel Ferin had warning enough, he might have had the school running around the house with buckets, soaking everything that could be soaked, but even so . . .

"Is there a spell," Issel asked Rhoan, "to make things wet from the inside? Wooden things?"

"I don't know. Maybe his favourite polish doesn't burn. He had us using plenty. Does it matter? Put the fires out, and let's see what we can find here."

She just assumed that he could do that; to be fair, so did he. He took the water pot back from her, and dipped his own fingers in it, to make his own kind of steam: no gentle mist this, no tease to the eyes, but rather a rolling bank that poured over the pot's rim and picked up more water as it went, enough to engulf the smoking heaps one by one and drench them with a dull and heavy hissing. More smoke rose up, clean and white this time; when that dispersed, there was nothing left but the smell of fire and the ruin of Tel Ferin's things.

That reminded Issel of his own little things. As soon as he had extinguished the last least flames, and Rhoan said, "Good, now we look properly," he left Gilder with her and was away to his window bed to see.

All his bedding was gone, dragged away to join one of the fires. The shutters were gone too, ripped off to serve the same brute purpose; but the loose board was intact and so was his wrap of greasecloth beneath, where he had kept it since the book was gone. He nestled that where he liked it best, inside his shirt, and went to find the others in Tel Ferin's apartments, gazing at an emptiness of walls.

The shelves had been pulled down and broken, heaped up for a fire that had failed to catch at all. The books, though—the books were simply gone. Paper burns, of course, but burned books leave ash and leather spines and half-burned pages; there were none here.

"He did know this was coming," Rhoan asserted. "He packed his books, and took them. With the school. It wasn't the Marasi taking them away, like they took Tulk and the others. He was betrayed, surely, but he knew before it happened; so he opened all the windows to let the rain in, he took his books and all our friends and, and, where did he *go* . . . ?"

Without us, she meant, and *how can we find him?*

And, perhaps, *how can we rescue Tulk and the others without him?*

Issel shook his head, to any or all of those questions. Gilder shrugged, and said, "There's nothing here, anyway. This place stinks. Let's get out of here."

"And go where? Do you think your house will be safe now, or anywhere?"

"Armina doesn't know where I live."

"No? Well, maybe not—but I expect Lenn does."

Rhoan said no more than that; it was enough. Gilder blenched. Those not betrayed already would spend the night wondering which of their friends it would be who gave them up, and under what persuasion.

All that Gilder said, though, he said again, "This place stinks," meaning *we can't stay here.*

"Yes, but it should be safe, at least." *We can stay here.* "They've been here, done the worst they can, found—well, whatever it is they have found, not much," *none of us,* "but they won't be back."

"You can't know that."

No, but she could hope. Issel would not take that frail thing from her. He said, "Rhoan's right, this house should be safe for tonight at least. And we don't have to sleep in the stink. There's an old pavilion in the garden, we can go there and sleep dry, maybe, if the Marasi didn't find it . . ."

THE Marasi hadn't found it, but by the time they made their way out to the pavilion they weren't going to sleep dry anyway. They went with armfuls of makeshift bedding, some scavenged from corners where the soldiers hadn't looked, some damp from being rained on, some wet and scorched from the fires; all of it getting wetter by the moment as they stumbled through the tangled plantings in the dark, in the rain.

"There may still be some cushions and covers out there," Rhoan had said, "but not enough for three of us. If any of that's still dry, we can spread it over the rest of this. Warm and wet asleep is better than dry and wakeful on a hard cold floor."

Issel went first to be helpful, to bring a faint light to all the water that he touched or carried; where rain dripped from his hair, where it scattered as he brushed against a branch, every separate drop gleamed iridescent and shed a glow around him, momentary phosphorescence like a falling swarm of fireflies. Even the fabrics in his arms were shimmering, he thought, just from the damp in their fibres, that his touch enlivened.

He looked down inside his shirt, and yes, all his wet skin was aglow. He must look dreadful, ghostly, revenant; he could hear Gilder's muttering behind him, Rhoan's nervous shortness of breath.

Only trying to help, give you something to see by . . . He might have let the light die, sulkily; stubbornly, he didn't. Only forced his way quicker between the branches, and heard the others fall further behind. They'd see where he was going; he would shine at them from beyond the trees.

Besides, Rhoan knew the way. She knew that there was bedding there already; she might be able to find it in the dark. She might have done that before, if never with him.

SHINING for himself, then, himself alone as ever, he stepped up from wet grass onto rough planking and through the open pergola into the shelter of the pavilion's walls.

It was a dark night outside, with neither moon nor stars breaking through, only a dim reflection of the Shine giving a little colour to the clouds. It was darker yet in here, and his own pale glow—*not a shine, no, don't use that word*—wasn't enough to light it.

He dumped his pile of soft stuff in a corner and went back out to the pergola, where rain ran down the leaves and stems of the plants that climbed the beams. One hand touched them, rain and plants together, and they gleamed bright and cold like moonlight, flickering like flame.

There were four rising beams and he lit them all, in time to see Rhoan and Gilder coming across the grass. They would think he'd done it for them; perhaps he had. He went back inside, and in this light he could see that there was another heap of bedding, in another corner. He went over and crouched beside it, thrust his hand in deep to see if it was dry—

———————

—AND fell back, yelling, as his hand felt the heat of it and the solidity, his nose caught the gamy reek of it and his eyes the movement as it stirred and rose.

His noise brought the other two running, where he thought that wisdom should have sent them the other way, into the safety of the dark. That's where he would have gone—well, if it had been Gilder who shouted. For Rhoan, he might have come. He hoped he would, and at the same time wished that she hadn't come for him.

She was there, though, and Gilder too, standing in the light with blades in their hands. The sight of them steadied him. He knew all the terrors of Sund and this was none of them, this bedding-beast; which meant it was something else, and nothing to be scared of, no terror at all . . .

He had almost understood it, in what little time it took him to turn and face it again. Now he was looking for a man and almost saw one, almost.

It was in that narrow gap between what he looked for and what he saw, that terror lay.

He was wrong again, as he always was wrong about what mattered. The bedding had fallen away as the huddled creature rose, and it was indeed one of the terrors of Sund. Issel was Sund, in all of its power and weakness and betrayal, all of his; and this was the finest and most refined of all his terrors.

It was Baris the dogtooth who cowered near-naked in the corner there. And never mind that he was clearly terrified of them and the world and everything within it, never mind that his terror showed entirely, Issel could still never stop being terrified of him. If Issel was Sund, he was most afraid that he was Baris too, or would be soon, too soon.

———————

ISSEL never could speak to Baris. It was too like talking to himself, his own ghost, his own dread future. He was glad to have Rhoan there, courageous, pure, incorrupt. She had nothing to fear and she knew it, as she knew how much he was afraid; she pushed past and went to the dogtooth in a way that Issel never could, touched him even, laid a hand on his arm and said, "Baris, be easy, you don't need to be afraid of us."

Was that true? Probably. The Marasi had been and gone, and no one here meant him any harm. Not even Issel.

The dogtooth looked little comforted. He did drop back down onto his haunches, slowly, slowly; but the tension in him was terrible to see. Every muscle was tight and trembling, his wild eyes shifted constantly between the three of them and the pergola, the garden, his way of escape. Except that four pillars of light burned there, and they must have seemed to him like iron bars or worse, a snare to catch a dogtooth, as though Issel had set them there deliberately to hold him.

Issel opened his mouth to deny it, to say *go, go if you want to*, he was ready to douse the light to encourage it. But Rhoan was talking to the creature, and if he gave her time, she might even get some intelligible speech in return.

Issel left the pergola's pillars blazing with their cold rainlight, and moved himself to stand between them, arms folded, an implacable silhouette. Gilder gazed at him cynically. Rhoan glanced round, scowling; she was harder to ignore, but he still didn't move, and after a moment she turned back to the dogtooth.

"Baris, are you hungry? I've some bread in my pocket here . . ."

A snuffle, a shake of the head.

"Well, all right, but say if you want it later. You must be cold like that, you are cold, I can see you shivering," which Issel supposed was one word for the tremble in the dogtooth's body, but he thought it was the wrong one. Deliberately wrong, he thought. "Wrap yourself up in those coverings again, there's no point in being cold."

Issel was cold too, cold and wet and getting wetter, with the rain on the breeze at his back; and that was the only dry bedding in the pavilion, that Rhoan was gathering up there and trying to dress the dogtooth with. Baris

snarled at her, and shrugged her off. This was the first chance Issel had had
to see the way his body was, the way it worked: the animal power and the
thick hairy skin—*the hide*, Issel wanted to say—that contained it; the con-
torted spine and shoulders, the joints that seemed almost to bend contrary,
as if all his skeleton was reshaping itself inside that coarsened skin. Likely
it was. Ordinary human bones could never hold together against such brutal changes. Issel knew the face was changing, teeth and jaw and skull and
all; he knew the fingernails changed, he'd felt the bite of those claws; so
why not all the bones else? Softened by the Shine, twisted out of their
proper being—yes, of course, how not?

Issel tried to straighten his own back, worked his shoulders mutely inside his clinging shirt, winced at the stiffness that he felt.

"Well, all right then," Rhoan went on, the soul of patience, "do as you
like, of course; but tell us, Baris, please tell us what happened here? Where
did Tel Ferin go and who went with him, who got away?"

Did you see anyone captured? was what she meant, but he might be too
slow to understand her. Certainly he was slow to answer. Issel gazed at this
slack, slobbering, shuddering creature and thought back to the fierce smile
he'd had selling water on the strand, Issel's first glimpse of his teeth. Or the
gloating strength in him when he'd captured Issel by the well, and later
dragged him before Tel Ferin. That Baris, the reliable servant was gone:
undone by tonight's shocks perhaps, or perhaps undone by the Shine, his
continuing degradation, the brain like the body slipping down to something brutal . . .

When the words did come, they were difficult to make and difficult to
hear. That could just be the combination of exhaustion and distress and
terror; it could be a sign of further corruption, the tongue struggling in the
misshapen jaw, the mind struggling to keep hold of the slipperiness of language. For certain, Baris used to speak more clearly.

No matter; since when had Issel cared about the dogtooth?

Since we met, since he maps out my future for me . . .

No. Not that. Issel would never go that far, down that road; he was
quite determined. There were sudden ways to stop it, if need be.

For now, he tried to lean forward without stooping, to hear what was
said and never show a hint of curve in his spine.

". . . He left me, the master . . ."

"Tel Ferin?"

"Yes. He left. He said there would be soldiers come, his wisdom showed it to him. He said he must leave, and his books. He put his books in boxes, and they carried them away."

"Tel Ferin's wisdom can't show him what's to come." It was Gilder who made the objection, but he spoke for all of them, Issel thought. And he knew what followed, the one name they knew who could show Tel Ferin what was to come.

"Never mind," Rhoan said quickly. "If they had so much warning, they should all have got away safely. Is that right, Baris, did everyone escape?"

"No." And after a long, heart-stopping silence, he went on, "I am here."

Issel tried not to huff in his relief. He could hear the same feeling in Rhoan, as she said, "But you're safe now, the Marasi have gone and we're here, we'll stay together and look after each other till we can find Tel Ferin. He must have told you where he was going?"

"He left me," again, and this was important; Tel Ferin had seemed to depend on Baris, all the rough work of the school had devolved onto his twisted shoulders. They found it hard to understand, why the master would leave his servant so. Odder still, that it took the dogtooth to explain it to them. Patiently. "He said, he would go with his books to another house. He took some of the young ones with him. More he sent to other houses," dividing the school between his friends the adepts, Issel supposed. "Me he said they would not take, into any house he knew. And so he left me."

As simply as that. He was dogtooth, he was tainted, the adepts would not accept him—and so Tel Ferin had abandoned him, and he'd known nowhere else to go.

"I hid," he said, "and the soldiers did not find me when they came. They were angry to find no one here. They would have burned it all, but the master told me to leave the house open. Let the rain in, he said. So they were angry again, but they went away."

They left him too, he meant; and welcome so, for sure, but he had been alone since, and bereft. Issel hated him and feared him, and could still feel sorry for him.

And could still wish him gone, or wish to leave him here; but Rhoan would not, and Gilder didn't care. So they nested, damply in separate corners of the small pavilion. When Issel gave up entirely on thoughts of sleep and went to sit under the pergola to watch the weather clear, he felt each of the others watch him on his way; and it was no surprise when there were shuffling, standing sounds behind him, soft footfalls coming, Rhoan sitting on the planking at his side.

"I thought that rain would never stop," she said.

"It always stops, it has to, or it would never have the chance to start again. Besides, we'd learn to live wet, like fish," an awesome prospect, to be immersed, inside the water, "and then we wouldn't care."

"Like we learn to live under the Marasi, you mean?"

Had he meant that? He wasn't sure. He said, "We still care."

"Only because they keep us caring, because they're ruthless and cruel and stupid. They could have governed us like the old council did, Tel Ferin's kind; we'd never have known the difference, and never cared a whit."

"D'you think?"

"I'm certain. Where we live, how do you tell who's sitting in the council hall and making laws? It's only because they fill the streets with soldiers, starve us and steal from us and let us see them at it, that's why we hate them."

Why we fight them, why we die. Issel just grunted; it was the only alternative to the question rising in his throat, *so why do we betray?*

But Armina wasn't *us*, she wasn't Sundain, she was slave; maybe slavery was indistinguishable under the Sundain or the Marasi, maybe she really didn't care . . .

He sank back into the silence of his bewilderment, his immeasurable hurt. After a while, Rhoan said, "Will you come down to the fountain square with me, in the morning?"

"With you?" He didn't know what that meant. He was going, of course; he hadn't stopped to wonder whether she would. It was his to do. If she came, she would have to come with him. He didn't have the words, either to explain that or to argue it; he shrugged and nodded.

"Thank you," for all the world as if the duty were hers and he just an escort, a companion doing the good turn of a friend. Then, "What did Joss mean, on the roof, when he said about you hurrying the man you took the urn from?"

If she meant it to be a distraction, she understood him all too well. A cold prickling shiver ran across his body, as though he'd just plunged head-first into a fresh pool of water.

"Issel? You'd best tell me, because I won't stop asking till you do. I know you have dark times in your story, but I want to hear them, I want to see. I want to see them all."

Hunched in on himself, with his arms around his knees and his face hidden, speaking from darkness to the sounds of her breathing, he found that he could do this, so long as he was allowed to do it bluntly and haltingly, the worst kind of storytelling, aching for interruption.

"I killed him," he said.

"What, for his urn?"

"No, not that. At least, I didn't think so," but he wasn't so sure now.

"Well, but you've killed others," and she was trying to find excuses for him before she'd heard the tale, and he didn't want that at all, he wanted meat for his guilt to feed on.

"He was the first."

"Tell me, then."

"It was after I came down from the roofs. Joss and the others, they knew what I could do, a bit," *little frog likes his water,* "and they didn't want me up there anymore. That made it harder, to live how I was living: running messages and stealing, mostly. And then I was, I was with Armina," and she had reshaped his life again, remade it around a death, gifted him an early murder, "and she sent me—well, she sent me here."

"Here? The merchants' quarter?"

"No, here. This house. She said that if I came here, I could claim an urn and be a waterseller. There was a beat close by, she said, and a well in the garden," although he'd never used it until the day that Baris caught him there, and had she foreseen even that? Or brought it about, guided him, misguided him, all to bring him here to this night with that morning to face ahead?

"If she knew about this house," and they knew that she did, she came and went almost as a member of the household, "and you needed a home and she knew about your talents, why didn't she just bring you, send you here anyway? Or tell Tel Ferin where to find you? She must have foreseen that you'd come here in the end."

"I don't know." He no longer knew anything about Armina, or rather he no longer understood her; he distrusted everything he did know. "That's what happened, though, she only sent me here for the urn."

"Where did you find it, then? Not in the house, surely? We'd have seen you."

"You never saw Armina, till she chose to be seen. But no, not in the house. At the gate," *where the wood is stained, I did that . . .*

He thought that she should understand him now, without his having to tell it. He let the silence sit until she nudged him, quite hard in the ribs.

"Go on, then. What happened at the gate?"

Perhaps she'd never seen the stain; perhaps she'd seen and never understood it. He said, "That's where I found him, slumped against it. The urn was leaning on the wall beside him. And he was—well, I didn't know what he was. Not asleep, not unconscious," not in his body at all, he'd thought, but wandering in some desperate other world where the sick go for a first and early taste of death. "He just lay there, slack like a body but still breathing, drooling at the mouth. His eyes were open, but I didn't think he was seeing me."

"Drugged, or spelled?" Rhoan hazarded.

"If there's a difference. If anyone can do that to a man, with drugs or magic. I don't know, I wouldn't know how. He was sick, I thought. Deathly sick, but that didn't worry me. If I'd never seen it before, it wasn't any sickness you could catch in Sund. I didn't stop to think if he'd been poisoned, maybe, by the water." To a boy used to sleeping in the Shine, all water had the sheen of poison to it; to a boy with Sund's own magic in his blood, all water carried pain and wonder in equal measure. "I just set to taking his clothes off."

"You took his *clothes*?" She was staring suddenly; the startled outrage in her voice made Issel turn his head on his knees there, just to look.

"Yes, of course. He was a waterseller, and I was a thief. He had the proper dress, and I needed it, if I was going to take his urn and his beat. He was a small man, I could wear his clothes."

"But—oh, never mind. You took his clothes," though her voice still balked at the shock of it. "What then?"

"Then I was going to leave him to find just where his beat ran, where the others in this quarter would face me off; but I was slow, I was still shifting the straps to make the urn hang best on my back, and he grabbed me. I'd thought he was nothing, gone, good as dead, but he came back, just enough . . ."

Just enough to curl his fingers around Issel's ankle in a soft and feeble grip, impossible to break. Issel gasped and stared down at him, eye to eye in the same world at last, and, "He couldn't talk but he could work his mouth, just a little, and I thought he was saying *help me*. So I did all I could do, the only thing I could think of, what I thought he wanted . . ."

What Joss had seen, or one of his informants: the knife in the dawn-light, so often sharpened it was more a needle than a blade, except for being sharp at every point. Issel had drawn it across the man's gulping, voiceless throat, the way he'd seen a hundred butchers do with sheep, with goats, with dogs in Daries.

He'd seen it and been close enough to smell it many times, but had still been shocked raw by the blood and the gush of it, so much and in such a hurry to be out of there, spurting halfway up the gate. Not spattering Issel or his new clothes, he'd been careful, cutting from behind as the butchers did and then jumping back when the bloodrush came, but it stained his memory, and he thought it stained his soul. It didn't matter that the man was surely dying anyway, or that he had—Issel thought—been begging for death; it didn't matter that Issel had killed others since. Nothing diluted, nothing could dilute that moment. Issel carried it ever-fresh, deep and dark and immediate and true.

He told Rhoan, as he had told no one else, ever; Armina would know anyway, and who else had ever been close enough to hear? She said the right thing after, which was nothing. It was some time before he realized that she was holding his hand in hers, and he only did realize at the moment when she let it go.

———

JUST before sunrise, they left the garden and the dogtooth waiting in it. Gilder came with them, of course; they had never imagined that he would not. Baris wasn't happy to be left, but they couldn't take him abroad in daylight.

No one suggested the roof-run. They walked slowly through the shadows, and never looked up to see if they were being watched or followed: down to the lower town, to the broken fountains in the broad square. The fountain basin was busy as always, and they could hide out in the throng. The foot of the bridge was guarded as always, and they could watch the Marasi come and go. The execution stage was still there, and about midmorning more Marasi came and did not go; swordsmen and archers, they set themselves in a perimeter about the stage.

Those archers would have made rescue impossible, even with a supply of Issel's wicked water, which they didn't have, which he would not ask Rhoan to help him manufacture. Three people simply couldn't do it, where three aimed arrows would be enough to stop them. Nothing to do, then, but lose themselves in the gathering, muttering crowd, and wait.

At midday, prisoners were brought to the stage in a wagon. No one more important than a sergeant was there to announce the offences— conspiracy, rebellion, treason against the Sultan who was lord of Maras-Sund—but the empire's finest had brought their flaying knives.

There was no hierarchy in death, no particular order, and no quicker end this time for the women. Lenn was third to die, and Tulk was fifth.

It was after Tulk had stopped screaming but before the skinners had finished their wet work on his body that Rhoan turned to Issel.

"You're going to do what Lenn wanted, aren't you? You're going to cross to Maras, and try to destroy the bridge."

It would be the bridge's makers he must destroy, the thing itself was a product of magic and untouchable; but, "Yes," he said. He hadn't exactly said it even to himself before this, it was just an inevitability; he couldn't imagine anything else to do.

"I'm with you," Gilder grunted at his side. He hadn't imagined that either, and didn't know what to do with it; but that was nothing next to Rhoan, when she said,

"So am I. Whatever it takes," glancing down at her hands, which could never be healed again the same way if they had to be hurt again.

Chapter Four

I T was Jendre's idea, her sudden passion, her unexpected and absolute rebellion. It terrified everyone she told it to, everyone she loved.

"I know where my sister is," she said, "and I know how to reach her; do you imagine that I can leave her be and live some kind of life here in sight of where she lies, knowing even a little"—*so little, too much*—"of how they keep her?"

And, "I know whom I love," she said, *you here, the three of you and my sister up the hill there, no more than that, what need more?* "I want to live my life with you, and no one else. Custom says, the Sultan says, the law belongs to the Sultan and so the law says that I must live it here, one voice among a thousand voices lamenting my dead husband through all my dreary days," as though she were dead too, as though her life meant nothing once her man was gone. "I say that I will not. His ghost has mourners enough, he doesn't need me to bewail him," except where she did, in her heart, a good man gone and she did miss him, "when I could be busy in the world, and save my sister," and never mind that it was his edict that she must save her from, he had held a cruel throne but he had still been a good man and kind to her, and she would grieve, but she would still save her sister.

And, "If Sidië cannot recover," she said, "we can care for her between us, and give her better care than she has now, but we can't do it here." Somebody would have to notice the young widow and her slaves coming and going, with and without food, in and out of some neglected corner of the house or the garden or the park. "So we have to leave," she said. "We have to take Sidië out of the hands of the magicians, and we have to escape beyond the walls." It was so simple when she spelled it out, she didn't at all understand their resistance.

And, "It's not just the harem, or the palace here," she said, "we have to go right away, outside the walls of the city. It's just too dangerous, else." If she could, she'd take them beyond reach of the empire altogether, across a border into lands unknown; but that was too far to stretch even in her imagination, far too far to travel. "My father says that half the young officers under his command keep a household outside the city," and it astonished her that she could say this without blushing, "which their fathers blink at and their mothers are not meant to know. No one would ask questions, no one would visit; we could live quietly together, Mirjana and Teo and me; we could nurse Sidië and be happy. And you could ride out to see us, Salem, as often as you were free, and no one would question you either, everyone would know that you had your own private pleasure house and nobody would care. Especially now that you are not to be married . . ."

"Not yet," Salem said, where he stood discreetly in the shadows of the belvedere, careful even on such a night of the wet dark, even here where they were—almost—sure not to be overlooked. "I must marry someone, and I must marry soon; my father is clear about it. But nothing else is clear, who holds power now under the new Sultan, where the lines of influence run. Marriages must wait, until the silt settles.

"Marriage is not a problem," he went on, and she heard the shrug far better than she saw it. "My married brother officers keep their little pavilions in the country, and treasure them until they can buy or build or inherit their own houses with their own harems, and bring their pleasures home. But—Jendre, do you know what sorts of women they keep in those little pavilions, and why they will not tell their mothers who they have?"

Amazingly, she could still laugh at him. "I grew up in a soldier's harem, fool. Of course I know. Do you think I care what kind of woman other people think that I must be, for you to keep me so? Besides, a widow who loves a handsome captain and flees her proper household for his sake, a wife indeed who dallied with him in her husband's house," and somehow this had started out teasing and was suddenly earnest, brutally honest, and it was an effort not to flinch from her own voice as she laid it out, "can you say truly that I am not that sort of woman who best belongs beyond the city walls, where she can be kept in some kind of silence, if only to keep secret her disgrace?"

"You grace whatever you touch," he said simply, and left her breathless. "And my family has lands beyond the city, and some of them are mine, where my father does not interfere. Yes, I could find such a pavilion, to house you and your sister and your people here in a decent privacy," and he very carefully did not say *I have such a pavilion already*, but she thought that she could hear the blood rushing to his cheeks, and wondered what poor girls she was displacing and what he would do with them now. "It would be harder to bring you back when I am married, when I have my own house, but even that might be contrived. I would like to have you close. But, Jendre, all of this: you are dreaming. We dare not risk it. You can have no idea what the penalty is, for stealing the Sultan's woman from the Sultan's own harem . . ."

"Oh, death, I am sure," she said, mock-brightly, as though it all meant nothing to her. "The penalty always is death, whatever the offence. But I am not the Sultan's woman now."

"Until death, you are his woman. Your death, not his own. Death for you and yours," and a gesture encompassed everything that was hers, Teo and Mirjana too, "death for me—this is folly, Jendre, even to talk about it."

Maybe so, but it was a grand folly. "It would be unbearable," she said, "not to talk about it, not to plan, not to make it work. To live, to sleep, to dream so close to Sidië, and not to try, never to have tried . . . No. If the penalty is so harsh, we will take better care; but it cannot be so hard, Salem. You come and go across the wall and never see a guard." He'd told her that; he hadn't thought to have his own words turned back on him, but couldn't deny them. "Easier than the new palace, you said, and far less sternly guarded," and she believed him utterly. She knew the place, where the cliff top overjutted the wall. She and her little friends had clambered about up there like monkeys, and her strong lover did the same with more ease and much less noise. So could she again, and her slaves too. How they should bring her sister out, she was undecided. In a sling at a rope's end, if necessary: between them they could haul a deadweight up. It was not so very far.

Less heedful than Salem, Teo was on his feet and pacing the pool's margin, a dozen paces up and down, ridiculously like a man of importance in the world. Mirjana was the opposite, sitting close beside her and very still, the image of submissive duty. Both of them were deeply afraid, she could read that, just as Salem was; and just as with Salem, it was not themselves they feared for.

She could love that in them and try to repay it in kind, to be fearful for their sakes; but she couldn't find a way to have that fear override her need to do this. She would spend her own life willingly, yes, and her friends' lives too if they were foolish or generous enough to give them her for coin. Just to try, to know that she had tried, that she had found her sister and done her best to free her. A general's daughter on campaign, she could overcome a pasha's boy and not break step; she could lead her own people in the certainty that they would follow, however reluctantly.

Besides, they might all argue, but they had no arguments to offer: only her own safety, which she cared nothing for. Theirs was precious to her, but she would still risk it recklessly for Sidië. That once admitted, what more could they advance? There was nothing left in the world that mattered, beyond these few people here and the other girl over there.

———

SO that was the plan, her plan, and they all worked to secure it. As swiftly as she could whip them to it, with only her tongue for a lash: now that it was decided—or now that she had overridden all their objections, at least, which amounted to the same thing—she couldn't bear a day's delay.

Nor was there much to wait for. Ropes, but Teo could find those; blankets they had, and dark clothing; a carriage and horses Salem could supply. He said that in these uncertain times, all the families that mattered in the city were hurrying their most precious possessions out to their country estates in sealed carriages. It would be no surprise to find the pasha's son doing the same, and riding guard on it himself. No one would ask, he said, what valuables they were that he was guarding.

Even finding and equipping a pavilion on his land, he said, he could accomplish in a day. Jendre snorted. *Don't disturb your other arrangements,*

Salem, I'm sure they can make room for us, and I'd be interested to meet them—but of course she said no such thing, she only felt grateful and urgent and begrudged him even that single day to shift his girls around.

———————

TIME stuck to her fingers like honeycomb, and she couldn't lick it off. It wrapped itself about her like wet silk, binding and confining, holding her still where she longed to run; the day seemed eternal, the night a blessing withheld, a promise to a child, *soon but not now, never now . . .*

Eventually, though, it did have to be now. The sun was obliged to move, however slowly; when it had slid all the way down—though she thought it hung on behind the clouds where she couldn't see it, she thought it gripped the scalded sky with claws to slow its falling—and when it had kissed good night to the far horizons, it had small choice but to set. It sulked, she thought, as it went, turning its back on the world, sinking into a heavy blanket of dull cloud; that was all to the good. She wanted no moon, no stars, no lights at all, no eyes abroad tonight. Every sense was treacherous, but sight was worst; it had the furthest reach and told the most, gave the most away.

Even now, even in the night, she must still wait. Whether anyone ever truly slept in the dreamers' pavilion, she did not know; but there were hundreds of women and their servants in the palace, and some of them would sit up late. This wasn't a normal night with Salem, when they wanted all the hours of darkness to be together. Tonight they needed the deep dark, when the world turned towards morning.

At midnight, she took her little troop of two softly through the house. Actually it was Teo who led them, a route he'd learned from Djago. None of it was exactly secret, but there were a lot of servants' stairs and corridors that she had never guessed at. Once they heard laughter ahead, two boys abroad on some private mission, probably illicit; she wasn't too proud to hide, squashing into a larder with her friends, the three of them fighting their own nervous giggles until the boys had passed.

Then there was a door, little more than a hatchway, one of many hidden ways out into the gardens, Teo said. This was a world they were leaving, and she was beginning to understand that she had travelled and explored only the slenderest shaving of it, only the topmost varnish.

There was nothing to regret in that. Of the three separate captivities of her life, this was the most meaningless: a harem without a husband, women in emptiness, meant to live in the memories of their lord, to keep that last least trace of him alive.

Did she betray him, in seeking to leave? Perhaps; but he was dead, and Sidië was not, and she felt not torn at all between the two of them. Even without Salem to run to, the running would have justified itself, if she could only take her sister with her when she went.

OUT in the air, with the warm wet breeze pushing at her, she took the lead from Teo. Not because she knew the way better, or because her eyes were sharper in the dark, or because she was wiser at walking on grass and avoiding the noise of gravel; none of those was true. It was only greed and weakness, that childish urge to hurry towards a treat not ready yet.

She paid the price of the greedy, of the weak, of the importunate. With her eyes blinded by hope and wishing, she missed what was close, what mattered.

A voice spoke to her out of the black gloom of the garden, and she thought her dizzy heart might fail altogether at the sudden terror of it.

"What, mistress, will you steal my favourite boy from me?"

She didn't shriek, at least her pride could be content with that. She might have gasped, but wouldn't admit even so much. She did startle, and stare around wildly and see nothing, no looming shadow, no accusing guard. It was only as the words themselves sank through the bitter shock of their coming, as she heard the voice that had spoken them echo in her head, only then did she think to look down.

Djago sat at the foot of a pedestal, between two crouching beasts of stone: a shadow among shadows, one creature more in a menagerie.

Once he was sure that she had seen him, he bounced to his feet and made a low bow, mocking perhaps but she thought not unkind. There was a chance at least that she had misunderstood him, that her guilty conscience was hearing what he had not said. At any rate she pretended, she said, "Oh, did you want Teo tonight? I'm sorry, I have a need for him myself."

"So I gather. In the darkness, in the rain, and oddly burdened . . ."

Teo's task was to carry the ropes and blankets that would make a sling for Sidië. She couldn't think how to explain them; instead, she prevaricated. "It isn't actually raining."

"It has been, mistress, and it will again."

"Which is why I chose to come out now. Don't you like to walk in the dark, Djago, when it's as wet as this?"

"Indeed, mistress. Not so far as you, perhaps, but see me, here I am. Walking."

At her side now and suddenly walking ahead of her, so that she had to jerk herself back into movement, where she had been so frozen to find him. Why he was there, she wouldn't start to guess; she was afraid that all her guesses would lead to the same conclusion, that he was waiting for her. What had Teo said, what had Djago been told or guessed or overheard? Was this betrayal, or misfortune, or conspiracy? She had no way to know, she could only wait for him to reveal himself; and he seemed loth to do it, swinging along inconsequentially and grunting at every step, as though nothing mattered in the world beyond the discomforts of the walk. She wondered if he were the goat who led the sheep so calmly to their slaughter; she wondered what he might know from Teo; because she could ask neither the one nor the other, she asked, "Does it not hurt you, to pull your mistress in that cart of yours?"

"Of hers, mistress, it is hers as I am; and yes, it does hurt me, especially to drag her and my weary carcass up the hill, but my pains are hers also, and always have been."

"Well," suddenly determined, "I at least have no claim on them, and will not take them from you. I am taking my people all the way up to the belvedere," more than she should have said, but she had to put him off somehow, "to watch the rain on the water there; you shall not hurt yourself further, to come with us. If you have anything more to say to us than a pretty good night, Djago, then say it here and go back to bed."

"Ah, mistress, my bed is not so comfortable either; but if you will pardon me the hill, then I am grateful to you. And if you could spare me your boy again when you come back to us, I would be more grateful still."

"Oh, you may have my promise on that," she said lightly, deceivingly. "As soon as we come back, he is yours for the asking."

"My thanks for your kindness," and he was gone; and Mirjana was already questioning Teo in a hissing whisper, and the boy was almost tearful in his denials, "I have said nothing to him, nothing, I have not seen him today . . . !"

"Enough. Mirjana, leave him now." But she took Teo's arm and said,

"I cannot give you the choice, I dare not leave you here; but if I could, sweet, would you come with me or stay with him?"

"Lady," he mumbled, "I belong with you," unless perhaps it was "I belong to you," she couldn't quite tell which, because he turned his head away and said it to the wind; but either way it was just exactly how she felt herself, with just that same touch of muddle to it, so she kissed his cheek with a sort of thankful possessiveness before she went ahead.

———————

THEY did go to the belvedere, and they did sit on blankets and watch the rain as it fell on the water. Jendre had half a suspicion that Djago might follow them up despite his protestations; she still hadn't worked out quite what the dwarf had wanted, and whether or not he'd achieved it. Best to show an innocent face to the night, to do the odd thing that she'd declared. Just in case there were sharp eyes out there, or someone low down sneaking through the bushes.

Besides, she had more waiting to do. If she sat where the rain could just reach her, then at least as she got slowly wetter she would know that time was passing, it hadn't clotted altogether, even though she could no longer sense it and there was nothing in her sight that she could watch, no drag of stars in the sky's net, no candle burning low . . .

———————

NOTHING, not rain nor wind nor dead of night could keep Salem from coming, or hold him the wrong side of the wall; nothing, not even the fear of a watcher in the shadows could keep Jendre modest at the sight of him, this one wet evening of them all.

She hurtled into his arms, and the cold discomfort of her clothes was an impediment but the wetness suddenly was not, almost an advantage rather; and the cold didn't last, and discomfort was negligible, less, meaningless . . .

After a while she heard a slap, a yelp, a hiss, "Don't *stare*, impudence . . ." and smiled as best she could, when her mouth was not her own.

A while longer, and one of them had to be strong-minded, determined, and clearly it had to be her. She moved her hands down to his shoulders, snatched a breath, and pushed.

And pushed harder, eventually hard enough or long enough; he took a step back, ran his own hand through the wet mess of his hair, breathed once and said, "What is it, then, tonight? I saw you yesterday, we were neither of us so . . ."

His voice faltered, his hand gestured for the word, and she couldn't supply it. Hungry? Desperate? Debauched, debased, delinquent? That last made best sense to her, but she wasn't about to impugn his honour, this night when she and all of them were dependent on it.

She shook her head and said, "Anticipation," a lie that he acknowledged gratefully; then she said, "Did you bring the carriage?"

"Of course. On the road below the hill, the horses couldn't bring it any closer. I can carry your sister that far."

And then there was a degree of fussing over ropes and such, all the ready details; and then she could speak to Mirjana and to Teo, their stern and loving mistress. "You two stay here, and do nothing yet. We will bring Sidië. If two of us can't manage it, neither can four. So wait, and listen for my whistle. If you don't hear that, or if you hear trouble, there," a nod towards the path that ran the other way around the water, "that is your way back to the house. Use it and be good, be innocent, know nothing of where I am tonight; I left you in my rooms and told you to stay there, that's all."

"Djago knows you did not," Mirjana said wisely, rightly, at just the wrong time.

"Teo: will Djago betray us?"

"No, my lady!" And then, hesitantly, "I don't think so. I don't know. But it was Djago who showed me the way out and let me go to His Excellence that first time . . ." Salem was always His Excellence to Teo, those times when he might overhear. Other times, he had other names or titles. It amused Jendre sometimes to listen to the boy, waiting for a mistake; it had never happened yet.

Tonight, nothing was much amusing. "You could betray him, then, in his turn?"

"I suppose, my lady," though there was nothing there to say that he would.

"Then we must trust to Djago's nice instinct for preserving his own small skin. You two wait here, as I say," the best protection she could offer them, just a little distance, "while Salem and I fetch Sidië."

And then she turned and walked along the margin of the pool, on her way to doing exactly that. After a moment she heard Salem's hurrying footsteps at her back.

NO need for misdirection, long detours down to the trees and up along the parade of shrubs. It was so dark, no one could see them coming until they were too close for any excuse to carry any weight at all.

Straight across the grass, then, and hope the building's shutters made it blind, as blind as she was, more.

Salem was at her heels, quiet as a young man could be, a soldier on a mission and obedient to her every gesture, ideal to her needs. She led him down the long side of the pavilion and then counted the shutters back, from one to four. The cords that should have tied them closed still hung loose, unknotted, hopefully unseen.

She signed to Salem, *Sidië, my sister's bed, down here to the left . . .*

Then, with all her courage where she needed it, in her hands, she worked the shutter open as silently as she knew how.

THERE was a spill of misty light, as before, but much more easily seen in this dead dark. It had a rank and magic sheen to it, and Jendre still couldn't name the colours that it carried in its shifts. But her sister lived in it, if that endless spell of dreaming could be called a life; Jendre could surely bear the greasy touch of it, long enough to go in and lift Sidië out of bed and out of the window, into the welcome wet of the rainy breeze.

Even so there was a moment more, a moment's unhappy lingering before she dragged her leg up and over the sill. She couldn't see anyone moving: no wizards, no women gliding from bed to bed and no hint of movement in the beds, only the slumped figures of the dreamers. The closest, directly below her to the left, that was still Sidië.

So she climbed in, and immediately turned to watch Salem, to snatch a last breath of clean air as he stepped long-legged over the sill to join her.

In the smoke, then, she pointed to Sidië's cot. He nodded, and moved around the other side. Both of them were looking over their shoulders constantly, still not seeing trouble, not seeing anything much in the shimmering, sliding fug.

Nothing to do, then, but lift Sidië on her blanket and maneuver her out through the window. In truth, it would have been good to know there were helpful hands waiting outside, but she would not involve the slaves here. She had to leave them some slender hope of denial, survival, or she couldn't have done this at all. Salem could take his own risks for her sake, if he chose; it was different with Teo and Mirjana. Once away from here, she would take all the help they could offer and not think twice, but this was a desperate and ignorant venture, and she would not gamble her friends' lives on a simple fling of hope.

Her own life, she did not care for. She gazed down into her sister's flaccid, bloated face and was surprised that she could care for that, when she could barely recognize it. The colours swam between them, iridescent and deceptive; she thought that the colours had got into her mind and were dyeing her own thoughts to match, turning them quicksilver, elusive, strange. She almost didn't recognize herself, she wasn't sure now who she ought to be. She blinked across the bed and saw a young man—Salem, but the name came late and slow and uncertain, almost a question in itself— down on his knees and fussing with Sidië's blanket. That was right, they were supposed to lift her by the blanket. Better than by the hair, which was lank and foul and she didn't want to touch it. Nor did she want to touch the blanket; something sparked in its weave and she thought of firefleas. There must be creatures that could thrive in this insidious smoke, and that would be a name for them. No good name for her, she was not thriving. She was kneeling herself and wishing that she could fumble as Salem had, anything that had a purpose; but her purposes were slid away and she had lost them, her hands were all empty of purpose and they couldn't even hold her up, couldn't hold to the side of the slippery, smoky cot, couldn't hold her in the world at all, the treachery of hands as she tumbled to the floor and through the floor, drifting on banks of colour where no hand could get a grip, no thought could hold her, she had nothing to do but fall through and through and through . . .

———

SHE woke—if you could call it waking, where it felt more like a long and bitter crawl up through dark and cold and pain—into the swaying shadows of a closed litter, and for a time she was deeply confused, she thought it was her wedding day. She had been drowsy, she might have dreamed, she could have dreamed a nightmare . . .

But this was no great palanquin softened with cushions and curtains and gauze, fit transport for the new bride of the Man of Men. Rather it was dark and cramped and brutally uncomfortable, a box of wood with narrow grilles high up; sitting on the floor as she was, or kneeling as she might, she could stretch her body and stretch her neck and still not reach to see outside. There was no room to stand. She'd have to balance with her legs bent and her shoulders hunched against the roof, her head twisted sideways, just to get one eye to a grille; and for what? Muddled as she was, still trying to think her way through a maze of smoke and dust, she knew none the less where she was and so where she was being taken.

Not as bride this time but back to the palace, that at least was right. Back to the harem, that too, in a sense.

This was a pinch-box, a black bier; she'd known them by a dozen ruder names, learned largely from her deplorable friends on the streets. Of course she had never been inside, never seen inside such a thing before—she'd only glimpsed a couple throughout her adventurous childhood, always at a distance and moving too fast to catch, with a trailing crowd behind too thick to squeeze through—but there could be no question in her mind. They were rare but potent objects, a common threat to wayward girls: *be good or I'll put you in a pinch-box and send you to the Sultan; if you wander off like that, the black bier'll come to fetch you, and you'll never be seen again . . .*

The women in the harem talked like that constantly, and of course as a little girl she had never believed them, she had never learned to be afraid of a pinch-box.

Now, she thought, would be a good time to take lessons.

A black box on carrying poles, on the shoulders of four strong runners. A black box with a heavy lock on the door, guards before and behind its bearers. A black box with a woman inside: always a woman—the men of the city faced other disciplines, no easier but generally less secret—and always a runaway, or what would she be doing outside the harem walls?

To run away from the Sultan was to steal his most intimate treasures. Wife or concubine or slave, it made no difference. The black bier would be sent to fetch back the thief; somewhere behind the slam of the harem gate, she would face her punishment. And of course the city never saw her again, but why should it? Even if she'd been kissed and cosseted and welcomed home, she wouldn't expect to cross the wall again before her master's death. It was only rumour that spoke of dreadful things, the cruelties of fire and iron and vitriol. But that was the temper of the city, to be cruel to the wayward; it could be seen daily in what was publicly done to criminals, to the mutinous soldiery, to the conquered. Rumour carried all the credibility it needed.

Sitting in that rocking darkness while the bare bleak light that filtered through the grilles tossed about her head like flickering insects, listening to the steady pounding of the bearers' feet, thinking that she could hear strangers' voices hoot and mock behind them—as she would have hooted and mocked herself, if ever she'd been able to catch up with a pinch-box— it was all too easy to picture the brutalities that awaited her. Her old lord was dead, but it was still a capital offence to run away. Worse, she had meant to steal her sister from those who dreamed the bridge. Even rumour had nothing to say about the penalties for such an offence. Treason of the highest order: the flinty men who made the laws must be murmuring together, how to advise the Sultan, what harsh way to death they ought to recommend. Or perhaps he would have ideas of his own. So new to the throne after so long confined, he would not be used to taking advice, and he might resist instruction; he might be very used to letting his imagination stretch into dark corners and play with what it found there.

If he chose to play with her, with her body, with her mind . . .

She had only one shelter from those thoughts, those swelling fears; and that was worse, because it lay in wondering what would happen to those she loved. She could forget herself in terror for Salem, Mirjana, Teo. Two of them she had tried to protect; they might even have had the sense to follow orders and sneak back to her rooms, when she didn't return from the pavilion; she still didn't believe that it would save them. It was too much the habit of the world to assume guilt all through a household, to punish the slaves as much as the mistress, to kill all as an example to others.

And as for Salem, caught with her as he must have been, intruder and conspirator, traitor, thief . . .

———

TIME that had been so weary yesterday was slick and savage now, eager to be at work. At work on her, and on her friends. She could be brave, she knew that, but not like this, locked in a box of darkness while horror waited in the light. Here she was a coward and she wanted to cling to her cowardice, to her fear. She could spend days, years, decades in this box, she thought, if only they would not pull her out of it. Let her just huddle with her imagination, picturing the worst inflicted on her, on Salem, on

Teo and Mirjana; so long as she could go on doing that, then the smallest and weakest little piece of her could go on whispering *see, not true, not happening yet.* And if not to her, then not to her loved ones either . . .

Perhaps not. She knew the folly of the argument, she knew that delay was feckless; she still felt an outrage that it all came so fast, the dull boom of the gate as it closed behind her, the sudden stillness of the pinch-box as the bearers set it down, the grate of a key and the sullen scrape of the lock as it unhinged. She was nowhere near ready to confront the world with all the hopeless pride of the self-condemned. She didn't want to leave the box; she wanted to plunge her fingers through the grilles for something to grip on to, she wanted to kick and scream to stay just where she was.

She did cower as the front of the box dropped with a clatter, she did cringe back from the daylight with a gasp that was treacherously close to a sob.

A voice said, "Will you come out?" and that was Ferres, she knew it immediately and then she wanted nothing more than to be out of that humiliating box. Hope would have flared within her, the most feeble and ridiculous of lights, *he is my friend and he will help me,* but she quenched it ruthlessly. She knew the man by his voice, but not by the chill that was in it; she would put no hope in him, nor anywhere.

Nor would she crawl out of this box like an animal, though it seemed to have been built that way. She could not stand; she waddled, then, flat-footed like a duck with her legs so bent she was still almost sitting down. A couple of short shuffling steps, and her head was free of the box and she could stand, and did; Ferres looked mildly surprised, as though he had expected her to grovel.

No doubt other girls had done just that, fetched back to a grim fate at the hands of the lord they'd fled. No doubt they had kissed his feet and wailed, promised anything and begged whatever least kindness he could supply. She would not do that. She would not beg for her own life, nor her friends'; she wished for a moment that he had understood that, before he opened the box. She thought he should have done. Hadn't they talked enough, for him to see what character she had? The more afraid she was, or the more angry, the less likely to plead. It always had been so. She would argue, she would fight, she would demand; she would not, ever, beg. Even when they took Sidië, when she had raged at her father, she had not begged for her sister's life or freedom. If she wouldn't do it then, she would not do it now. Not from the eunuch, nor from his mistress either, though the Valide Sultan might hold all their lives within her gift.

Was Jendre too proud? Perhaps she was; she thought so sometimes, often. But a life that could be begged for, that could be won by pleading, that was too cheap; it was no life worth the having, it held no value in her eyes. She could only hope that her friends would think the same.

"Come."

Ferres had his usual entourage; he had others, guards with scimitars, either to defend him and his against any madness of her own or else simply to emphasise her disgrace in this place where once she was a power, a wife favoured by her lord and husband.

Favoured by Ferres too, or so she'd thought. She supposed it was himself he favoured ultimately, first and last; no sacrifice, then, to give her up to knives and coals and screaming. But then he'd known all those himself, when he was cut; why would he be merciful to others?

Besides, he had no power to doom her, nor to save. He might have influence, but little enough of that. He was master of the harem, perhaps— and a great survivor, if he held that position still—but it would be his own master who would decide her fate, unless it was his mistress. She couldn't guess which of the two would be more cruel.

───────────

SHE wasn't sure where in the harem she was: some undiscovered corner, the place of punishments, not normally shown to women till they needed to discover it. There was a small shadowy court, overlooked by high walls with narrow windows barred against any invasive sun; there could be no other purpose to the bars. Nothing here gave any prospect of escape. Not the locked gate, nor the guards at every doorway, nor the dank and foetid air itself which smelled and tasted as though it had not left this darkling place for years, for generations. She wanted to hold her breath against it. It spoke of bitter sweats, of pain and fear and nothing that would naturally come to womankind but must be brought by men. There was a whipping post in the court, rubbed smooth by women's bodies; she thought that was the least of what was here.

Ferres and his escort conducted her through one of those watched doorways and then down, one flight of steps and then another. She wondered why the grim and the ghastly must always be buried. People could build towers as well as dungeons; why did they never make a torture chamber at the height, where at least there could be air and light and perhaps a bird fly past the window as you screamed?

The question answered itself, of course. Air and light and birdflight would work against the purpose. She shrugged inside, and went on down.

THE steps brought them to a hallway, where another door gave into a vaulted, pillared chamber, lit by many lamps. Here was justice waiting to receive her, all too swift and certain. There were guards and eunuchs lining the walls on either side; at the end was a dais where nobles and generals stood behind the Valide Sultan, who stood herself beside a throne that held the Sultan.

Here is a man who waits for women, she thought, and wondered what that meant, if anything at all; and then remembered with a pang that her own Sultan had waited for her, that first night when she brought him an ortolan, and so of course it meant nothing. And why would it matter, anyway, to her? Too late for insight. Too late for breathing, almost. Her chest was oddly tight, she struggled for air, but she might as well not bother. She was glad to have eaten so little yesterday; why trouble her digestion with the work?

Ferres led her forward, to where a plain reed mat was laid out on the floor before the dais. He prostrated himself, but not on the mat, beside it. The mat was hers, then. She knelt there, gracefully, submissively, lowering her head; and then she sat back on her heels and raised her eyes. She was still her lord husband's widow, even here she had a position that they could not take from her, and she would not grovel.

What she would do instead, before anything else, while they were still gazing mutely down at her, she scanned the ranks of observers behind the throne. Her father was not there. That was sheer relief; it would have been terrible for both of them if he had had to watch this, while she knew that he was watching. If his absence meant that his position was suspect or perilous or lost, if she had balked his rise, then she was sorry, but it was hard to care too deeply. If a man will sell his daughters, he cannot be sure of profit.

Neither was Salem's father present, and that did look deliberate. A general was only a general, but the pasha was a power in the land. Or had been. That was the old dispensation. Salem had not complained of any loss of influence, specifically—but his marriage had been rethought, and he had been eager to come to her, a young man in pursuit of compensations . . .

No matter. Their families were no part of this; that was useful to know, and it spared her one degree of grief. Beyond that, it could not matter.

She would not look at the Valide Sultan, for fear of blushing under that hawk-woman's sardonic eye. She looked at her son instead, the new Sultan, not to be seen avoiding his gaze for shame; and she saw what she had seen before, a corpulent man not ageing well, not like her lord, neither shrewd nor capable. He met her eyes and dabbed at his mouth with a handkerchief, and she wondered how many women there were now in his harem, and how busy he had been in their enjoyment.

"Well. Here she is, then." It was the Valide Sultan who spoke, who must have felt that the silence had endured long enough. The brisk snap to her voice offered Jendre no hope, no dream of hope. "The girl who would run from her lawful place, and offer great harm to the empire in her running."

Here I am, yes—to face the woman who would poison and kill her own son, to keep a safer grip on the throne. Jendre did not and would not say that, it would sound too much like pleading; she hoped that perhaps the Valide Sultan might understand it, simply from her stillness on the mat there, her refusal to look anywhere but at the man on the throne.

Who stirred, now, and spoke to her; who said, "Why did you do these things, little pretty?"

His voice was oddly high and hollow: not like a eunuch's exactly, nor like a boy's, but on a par with his smooth round face and figure. Perhaps it had grown too big on too little substance, there was not much matter in the mind behind it. They had called him mad, but she thought simple might be a better word.

There was a stirring, almost a muttering among the men behind him, a sudden stiffness in his mother, and it all said *why is he asking questions, what do her answers matter? She did do these things, there is no dispute of that, so let her be condemned and so an end* . . .

But he had asked, and she would answer him.

"I suppose for love, Your Magnificence," and oh, how strange it was to use those words to the wrong man altogether. "I had loved your brother, my lord and master, and I would have stayed with him forever and known myself privileged to do so," and not a word of a lie in this, she was too proud again, "except he died and left me, and so I was alone. And I could mourn his ghost all my life as the law would have me do; but a harem where he walked was a garden, and a harem in his everlasting absence was a cage, and I was fretful, I wanted to be free."

He nodded, and murmured, "I know how it is, to be caged. And to wish for freedom. To be caged for a corpse's sake is folly, even if my precious brother makes the corpse. I saw the corpse, you know. I asked to see it."

"I saw him too, Your Magnificence. I should have been with him as he died, but I was led away."

"Of course, you are the girl who gave him the bird that killed him." He spoke as if he worked out all the ramifications as he went, like a child doing sums on its fingers. "Not your fault, my mother says, you did not know. But if you had not done it, I would still be in the cage."

It was, she supposed, true. Perhaps she should use her own fingers more; she hadn't worked it out that far, that he had cause to be grateful. His gratitude was more properly owed to his mother, but he could not know that. *Your Magnificence, I am delighted to see you free, it is what I worked and prayed for*—no. She would sooner die young and foolish, honest and in agony if need be.

Need might not be, but that wasn't clear yet. He said, "Your yearning to break free, I understand. But why would you seek to break that work that gives us power across the water?"

"For love, Magnificence, as I said. That was my sister I went to rescue, no more than that." *No worse.*

He said, "Ah, I can understand that too. I could have wished for such a sister, to rescue me"—and he said it in defiance of his mother, who stood at his side and tapped her throat with two fingers in a gesture that Jendre understood only too well, she had seen its work twice too often, and two men dead.

If the Sultan understood it, he showed no sign; she was surprised to find him so rebellious. So, she thought, was his mother.

He said, "There can be no punishment, for what I would have wished to do myself. She cannot have her freedom, this girl, she is married yet to my great brother and his ghost still claims her; but she shall not suffer for the wanting of it. And all the harm she meant among the sleepers was to take one that she loved, we could have spared the one. She shall go back to the Palace of Tears and weep her life away among her sisters, but there shall be no punishment else."

"But, oh my son, my lord—" The Valide Sultan did not sound defeated, and Jendre quailed at her tone.

"Yes, mother mine?"

"What of the man, the pasha's son, found with her? In the harem of ghosts where he was forbidden, among the sleepers where he was twice forbidden . . ."

". . . And in her company all through, three times forbidden," the Sultan finished for her, smiling happily at the chant of it. "Was that too done for love, girl, his for you?"

She swallowed, faced him directly where she could not face him down, and said, "And mine for him. Both those, Magnificence, yes. He would have sheltered us, my sister and myself; and I had lost my lord your brother, and . . ." *And I cannot bear to lose him too*, but the Valide Sultan was tapping her wattled throat again in her little signal that meant death.

And it seemed her son was still listening to Jendre and not to her, because he said, "Well, if the girl so much desires the young man's company, then that I think is easy. She must have it, she must keep him with her."

And he sat back, fat and contented, and giggled, and wiped his mouth with his handkerchief; and Jendre stared at him, trembling, feeling the dark close in around her like a pinch-box. Swift to feel an impending dread, she was slow to understand it, slower yet to give it credit. Meantime his eyes shone as he gazed at her, all sharp and cruel curiosity.

Chapter Five

OWN in the Shine was Issel, dreaming of destruction.

He was very much afraid, which was how he knew he was awake.

THIS time, for once in his life, he was not alone. He had his friends about him, his little army of the night.

There was Gilder, whom nobody knew.

There was Rhoan, who had been hurt too badly, in her heart and in her hands, who knew only that she would have to be hurt again.

There was Baris the dogtooth, who was already lost, twice lost, twisted all out of shape and then discarded.

And there was Issel himself, who had no word for what he was, except that he was frightened.

That made four, and they were setting off to bring down an empire.

THE first that Issel was glad to have, the first to be useful, that was Baris.

THEY were on the strand and looking for a boat. Issel might have been vindictive, he might have led them straight to his old master's, the boat he had been kicked out of; but that was another life, and he didn't care anymore.

It was strange, how the world had changed around him. What used to matter was falling away, like peel. What was left seemed very different, more dangerous, more hurtful.

So he headed for the first boat they came to. There was a boy, wrapped in a blanket, not sleeping and trying to be brave. Under the blanket, Issel was sure he held a knife; he was sure the hand that held the knife was trembling. It didn't matter. Neither mattered, the knife nor the tremble. Issel showed him Baris.

One glance at the dogtooth in the Shine, and the boy whimpered, scrambled out of the boat, tripped over his blanket as he fled. Issel watched him go and felt the rip of his own soul parting. *That is me, there; and here I am; and which of me is true?*

That was not the limit yet of Baris, on that night. He had a strength past human, in his distorted frame. He set his hands to the sternpost of the boat, dug his bare feet into the shale, and pushed. By himself, he pushed the boat to the water's edge and floated her, which the other three might have found difficult between them; then he took the oars and was clearly set to pull them all across the river to the further shore, which Issel had been sure would need all the strength of all of them to reach.

For the first time he wondered about Baris, what kind of man he'd been before. To be so poisoned by the Shine, he must have been a waterman, his life down here below the bridge. Another reason to be glad of him, that he had this easy skill with boats to marry to his strength.

Gilder knew what he was doing, too. Gilder took the steering oar. Rhoan only huddled among the nets, in nobody's way except her own, not wanting to look ahead to the lights of Maras or behind to the darkness of Sund.

Issel sat close to her, touching close if she wanted to touch, which she did not. He'd thought he would be the one to be huddling, so close to so much water; he remembered his last time, his one other time in a boat, and thought this would be dreadful.

But he looked up at the bridge, at the way it cast the Shine across the river and across the lower towns on both shores, not like a light at all but something sicker and more solid, a veil cast over corpse-light, and he wanted to bring it down. If Maras must come with it, let it come.

He hated the bridge, and how it polluted the water, and everything its glow could reach; and without his thinking about it, his hand had reached over the boat's side to trail in the water, to feel the tug of it between his fingers and the power of it, the corruption of it, the strength of it rising in response to his, inside him, not a tingle but a gripping, gasping fury. And of course he was afraid, but he could use that fear too, a taint in him like the taint in the water, he could use them both; and—

"Issel."

That was Gilder, and his own name was a warning. He looked around, and the small man nodded sideways, to the river.

Issel looked over the boat's side, and saw how his hand was cutting its way through the water, a negligible moment in the pull of tides and currents; but from his fingers and back towards the Sundain shore, the wake he'd made was lit up in all the colours of the Shine, a drifting shimmer that held its own place in the river like a sign, a defiant declaration, *we are coming*. Like any wake, it was broad beyond and it narrowed to a point at his fingers as they went, and to anyone who saw it from either bank it must have looked like an arrowhead, like a spearhead aimed at Maras, thrusting clean to the heart of empire.